THE SCOURGE OF DESPAIR
THE SANCTUARY SERIES, VOLUME ELEVEN

ROBERT J. CRANE

OSTIAGARD PRESS

The Scourge of Despair

The Sanctuary Series, Volume 11

Robert J. Crane

copyright © 2020 Ostiagard Press

1st Edition.

This book is a work of fiction. Names, characters, places, and incidents are products of the author's imagination or are used fictitiously. Any resemblance to actual events or locales or persons, living or dead, is entirely coincidental.

The scanning, uploading, and distribution of this book via the internet or any other means without the permission of the publisher is illegal and punishable by law. Please purchase only authorized electronic editions, and do not participate in or encourage electronic piracy of copyrighted materials. Your support of the author's rights is appreciated.

No part of this publication may be reproduced in whole or in part without the written permission of the publisher. For information regarding permission, please email cyrusdavidon@gmail.com.

CHAPTER 1

Vara

"I never should have left him," Vara whispered to the evening winds, and not for the first time. It had become a mantra of sorts for her from a mere hour into her airship journey away from Reikonos and to Termina, the city of her birth.

"But you did, and I wish you'd stop saying so," came the quiet voice of Isabelle over her shoulder. Her sister stood behind her, their reunion only a day past after being separated for a thousand years. Isabelle, for her part, had looked none the worse for the time. Now in her 1200's, she was less than a quarter of the way through the elven lifespan. Her tresses were still fully golden, her pale skin showed not a wrinkle. When she'd opened the door to their parents' old home, it might have been a scene from their lives a millennium ago, save for Isabelle had never before worn such a look of shock. Such was the effect of seeing her "dead" sister, Vara supposed.

"I retread my error every moment I'm away," Vara said. She stood upon the bow of an elven airship, its sleek, curved lines a pleasant departure from the blocky, less elegant ships that seemed ubiquitous upon the docks of Termina and Reikonos. The Amatgarosan ones, in particular, looked a bit like a flying brick when they cut through the air. None of that here; elvish design was always focused on things that looked beautiful, that lasted. She'd been drawn in immediately by the one in Reikonos, and found the shipmaster a stunned man indeed, and one who knew her face. That had inspired free passage to Termina, which she'd taken as good fortune at the time.

Not so, now. She mentally flogged herself again for leaving him in the heat of anger. She'd been foolish, she'd been intemperate, she'd let her own idiocy carry her away in his hour of need. Certainly, damn the man for his profligate use of his implement in the past, especially with that dark elven swine. But that was no reason to leave him – and the others, she supposed – facing Malpravus and his ilk in charge of Reikonos.

"I note you're not quite as broken up in contemplating how you left the others in the twist." Isabelle sidled up next to her. Her voice was cool and clear, like the evening air as it greeted them rushing across the bow of the ship. The darkening land lay before them, seemingly endless, though it was anything but. Ahead, already, the sun sparkled its last light across the once-Torrid Sea.

"I do feel bad about it," Vara said, watching the sparkles on the water. Reikonos was a spot in the distance, growing larger by the minute. Between them and it, though, lay a writhing mass of–

"Bloody scourge," Isabelle whispered. Now that she, too, was at the edge, they were clear to see.

They were packed to the horizon, a seething, writhing mass of gray bodies. They warred with each other, not in any organized way but rather in the manner of a mob. Climbing, pushing, inadvertently clawing for purchase and for better position, they all pointed in the same direction–

Reikonos.

"There it is," Isabelle whispered. There was no need for volume; they were both elves, with the elongated ears and all the added hearing attendant their long-lived race.

And indeed, there it was, a gray blotch on the horizon. Wall stretching round its length, the tall Citadel anchoring the center. It was more cut up into districts than she remembered, but then, she'd never given it a good inspection from the air, really. The closest one could have gotten in the days of old was to look out of said Citadel, and the only time she could recall doing that was when the city was burning during the dark elven invasion, pillaging already underway and a thick black pall hanging over everything.

No, it certainly looked different now. Statues stood where before had been empty greens for grazing livestock. Smokestacks loomed like sentinels over other districts, piping black and gray soot over the skyline and giving the city a perpetually hazy look.

Vara wrinkled her nose as she looked down. "I'm at a loss to guess which smells worse, the city or the scourge."

"It's a near-run race," Isabelle agreed, wrinkling her own. "It makes me very thankful that in spite of Termina's current...status...problems...entire disposition, really...that it was designed by elves." When she caught Vara's curious look, she added, "We know how to build a sewer system that holds in the smells." She lifted an immaculate white sleeve to her nose. "And the scourge are across the Perda from us."

"Do they stand there and wait for the waters to part like an army seeking for an opportunity to invade?" Vara asked.

"Indeed they do," Isabelle said. "Day and night, for a thousand years. Their numbers do not wane, no matter how many fall into the waters never to rise again." Her brow puckered. "Though I think by now they're nearly forgotten in the background noise of city life. Too many distractions, and they're far too distant."

"You...forget about them?" Vara looked down as the airship's shadow swept over the gray masses. Some seemed to try and leap up to reach it as they passed. Futilely, of course; they were hundreds of feet in the air.

"Other than during a rather dramatic drought about three centuries ago," Isabelle said, "they don't really pose much threat so long as you stay aloft." She shrugged her delicate shoulders. "So, yes, they remain almost forgotten across the river, much like the old human settlement that used to stand upon its banks."

"Santir," Vara said, turning her eyes back to the horizon. Cyrus was out there, somewhere, in that gray city that grew closer with every passing moment. The whip of the airship's blades carried her closer to him, closer to erasing the terrible mistake she'd made in leaving. But she'd brought Isabelle back; that was not nothing. Now, at least, they would be a few more against a seemingly impossible enemy.

"Do you remember when you were a child and...?"

Vara blinked, not needing even a small amount more of a clue. "And Father used to take us–"

"He took you. I was an adult at the time. If I happened to be in town he would allow me to tag along."

"You're barely an adult now," Vara snapped back. Then her tone softened. "He'd take us across the river to that human sweet shop."

"They did the most amazing things with our sugar," Isabelle said wistfully. "Hard to believe; they could grow it down in the southern lands above the desert, ship it to us, and we would make of it – well, nothing almost. A flavor for our tea. But them..."

"Those cakes," Vara said, closing her eyes.

"Yes," Isabelle said, relish in her voice. She was savoring the memory. Then, the spell seemed broken. "There is a similar shop in Termina even now. A human one, of course."

"Of course," Vara said. "Our people wouldn't want to be accused of having any actual flavor in their lives."

"Quite."

Vara lurched; for a moment she thought the airship had jerked, but it had not. She caught the rail with a mailed hand, wood clanking against her covered palm. Something seemed to have happened in her gut, something that had almost bent her double. It was subtle yet not; seemed outside of her yet vibrated through every vein and nerve.

"Are you all right?" Isabelle asked, hovering at her elbow.

"I think so. I felt...very odd there for a moment. As though something tore the breath from me for a moment, like some dark knight's spell."

"Curious," Isabelle said, and then they lapsed into silence.

The feeling retreated, fortunately, leaving only a coldness in the pit of her stomach. She could not shake the sensation that something had indeed gone wrong, and not far. Something to do with–

"Sanctuary." Isabelle surely heard her, yet she said nothing. Still, Vara could feel her sister's concern and her eyes upon her.

Vara stared at the gray city ahead, as they grew closer. The dockyards were right there, past that wall, the one only a few miles in front of them. Why, they'd be there in–

A scarlet light flashed ahead; Vara jerked her head away to avoid being blinded.

The airship rumbled beneath them. Isabelle cried out and Vara ducked low, her armor's natural augmentation to her dexterity and speed giving her a moment to reach out and seize her sister's hand as the wooden deck squealed under the force of the sudden change in bearing.

Vara forced her eyes open against the blinding glow. A red light like a beacon shone into the sky from the top floor of the Citadel. It coruscated energy, bolts of white-hot power running through it like scarlet lightning. Then it started to change–

"What is that?" Isabelle asked, a question echoed in one form or another by the elven crew behind them. She did not fight against Vara's hand on her elbow.

There was only one answer, of course:

"Malpravus," Vara whispered.

It played out before them almost silently, a drama more visually exciting and terrifying than any play she'd ever seen in any theater or amphitheater in the human world or the elven. The red beam of spellcraft expanded out from the Citadel–

"The power," Isabelle gasped. She could feel it; Vara could feel it, too, though perhaps not as much as her sister, with her longer history of magic.

It ballooned forth, expanding upon the city itself like a dome of light swelling out. They watched, breathless, minutes leaden like hours as it spread building by building, district by district, encompassing the whole of Reikonos.

Airships were beginning to take off now from the dockyards. She could see them rising up, even as their ship took a hard turn to the left, veering away from their approach.

"What are you doing?" Vara cried out. She couldn't help herself; all she could think of was that somewhere down there was–

Cyrus.

"We can't go into that!" Captain Beniye called back from the high quarterdeck overlooking them on the main. She opened her mouth to argue–

Isabelle clamped her hand onto Vara's wrist, and when she

turned to look at her sister, found Isabelle's blue eyes glowing with worry. "That...that thing, that light...it's death."

Vara could scarcely argue with that. She watched it crawl across the city slowly, almost lasciviously. Airships surged from behind the wall now, pouring out like bees leaving the hive. Two crashed together and an explosion ensued. She watched hundreds of lives end in a blaze, the wreckage falling and spreading as the red light only grew, stretching to the borders of the city–

But she could not look away, even as she – *she knew* – this was the death of everyone in its path.

The red light reached its crescendo, coming forward the last mile and crossing the great, gray wall that ringed the city. One last ship dashed out of reach, and the ringing of a bell behind her reached her overwhelmed ears. The ship was turning, Vara trying to watch the red light even as it grew larger, expanding, reaching across the gray wastes of scourge, their teeth snapping as they reached a frenzied pitch, leaping and crying out in guttural tones below–

One last bright flash...and it was gone. The ship was turning, rolling over in a hard arc to the left, and Vara was hanging on the rail, looking back as the light died. It pulled back like a retreating army, all the way to the pinnacle of the Citadel, and then twinkled for only a moment before it shot into the sky, vanishing above the clouds.

Below, among the scourge, a silence fell. The clack of teeth and jaws was over, the sounds of a ravening horde somehow sated.

And beyond, over the rail, across the void, behind the city walls...

Reikonos was silent as a tomb. Vara blinked; the light of the spell still burned in her eyes, and she wondered if it would ever fade.

Into that silence – of Isabelle, of the crew, of the scourge –

even the turning blades of the airship seemed quieter now that the red light had faded – a single word escaped her, like sudden thunder on a clear and quiet night.

"Cyrus..." she whispered.

A single tear fell across her cheek.

CHAPTER 2

Alaric

Reikonos was dead. Of all the certainties he had known in his life, this seemed most certain, for it fell well within the framework of his experience.

"You're sure they're all...?" Guy Harysan – short, irksome, improbable, and yet a hero nonetheless, now carrying Praelior – asked. He held a stubby finger up, running it emphatically across his neck. Night had fallen, and a pall hung over Reikonos even beyond the usual smoke. Beyond the roaring whip of the *Yuutshee's* blades churning to keep them aloft, there seemed to be a curious quiet that Alaric could feel, but not hear.

He could feel it all the way to his bones, a silence of death that reached across the gap between them and the outermost wall of the city. The gray stones were far enough that he could no longer see them individually, though he'd noted the divide between them only minutes before, in the midst of the battle. Cannon-firing, spell-weaving, and somehow he fixated on the mortar joint between two stones for a moment, breathing it into his memory for reasons he couldn't even articulate.

Truly, the shade was that of a tombstone. And every stone in that wall might as well be one now, for the city...

It was dead. Truly, truly dead.

"I am certain," Alaric said, staring over the *Yuutshee's* rail. Guy stood next to him like a shadow.

"It could have been us," said the man, clad all in black. Another shadow, this one attached at his left arm. Alaric favored him with only a bare look, but it was enough to catch his attention. "I am Edouard." He offered a hand. "Edouard Boswin."

"Don't take 'is hand," Guy said, shaking his head furiously.

For this, Alaric felt the need to turn and look at the smaller man. "Why not?" He caught Edouard's crumpling posture out of the corner of his eye.

"Ain't it obvious?" Guy threw out a hand to indicate the man in black. "What 'e is?"

Alaric turned slowly. "What are you that has Guy here so terrified I might touch you? Survivor of some plague, still bearing its effects upon your flesh? Son of some dishonored traitor, brought low by name and blood?" When Edouard merely hung his head in answer, Alaric said, "Speak, friend. For there is no judgment from me on any of these scores."

"You saved my life," Edouard said, head still hung. "No one else would have done that." He nodded at the sword he'd returned to Alaric – Aterum, already back in its scabbard. "Gave me that...that magical weapon of yours to aid my climb. That was more decent than I deserve."

Alaric cast his gaze back at the dead city, gray and forbidding...and entirely his fault. "I don't know what it would take for a man with as checkered a past as Guy's to think ill of you, but let me assure you...I have just this day become responsible for the death of a whole city," and he looked at Edouard once more, "and so I have no room to judge you, for my judgment is entirely too occupied pronouncing my own guilt at the moment."

"I'm an executioner," Edouard said. "The headsman. One of the ten." His lips moved as though there were more to say but he couldn't find it. Instead he bowed his head again.

"They're cursed, Alaric," Guy said, and snorted as though he wanted to spit. "They kill, you know...everybody. Everybody accused of a crime, anyway. Anything worse than pickpocketing and..." Guy ran his finger across his neck again, just as he had when indicating the city a moment earlier. "'hoo wants to be around that, eh?"

"I didn't pronounce the sentences," Edouard said sadly. "I just carried them out." He started to turn away, to shuffle away.

"A city just died here," Alaric said. Something stirred within him. He looked to the quarterdeck, where Captain Mazirin was speaking to the man at the wheel that steered the big ship. "A whole city. Millions of lives, with all their attendant pasts, jobs, and dreams." He wanted to be up there, talking to the captain, but something rooted him to the spot...

The city. Somehow the fading glow of the red spell seemed to linger in his vision, as though burned into his sight. It would fade, he knew, for this was not the first time he'd seen it cast. No, indeed, it was not even the first time he'd seen it cast on this very spot.

It was, though, he hoped, the last time he would see it done, here or anywhere.

"It would not be a terrible thing if the city claimed one more before it fades into the mists of time," Alaric said, looking at Edouard. "You carry a dark shame with you like those clothes." He nodded at the black. "If you wanted to...you could leave them behind upon the pyre that this place will soon become."

"But...I would still know it's me," Edouard said. He looked at Guy. "You would still know...what I've done."

"Oh, I wouldn't worry about Guy," Alaric said, planting a

hand on Edouard's shoulder. "He has sins enough of his own to bury." He shot Guy a very significant look and watched the smaller man turn away. "There was a time when, in the ruin of a city, I made a similar choice. I cannot promise you it will be easy. Redemption is not a simple decision; it is a path you will walk every day, trying to atone whatever dark deeds you might have in your past. But if ever there was a moment you wished you could leave all that you were behind and begin anew...this is surely it."

And he turned, stalking off toward the stairs up the quarter-deck, fixing his gaze – and his intentions – upon Mazirin, who stood there, speaking feverishly with her subordinates, a whirlwind of activity in a place where everyone else seemed still too stunned to move.

CHAPTER 3

Shirri Gadden

The airship engines produced a strange whine, the wooden bow slicing through the winds of the night. The clouds had all cleared off some miles ago, leaving Shirri Gadden staring at a black sky over hilly, dust-filled lands below, not a speck of grass or a single tree to break the monotony.

She'd been staring over the edge like this for miles and miles, Reikonos having long since disappeared over the horizon. Where were they even heading? She did not know, nor did she particularly care. Beside her, her mother sat in silence, fussing with her robes every now and again. Past her stood Hiressam, his statuesque face turned toward the horizon.

"Where are we going?" Shirri asked at last.

Her mother looked at her; Hiressam stirred out of his statue stillness. He answered. "Southwest. Termina. Pharesia. Perhaps Emerald or Amti, maybe even somewhere else in the southern lands. Hard to say."

Shirri nodded, head sinking back down again. They'd made it aboard this airship just as it crested the wall. It had been a near thing; one moment they'd been fighting a battle for their very lives, the next the shouts and clamor of the war had given way to other ones, more fearful and less feral, somehow.

It was then that she'd seen the red pillar of magic. Seen it turn into an expanding, coruscating dome that came for her. Came for all of them.

So they'd run. Made it to the side of the airship, and looked back as the city of Reikonos was overrun by the spell, the battle over and definitively lost.

"There went the revolution," Shirri whispered. Of course they all heard her.

"It was always but a foolish notion," Pamyra, her mother, said quickly. Was it Shirri's imagination or did she seem redder than usual? Abashed because she, for a moment, believed?

Now it was Shirri's turn to palm at her robes, straightening out a crease, though it would have little effect on the bearing of her life anytime soon. "You told Alaric you would fight for a cause, at last."

"And see where that got me," Pamyra said with a heavy sigh. "In over my head. Over our heads—"

"I was already over my head when they found me," Shirri said. "Little chance I was going to make it through the night." There was a strange courage growing within her. Every hopeless word her mother breathed seemed to inspire Shirri to go in the opposite direction out of sheer defiance. "They bought me days. And if this had happened while I'd been hiding, as I wanted to?" She looked over the edge of the deck and again saw the furrows of the dead, rutted land slipping by below her. "Well, there was little chance you or I would have been in a position to catch an airship before that spell-magic caught us."

"For whatever good it does us," Pamyra said with exasperation. "Do you not see that wherever we end up, we face the same conundrum, even absent the Machine dogging our tails?" She pointed to the aft of the ship. "That thing that destroyed Reikonos? It is still out there, and if I may hazard a guess, it is merely getting started."

"'It' has a name," Hiressam said. "And the name is *Malpravus*."

Pamyra produced another noise of exasperation. "Is that supposed to mean something to me?"

Hiressam cocked an eyebrow at her. "Malpravus was the Guildmaster of Goliath, Sanctuary's foremost opponent in days of old. He allied himself with the forces of darkness at every turn – the Goblin imperials, the dark elves under command of Yartraak, the governments that sought our annihilation as heretics. Always he sought for himself the power of the very gods." He looked back as well, as though he could see Reikonos in the distance behind him. "It would appear he finally succeeded. Or rather...ascended."

"Be that as it may," Pamyra said, "it – he – whatever you wish to call the cause of that red spell of extermination – is still out there. It drained a city in mere moments, and I cannot believe that whatever this Malpravus's ambitions, they will be sated having exsanguinated one city alone when there are so many available." She settled back on her haunches, exhausted. "No. Mark my words. This is but the beginning."

Shirri stirred at that. "Then...shouldn't we warn them?"

Pamyra turned her head to look at her Shirri. "Warn who? For who would believe such foolishness? The age of magic is done, daughter mine. Conjurers can scarcely produce a flame the size of a brazier at this point. Who would imagine that what we just saw could be achieved?"

"Surely someone would," Shirri said. "It's not as though there's no evidence."

"There won't be for long," Hiressam said stiffly, and when

Shirri cast him a questioning look, he added, "The city will burn. Untended fires, no one to put them out or even slow the spread. Hell...it is likely already afire. It will be ashes three days hence."

"And with nowhere for the residents to have escaped," Pamyra said, piggybacking neatly on Hiressam's statement, "they would all have died of the fire, you see. No magic necessary, just a tragedy of modern life."

Shirri looked to Hiressam to see if he would dispute this arrangement of facts and logic, but he turned his eyes back to the horizon. "So...there will be no proof of what we saw?"

"Only the witness that we bear," Hiressam said.

"Which will hardly be enough," Pamyra said.

"But surely–" Shirri began.

"Surely nothing," Pamyra said. "For who would want to believe such a tale? Magic of old come back, and mighty enough to destroy whole cities? We should be lucky if the authorities wherever we are going do not throw us immediately into the nearest lunatic asylum to merely still the annoyance we cause." She shook her head. "Ours is a tale no one will want to hear, for even if it were accepted as true...what would anyone do about it, in these days with so little magic?"

There was little Shirri could differ with in the conclusion, though she spent long minutes pondering it. How right was her mother, that no one would want to hear of these dire tidings, of troubles nearly inescapable coming their way. There was struggle enough in the world already. Who wanted to look for more beyond what already lay on their own doorstep? "What next, then?" she asked, feeling quite crushed under the weight of all this.

"We go where the airship takes us," Hiressam said simply. Pamyra did not argue this; apparently it, too, was a conclusion as inescapable as the last series presented.

Shirri gathered up her courage a few moments later to ask, "And then?"

But no one had an answer for that. Not Hiressam, not Pamyra...and certainly not Shirri. So she busied herself by watching the dead, lifeless land slip beneath the airship's bow like waves on an ocean, bearing her at last to a new land.

CHAPTER 4

Vaste

"Look upon me, the greatest fool who has ever trod foot upon soil," Vaste said, staring into the growing darkness enshrouding the airship as it cut through the skies under the faded moonlight. "And now...board, I suppose." He stared at the planks that composed the ship's deck, stained a dark coffee color.

"You have competition." Vaste's companion spoke from next to him, similarly upon the ship's deck, but he wore no robes, no easy cloth. Nor was his skin the same slime green as Vaste's. His was yellow, but the shape of his body was similar. Except the ruddy bastard was covered in muscles from head to toe. His head was bowed, though, the picture of despair. "I swore to serve the cause of honor, but have participated in the destruction of a city. If you are a fool, clearly I am the bigger one, for claiming to defend ideals but working for the Lord Protector." He let out a bellowing guffaw. "Lord Protector indeed! Even his name was a lie, for what did he protect?" He glanced over the railing, but the ruin of Reikonos had already receded over the horizon behind them. Nothing was ahead but night.

"Right, that's all well and good, you being a gullible moron and trusting the land's most evil villain," Vaste said, "but I'm talking about a much deeper deception. I fell in love with a non-real person. An invisible person. A ghost, if you will. Because I am so actually pathetic that I could not find a woman, and thus my – I don't really know how to define my relationship with Sanctuary in words – my spiritual retreat? It created a woman for me. Out of pity."

Qualleron's eyes narrowed. He seemed to be contemplating this. But then he opened his mouth, and the illusion of understanding was broken. "These men who run the airship. I am concerned about them."

Vaste tossed a perfunctory look over his shoulder. Yes, there were men running the airship. Yes, they were staring at the two trolls splayed on their deck with great suspicion. "They're looking at us like we don't belong here. Because we don't."

"I don't like it," Qualleron said. His sword was across his lap, the blade chipped terribly.

"Of all the things that have happened in the last while, this is the one you find most objectionable? Not the dead city, not the demi-god who absorbed enough magical energy to – I don't even know what he's capable of at this point, and I'm not sure I want to – and not me, who fell in love with a damned ghost–"

"I am concerned about many things," Qualleron said, getting to his feet and brushing the dust off of his armor. "Those in the past I can do nothing about. But this..." He watched the airship men very carefully. "Getting cast off in the middle of these lands would be very trying on us. You more than me."

"Fool, I've got no will to live," Vaste said. "If I drop, I'll clobber myself in the head with this," he brandished Letum, "and my problems will be over. Falling into the middle of scourge lands and becoming the first good meal they've probably had in ages would be a fitting end for my imbecility."

Qualleron was sending sizzling looks in the direction of the crew. "They will try nothing – for now." He settled back down on the deck, ponderously slow. "I have cowed them."

"Does that make you a bull?" Vaste asked, not really caring about the answer.

Qualleron cocked his head. "Oh, I see. Your language is funny. I used the colloquialism–"

"I don't care why you think it's funny, or that you think it's funny at all, really." Vaste hung his head. "Can you just...leave me to my misery?"

The yellow troll was quiet for a moment. "No."

Vaste snapped his head up. "Why the hell not?"

Qualleron made a small show of turning to look around them. "You see how little space we have here. I believe if I were to leave you, put some distance between us, it would activate the territorial nature of these men." He looked at the airship crew suspiciously; Vaste could scarcely see them in the dark and cared little for their dirty looks. "We are heading westerly. By the morning we will be on the other side of the river, safe from the dead ravagers–"

"They're called scourge."

"Once we are there, I do not care if they put us out," Qualleron said. "We have hardly paid for the privilege of this voyage, after all. But to see ourselves thrown to certain death? That would make these men more dishonorable, and thus–"

"I don't care what arcane calculation you are running in your head to determine who is the least honorable in this situation and thus most worthy of being thrown overboard or murdered," Vaste snapped. Then he pitched over onto his back, staring at the cloudy skies overhead, the dark of night having closed in on them. "I don't care about any of it anymore." He pictured Cyrus in his mind's eye. The dumb bastard had gone to fight Malpravus deep in the city.

Clearly, he was dead.

Curatio had left to go to Sanctuary and never returned. Sanctuary had fallen.

He was almost certainly dead.

Alaric had been fighting in the yards. Had he made it to an airship before the wall of red magic had swept fully over the dockyards?

Probably not. Which meant they were likely dead as well.

Only Vara was safe, and looking like a genius for having escaped the trap of death that was Reikonos before the end had come. He dragged himself to the edge of the airship and looked under the short rail that stood waist-high to a human but barely knee high for him. Getting his head beneath it took some effort, bumping the shoulders a time or two, but...

There, beneath them, the dark ground slid beneath the airship. No grass, no trees, just dead earth under waxy moonlight. An ocean of dead land, seemingly endless. Ahead, he could see nothing but the dunes of earth, and behind...

Well, there was nothing back there, either. Not for him.

"Vara," he muttered. She was out there, somewhere. She'd gone to Termina, he'd heard. Honor probably dictated that he find her, tell her about the unfortunate deaths of...well, everyone.

And after that?

"They will not make their move tonight," Qualleron said, still staring suspiciously at the airship crew. They weren't huddled, exactly, but they were certainly giving the trolls a wide berth.

"Marvelous," Vaste said, almost wishing that they would. "That gives me a whole sleepless eve to consider what happens when they do. And I do love having death and murder for breakfast after a long night's fast."

"It will come to that, I think," Qualleron said.

"You're so gods-damned reassuring," Vaste said. At least he'd be rid of Qualleron soon. Perhaps even as early as the morrow, depending on how things went. He turned and stared up at the white-glowing clouds. It was going to be a long night, and a sleepless one at that.

CHAPTER 5

Cyrus

He woke to the sound of grinding metal and a feeling of falling out of the sky. Cyrus had felt such things once or twice in his life, most recently when he'd been launched out of the Citadel by Malpravus and suffered a grievously rough landing upon the cobblestones of a Reikonos alleyway.

This, though...was different.

Panicked shouts permeated the bubble of unconsciousness that ringed him. He blinked open his eyes to find himself in semi-darkness, a lamp burning on the wall with a pale, flickering flame.

The dark elven language had always been uncomfortable for him, but now it was ever so much worse. Someone shouted imprecation somewhere outside his field of view, but it sounded different, shorter, sharper, barely recognizable. He looked; the thud of the men hitting the deck above rang out. He'd been unconscious, then something had happened, and now he was awake. His head ached, regretting being stirred. Also, his helm was missing, along with at least one boot, which he recognized because of the rough sense of wood pressing against his heel.

Cyrus sat up. Sure enough, five dark elven men dressed in ragged clothing rolled and fell into walls with the dipping of the small space around them. It was all wood, save for the black iron bolts that held the place together. They'd been undressing him, but now they could not keep their footing. One was cradling a broken arm, another caught his flying boot in the eye and screamed.

An airship. The answer came to him swiftly. Surprisingly so.

Another answer came quickly thereafter.

"Baynvyn," Cyrus muttered. "That son of a bitch. Literally." His left boot landed beside him with a clank as the airship leveled out. He grabbed it and plunged his foot back into it as the men around him moaned from the abruptness of their landings. One appeared to have gone unconscious, near-black blood sprouting from a wound in his scalp.

But Cyrus had little time for them. He found his helm and rose, gathering his footing on the uncertain, pitching deck beneath, and stood, throwing out a hand to either side to catch himself as the world shifted wildly to his right. His gauntlet clanked against the wood, and he waited to regather his balance.

It did not come in time.

All that shifting, all the pitching gave way to a much more violent lurch. A great splintering crash echoed through the wood beneath his fingertips, and Cyrus was thrown forward with the collision. He tucked his head close to him, drawing in his knees as he was hurled physically through the air–

Cyrus smashed through one, then two, then a third wall. Strong, sturdy wood planks gave way beneath the power of his armor, and sawdust and splinters filled the air as he rolled and came to rest, clinking against something sturdy and iron–

"A cannon," Cyrus whispered, gauntlet clanking against the

ugly, rippled iron surface. He shoved off it and broke into a run, making for a hint of light in the distance, visible barely through the near darkness.

His boots rang, and low-hanging deck beams threatened to decapitate him with nearly every step. The distant light resolved into stairs and a twilight purple gleam shining between the boards overhead.

Cyrus flung himself up the stairs as a hard groan ran through the ship. It was settling, then. The earth was snugging it into its embrace, and without a dock to hold it upright...

The whine of the engines and the whistle of steam were an auditory clue as to what was happening now. Machinery was failing. Which was disconcerting, if only for the fact that they were almost certainly over the wall, beyond Reikonos's bounds.

Darkness and a half moon rested overhead, but still he could see the lands beyond the edge of the airship. Bleak and rippled, bereft of even a sign of life, this was scourge country. He'd seen them with his own eyes past that moat, the gray, rotting flesh in endless waves, waiting for some life to come their way so they could sink their snapping jaws around it.

Cyrus shuddered. He'd had enough encounters with the scourge to last a lifetime. Leaping into the dusky evening, cool air flooded into the cracks of Cyrus's armor, waking him out of a warm stupor that had shrouded him since he'd come to below. He breathed a healing spell and felt better. What had happened? Well, that seemed obvious upon reflection.

Baynvyn had clocked him, dragged him aboard his airship, and taken off. Now here they were, beyond the wall, and the ship was grounded for some reason.

The deck was a frenzy of moans and barely moving bodies. The crash had flung the crew about, and they were scattered everywhere; thrown up to the edges of the ship, tangled in rigging, impaled on...well, whatever equipment they had on the deck. The occasional scream punctuated the night, and with a sweep, Cyrus took it all in and found his target.

He was upon the fallen Baynvyn in seconds, ripping Rodanthar from his son's grasp and drawing the most surprised look in the process. Baynvyn stared at him through squinted eyes, though they seemed slightly dulled. "What are you doing up here?" Baynvyn mumbled.

Cyrus rustled his fingers around the edges of Baynvyn's belt, searching. Ah. There.

Taking Epalette, he breathed another healing spell and took his time saying exactly what was on his mind. "I'm preparing to save your ass, that's what I'm doing." Cyrus glared at him, feeling a tingle in the back of his mind at the familiarity of those words. He looked around again. "What happened?"

"Strained the engines when we took off so fast," Baynvyn mumbled, though his voice was getting clearer. He tried to stand, but failed. "Made it about ten minutes before the main failed." He waved a nearly limp wrist, blinking furiously as though trying to shake off a head trauma. "Emergency landing."

"Crash, more like it," Cyrus said, striding over to the side of the ship. The blades were still turning on the main shaft overhead, albeit very slowly. They reminded him of a windmill rather than a hard-churning crank of the sort he'd seen on other airships in flight. "Is it reparable?"

"We'll need several minutes." Another man appeared from behind him. He was dark-elven, wide-bodied, and straitlaced as anyone Cyrus had ever seen. His uniform had been creased perfectly before this crash, Cyrus would have staked his sword on it. "I need to get down to the engine compartment. They were trying to effect repairs before...this, but..."

"They failed," Cyrus said, brusquely, because this was a moment that called for efficiency. "Get it done. I'll buy you some time, but I can't promise much."

The man stiffened, anger flashing across his dark features.

"You are a prisoner, and I am the shipmaster of this vessel. You do not tell me—"

"Do I look imprisoned?" Cyrus asked, the dual godly weapons in his hand probably causing his speech to come out extremely clipped. He didn't care; in fact, he welcomed it. "Are we in the middle of the lands where the scourge run free and wild and eat anything that falls out of the sky?"

The shipmaster stiffened slightly, but his chastening was obvious. "Yes."

"I'm a general and probably the only functional fighting man aboard capable of repelling those things," Cyrus said, staring down the shipmaster. "If you'd prefer, though, I can leave, and probably outrun them." He flashed the twin blades. "Your call – *Shipmaster.*"

The shipmaster looked as though he'd had something reasonably uncomfortable shoved into his gullet.

"Just go along with it, Hongren," Baynvyn said blearily. He seemed to be coming back to himself somewhat. "There's no chance we make it clear of the swarm coming our way without his help."

"As you say." Shipmaster Hongren gave Baynvyn a curt nod. "I will get to the engine room immediately."

"You might want to get the men ready with those cannons," Cyrus called after him as he bolted down the staircase belowdecks. "I don't know how many scourge are coming, but I'm guessing it's a lot." He stood tall, trying to see over the rails that lined the deck edges. In that direction it looked clear to the horizon.

He spun. There was no seeing over the quarterdeck, so Cyrus leapt, coming down next to the ship's wheel, which stood unattended. No sign of movement across the flat, dead, dusty plain in that direction. He swiveled to look to the right—

Ah.

"There you are," he muttered, for there they were, indeed.

Reikonos was barely visible, the Citadel tower just a spiked shadow in the looming darkness, really, no sign of the walls or moat. But the Citadel...yes, he could see the top of that, where Malpravus had plotted his damned evil, had done–

No time for that recrimination. "Shit," Cyrus whispered. He gauged; the scourge were five minutes away, perhaps ten if they moved slowly.

A thousand years with barely a meal landing in their forsaken territory? "Maybe four minutes," he breathed.

Thumping footfalls on the deck made Cyrus whirl.

"Just me," Baynvyn said. A slick of navy blood wended its way down his temple. It was crusted over by his spell, and a clarity was beginning to return to his eyes. "Can I have Epalette back, please?"

"No," Cyrus said, and leapt over the aft rail. He cast Falcon's Essence on the way down, and was spared a broken leg as the spell light flared around his hands. He stepped down to the earth in the shadow of the ship's stern, as easy as taking a stair.

"If you die, we'll be left defenseless!" Baynvyn called down to him. He hung over the aft deck rail, gaze flitting from Cyrus to the ravening horde coming across the horizon. "That's my mother's blade!"

"Then I guess you'll be motivated to help me get back aboard when the moment comes." Cyrus watched the growing shadows on the plain ahead, growing larger with every passing second. "Otherwise you can kiss your dagger goodbye."

CHAPTER 6

Vara

The night had closed in and the red glow of the spell had faded from her eyes by the time the airship had arrived at the scene. Now a new glow was rising behind the city walls, the light of fires unwatched and uncontained by the people of the city. Roofs had taken to flame here and there, spots of light shining in a field of dark, like a holed blanket thrown over the head on a sunny day.

"Vara," Isabelle said softly, gently. Her voice had changed in the intervening time since last they'd met; her patience had grown.

Vara's had waned. "What?" Especially now.

"There is little to see here," Isabelle said softly. The crew was crowding around the bow with them, leaving little in terms of a respectful space. They were pointing, talking – gawking, really. "You know that spell. You know what it does."

Vara's teeth clenched, and she had to pry her jaw apart to

give reply. "You cannot be certain that this spell is the same spell as – oh, to the hells with it." She clenched a fist, wanting to hammer something desperately. Of course it was the same spell she'd seen Malpravus use against the entirety of Goliath, sacrificing them on the pyre of his ambition.

Isabelle said nothing for a long moment, letting the hushed voices of the crew be the only break upon the evening's silence. When she did speak, it was, somehow, gentler still. "There is no surviving that."

"There was no surviving the God of War, either," Vara said, "yet here I am."

"But you said yourself," Isabelle was calm, measured – and damned irritating for it, "you felt the pull of Sanctuary in the moments before the spell. That it...died."

How to respond to that? She kept from losing her mind, but only just. "I felt something," Vara said. "that does not mean–"

"But you cannot fade any longer? You cannot retreat to the ether or whatever you call it?"

Vara's jaw tightened once more. "No."

"Then what could that mean but that Sanctuary is gone?" Isabelle asked. "The spell...it would have required great power." She fiddled with her hands, finally settling on crossing them before her white robes. "Great magical power is not easily found in these days, I can assure you. The reservoirs are dry. If I may suggest–"

"Just say it," Vara snapped. "Malpravus drained Sanctuary and used it to prime the pump of his spell which sapped all the life in Reikonos." She wheeled on Isabelle. "Why pussyfoot around?"

Isabelle did not hem, nor haw. "Because I want you to come to the realization in your own time that–" And she halted there.

Vara turned back to the cityscape, picking out a house in the distance whose thatched roof was already fully engulfed. "He is not dead."

"Is it your brain or your heart which makes that determination?"

Vara pursed her lips as she considered. "I am not certain, I simply know that it is so." She straightened her bearing. "He lives. I feel it."

A small, almost muted note of exasperation escaped Isabelle. "Very well," though, was what she said, in apparent defiance of her true feelings on the matter. "What do you wish to do about it?"

Now Vara wheeled again, but not at Isabelle. She scoured the deck of the airship for her target and, once found, went for him immediately, as certain of her course as an arrow that had already left the bow.

Captain Beniye waited on the top deck of the airship next to the wheel, surveying the destruction and dictating a letter aloud to a small-boned elven woman with a large book across her lap who sat just behind him. Vara ignored what he was saying for she did not care, and stalked up the stairs to the quarterdeck, barely keeping herself from skipping it altogether and leaping up beside him. Isabelle followed, making more quiet noises of exasperation but arguing none.

"Captain," Vara said without preamble or for him to even finish dictating his current thought. His eyes lit in surprise; Captain Beniye was an older man, close to the turn that all elves took if they got old enough, the one that brought the final deterioration of their physical bodies in the last century or so before death. He still had the sharp angles of bone structure one might associate with youth in a human, but they were softening distinctly, hints of jowls beginning to form. "I need to land in the city immediately."

Beniye's eyes were an earthy mix somewhere between green and brown. He was judicious in his reply, but swift: "Impossible. If they are all dead, the dockyards will be quite inoperable to us." He waved a hand in the direction of a familiar section of Reikonos. "There will be no landings in the city now."

"Fine, get me close and I'll jump off myself," Vara said, pointing at the wall. "That should be easy enough."

Beniye paled. "How would you get back aboard, though?"

Something about that struck squarely on Vara's nerves. "What do you care? I'll not be your problem anymore."

Beniye now flushed, a deep scarlet. "Shelas'akur...you have just returned to us. Forgive me, but I cannot see myself casting the last hope of the elves overboard as though she were some excess ballast."

Vara closed her eyes, trying to decide how to respond to that. It was both kinder and yet more condescending than she might have imagined, as though she were some glasshouse flower, too delicate to be allowed to make her own way.

"It has been a thousand years, Captain," Isabelle said, taking up the cause with admirable delicacy. "I should think it would be obvious by now that our days of hope are passed. Now the elves of the south have taken up the torch."

Beniye's crimson hue deepened slightly, and he averted his eyes. "I just thought – with Lady Vara returned to us, perhaps–"

Isabelle shook her head gently. "The shape of things is too far bent to imagine it will ever go back to the way it was before. My sister has family in Reikonos. She needs to see for herself. How best can we do that? And most safely?"

The captain swallowed visibly, then turned his calculating eyes upon the city. "We have a rope ladder, and there is space enough in the city parks."

"Drop me over there," and Vara pointed to the wall on the far eastern edge of the city, "that would be best." She caught the glimpse of puzzlement from her sister. "See that statue?" She pointed to twin stone edifices, two men hewn out of rock and raised high above the buildings surrounding them. "That's not so far from where Sanctuary was." She felt that curious tug within herself. "It would be a good place to start our search."

Beniye sighed audibly, but nodded. "I will see it done."

"Excellent," Vara said, feeling like she'd finally extracted a hard-won concession from this negotiation. She looked to her sister, who had a knowing smile of the sort they might have shared back when Vara was a child and Isabelle a young adult, both in a city of interminable elders who had little memory of childhood. "Then that is where we begin."

CHAPTER 7

Alaric

The quarterdeck was surprisingly quiet, Mazirin's voice barely audible over the churning sound of the airship's blades turning above them. They seemed oddly muted, though perhaps that was because in Alaric's ears, he could still hear rushing blood and the silent scream of that red mass of magic running through the city, his city–

He blinked, and his vision was still blotted with the red light, some afterimage of the horror he'd witnessed. Twice now, he'd seen that city destroyed and been powerless to stop it.

Alaric turned his attention to the brown-coated captain, with her braided ebony hair hanging around her shoulders as she gave her orders to the man at the wheel. He did not understand her language, but her diction was clear and there was little doubt she was sure of what she was doing even if, for the moment, he had no clue what he was to do.

"Where are we going?" he asked, not waiting for her to finish her conversation. He almost regretted speaking out of turn as soon as he'd done it. Almost.

She turned to him slowly, coolly. In her eyes he saw the icy reserve that he'd associated with her had returned. It had disappeared in the moments when she'd brought her ship in close and rescued him, when she'd fallen out and he'd caught her in his arms. All that was gone, now. Her guard was back, the ice had frozen once more within her.

She finished whatever she had to say to the helmsman, and then she drew herself up stiffly. "I am required to report this incident to the nearest Amatgarosan outpost. Immediately."

A dull pain radiated behind Alaric's eyes, and it seemed to slow his deciphering of her meaning. "Where is that?"

"It is called Xiaoshani," she said. "It is two days from here."

Alaric shook his head slowly. "There could be survivors back there." He didn't feel a need to point to the city behind them. "I need to–"

Mazirin's eyes did not show any reaction. "We are not going back."

Alaric stared at her. "But–"

"I risked my crew's life once already," Mazirin said, and there was a raw anger chafing beneath the surface of that ice. "I will not do so again. I have my duty." She looked away, and when she spoke now, there was less sting in her words. "Also...there was no surviving that."

Somehow that only made Alaric see red, as though he were not already seeing it endlessly, burned upon his very eyes. "You don't know that."

She raised an eyebrow at him. "I do. And if you consider it with your head rather than your heart, you would know it, too."

"I can't just leave them–"

"There are only bodies to leave," Mazirin said, and now her voice had achieved something almost in the range of gentle. "You saw what that thing did." She pointed behind them, as though he did not know which direction he wanted to head, which direction his almighty failure lay. "There was no stopping it – and no surviving it."

Alaric stared down at the much smaller captain. "I...I need to know if–"

"I have standing orders," she said, and she straightened her back. Gone was any pretense of warmth, too. This was a decision made, and her very bearing told Alaric that any talk would count for nothing. "Xiaoshani. Two days."

"Where is this Xiaoshani?" Alaric asked. His head felt as though it were spinning, and any control he'd had of his heading was lost now unless he wanted to leap over the edge. Part of him contemplated it, but found the option lacking. In survivability, in prudence.

And with a glance, he saw again Guy and Edouard, waiting at the rail below. They were both watching, and Alaric felt his resolve tighten in that moment.

"Captain," Dugras said, coming up the steps to the quarterdeck. "The engines will hold until we get to Xiaoshani."

"Thank you," Mazirin said, then turned away from them both.

Dugras looked up at Alaric, and he realized suddenly that the dwarf had spoken in his language entirely for his benefit, perhaps to make him feel included in this moment when he could easily have said whatever he had to in their own language, leaving it an utter mystery to Alaric. "I'm sorry about what happened to Reikonos," the engineer said. "That was truly terrible. I haven't seen its like since...well, ever, really."

Alaric cocked his head. "Thank you. I am only glad that there was no harm that came to yourself, your captain, or your ship." He looked up to find Mazirin's back to him. "You truly went bravely beyond any requirements given the situation, and I feel fortunate that you were not harmed by being caught in the middle." He lowered his gaze, finding a scarred piece of wooden decking to focus on. "Obviously I cannot say the same for...so many others."

"It's not your fault," Dugras said. But as reassurances went, it was both flimsy and hollow, entirely unsuited to the task at hand. Such was the lot of falsities said for comfort, though, and as such Alaric found no comfort in it.

"I appreciate you saying so," Alaric answered. "But I think we both know that if I hadn't prompted this things might have gone very differently." He looked out to the left and found glittering moonlight running parallel with the *Yuutshee* against the surface of the once-Torrid sea. "This is simply a failure I will have to live with."

"Right," Dugras said uncertainly. "Well...no one could have guessed–"

"Thank you for your attempts to assuage my guilt," Alaric said stiffly. "But they are unnecessary." He clasped his hands behind him, realizing that in his own way, he was mirroring Mazirin's posture when she indicated the conversation was closed. "My complicity is obvious, and I will deal with this," he said with surprising feeling, stirred deep to the bones of him, "when I can." He forced a smile. "It appears I will have at least two days to do so. And to decide what...if anything...is next."

With a bow of his head, Alaric turned from Dugras. He caught a flash of movement out of the corner of his eyes. Mazirin was looking at him, but looked away as soon as she caught him doing so. Whatever dance they had been doing, the two of them, this seemed another part of it, but Alaric had not the will to figure out his own move, nor the inclination to make it. Instead he focused on keeping himself upright on his weary legs, and holding in the sickness of his heart at the thought of what had happened this night, and maintaining the braveness of his face as he descended from the quarterdeck to where Guy and Edouard watched and waited for him – very possibly the last surviving remnant of Sanctuary.

CHAPTER 8

Cyrus

The scourge churned across the empty earth between Cyrus and the horizon. He had to admire what they'd done, really; there was not a tree, not a blade of grass, anywhere in sight. Whatever else these endless, surging beasts were, they were effective destroyers of life. Why, they'd turned the once verdant plains and forested lands south of Reikonos into a near-desert, hard-packed dunes lit by the moon breaking through the clouds.

"How are you faring thus far?" Baynvyn's voice reached Cyrus's ears; his voice still sounded cottony from his injury.

"The enemy has yet to arrive," Cyrus called back drolly. "I'm in little danger from anything but a turned ankle upon this blighted ground until they get here."

"Right," Baynvyn called. "Well...perhaps try not to move around too much, then. The earth looks a bit rutted."

Cyrus rolled his eyes. His son was not wrong, but neither

was he helpful. Mobility would be key in the coming fight. "How go the repairs?"

Now Shipmaster Hongren answered. "We need ten minutes to fix the lift engines and get her aloft. After that, we can assess the damage to the ones that propel us forward, free from worry of these things swarming us to death."

Cyrus looked back to find the shipmaster at the rail next to Baynvyn. Both looked down at him as though he were some animal in a far-flung arena about to fight for the pleasure of the crowd. "Do you have a rope ladder?"

Hongren stiffened as though he'd been struck by a bolt. Then he disappeared, presumably to hunt for said ladder.

Cyrus turned back to the encroaching scourge. There were many of them, too many to count. Yet fewer than he might have expected given the number clustering around Reikonos. Perhaps Malpravus's vile spell had eliminated a few of them?

Well, one could hope. But hope was hardly a winning battle plan, and not the only thing Cyrus Davidon had at his disposal.

"All right, all right," Cyrus muttered to himself, gripping Rodanthar and Epalette. Yes, mobility would be key to his defense of the airship. The scourge moved quickly, struck hard, and had overwhelming numbers. They could also climb in ways that nearly defied belief given their lanky limbs and stout bodies. Their strength was considerable, animal in its way. To be caught beneath a surge of them would be death, even for him, armored as he was.

"What are you going to do?" Baynvyn called down to him.

"Fight them, of course," Cyrus called back, already mentally working through the options. The ground around was of little tactical use; it was merely uneven plains, but with no steep, sweeping gradients or canyons for him to use as a chokepoint. Not that such a thing would work against the climbing scourge.

No, the only geographical feature that worked against them was water, and there was none of that between here and Lake

Ashea. Assuming that lake even still existed in these forsaken days.

"But how?" Baynvyn asked. Persistent little shit.

"With great alacrity and dogged persistence," Cyrus offered, for it was, truly, all he had. If they pinned him down, he would be dead, and the airship shortly thereafter. If he were to be drawn too far away from the ship, then, too, it would be overwhelmed, and eventually they would get him, given that there was nowhere for him to go between here and the river Perda, hundreds of miles to the west. Even with two godly weapons in hand, he did not favor his odds of running that far.

"That's not much of a strategy."

"But it beats the hell out of standing still and giving up," Cyrus said, not caring whether he was heard or not. The wind had a chill to it and was finding the gaps in his chain mail. It tugged at his underclothes like the fingers of a lover, him feeling quite bound by all the cloth and metal. The scourge were now a mere hundred feet away, a great crashing wave of death that he could already smell. The scent of rot filled his nose and choked to the back of his tongue like a necromancer's pet shoving a skeletal hand into his jaws.

Baynvyn gagged behind him; he smelled it too, then.

"In the last thousand years I'd forgotten how much these things reek," Cyrus said, mostly to himself, swinging Rodanthar up to a high guard above his head and putting Epalette out in front of him at just above waist level. He bent his knees slightly; they'd leap at him, and the dagger would catch them close, the sword would swing from on high with great power.

Now that they were near he could see the splits in the heaving mass of dead, gray things. They were not just one writhing wave, but individual scourge with their black eyes and wrinkled, elephantine skin.

They came upon him both more quickly and more slowly than Cyrus anticipated, and he wondered at how those two contradicting ideas could even coexist. On one hand they seemed to ooze toward him like gray syrup rolling across the plain. On the other they were upon him in great number, as though they leapt up quickly in the last second, and he began to swing to counter them coming at him–

Limbs flew, torsos were ripped cleanly in half. Cyrus waded in, shouting at the top of his lungs, summoning the battle fury that had seen him safely through so very many fights. It was not enough to be cold, no. Mere calculation could not win this day, would not keep him alive in the midst of the coming storm of teeth and claws and death. One had to hate the enemy, to want to see them dead. Admittedly, this was easier with scourge than with a human foe. The black eyes were deep and pooling, like oil dripped into large dots upon the gray faces. His blade found home and a scourge head went flying.

"Don't stop!" Baynvyn shouted, perhaps in expectation it might have some effect on Cyrus's plans.

It didn't; Cyrus bent slightly and sprinted to the side, running with Rodanthar's blade turned out against the tide of scourge flooding at him. He still shouted, top of his lungs, for he needed to hold their attention. A glance back proved that yes, it was working–

So he threw himself into them, and his arms worked madly. Now there were no individual scourge again, only a faceless mass coming at him endlessly. He was in their midst, and his vision was a tunnel that was black around the edges. There was whatever target he was swinging upon in the moment and little else. Cleave this one's head off – done. Catch this one on Epalette and drag the blade from arse to throat, sending the creature yelping back into its fellows, who trod it underfoot until the whimpers died.

Cyrus flailed wildly in a controlled dance of death. The twin blades gave him extra time, and every moment of it was necessary. He carved his way through the scourge in a bloody swath, shouting and yelling and kicking and spinning because they came from nearly every direction, every moment. He would no sooner batter one back than another would appear at his heels trying to land teeth upon him. They would often succeed, too, and a dozen little breaks in his skin left him bleeding from the knees, the thighs, the left hip – anywhere they'd managed to catch that his plate didn't quite protect. The chainmail did not break, but neither could it hold back entirely the pressure of those jaws, relentless and driving like one of those steam engine machines he'd seen in Reikonos.

A breathed healing spell here and there stifled the pain; it was hardly unmanageable in any case. The bites were but wicked stings, shearing force applied to his chainmail. He gritted his teeth and struck wherever he felt it, making it stop every time–

But there were so many, and then came the one he could not stop.

It was at the ankle, and he swung when he felt it. A scourge grabbed him as he sprinted, shoving his way forward and making a hole in their ranks. That was all he was doing, cutting through them. Keeping one step ahead of the ocean of ever-snapping jaws.

This one, though, caught him at the exactly wrong moment. The scourge's open mouth moved just so and caught his foot as he was moving forward. No mere bite as he passed, this one captured his whole boot in its mouth. He struck, of course, planting Epalette squarely in the top of the thing's head, but–

It already had him, and the strike made it jerk, a final spasming of its jaws locking the hold tighter, for it had him solidly.

The scourge died, but it dropped as it did, and Cyrus dropped with it, caught by the weight of the creature and already on one foot. It tugged him like a snare, pulling him to the ground.

He yelped as he went down, swinging Rodanthar and

Epalette both in a mad attempt to clear the space around him before he went down. This was an unforeseen complication; he hit the earth heavily, shoulder crying out as he landed, the armor plating absorbing the impact.

But nothing could absorb what came for him now.

They were on him in a breath. Biting, scratching, clawing, an infinite number of scourge, all sweeping upon him like water in a sea. He bowed his head to protect his face, the most vulnerable part of him, and heard the claws and teeth strike plate mail and chainmail and the top and sides of his helm. For they were all over him, in every direction, an unceasing tide of teeth and claws and violence–

And they would not stop until they had torn him apart.

CHAPTER 9

Vaste

He woke to blows raining down upon his head, to the thump of clubs and the men of this ship trying to split his skull, and to his surprise, Vaste cared muchly.

"Stop...that!" Vaste said, taking hold of Letum and whipping it across six strong men. He swept them away like refuse before a broom, pushing rather than striking, and they were bowled over like stalks of wheat in a wind.

"Ah, now you awaken." Qualleron's dry voice ran out among the myriad of bruises and pains that ached Vaste's head. He stood off some ten feet, that mountain of a sword before him, and twenty men with weapons of their own, some bladed and serious, some makeshift like wrenches and wooden implements, extended before him and clustered together with the aura of fear about them. They made no move toward the warrior troll. "You did not hear my struggles?"

"I didn't hear anything until these morons began clubbing

me," Vaste said, brushing fingers against his scalp. Knots were already forming there, and he muttered a healing spell. It helped little. "Probably they were trying to reduce me in intelligence so that I would be equal to them; the joke is on them, though, for at this moment I would welcome being so stupid and ill-aware of the world around me, if I didn't have to match them in terms of personal hygiene."

"It is probably a package deal, intelligence and grooming," Qualleron announced in a booming voice, surprisingly jovial for a man – troll – who held at bay some twenty others at the point of his sword. "I think we have outstayed our welcome. Perhaps we should together leap over the side."

One of the sailors who'd taken a club at him waved his weapon at Vaste, pitching anger at him in a foreign tongue. Vaste wagged Letum back at him warningly. "I find this to be a most cruel eviction, another indignity piled on top of many worse. But if it gets me away from these smelly men..." And he eased to the side of the ship, placing a hand on the edge and looking over. "Why, we're still thirty feet from the ground."

Wavy plains lurked below, the smell of fresh-tilled dirt mingling with the oil of the airship and the toxic steam that somehow followed them, as though creeping between the planks of the ship's decking. Still...the drop was sizable.

"I'm not jumping from this ship unless you bring us lower," Vaste said, looking back at the men, who'd crept in on him while he'd been looking. He feinted at one, threatening to take his head off with Letum but settling for a solid bonk that knocked him to his knees instead. "Take us lower."

"They don't understand you," Qualleron said. "Few bother to learn the backwards languages of this land. And why would they? There's little profit in it." He bellowed something in perhaps that same foreign tongue, something that sounded smooth and yet deep, when spoken in Qualleron's voice.

The humans talked amongst themselves. Swarthy men, ill-kept, they reminded Vaste of the desert folk, though minus the spiffy robes. These men wore vests of poor cloth and looked like they might be as pale as Vara were they not under the perpetual sun. One of them answered back to Qualleron, though he sounded smoother still.

"They will take us lower," the larger troll said, his yellow face implacable. "Then they want us to get off without complaint."

"I will complain as much as I damned well please," Vaste said. "And to all the hells with them if they don't like it. It's not as if they can understand me anyhow."

Qualleron spoke back to the men, and they rumbled and talked amongst themselves, still brandishing their weapons and makeshift weapons and looking very worried about the whole thing. "I have told them what you said," the yellow troll let a small grin leak out, "and they agree that they do not care if you whine about your lot so long as you get off this ship."

Vaste snuck another look over the edge; the wheat field was gone, replaced by some other crop, beans or some other close-to-the-ground vegetable. The pace of the ship had slowed nearly to naught, and he felt now they were only a mere few feet from the earth, perhaps fifteen or so.

The squeak of the deck made him look up; Qualleron had sheathed his sword and stood beside him, peering over. "This is, I think, as good as we will receive. If they bring the ship too low, they risk to rip the bowels of the vessel out upon the earth."

"I'd like to rip their bowels out," Vaste grumbled. He caught a scowl from one of the closest men. "Oh, piss off. I know you can't understand me. Take your hateful eyes and shove them up your arse as a laxative. Or mayhaps I'll do it for you."

Qualleron bellowed a laugh. "Does this abuse you heap upon them make you feel better?"

"Not particularly, no," Vaste said, steeling himself. The ship had come nearly to a stop now. "But seeing as they're ejecting me over a foreign land without reckoning for where I am or where I'm meant to go, I don't feel very bad about it." He grasped Letum in both hands, put first one foot, then the other over the rail and stood upon the edge of the vessel. "Why, I ought to set a small fire on their vessel before I go—"

"No," Qualleron said, and gave him a shove.

The world went decidedly topsy-turvy, the ground rushing up to meet Vaste. With Letum's aid, he managed to turn a whole flip in midair before he crashed down, going from seeing the dark earth and green plants rising up to meet him to a flash of the horizon and then the slowly bluing skies above. The sun nearly blinded him, shining out of the east, then his arse hit the ground in a decidedly unsubtle manner, and one of these damnable vegetables snuck its way up his robe and molested him in such a way as he could only have hoped Birissa might have, given enough time.

Of course, there was no time, and she was a construct of his fantasies brought to life and then death by Sanctuary, but still.

"I hate vegetables," Vaste said, lying firmly upon his back with his robe risen entirely too high for his comfort.

"They make you strong," Qualleron said, landing much more lightly, and upon his feet, damn him. He offered a hand, mailed, with a squeak of the joints, to Vaste as aid.

Vaste swatted it away with Letum and basked in the pain along his arse, his glorious arse. "Perhaps if taken orally. I cannot imagine this particular plant is making me stronger, trying to enter my body as it is." He brushed at it, felt the sting of it leave his clenched buttocks. He sat up, looking around warily. The ship was already rising above them; the refuse cast off, the men aboard clearly had no desire to linger. "Where are we, even?"

"I believe we are across the river the folk of this land call the Perda." Qualleron stood with his legs firmly planted, looking around as if he were simply seeking out some point of interest.

"Wonderful," Vaste said. "Then we're in the territory of the elves or the humans, and I care not which because they both probably hate me."

"Really?" Qualleron mused. "What did you do to earn such enmity?"

"I exist," Vaste said, rising slowly to his feet and muttering an incantation to soothe his savagely wronged arse. "Also...I probably mouth off a bit, though clearly that's secondary to the whole 'existing' thing."

Qualleron laughed loudly, a deep belly laugh that thundered over the fields and overcame the sound of the retreating airship, now some distance off and the noise fading as it headed south. "You strike me as a man whose mouth gets him in more trouble than his mere presence."

"Well, who the hell asked you?" Vaste stood up, feeling the squeak of vertebrae in his back as he straightened. Looking around in all directions, he saw...

Nothing, really.

Vegetables, vegetables, and more vegetables.

Not a road, not a house, not a town.

"Come," Qualleron said, and beckoned him south, following the trail of the airship. "Let us begin our journey."

"Counter-proposal," Vaste said. "Why don't I plop my delicious arse down right here, avoiding all nearby flora, and you can just go on without me?"

Qualleron had taken a few monstrous steps, and now he paused, cocking his large head. "Why?"

Vaste sighed. "Because why would I go on?"

Qualleron just stared at him blankly. "You'll have to eat."

"Well, if your thesis about the dietary soundness of vegetables is accurate, I have plenty to eat right here," Vaste said, waving his hand at the fields around him. Another sigh, and he felt it to his bones. "Why should I go? My friends are dead. Reikonos is asunder." His legs wavered, but he did not plop down as he might have wished to.

"You must have some reason to go on," Qualleron said, staring back at him, the sun framing his large, muscular, armored body in the rays of its light, "for you have risen from your fall. Your heart has already spoken. You are ready to carry on. Let us go."

"What?" Vaste bristled. "No! You are mistaken. Or my heart is an idiot. I won't rule that out, since it did just fall in love with a phantasm." He sighed. "Qualleron...I don't know how I can go on given this ruin I've just seen done."

The larger troll took a single step toward him, landing a hand thunderously upon his shoulder, the metal of the gauntlet laying real weight upon him. "It is simple," Qualleron said. "You will put one foot before the other and follow me onward to the next village, where we will break our fast on something other than vegetables and you will regain your will."

Vaste blinked. "That...that cannot be it. That's not a plan."

"It is a plan," Qualleron said, winking at him, and starting away, armor clinking. "And we shall follow it until the hand of fate steers our next move." He did not slow, either, cutting his path across the field of green, dark earth given a golden tinge by the sun's morning light.

"Well, it's a shit plan, then," Vaste muttered. "And I can only imagine where your hand of fate wants to go, and it's probably going to find some vegetable remnants there." But he found his feet moving, however reluctantly, to keep pace with the yellow troll from the far off land, though with every step the burden in his heart did not lessen one ounce.

CHAPTER 10

Vara

"Who the hell is that supposed to be?" Vara asked as she took the last step off the airship ladder. She was talking about the nearby statue, fifty feet tall, armored and helmeted, with a grand sword and sharp lines. Her feet sank into the thin, well-trod grass, the soil denting beneath the weight of her armor and herself from the ten-foot drop.

Beniye had gotten them as close as he could. Bringing the airship down between the twin sculptures in this ocean of green in the midst of the rat trap city of brick and wood, with the plumes of black smoke already rising all around them, it hovered a mere forty feet off the ground, and the ladder had only been thirty long.

"I believe it's meant to be your esteemed husband." Isabelle hung over her, swaying rather heavily from Vara's departure from the last rung. "Catch me?"

"Catch your own bloody self, cleric," Vara said, favoring her with a sour look. A whispered healing spell mitigated some of the discomfort in her ankle from the leap. "You'll find landing on me to be an unpleasant prospect given the curves of my armor."

With a muffled sigh, Isabelle let herself drop, landing in a crouch, her white robes whispering beneath the heavy thrum of the airship's engines and the whip of its rotating blades. She seemed to manage the thing delicately, at least as such things went. Her pale, unlined face evinced a hint of discomfort, and without a word from her lips, her fingers were bathed in a light glow. "I come all this way and you cannot even give me the courtesy of a soft landing."

"You want to land on my armored arse, maybe break your tailbone? I'll throw you back up, you can give the dismount another go."

Isabelle smiled lightly. "Your face...I had forgotten it, the lines of it had become smoothed and faded in my memory."

Vara felt the frown pluck at her brow as she peered past the trees into the glow of the dead city at night. "I do not have lines on my face. I'm barely thirty-five...well, for years lived in the world. If you don't have lines, I can't imagine I do."

"Perhaps it's something about the grim set of your jaw," Isabelle said wistfully. "That tireless determination that you used to unleash on Mother and Father had faded into the recesses of my mind as well."

"Bit of a dead letter, that," Vara said, peering through the swaying trees and feeling the warm, dry air coming from the fires in...well, every bloody direction, it felt like. "This way...I think."

"Where are we going?" Isabelle fell in beside her, favoring one leg over the other. Probably twisted her ankle, then. Vara murmured a healing spell of her own. "Thank you, but I rather think I can manage it better than you."

"It's hard for me to tell what you're capable of these days,"

Vara said, falling into an easy march step. She left the grass behind as it gave way to cobblestones just over a curb, and the green of the park surrendered to the wood and clapboard buildings in this part of town. "Magic being what it is."

"Speaking of dead letters, are we?" Isabelle said, and she stopped in the middle of the street, the gentle scratch of her sole upon the cobbles just barely audible under the whipping of the airship's engines behind them and the rising hiss of a wind through the buildings ahead.

Vara turned. "You talking about magic in these days? Or...that?"

That happened to be a corpse in the middle of the road. It lay there without sign of ill deed, no blood spilled, wound gouged or even a hint of murder.

Isabelle stooped beside it. *It* was once a woman in a sundress, but now it was cold meat, left unforgivably to moulder here on the stones of the road. She brushed the woman's bare forearm. "Cold."

"Again, you'll have to specify. The corpse or...all this?"

"In every case, it could well be both," Isabelle said, taking hold of the woman's – now corpse's – jaw and turning it to either side. There was some small resistance, the cold grip of death's immovable hold not laid entirely upon the body as yet. "Not a hint of violence upon her, yet it was done nonetheless."

"Malpravus," Vara said, almost a growl. She turned her eyes forward and began to stalk ahead. "This is his mark."

"But there is no mark."

"That's how you know it's him," Vara said. "Death is what he gives, and in such large and cruel measure."

They passed more corpses; men, women, old, and young, there was no discernible difference and no hint of mercy. The faces were turned in almost the same direction–

The one in which they were heading.

"Are you quite sure you know where you're going?" Isabelle

asked, her robes rustling as she held them up to keep the hem from dragging on the bodies that were growing thicker in the street. As if they'd all run out of doors to see the death that approached.

But how would they have known, Vara wondered? She caught a reflection upon a high window to her left – fire from some streets away, glinting down to her over the lower buildings to her right.

Ah! That was it, then. The light through the windows, reflected red as death. She nodded slowly as she walked, threading around the bodies, in equal measure giving them the dignity of space by not treading on them but also needing to make her way through. "They saw it coming through the windows," she whispered. "Saw that red light of death mirrored in window and glass."

"You saw it before, didn't you?" Isabelle asked.

Vara nodded slowly. "At the temple in the Waking Woods, when Malpravus first learned that evil spell. He meant to turn it loose on all, but ended up sacrificing his own army before anyone."

A shadow crossed Isabelle's perfect features. "And now he has turned it loose upon his own city. Fitting, I suppose."

"Yes, he's all about building a pyre of his own apotheosis while using the little people as kindling for his ascent," Vara said, ducking down an alley. The chop of the airship's blades followed them, Beniye keeping the ship apace but above, watchful.

"If you're right, then he has now ascended," Isabelle said. "What do we do about that?"

Vara felt her jaw tighten. "First, we find my dear husband." Because he was alive, he had to be. "And then..." She felt a momentary quiver in her stomach, no more than a flutter of possibilities, grim and terrible. "...Well...then we'll figure out what comes next."

CHAPTER 11

Cyrus

Cyrus had fallen, and it was an almost perfect reproduction of all his nightmares from his many years of battle.

He'd fallen before, of course, in war and in conflict. Felt the bite of death's hard teeth upon his flesh, dragging him into the darkness, knowing that if not for a well-timed resurrection spell, it would become eternal.

There had been that first time in Enterra. It had been an eye-opener for him, a warrior that had always operated without a healer who knew the resurrection spell. He'd fallen in the darkness of those caves, felt the touch of death upon him, the swift silence and bleak end that signified the stop of all things Cyrus. It had come without mercy, sharp claws glistening in the dark as he was seized by the strong hands of death.

He hadn't thought, at the time, he'd ever suck in a breath ever again. But he had.

This was different, however. Though he was wrapped in strong armor, enshrouded in strongest chainmail, the teeth of the scourge bit into his flesh all around the edges. Hard, pinching spikes of pain dragged across his flesh, trickles of warm blood cascading inside the protection of his armor and hinting that there was no protection, not from this dogpile of stinking, rotting flesh.

Cyrus sucked in a breath and nearly choked, the desire to retch much stronger than the one to scream. The weight of the things was all upon him, the jaw still clamped on his ankle, dragging him down even as he fought against it, trying to pull at his leg to rip it from the dead mouth.

No matter, though. Now they were upon him, upon his back, weighting him to the earth under failing arms. One had pinned his left arm, with Epalette in the fingers, to the very ground and was clamped around his wrist, dragging at it. It bent in improbable ways, impossible ways, really, the joints screaming out in protest at this abuse, and he felt his grip upon the dagger loosen, threatening to give way.

It was over, though, wasn't it? Cyrus tried to push up, but another scourge, or maybe five, were upon his legs. Their weight was not insurmountable, if he might have a moment to brace himself, to prepare and thrust upwards against cruel fate. There was no such moment, however, and no leverage. His knees, dragged by every thump and impact from gathering any purchase beneath them, found no ability to plant themselves so he could use his great strength to rise. Every time he flexed them he was knocked forward another inch, and he collapsed.

A thundering BOOM! from behind him caused a strange shudder to run through the scourge pile upon him. A wobble of momentum ran through the legs and feet and claws all perched upon him and then upon the scourge piled atop them – it was a darkening that Cyrus was experiencing, the sight of the ship vanishing under the endless scourge, growing like a tower upon his back and snapping at one another, each seeking for a morsel of him.

But the light, the noise! That stopped them for a bare moment, and splatters of black blood trickled down upon him.

One of those guns, the cannons upon the ship. They must have fired.

The scourge upon him were still impossibly thick, but Cyrus had his moment, and he used it to get his knees beneath him, to clutch the strength given him by Epalette and Rodanthar, to lift against the weight of all the fiends stacked upon him—

Cyrus moved. The scourge atop him shifted like a falling tower. His resolve increased, and he stabbed up, catching a scourge in the belly and making it squeal. Dragging his blade toward him, Cyrus thrust himself to one knee, Epalette and the hand clutching it a mere fist against the ground to give him stability as he put everything into rising.

Another crashing boom, and something hard and fast skipped by him, splattering him with thick scourge ichor like stinking oil. It spattered across his helm, and he blinked to avoid catching it in the eyes. He did not let it stop him, even as it distracted the scourge. He cut into the ones above him blindly, ripping one, maybe two of them apart based on the sounds. They began to skid off his backplate, and he turned and swung his blade even as more surged forward, threatening to again knock him off balance, to put him to the ground helpless, but this time on his back.

"No!" Cyrus shouted, and another boom – no, a flurry of them – echoed from the side of the ship. He caught a glimpse of a line of fire this time, smaller, cascading. Rifles at the edge of the deck, he realized, shooting into the scourge that had made it past him and were climbing up the ship.

Too few. Entirely too few, he knew as the scourge rushed around him like a river. He was exposed, thirty feet out from the ship.

"Cyrus!" Baynvyn's voice carried, even over the sound of the feral beasts that crowded all around Cyrus. "You're too far out!"

"I noticed that," Cyrus said, burying Epalette in the exposed belly of a scourge and then throwing it overhand into a clutch of its onrushing fellows. It bowled them over, freeing him for just a moment from worrying about attack from that direction. Like a spoiling strike against an army about to rush, it knocked them off their offense, at least for a breath.

But a breath was almost all Cyrus had, and then they were upon him again from every other direction. One hit him in the leg and his joint creaked beneath the blow, which was like a good, solid kick. He cringed and tried to ignore it, but the twinging within his knee told him damage had been done.

Another knocked into his back, and Cyrus could but swing wildly, trying to defray some of the attacks from the front as he stumbled forward onto a scourge that was coming low from the side. It voiced its displeasure, and he took little notice of it even as he buried Rodanthar in its skull.

Too many. Entirely too many.

This, then, was the same problem he'd foreseen, coming to fruition. In all the battles he'd ever fought, against dark elves and gods and trolls and men, truly the scourge were the most implacable. They would bury him with their numbers, and think nothing of it, for none of them thought. None saw him as anything other than meat for their bellies, life to be devoured. The cruelest joke the God of Death had ever unleashed on them was these, his last, parting gift.

The smell was devouring. Their weight was upon him, and with it that stink that pressed into his lungs like long-rotten flesh. It dared to choke him, but he couldn't stop long enough to retch, swinging as he did, sword and dagger, trying to keep them off him. They surrounded him, like wolves upon every side, yet he swung, pressing the bottom of his helm tightly against his armor, feeling the quartal scratch and drag against his breastplate as he tried to keep his neck tightly protected.

This, then, was the end. Another boom of cannons, and the flood subsided for perhaps a moment. The rumble of a thousand weighty feet upon the soft soils came like distant thunder, transmitted through his armor and into Cyrus's very bones, and it was as if he were in Luukessia again, a thousand years before, feeling the death of all that is, that was, that ever would be in that land coming for him.

But now...it was in Arkaria.

His home.

Blood thundered in his ears, a thousand pinpricks ate at his skin as claws ran continuously across his armor. There were so damned many, and his ceaseless swings could not get rid of enough of them. Black ichor spattered his face. Snapping teeth would be visible for a moment through the flood of gray flesh, then gone as he cut the thing in half. He wielded his blades wildly, always hitting some target, and yet still they came, from either side, from above, from belo–

But no. No, they did not come from below.

Cyrus kicked and found dead flesh; the corpses of a dozen scourge fell from him. To his right he stabbed and slashed, and whirled to the side, rising back to his feet.

The flow had abated, and he found himself surrounded, still, but only by three – then two, as his blade cut home.

There was no end of them, certainly, and they were focused upon him. A sea of gray flesh, as far as his eye could reach, extended out to the horizon.

"What in the hells of the depths...?" Baynvyn's voice made its way to him over the growls of more scourge than he could count. "What is that one doing?"

For there was one, one lone scourge before him. For a flash, he recalled Drettanden, large and wretched, leading the others of its kind in a quest for Cyrus's very blood.

THE SCOURGE OF DESPAIR

But Drettanden had been large; too much soul to fit into a normal scourge. This one was normal enough, but surging and snapping and clawing and ripping and tearing at the other scourge coming forward. Drettanden had been a leader, commanding them.

This one fought them, ripped them apart swiftly, and without fighting resistance from its own kind. Instead, they had come to a halt before it, a dozen or more gray bodies at its feet, ripped asunder at the throat and gut by it.

Cyrus staggered back; his legs were weak from the battle, and all around him he could feel the scourge desiring to press in, to devour him. They were close, he could tell, to breaking this odd truce, to surging in and making good what they'd tried to do before this thing – this one scourge – had stopped them.

"The engines are back online!" Hongren's voice filled the air, seemingly to the horizon. "We need one more minute to spool them up!"

A low, terrible growl reached Cyrus's ears, and he slashed as a scourge leapt the truce line and died, torn in half by his blade. He watched, scalp tingling. "I'll try and keep them off you for that long," Cyrus called back, not daring to look at the ship. The scourge had stopped their reckless advance, and a good thing, too; they'd have long since spilled around it and swarmed the sides if they'd but maintained their aggressive posture.

The scourge – that lone scourge – did not look at him. Indeed, he saw nothing but its back as it shuffled from side to side, growling and snapping and killing its fellows here and there that dared to stick their faces forward. It grabbed one by the throat as he watched and tore it open, black spraying out like oil from some wretched machine.

"What in all the hells is happening down there?" Baynvyn called out to him.

Cyrus didn't dare look back. The press of the gray devils was shuffling closer to him, and he could feel the thin thread of uncertainty holding them back, like a ravening wolf held at bay by a spear and little else. "You can see as well as I can. This scourge in front of me," he nodded at it, as if that mattered, as though acknowledging it somehow gave it power, gave it gratitude, would keep it helping him, "is really saving my..."

A tingle across his scalp was his warning that he'd tumbled to something.

The scourge looked back at him and wagged its backside significantly; there was something like regard in its black eyes. They looked somehow...less dead than any of the others.

Cyrus did not relax his guard, but the tingle spread down the back of his neck, triggering goosepimples along his arms, beneath the sticky, warm blood as the realization chilled him, and he looked into those black eyes, sure that this, indeed – beneath the gray flesh, beneath the stray hairs and wrinkled, elephantine skin – was a soul he knew. Knew – and had not seen in a thousand years, because she had gone into the embrace of death just before the rise of the scourge...

"...Niamh?"

CHAPTER 12

Vaste

"Did you know...?" Qualleron's rich bass voice echoed as he and Vaste strolled down a small path cut through the middle of the field. Birds chirped in the morning air, and Vaste could hear nothing but them and the sound of his own heavy footfalls with Qualleron's a thousand, a hundred thousand times an hour.

Or, at least, he could have heard only that, if not for Qualleron's endless nattering.

"...and then, when the Duchy of Vicienne called, I answered," Qualleron rambled, ambled, and wouldn't shut up. "We set out on a day much like today, through the rolling hills of that green country." He turned his broad, yellowed face to Vaste. "Have you ever been to Vicienne?"

"I haven't even heard of Vicienne." Heat pinched at Vaste's cheeks, and not from the sun or the day. This was his blood, rushing, lighting him up in the face. Couldn't he be left alone with his thoughts, with his humiliations? The pain of Birissa was still keenly felt, the thought that the ark, a thing he hadn't really ascribed any intelligence to, so pitied him it had created a dream lover out of whole cloth just to satiate his pitiful desires...

"You would like it," Qualleron said, nodding his mighty head, clearly assured. "The women are warm and welcoming to our kind. All sorts of women." He kept his face pointing forward, but the slightly amber tinge to his cheeks suggested this was not idle advice, but tailored specifically to his audience, and about as subtle as an anvil to the side of the head. "Human, elven, dwarven...gnomish, if that's your sort of thing–"

Vaste, ready to unload his frustrations, instead almost tripped over his own feet. "How in the hells does that even work, a gnome and a troll?"

"There are ways," Qualleron said, a glint in his eye.

"Gnomes are all of two feet tall at most! And I'm short at seven!"

Qualleron shrugged dismissively. "I leave the details to those who are interested in that sort of thing. For my part, I simply enjoyed my tour in the Duchy with more common pursuits. The food is exquisite. Their command of dough, for instance–"

"Oh, feck off with your dough," Vaste said, the curiosity about the physically improbable pairing of trolls and gnomes now past. "Why must you persist in this endless blathering? Do I seem in a mood for conversation?"

"You seem in a mood, that is certain."

"Well, I am in one," Vaste said, turning his eyes back to the road ahead. A woods loomed, broad and old ahead, mighty chestnuts and yew trees waiting, acorns strewing the hillside road. "And it would be much aided if you would cease this interminable travelogue and let me mourn my stupidity in peace."

"Well," Qualleron said after a brief pause, "I would but for my own experience, you see."

"What the hells does that even mean?"

"It is a simple thing," Qualleron said. "Obviously, I have spoken much of my experiences walking this world."

"Yes, and for a change, could you perhaps speak of your experiences *riding* this world? For I am quite tired of hearing of walking, especially because my feet already ache. Not to mention my bottom."

"That reminds me of another tale of the Duchy of Vicienne–"

"What, my bottom hurting? Yes, I imagine many bottoms hurt in Vicienne, if the elven, dwarven, human, and gnomish women insist on getting bawdy with troll men," Vaste said acidly.

Qualleron almost tripped over his own feet, and a low, bellowing laugh escaped him, sending the birds hiding in the fields all around them into the air as though he'd clapped his mighty hands. The troll bent almost double, wheezing as his laugh came to a slow end. "Yes, yes, that is quite funny. I see. Buggery, you call it, I think? Humorous."

"Yes, troll buggery is absolutely hilarious," Vaste said, rolling his eyes as he continued down the path. The first trees loomed before him, and the path wended up a natural hill, then down ahead, out of sight over a knoll. "Unless you're the one receiving it, in which case I imagine it becomes rather less funny and rather more painful."

"Indeed," Qualleron said, and his laughter died as quickly as it had started. They walked in silence up the hill and then it began to wend down, curving past a thick knot of trees, the undergrowth so dense that to stray from the path seemed not only inadvisable, but maybe impossible without a sword to hack one's way through. "Did I tell you yet about the ruin of the land of Prenasia?"

"No, but I'm sure you're about to," Vaste said, and the seething in his heart seemed to take new life. He'd reached his limit; enough of these stories of a wider world he gave zero damns about. He was resolute; he would tell Qualleron where to stick his many tales, and his only consolation should be that it wouldn't hurt as much as putting a troll member there would.

He'd set himself to open his mouth and deliver the missive of his heart – *Shut up, already* – when Qualleron seized him firmly by the shoulder. Vaste's gait was interrupted, so strong was the effect of the mercenary's hauling him back a step. He prepared to deliver an even angrier reproach, and straight to Qualleron's face, but–

Qualleron's face had gone stony, his eyes searching not Vaste's response to his rude manhandling of his person, but something...beyond.

Vaste kept from stumbling over his own feet, then righted himself again. He somehow held back his desire to unload his frustrations – numerous and comprehensive – and turned, instead, to see what Qualleron was icily surveying.

It was bodies. Twenty, thirty, maybe more. Strewn about, hacked to pieces, crimson staining the leaves. The rich, earthy aroma of the forest was cut with the tang of blood hanging thick in the air.

"Well, here I thought I was having a bad day," Vaste said bitterly, "and then these chaps had to come along and show me how much better it could be."

CHAPTER 13

Alaric

The sun rose on a shining sea, sparkles dancing and shimmering upon the glassy surface. The wind whipped over the bow of the *Yuutshee* and made a thunderous noise as it blew his long, graying hair back behind him. And beyond, where his eye met the horizon, Alaric saw something he figured he'd never lay eyes on again.

"That's the dead land, that is," Guy said, squinting at the green beyond the shore, lit beneath the rays of the rising sun.

"It is called Luukessia," Alaric said simply. "Or at least it was, when last I was there."

Guy stared at him. "Mate, that land's had scourge on it for a thousand years. You want to tell me – oh, whatever, I suppose, if you were with Cyrus bloody Davidon, maybe you were scarpering about a thousand years ago."

"In point of fact," Alaric said, unable to escape a wry smile, "this was ten thousand years ago. Eleven, now, actually."

"Yeah, awright," Guy chortled.

The soft, shuffling footsteps of someone else approaching from behind made Alaric turn his head. Dugras came upon them hesitantly, with his now-customary reluctance, as if intruding into their small corner of the *Yuutshee's* deck. "Hello," he said, with great stiffness. "How fare you?"

"The sun rises," Alaric said, "whether we want it to or not. And so goes life."

Dugras raised an eyebrow. "That's very, uhm...profound, I think?"

"Yeah, he's just full of profundity," Guy said. "And me, I'm full of profanity. So what the hells do you want? Fresh air?"

"I do like to get out of the engine space every so often," Dugras said. "But it's not just that." He kicked a small foot against the grain of the wood decking. "I always like to see this dead land before we get too far into its interior." He cast his eyes over the bow. "It seems to get uglier the deeper you get."

Alaric stared out over the last vestiges of the diminishing Sea of Carmas. "Then it is still filled to brimming with scourge?"

"No," Dugras said. "Not like Arkaria, where death is instant and certain. Here, if you crash in the right spot, you may survive a day. But enough remain to pose a permanent hazard." He chuckled. "Which is why so few dare to tread here."

"Except the Chaarlandian pirates," Guy said cheerily. "I hear they bloody love the place."

Edouard made a choking noise. "That's here?" His eyes wide, he looked back over the shores of Luukessia. "Oh. Oh, my."

"Relax, gentlemen," Dugras said with a smile. "Chaarlandian pirates know better than to attack Amatgarosan vessels."

Edouard remained pale. "Are you sure?"

"Pretty sure," Dugras said. "Amatgarosan freighters have teeth, after all," he pointed at a small cannon at the bow rail upon the forecastle, "and we have the might of the Empire behind us. They won't dare to harry us."

Alaric stared at the fore of the *Yuutshee*, watching the last sparkles of the seas fall away beneath them. With that ominous tempting of fate ringing in his ears, he stared ahead, seeing only empty earth, blighted and dead, as dark as what they'd left behind in Arkaria. Two homelands destroyed, now.

CHAPTER 14

Shirri

"Have you ever been to Amti?" Hiressam asked as they stood at the edge of the deck, watching the city loom larger and larger in view.

Shirri had not, and she said so. Hiressam merely smiled and added, "Then you're in for a treat," as though this were the only thing they had to worry about today.

Pamyra huffed at her side, but Shirri scarcely noticed. The wind was whipping at her hair, a warm one, out of the south, and the thrum of the airship's engines had become a strange companion to her over the course of their flight, which had lasted the night and into the dawn now bearing down on them from their left with startling brightness.

And soon enough – she saw it, indeed.

Shirri knew the history of Amti, of its settlement in the ages past, the days of her mother. How it had sprung from the immensely tall trees of the south, hidden from titans within the monstrous trunks, cities unto themselves encased in the wood but open to the sky above.

That was the past, though. Amti now...it was a different thing altogether.

The titans were gone, and with them, the need to build within the safety of the trees. Indeed, though the Jungle of Vidara still remained at the city's edge – the old town – now it sprung like any city across a plain, a city of wood and immense buildings carved out of the trunks of the trees where a mighty jungle had dwelled. Now tamed, broken to the will of the elves of the south, countless homes and buildings and markets stood where once the trees and vines held dominion. The tall, hollowed trunks towered into skies, four and five story buildings sandwiched between them that held closer to the terra firma below.

Sunlit sparkles ran across the surface of Lake Ashea at the southern edge of town, and the airship docks waited almost at the edges. They landed with but a bump, and Shirri found herself being ushered down the stairs the moment they were able, their uneasy benefactors among the crew eager to see them gone. They chittered at her in a strange language, one of Coricuanthi origin, she believed, by the dark shading of the crew's skin.

Their meaning was clear, though – *okay, you're safe now, get out.*

"They couldn't even spare a crust of bread for us," Pamyra muttered darkly as they wended their way between the airships at dock.

"In fairness, we never asked," Hiressam said, taller than them both and watching the surging crowd around them with his head in a constant pivot. "I didn't feel right about it, given we were already stowaways. At least they left us be, and didn't complain when I refilled our skins from their rain casks."

Her mother's face was sour, though. "I'm surprised they didn't begrudge us even that."

"Have a trace of gratitude," Hiressam said. They were in a break in the crowd, a thin spot where the docks ceased and suddenly movement was unencumbered by obstacles. Those disembarking now seemed less in number than a moment before, a surge all pushed through, and Shirri found herself once more with space to breathe.

Pamyra raised an eyebrow at that. "Gratitude? For what?"

"For our lives, of course." Hiressam paused, turning all his attention upon her. "We survived what so many did not."

Pamyra's eyebrows twisted down in angry lines. "We brought about that through our meddling. Their deaths–"

"Are not our fault," Hiressam said. "Nor our choice. We – excuse me?"

Shirri turned. A woman was standing behind her, having approached so quietly that her footsteps hadn't even been audible. She wore a green cloak that seemed burnt about halfway down, and a cowl hid half her face. Still, intent eyes peered out in undisguised curiosity. "Yes?" Shirri asked, feeling a bit put out by this sudden appearance. "Can we help you?"

"I saw you coming through the crowd," the woman said, her voice a bit reedy, as though it were scarcely used. "You're in from Reikonos?"

Hiressam's face fell. "Yes. The last in from Reikonos, I expect."

The woman was quiet for a moment, studying Hiressam. "I know you. What is your name?"

Hiressam's brow puckered. "If you know me, what need do you have to ask my name?"

Shirri took notice at last of the weapons the woman was carrying. A bright green, intricately carved bow was slung over her shoulder, and a quiver of arrows with their fletchings out hung beside it.

A bow? Who carried a bow in these days?

"It's been a long time since last we met," the woman said, peering out at Hiressam around her cowl, one eye only visible, "but you were of Sanctuary, weren't you? One of the chicken-hearted that left before the end, I think."

That practically drew a gasp from the staid elf – well, not quite, but close enough for him. "I was," he said, hand falling to his sword. "And you are?"

She lifted a hand to her cowl, and then pulled back her hood. A half dozen light scars crisscrossed a sun-worn face. Her ears were smooth and round, those of a pure human, which made the bow slung on her shoulder an even stranger thing. Sure, a few elves here and there still carried them, their long experience such with the ancient implements and their stubborn refusal to step up to a firearm understandable.

But a human with a bow?

...Why?

Now, Hiressam did gasp. "I know you as well."

The woman looked easily at him. The most prominent scar, a twisting one that looked like a claw mark across her right cheek, was angrily red. "I'm not surprised you would. Though when last we met I wasn't quite as blemished as I am now."

"Who is she, then?" Shirri asked, finding her voice.

"This is Calene Raverle," Hiressam said. "Chief Ranger of Sanctuary at the end."

"Aye, I was," Calene said, her gaze proceeding over Pamyra and then Shirri in slow, analytic fashion. "And I have come here because a rumor reached my ears from Reikonos that would affect us all – at least those of us left. But before I can catch a ship, here you come, strolling right off, bickering." She took a step toward Hiressam, and something in it reminded Shirri of a hunter circling her prey. "Now tell me true," and her eyes glowed, fiercely. "Has Cyrus Davidon returned?"

Hiressam bowed his head. "It *was* true. But Reikonos is destroyed, and Cyrus along with it."

Calene stared at him flatly for a moment, then turned, her cloak with its scorched hem at mid-back rustling behind her. "Come with me," she said. "I want to hear more of this. *All* of this, in fact."

And she stalked away, leaving Shirri but to exchange a glance with Hiressam, whose eyebrows were raised at the curtness of the demand. "We have nowhere else to go," he said, "and I don't know about you, but I have little gold in my purse."

Shirri nodded, and saw her mother grimace, then scoff. But the decision was made, and the three of them followed the peculiar woman in the burnt cloak with the bow strung across her back out of the dockyards and into the rush and chaos of the city proper.

CHAPTER 15

Vara

It was not that the scenery was repetitive (it rather was), or that the corpses seemed endless and in perfect repose (they were), or even that the fires were spreading with such rapidity as to make Vara fearful, as the flames leapt out of broken windows, crackled within storefronts, and even blazed freely in three-story apartment dwellings.

"This near quiet other than the fires is...unsettling," Isabelle said, perfectly encapsulating Vara's feelings on the matter.

For quiet it nearly was. But for the crackling of the flames, or the chop of Beniye's airship blades as he followed behind them down the street some two hundred feet or so, Reikonos was, simply, dead.

"Come now," Vara said, dodging down an alleyway, for ahead two tenement buildings blazed to the heavens like braziers before an altar. "You have elven hearing, do you not? Has it diminished in your fading years?"

"Had I remained in Termina, I believe I would have had a great many years yet before me," Isabelle said, picking around a fallen corpse, lifting the hem of her long white robes to do so. "Here, I become rather less certain."

"Well, we wouldn't want you to experience uncertainty," Vara said, cutting through onto another main street and pausing to look about. This was one that she was certain she'd walked along, and not that long ago, either. Stroking the smooth flesh of her chin as she stood in contemplation, she listened and heard the fall of a building some ways off in the distance.

"Yes, you seem to have plenty enough of it for both of us," Isabelle said, finally having caught up. She huffed, standing in the middle of the cobblestone street and looking about. "There are rather a lot of fires."

She was right, of course, as infuriating older sisters tended to be. "Less than in the dragonlands," Vara said, still deciding on the direction. "Are there still dragonlands?"

"Not many," Isabelle said. "Firoba has made great industry of dragon hunting, and that area of southern Arkaria is a favored ground for it. Binngart in particular does a booming trade in their scales, bones, hide, and teeth. Or did – when they were more numerous."

"I find myself oddly cold to this news," Vara said, sweeping her gaze past a shop with shattered windows, nothing but darkness within. "Ah. This way."

"It doesn't bother you that the dragons are being wiped out?" Isabelle asked, hiking her robes to follow with a swish of soft fabric. "That given time, they'll be extinct?"

"Perhaps it's that I saw them administer a similar sort of mercy to the titans of Kortran," Vara said, "so no – it does not bother me overmuch, especially not in comparison to the ruin of rather more worthy species that I assume were destroyed in the rise of the scourge, such as the dwarves of Fertiss, and the goblins of Enterra."

"There remain a few here and there, expatriates, and now mingling blood with their kin from overseas," Isabelle said as they took a turn down a side street marked by the corner building rather dramatically on fire, flames pouring out of all its windows. "And I notice you do not make mention to mourn the gnomes."

"Did I not?" Vara asked. "Yes, what a tragedy."

"That they died? Or that you forgot them?"

"Certainly one of those. Ah!" Here she stopped, at the opening of an alley. Darkness reigned within, and Vara found herself staring through the mouth, missing the gaslights, which had apparently gone unlit this eve. "This way."

Checking to make sure Beniye had not lost them, she confirmed the position of the airship, then started down the long alleyway where she and the others had ended their thousand-year interregnum and saved Shirri Gadden from her assailants. Only days past now, it already felt like years gone by between that event and now. So much had happened since...

The world had changed on them rather dramatically. That the scourge had come, and Malpravus had climbed his way to the top of the heap of what remained of Reikonos, were shocking things. Cyrus having a son...

...Well, that should have been less so.

Yet it wasn't. It had shocked, and more than that. It had dug a hot blade into an old wound Vara had long since thought sealed. Apparently not, though; some festering lesion remained in her soul of the resentment built up around Cyrus's time with Aisling. That their Sovereign-induced dalliance had resulted in a child...and one that was now their enemy...

Perhaps she'd overreacted. These were, after all, the consequences of sins of judgment he had long ago atoned for in her eyes. It was just such a sharp rake to the eyes, such an affront to her heart.

It was only after she'd been on her way to Termina that the

thought had occurred to her: it was not completely out of the realm of possibility that, had things gone a bit different, or she'd forgotten her *ventra'maq* one month in the heat of planning some expedition, that she might indeed have been a mother to some bastard of Archenous Derragnault's patrilineage.

Would it have been her fault? Well, at least half. But should Cyrus hold her responsible for, and be angry at, such a long-ago sin of bad judgment?

That thinking had allowed reason to prevail where fury had taken hold of her.

A building burned a block over, and black smoke clouded the alley, making it harder to see. Winds were whipping everywhere, and the air was hot and dry.

"Are we close?" Isabelle asked. She coughed lightly as a thick curl of smoke floated over them.

"I think so," Vara said, wondering what she might find. That curious prickling within had made her wonder; was Sanctuary still here, even? And if not, what might she discover?

She did not have to wait long; just a moment or two for the winds to briefly hold, and then the clinging smoke seemed to part.

The place where Sanctuary had appeared, where it had been...

...Was but a vacant lot in the middle of the alley.

"Gone, indeed," she whispered.

And less than a block away, something exploded as fire touched a thing it was not meant to touch.

Vara's armor rattled, slapping against her chain mail, and the mail against her flesh. Isabelle stumbled, and Vara caught her, hand already upon Ferocis.

The brick wall behind them crumbled at the mouth of the alley, and some large, black machinery disturbed by the explosion pushed through. Flames came with it, littering the wreck of brick, of metal, with patches of glowing orange that slowly began to spread across the new mountain blocking their retreat.

"What now?" Isabelle asked, Vara's hand still clenching her elbow.

"Now...I believe we should move on," Vara said, watching the flames spread across the street from the alley mouth, flung there by the explosion. She'd lost sight of Beniye's airship in the haze now hanging above, and that, coupled with the fact they could not go back the way they came, was cause for concern. "And swiftly – while we still can."

CHAPTER 16

Alaric

Upon the quarterdeck, something was shouted, and Alaric heard it through the edge of tiredness that fogged his mind. Night had fallen, and lamps shed soft light every few feet. A white haze shone through the clouds where a crescent moon was hid behind thick tufts of white. There was a chill in the air as the *Yuutshee* churned through the quiet night sky.

"What was that?" Alaric asked, turning his head barely; he had heard the words shouted, but they were in the Amatgarosan language, quick and snappish.

"I'm not exactly a linguist," Guy said, "but I think it's something 'first.'"

"First marker," came a voice from behind them. Alaric turned and found Dugras slowly dragging his way across the deck where he'd just emerged out of the staircase belowdecks. "We're about to reach the old castle we use as a navigational aid."

Alaric turned his eyes to the shrouded, shadowed landscape below. They had been traveling for a day and a sameness had loomed once they'd reached Luukessia. The green of the edges had slowly given way to bleak gray, the forests half-eaten by scourge, the grasslands mostly dirt, and the lakes turned murky from unhampered soil runoff. Had Alaric any affection left for his old homeland, it would have been put to the death today. "Old castle?"

"Yeah, there's an old castle square in the middle of the continent," Dugras said, shuffling over for a moment. "At it, we turn due southeast, for the immense old tower, stay on a line for that for a day, make a slight adjustment to bearing at the coast, and boom, we'll be at Xiaoshani by nightfall tomorrow."

"Excellent," Alaric said, though he did not feel excellent. He felt nothing of the sort, really, only tired and ready for some measure of sleep. "You are out and about again, my friend, yet you do not have the excuse of wanting to see this dead land."

"I need a break from belowdecks every now and again," Dugras said, shuffling up to the edge. "Besides, I'm off duty now. Sort of." He loosed a forceful yawn. "If things go pear-shaped, I'll have to rush back down, but until and unless...I'm free. Has the captain assigned you accommodations yet?"

"We have three very stretchy, very swaying hammocks in the far corner of the crew deck," Guy piped up. "I spent an enjoyable afternoon swaying my way through a nap. Or trying, at least."

"It's a bit of an acquired skill, sleeping on a moving airship," Dugras said with a quicksilver smile. "Fortunately for you, this is a freighter, where we do care about our crew's comfort. The military airships? They keep everything battened down at all times, and execute turns that make you sick."

"I'm already windsick enough as it is," Guy said. "Can't imagine it getting much worse."

"Dugras," Alaric said, peering out across the featureless

expanse, "you mentioned the first marker. Where is this old castle of which you speak?"

"Uh, it'll be ahead," Dugras said, making his way to the rail beside Alaric. "It's called out when the lookout spots it with his looking glass, which means out of sight for us, probably. But we'll be upon it in moments." He peered his almond eyes into the dark. "Ah – there, you see?"

And Alaric did see, though with some difficulty at first. It was a mere shade on the obsidian landscape, a phantom looming out of the formless mass beneath them, with little moonlight to show it to them, and the lanterns blazing upon the deck insufficient to the task of illuminating dead Luukessia a thousand feet below them.

But soon enough it did break from beneath the shadowed layers, an old keep in a perfect square, the walls crumbling and dead vines crawling up the sides. There were three new towers at the compass points of the inner keep, and in the center, where once had been the tower where he'd lived and grown up, now there was a recess like the center of an arena, and more vines crawling into the craterous middle.

The Garden of Peace, Curatio had called it, when describing it to him during their thousand years in the ether. There he could see the direct result of his decision not to return to his land. It was almost as convicting as the dead gray of Arkaria that he'd left behind; his choices were written in dust everywhere, in the countless dead in this little corner of the wider world. Certainly there was blame enough to go around: Mortus had done evil enough, as had Malpravus, but...

Alaric had challenged their evil, and it seemed more had flowed from that decision; what good had he done, given all the ruin of nations he had left behind everywhere he'd done his work?

"I like to see this, too, if I can," Dugras said, rubbing his eyes. "It's hardly as inspiring as the coast, but it reminds me that people have been around for a long time. They say this ruin was inhabited for thousands of years."

"Sounds like a load of rubbish, mate," Guy said.

"It was called Enrant Monge," Alaric said, feeling not a trace of self-consciousness for what he knew was about to say, "and it was the place I was born, some eleven thousand years ago. After I was removed to Arkaria at the hands of Protanian slavers, the monarchy fell, for I was the last heir of this land, and it broke into three kingdoms. This became the place for mediation of disputes, maintained by a monastic order, and it was in continuous habitation until the scourge came, when Cyrus battled them across this land, at which time it fell to them."

A silence so quiet you could hear a scourge-claw click fell over them, broken by Guy's somber, "You know...I actually believe every word o' that."

"Me, too," Dugras said. "How much has my life changed that it all seems plausible after all I've seen?"

Alaric felt a chuckle escape him, dark and rueful. "It is a simple joy to believed, especially with a life story as outlandish as mine has become."

He looked down at the castle, growing closer with every moment. Another shout came from the quarterdeck, and a rattling from the back of the ship was followed by the slow turning of the ship. Alaric stared at the place of his birth, and what would likely have been the place of his death had events taken but a different turn so long ago...barring his falling in battle in some rebellion, his bones would lie beneath the graveyard in the keep even now, along with those of his ancient brethren.

What would have become of Luukessia if he had come back, had not stayed in Arkaria? Would the land still be a graveyard? Or might it bloom with life even now?

"Under the boot of Mortus," he whispered to himself. But

was that slavery and postmortem capture worse or better than the fate of all men of Arkaria and Luukessia now?

Another shout from the deck above split the night, a crack over the thrum of the engines and the blades whipping overhead. This was sharper, loud not for the sake of announcement but with a tinge of something else, recognizable to Alaric's ear in spite of the language barrier–

"Damn," Dugras muttered, turning his eyes toward the quarterdeck.

"What is it?" Alaric asked, his fatigue fading into the murmuring background as a new emotion, worry, rose like Enrant Monge from the darkness.

Dugras's small frame had stiffened; his bearing had changed utterly. "There's a ship coming up behind us, in the distance." His expression was taut. "And given where we are...it might well be pirates."

CHAPTER 17

Vaste

The bodies stretched the span of the forest floor, scarlet blood dotting the green leaves and nearly black against their tunics. They blended into the dark under the canopy of leaves and needles nearly blotting the sun above. The scent of rich earth mingled with metallic blood in Vaste's nose, and he sighed deeply at the scene before him. It was hardly the worst slaughter he'd laid eyes upon in the last day, though there was a certain violence about this that the destruction of Reikonos had lacked. The red spell had been bright and sudden.

This, though, had a slow consideration to it. The wounds were tight, stabbing rather than the more indiscriminate hacking and slashing that came from a fight. He took a step over to the closest corpse and gave it a nudge with his staff.

It turned over immediately, displaying a dirt-stained face. Dead leaves clung to the liquids on the dead face, and dull eyes did not meet his own as Vaste peered at the body.

"Human," Qualleron announced, hovering over Vaste's shoulder.

"Yes, I noticed that, too," Vaste said. "Because I have eyes, you see."

"Heh," Qualleron said with a hearty chuckle. "'I have eyes, you see.' Very droll, your wordplay." The bigger troll moved past him and squatted beside the body.

"That wasn't even wordplay, you oaf," Vaste said. "Just an observation." He moved to let Qualleron have this body to poke and prod at; he had little interest in doing that, and besides, there were others to choose from if he decided to give it a go.

"Are they all human?" Qualleron asked. His voice seemed to bounce off the trees, echoing through the forest dell, and off the hills rising on either side of them.

"How should I know?" Vaste asked, walking past another, his staff touching the bed of pine needles and long-dead leaves covering the forest floor. He reached out and gave this one a nudge, and that was all. It was that was needed with Letum, and the body rolled over, once more turning a bloody face to the sky. One leaf clung to this fellow's cheek and another to his forehead, giving him the appearance of having a very strange tree-born disease.

"Would you mind looking?" Qualleron asked, quite mildly to Vaste's ear. Almost as if he were having a good time.

Vaste sighed, deeply, impatiently, then brushed a leaf off the dead man's face. It had been rather huge, and blocking the curve of his ear, which was, he found, not at all pointed. "Another human."

"Mm," Qualleron said, as though this made some sort of sense to him.

Vaste frowned, then moved to the next body. "Human." He picked his way through them, avoiding the pools of blood gathering on the forest floor. He nudged another, and it turned enough he could see its dead eyes and rounded ear.

"Human. I think we can safely say they're all – AHHHH-HHHHHHH!"

"Help me," the body said, latching a cold, wiry hand upon Vaste's ankle beneath the robe.

Qualleron was beside him immediately, sword flashing high. It stopped at around Vaste's waist, and the mammoth troll pointed it aside and dropped to a knee carefully beside the quite-living body. Instead of cleaving the hand from Vaste's ankle, he brushed it free gently, and took it in his own. "You have been wounded in battle," he said in a low, almost comforting tone.

Well, others might have found it comforting. At the moment, Vaste was still trying to recover his calm, having nearly struck down with the point of Letum and separated that human from his head by sheer, terrified force.

The human gasped, and Vaste looked upon the thin neck and dirty hair, long and tangled in a messy bun.

A woman. Her frame was thin, her breath coming raspy, her neck partly open to the air, dirt clinging into the wound. "S...slaughtered," she whispered. "Not...battle."

Vaste had questions about that, but he held them inside. Questions like: Why were there humans being slaughtered in northwest Arkaria? Also: why had she grabbed his ankle? Why not just make a vague grabbing motion toward his head, safely out of reach? The flesh of his leg was crawling at her touch, and he could feel sticky blood upon his skin, and it made him shiver and feel faint.

"You should be still," Qualleron said soothingly, then, with a look to Vaste. "Do you have some magic that might be of use here?"

Vaste surveyed the wounds before him and shook his head. "Whatever healing I might cast on her would simply prolong her pain and postpone her death." He motioned with Letum at her chest, where her rough-spun tunic was drenched with blood. "Her throat is opened, but only barely; her heart is pierced, but tightly. Either this happened very recently, or whoever did the job is a master with a blade."

Qualleron grunted and gave him a nod, turning his attention back to the dying woman. "You know you are dying?"

Her eyes were fluttering, but they found his easily enough, and she nodded, then was racked with a cough that brought up blood. "They left me alive...to be messenger." She coughed again. "Knowing I'd live...just long enough to be found." A racking cough was followed by a bitter smile. "Told me so."

"Who did this to you?" Vaste asked, finding himself strangely drawn in, against his will. Did he not have problems enough of his own?

The screech of a bird above made her search in the distance above them. Then she blinked, and her eyes fell back to earth, back to her pained and dying body. "Elves...of course..." Another racking cough came now. "Who else...?"

Elves killing humans. In northwest Arkaria, where humans hadn't even really lived in his day. Hmm.

"Not sure I'm going to make it until they get here," she said.

"Wait," Vaste said, small chill running across his back. "That's the second time it's been mentioned that she was to be messenger to someone. Who exactly are we waiting for here? Because maybe we should leave before they find us in the midst of a field of slaughte–"

"Too late," came a whispered breath, and Vaste felt a blade at his side. He didn't turn, as other footfalls rushed in around him, humans clad in green tunics like hers, their eyes filled with hate at the tableau of death laid before them, and, he felt himself suddenly, unexpectedly worried...for both himself and Qualleron.

CHAPTER 18

Cyrus

"Niamh?" Cyrus asked again, into the rising sound across the dead fields of Arkaria. As far as his eye could see, gray, writhing flesh stretched to the north like an endless sea of wrinkled, rotten scourge. The stink was enough to make an open sewer seem pleasant by comparison.

And there, before the army of the dead, was one that looked not a whit different in anything but bearing. Where the others had black eyes, soulless in their depths, in this one he saw just the barest hint of a spark of light.

A flicker of recognition, of knowledge, that he knew the soul within. It was a thing he'd learned in a thousand years of the ether, the feel of a soul he'd met, a soul he *knew*. It was a sense, one he'd felt in the throne room of the Citadel, that horrible feeling that something was wrong with the person he was looking at.

This was the inverse; the inside of the barrel did not match the contents stenciled on the outside planks. This scourge was not filled with depthless hate for life; it had something else within it, a spark that all the others lacked.

It was an idea that warred within him, the thought that this rancid form, this twisted body, this four-legged horror could be the vessel to hold the pure, white light of the red-haired, fiery druid he'd known a thousand years ago. Yet the eyes...

And she stood between him and death, sure and certain.

"You're saving my..." He said, experimentally.

And the scourge was still, for just a moment, and then it shook its tail at him again, and...

He knew.

"Niamh," he whispered, the sick realization settling in the pit of his stomach. "Mortus...he trapped you..."

A scourge leapt from the left, and Niamh swept at it, battering it back with claw and tooth, and the truce held. The line of scourge hissed and drooled, their dead eyes fixed on him and beyond him, where the creak heralded the rising of the ship from the earth.

"Cyrus!" Baynvyn called. "If you mean to leave, you had best be heading this way!"

"If you want your dagger, you'll wait just a second!" Cyrus called back, without a trace of a shit given. "Niamh..."

The scourge nodded, almost imperceptibly, then flicked its distorted, overlarge head toward the airship, and the message was unmistakable: *Go*.

Another snap, and one of the scourge came forth again, this time at her–

Cyrus lashed out, and its head was parted from its body at the near-lack of a neck. He knew in the moment what he'd done, and would have cringed, but there was no time. "Go!" he shouted back at Niamh, or what she had become.

She did, and followed, as all hell broke loose around them.

"You might want to hurry!" Baynvyn called, oh-so-helpfully.

The airship was rising, now twenty feet up, the side nearest him dipping slightly, his son – if he could be called such, the bastard – hanging tight to the rail.

"You might want to shut the hell up before I give you a thousand years' worth of the back of my hand, son," Cyrus said, getting almost underneath the rail. He could outrun the scourge easily, but they had numbers on their side, endless damned numbers. "Come on," he said to Niamh, who evinced a singular moment of doubt. Or maybe befuddlement at the reference to Baynvyn being his son; it was hard to tell.

Didn't matter. Reversing his grip on Epalette and Rodanthar, he grabbed her and seized her forward, launching her up and over, then following with a leap of his own.

He came crashing to the deck like Vara in one of her mighty jumps, though less gracefully by half. He managed to roll out of it, coming up before some unfortunate dark elf who stared at him with wide eyes and upraised hands. "Did I almost land on you?" Cyrus asked, pointing his hilt at the man.

The man's mouth moved a couple times, trying to form words. "No – no, my lord. And if you had, it would be fine. I'm blessed with extra cushioning should you need a soft place to land." He cringed, baring his teeth painfully.

Cyrus stared as the ship lurched. "That may be the saddest thing I've heard a man ever say."

"What wretchedness is THIIIIIIIIISSSS?" Shipmaster Hongren shouted, his voice high and terrified. His dark eyes were alight on the Niamh-scourge, and his mouth agape in horror. "SHOOOOOOT ITTTTTT!"

"On second thought, that is," Cyrus said, bringing his blade, flat edge down, onto a sailor's pistol, knocking it out of his hand before he could fire. It discharged upon hitting the deck, blasting like a cannon and sending its metal projectile skyward, where it dinged off a rotor above. "Get ahold of yourself, Shipmaster!" He stalked over, interposing himself between the rising mob of the crew and Niamh, who huddled by the edge of the rail, looking like a threat to absolutely no one. "This scourge is my guest – and thus, yours."

Hongren's face was navy with outrage, his eyes wide, almost swollen. "You, prisoner – how dare you!"

"I just saved you, that's how I dare," Cyrus said. "If you had a little more daring, perhaps you could have done a bit more to help that process. Instead, I got help from a scourge – who is an old acquaintance of mine, by the way, so treat her with a bit of respect." He drew up to his full height, which was quite enough to quell most humans. Among the shorter dark elves...well, he could sense the crew being cowed.

Still, his proclamation went down like a troll in a cotillion. The stir of anger, of confusion, ran through the handful of crew on deck. "You know this...this thing?" Baynvyn asked. He was still holding the rail as though afraid to let go. Cyrus watched him, and it seemed he missed his dagger. His eyes flitted to it, in Cyrus's hand, after he finished speaking.

"I know her well," Cyrus said, "and so did your mother." He kept his blades pointed unthreateningly away, but decidedly present. They might try and put him in chains again, after all, and he had no intention of letting them. "She stays with me, and I stay aboard until you find a nice, scourge-free place to drop me."

Baynvyn shook his head slowly. "We are bound for Saekaj Sovar. You are to be presented to the Sovereign, on his orders." He eyed the Niamh-scourge. "And he will not allow...that...within the city."

"What's his name?" Cyrus asked.

Baynvyn stared at him blankly. "Surely...surely you know."

Cyrus stared back, then sighed, keeping Rodanthar and Epalette tight in his grip, the metal squeaking as he squeezed in frustration. "It's still Terian, isn't it? That bastard. He's got that axe, he's a thousand years old and still clinging to power."

Baynvyn looked ready to leap forward, his eyes narrowing and his voice turning cold under the thrumming engines. "You mind your tongue. The Sovereign is a great man, a hero of our people, and–"

"A collection of scabrous sores bound together by inhuman quantities of carnal lust and the occasional bawdy joke," Cyrus said. The atmosphere on the deck changed, then, and he could feel it. The sailors rumbled quietly amongst themselves. "Well, I'll just have to talk with him about this matter, because she–" and he pointed at Niamh, "–is a mutual friend of ours." Keeping his weapons at his side in case the sailors decided to do something foolish, Cyrus lowered his voice to mutter, "I'm sure even at a thousand years of age, Terian can still be reasoned with...after a fashion."

He put his back to the deck rail and let himself slide down, the Niamh-scourge close at his side. "We'll just wait here, you and I," he said. The scourge whimpered slightly, and curled tight to him. It felt so strange, and the smell was unpleasant, but he more than tolerated it. He rested a hand around her side, settled in against her, and let the airship carry them on under the dark of night, pierced only by the moon and the torches scattered around the deck. The light flickered on the faces of the dark elves watching him, and Cyrus watched them, knowing that a moment's rest might turn out just as well for him as falling asleep in the face of the scourge.

CHAPTER 19

Vara

The air was black with thick smoke and growing miserably hot, seemingly more so with every passing moment. Vara was quite conscious of this fact, feeling the breath of flame-licked air rushing down the alley behind her as she broke into a trot, trying to escape the stifling smoke and endless, growing heat.

"Our situation seems to be getting more desperate," Isabelle said. "Sanctuary is gone–"

"You needn't rehash the chain of poor luck we've just experienced," Vara said, sharply as, well, ever, "as I have been present for every lick of it." The muscles in her legs protested lightly at the rough treatment.

Isabelle was breathing heavily, interspersing the occasional cough from the acrid stink blowing toward them from behind. "Let us be clear: I will rehash this as much as I care to, for you have led us, rather stupidly, into a situation that could have been avoided had you merely taken one simple fact of the world to heart—"

"I don't care to hear this—"

"Cyrus is dead," Isabelle said, dragging hold of Vara by the smooth edge of her pauldron, whipping her around. Her eyes were big and blue and watery from the smoke. "He cannot be the lone survivor of this massacre—"

Vara turned round, feeling the resistance of her sister's grip upon her, and nearly toppling over at the strength of it. With eyes blazing as her feet lost traction upon the cobbles, she righted herself only after catching a hand upon Ferocis. Coming back up, she felt the scorching heat of her glare settle on her sister's gaze, which was steady. "How in the hells...? Your grip is strong as a troll's. Stronger, even."

Isabelle shifted her robes aside to reveal a length of wood in her hand only a foot or so long and with a red tinge. It had real mystique, and Vara felt drawn to it somehow. "This is Amoran, the Wand of Love. It's hardly the equal of the sword on your belt, but it suffices to let me move my own piano on the occasions I tire of its placement in its current corner."

"Small wonder you've aged so gracefully," Vara said, twisting her shoulder to pull out of Isabelle's grasp. With her hand on Ferocis's hilt, it was marginally easier. Heat was billowing out of a building to her left. "We should continue moving."

"And dodging my argument, I note."

But Vara ignored her, plunging ahead instead into a street filled with buildings belching fire from their windows. The brick was beginning to crack in some places, and she even saw a wall fall, flames pouring out of the space where it had been a moment before. Wood burned with ease, and Reikonos seemed mostly wood with brick as facade, but a plaster upon the warts beneath.

Now, the flames of ten thousand untended hearths were

being unleashed from behind those amenable walls, and the result was an inferno.

"This is rapidly becoming unsurvivable," Isabelle said, holding a hand to her face and blanching from the heat of the street. "You believe your husband made it through the spell – fine. I see no reason to argue that just now. But surely you must concede that this place is going to become the gravesite of us all should we remain here much longer. Either he has found a way out or he will burn; there are no other options."

Vara set her jaw; the logic was unassailable. Also, the heat felt as though it were tanning her fair flesh, at least that which was exposed. She could almost feel the skin roasting on her chin, and her armor was starting to glint with warmth. "Yes. That much is true."

"Then surely you see," Isabelle said, coughing lightly as an ill-timed plume of blackest smoke blew their way, "we must evacuate before this gets worse. We should flag down Beniye, find a place where he can put down that infernal ladder, and then leave before we are cooked to char."

Vara looked around once more; this street was utterly engulfed, a valley of fire, and she could barely keep her eyes open against the raging flames. Looking back, it was more of the same, perhaps a bit milder than what lay ahead, and to either side there was but the alley through which they'd just passed, half-crumbled, impassable, and no path back. "Yes," she said. "He would have found a way out before things got this bad."

"Reason, at last," Isabelle said, "or at least a portion of it. Which I will take, in this pinch." She grasped Vara's wrist and nodded behind them. "This way, I think, is our only path."

Vara let herself be led. It was a strange waning of the spirit she felt, a small surrender that stole more than a drop of her will. Still, Cyrus had to be alive.

He had to.

He'd just...well, airships had made it out before the end. Perhaps he'd been on one of them. Or...surely there were other places he might have gone.

But where?

The buildings on either side of them raged with fire and black smoke billowing up, the heat assailing them as if blown out on the tongues of angry dragons, threatening to kiss them with fire as they dragged their way through the middle. It was an act of threading, trying to be in the middle of the street as much as possible, to keep steady in the center and not be overwhelmed.

"This is...quite difficult," Isabelle said, tears glinting on her cheeks. From the heat, Vara was assured. For her own were distinctly misty, wetness sliding down, and not out of any misplaced belief in her husband's doom.

The smoke parted for but a moment as a strong gust blew through, and Vara flinched as though punched by a fiery hand; above she could see sky, and the Citadel, its top sticking up above everything through a momentary parting of the black clouds.

"How will Beniye find us in this?" Vara asked, listening for the chop of the airship's blades. It was futile, though; all she could hear was the crackling of fire in all directions. Even the gust had made little noise compared to that.

Isabelle froze, stricken. The thought had seeped into her consciousness, too, then.

Another gust blew through, clearing the air above them just a bit, and giving them a momentary vision.

There was no airship overhead. Nor anywhere nearby.

And then the choking, black clouds covered up the darkening skies once more, and they were left with only the surging fire as their light.

CHAPTER 20

Cyrus

"How do you even land at Saekaj?" Cyrus asked after about an hour of continual flight. Baynvyn had gradually eased close to him, hugging the rail, though the rest of the crew had moved on, back to attending to their duties. Niamh's gray, wrinkled head rested on Cyrus's leg, and with every breath she took he held his own, for the stink was terrible, akin to a time he'd stumbled across days-old dead on a battlefield.

Baynvyn looked at him blankly, then, apparently, got it. "There's a tower now. Built a little over a decade ago. Spiked protections at the bottom and sides of the platform so the scourge can't climb it."

Cyrus pondered that a moment. "But how did you build it without them attacking and overwhelming you during?"

This prompted a rather smug smile upon Baynvyn's already smug face. "With great alacrity."

"And many casualties, I'm sure," Cyrus said, rolling his eyes.

Holding back a perimeter of scourge during a construction project of that sort, by necessity, would have been a costly endeavor.

"Very few, in fact," Baynvyn said, his eyes sweeping the horizon, dark hair stirred by the winds coming over the bow. "Mostly down to falls by workers as the tower took shape, and not...well, what you're surely thinking."

"Boy, I've fought the scourge in just about every conceivable environment," Cyrus said, well tired of his attitude. "I know what it'd take to build a tower in the middle of Arkaria with them coming at you from every angle, and the idea that you'd only suffer a few deaths, and those from accidents – well, it's laughable."

"Laugh away, then," Baynvyn said. "But do so quickly, because we are arriving, and I suspect you'll want to see the tower, won't you?"

Niamh lifted her head, and Cyrus stood, concentrating on Epalette for a moment. Baynvyn was looking at him, and then, a second later—

"So you do know how to use it properly," Baynvyn murmured.

Cyrus walked as quietly as he could a dozen paces away from his son, not deigning to answer. Niamh's eyes followed him, though; the scourge had the measure of him, either by smell or by the wavering of light around Epalette's vanishing effect. Still, his aim was to not get brained by his son. Which seemed a distinct possibility. Always, maybe.

Presently, the tower came into sight. Like a tree from the lands of the south, it extended up over the blighted plain what seemed like miles into the sky. A black pillar for a black land, it bloomed at the top as if a dark flower, opening up to platforms, spikes jutting from the undersides like thorns on a rose.

From where he stood at the edge, Cyrus could see the

wreckage of a dozen airships in the shadow of the tower, covered over by a writhing mass of living gray.

"They're everywhere," he breathed, and felt Niamh brush against his calf, as if to drive home the point. She lifted herself up on those comically distorted legs and peered over the rail into the faint mists that clung to every surface. Not enough to obscure vision, just enough to cast a pall over a once-sunny land.

"Now you see it," Baynvyn said, once again at his back, ever the rogue, and Cyrus side-stepped, putting enough distance between them so as not to have to worry immediately about a blade between his ribs. A sharp memory of Baynvyn's mother doing just that came back to him, and he turned a wary eye upon the man.

"Now I see it," Cyrus said. "What happened to the Waking Woods? The Scourge?"

Baynvyn's lips puckered, twisting in amusement. "Well, that's an interesting–"

The ship rattled beneath their feet just then, unsteady, as though a titan had given the thing a slap across the belly. It was followed immediately by cries from belowdecks, a shout from a metal trumpet that jutted out of the wood nearby.

Cyrus turned to look at Baynvyn, but found the rogue's face a stiff mask. "Are we going to make it?"

"Too soon to tell," Baynvyn said. He rested his hands on the rail, apparently calm in the midst of this new crisis.

The ship began to sink in the air, the tower that had been far below suddenly gaining distance with great speed. Cyrus steeled himself mentally for the crash.

Another hard shudder ran through the vessel, and they seemed to slow, the air rushing across Cyrus's face reduced as the ship twisted sideways.

"Ah," Baynvyn said, casting his eyes to the quarterdeck where the wheel sat, and the shipmaster barked in dark elven, too fast for Cyrus to catch much beyond a word here and there. "He's bringing us in sideways to slow our descent."

"That'll be great – until we capsize like a ship in the surf," Cyrus said, preparing to hold to the rail.

Baynvyn turned to stare at him with slitted eyes. "Are you thinking of the time you faced Tempestus, God of Storms, upon his own vessel?"

"Admittedly, it's been a while," Cyrus said, "but as I recall, I'm the one who ordered the capsizing of that ship." He cocked his head. "Was that a test?"

Baynvyn looked away. "Perhaps."

He's still unsure it's actually me, Cyrus realized. *Or at least still reluctant to admit it.*

The ship's board squealed and groaned like the old barn Guildhouse in Reikonos when a hard storm blew through. They fell through the air as Cyrus might imagine a brick dropping in a low arc after a hard throw. That pillar of black, the blooming flower of death in the midst of the endless swarming scourge, drew closer.

A sharp, barked order from the shipmaster righted them once more, and now Cyrus could see on the edge of the tower a dozen ship docks fanned around the petal-like edges. Their vessel came around on a slow curve, another shuddering bump dropping them a dozen feet. A look skyward showed Cyrus a plume of smoke belching from one of the turning shafts overhead. It didn't seem it would last much longer.

Small navy dots resolved themselves below, and now he could see they were dark elves moving about. One waved lit torches in the air as if doing some sort of pyromantic dance, beckoning them forth. It was only a few more minutes and he felt a hard thump that jarred him–

Cyrus turned in anticipation and found Baynvyn there, reaching out. He thumped his son's hand aside with ease, then moved away swiftly, both blades giving him the ability to do so without difficulty. "No," he said simply, and then walked to a gap in the rail. From there, he could see a ladder being walked to the side by a member of the ground crew.

"You really are Cyrus Davidon," Baynvyn muttered, rubbing his wrist where he'd been cuffed.

"Yes, and someday you'll truly believe that, with all its precarious implications for your life," Cyrus said. Beckoning to Niamh, he brushed aside the crew member waiting to do...whatever it would take to put the ladder there, and went right up to the edge. "On that day, come find me. We'll talk, we'll reconcile – I might even give you your dagger back."

"You can't leave me without it," Baynvyn said, a certain desperation rising in his voice.

"I can't trust you with it, that's for sure," Cyrus said. He knelt, then nodded to the scourge that had come to his side. She stared at him blankly for a moment, then seemed to realize what was being asked of her. Without further hesitation, she climbed upon his back, taking care not to rake him with her claws.

He stood, getting the balance right. Without hands, she was left to hang there, making a whimpering noise. "It's just for a moment," he whispered.

"You cannot leave," the shipmaster announced. He stood on the stairs to the aft deck, looking quite alarmed.

"Well, I don't think I can stay, so..." Cyrus shrugged. "...Thanks for the ride, but I've got to go see an old friend – and I doubt you'll be helping me with that, seeing as you all would rather I end up in – what's that prison you have? The Depths? Well, I've got other plans."

And with that, he stepped over the edge, taking care to hold tight to one of the Niamh-scourge's forelegs.

They dropped twenty feet and Cyrus muttered Falcon's Essence on the way down. It was not quite as gentle as taking a mere step, but it wasn't as dramatic a fall as it could have been. Niamh whimpered in his ear, and the dark elf with the ladder screamed as he saw a black-armored warrior with a scourge on its back dropping toward him like sure death.

Cyrus landed and shoved the man with the ladder out of his way as a great hue and cry was raised on the deck of the airship he'd just departed. He didn't wait for said cry to resolve, but instead took off at a run, sprinting between this airship dock and the next.

"Where did he go?" someone shouted from above. Cyrus didn't bother to answer, or wait to hear the answer.

He'd seen the layout from above, the great flower petal. At the middle, there was something to traverse the stem– an elevator, a staircase, some way to get down into Saekaj. That was where he needed to aim, right for the center of things.

"We'll find Terian," Cyrus said, listening to the shouts grow louder around him. The place was in a real stir now, though he was concentrating, Epalette in hand, intent on keeping himself masked from sight. If he could make it inside, disappear into the city, well, that'd be for the best. He could reach the palace before the alarm was raised, get to Terian and settle matters.

"Close the gates!" Someone bellowed behind him, taking up a call shouted from the deck of the ship he'd come in on.

That, then, was the plan. Lock him out before he could get inside. Well, that might have worked on the warrior with Rodanthar in his hand, but he wasn't just relying on that. Not now.

Gripping Niamh, keeping her snug with his wrists, blades clutched in hand and crossed in front of him, Cyrus sprinted for all he had. Every step across the black surface of the tower, he felt the weight of the scourge upon his back like a great knapsack. "I would never complain to a lady about her weight," he said, very mildly, "but..."

Niamh loosed a small whimper, and he could not for the life of him determine whether it was annoyance or critique.

Ahead, the tower's center was a large structure, cylindrical, with open doors large as city gates. Cyrus peered into the torchlit dark within, trying to see what waited for him. Half a hundred dark elven men, all with their attention in his direction, certainly – clerks, laborers, guards, traders and captains, with so many stacks of sacks and crates piled inside as to obscure much of the ground within. At least six airships rested on the petals of this level of the tower, and he could see dark spots in the distant, dark skies hinting that more were always coming. One seemed to be taking off even now, a wash of air coming from his left along with the noise of those spinning blades above the deck.

Ah! Cyrus could see now, an arrangement of platforms at the center of the building's inside. Four or so wide platforms in a gulf that opened to below. The platforms were loaded with cargo and in a configuration that reminded him of a mouth with teeth knocked out. There seemed to be other platforms missing, probably down the central shaft of the tower.

That was it, then. That was his entry.

Steering around a guard, Cyrus dodged, catching a flicker of concern in the man's eyes as the illusion of Epalette crossed before him. Cyrus had seen it before, that curious wavering in the air the dagger produced. Hell, he'd been behind it before, too, using it to hide himself from sight with Aisling's aid.

"I could get used to this," Cyrus said, keeping his eyes on the guard he passed, and taking them off the path ahead for just a moment too long.

Something strong and solid struck him, catching both blades and driving them back into his chest. They clanged like a temple bell, and his wrists pinned Niamh's forelegs against his armor, causing the scourge to emit a fierce squeal of pain.

Cyrus, for his part, felt the impact across his chest, and hard, at that. It drove him off balance, running into the invisible wall of what struck him, and before he could get his head around to see what he'd even hit, he was falling back, landing on Niamh, who squealed again. He tried to twist sideways to avoid crushing her, and his armor rang out against the metal decking, loud as a bell gonging.

"Don't get too used to it," came a scratchy, harsh voice.

A familiar figure loomed over him, a wide-bladed axe held in his hands. He wore the armor of Alaric Garaunt, though the helm was missing, and instead of Alaric's gray hair, eyepatch, and tanned flesh, duller, navy skin stood in their stead, along with blazing, hateful eyes that matched perfectly the scowl upon the face of the man who had knocked Cyrus to the ground.

"Oh, good," Cyrus said, rolling quickly to his feet. "I was just coming to find you." He could feel the tension in the air, the rage radiating off the man in front of him. "Or rather...*we* were."

Terian Lepos lifted his axe in front of him, and without a word, let the blade explode into flame. "How fortuitous, because it saves me the trouble of tracking you down..." he said, the flames lighting his eyes, illuminating a deep rage, "...so I can kill you."

CHAPTER 21

Vaste

The humans flooded around him, some thirty or more, clad in cloaks of green that reminded Vaste of the rangers of old from his day. They carried bows and arrows, too, most of them, though here and there he saw flintlock rifles of the sort he'd seen in Reikonos. They were a dirty, bedraggled lot, and at his side, a dagger poked into his ribs, threatening to tear his robes and then go deeper.

A woman held it, her eyes focused spitefully upon his, watching him for some sign of resistance to plunge it into his side.

He did not give it.

"Check her," the woman ordered. She was tawny, smudged with dirt enough to take the pale sheen off her face. She came up to perhaps his armpit, tall for a human woman, though hardly on the level of Cyrus Davidon. In her other hand she held a flintlock pistol that was worn and battered, and the gambeson beneath her green cloak was weathered and gray.

A human man half a head shorter than her pushed past Qualleron, who sheathed his blade without complaint and rose, his hands lifted to either side in what seemed the universal gesture of peace. "We have no quarrel with you, humans. We stumbled on this place in following the road, and had nothing to do with this slaughter."

The woman with the dagger favored him with a piercing look. "Perhaps you did not. But perhaps you are lying, as well. We'll see to the truth of it soon enough."

"Oh, will you?" Vaste asked, finding his annoyance on the wax, perhaps partially driven by the dagger poking in his side, but mostly by the day he'd had. "I'm sure you'll make a thorough and impartial investigation of it before coming to murderous conclusions and executing us."

"We had nothing to do with this," Qualleron said quietly. "There is no need for executions. They will see."

"She's not going to live," the man said of the dying woman, who, as if for emphasis, coughed another geyser of blood that flecked his face and spattered the hem of Vaste's robe.

"Of course she shan't," the woman with the knife muttered. She seemed to be pondering.

"We are travelers with no stake in your fight," Qualleron said. "We did not ask to come to this land, we were dumped here."

"Life's just filled with injustice," the woman said, flashing a hateful smirk. "Small and..." she gave Vaste a surveying look, "...large."

"Among my people, I'm considered quite fit," Vaste said sourly. "A perfect specimen of beauty, in fact. Especially my arse. It is the stuff of legends, and arias are sung to its magnificence."

"Then it'll be long remembered even after the maggots

consume it," she said, and he could feel her tense to deliver a blow.

"Oh, enough of this shit," Vaste said, and brushed his arm back with the speed of Letum. He trapped her hand, useless, between his wrist and side, pinching it so that she let out a cry and loosed her grip upon the dagger, which clattered to the ground. With a hard twist, he pulled her off her feet and sent her hard into the nearest tree.

One of the humans moved at his side, and Vaste swung, instinctively, with Letum, catching him across the knees. A great, splintering crack rang out in the forest, and it took a moment for him to realize that, no, it was not the sound of a gunshot, but of his staff smashing hard against bone.

The human screamed and flipped forward, landing hard upon his back. Vaste rapped him upon the nose, and his eyes glazed over, crossing as they stared up at the heavens, his mind gone from this fight.

"All I want is to be left alone!" Vaste bellowed as the humans nearest him charged, blades in their hands, swarming at him as locusts, but flying with such slowness as to seem like dawdling bees tarrying around a flower on a summer's day. "Yet even this smallest of requests cannot be answered by the universe, by the world, and instead of peace and a chance to mourn my shit fortunes, I stumble into a slaughter and receive the blame from you daft twits. Well, I have problems of my own!" He leveled a man charging at him, smashing Letum so heavily across his chest that the man's legs flew up ahead of his body and he drifted through the air like a gently tossed ball until he smashed into a nearby tree.

"Are you sure this is wise?" Qualleron asked, now at Vaste's side, his sword drawn for action but held before him, defensively, keeping a half-dozen humans at bay. "Need we be so harsh?"

"I have had it with ALL OF YOU!" Vaste let his voice boom

out as he struck the pistol from one man's hand and it hit the ground, blasting skyward as it expelled its chemically-propelled projectile. "I will take *no more of this.*" And he swung Letum around in a hard circle, causing every human even close to him to try and leap back, with varying degrees of success. He caught a couple of them in the ribs and arms, and heard the smack of staff on bone, the sharp intake of breath at the impact.

"Let him go." This from the woman who now lay at his feet, thrown down when he began swinging madly. She cradled her own pistol, but it was pointed down.

"But he's just–" one of the men started to say.

"Our war is with the elves, not these two," she said, picking herself up and dusting herself off. Dirt billowed free of her green cloak, and a streak of blood ran down her chin where she'd been struck during the battle. She looked at Vaste with a steely eye. "Leave these lands. Before you get drawn into this mess of ours."

"I want nothing more than to do just that," Vaste said, and with a flourish of a bow that had more than a little mocking in it, he swept his robes up and strode off, heading for the top of the hill, plunging forth in the direction they'd been going before this unreasonable detour had thrust itself upon them.

Qualleron's heavy steps followed behind him, and the bigger troll said, "Thank you. We wish you all very well, and good luck in your blood vengeance."

Vaste did not look back, though he could feel the angry eyes of those humans boring into him as he trudged, with a newfound energy, up and over the hill.

He did not quite breathe again until they were all out of sight.

CHAPTER 22

Alaric

"Wait here," Alaric said to Guy, who stood curious, and Edouard, who stood silent. While Dugras turned and retreated belowdeck, the captain herself appeared, passing him with but a word. She ascended to the quarterdeck and Alaric waited only a few moments, then followed. He found her at the back rail, with a peculiar tube in hand, peering through it into the dark vastness beyond the back edge of the ship.

He felt torn, standing there beneath the beating blades of the airship rotors. Like pillars they towered above, turning endlessly, the whip of the air off them like a breeze upon him, finding the cracks of his armor. But he could sense a greater disturbance emanating from them, the turning at a speed beyond the eye's ability to fathom, so that it looked like a series of discs hanging above him in the faint moonlight.

Mazirin was utterly focused, her figure shrouded in her brown coat, the hem whipping lightly in the breeze just below her knee. She cocked her head slightly as he approached, then pulled the tube from her eye and said something in her own language which sent two of the men around her scuttling forward, robe-like clothing flapping.

She turned her head slowly, casting a wary eye upon him. "You cannot keep yourself away from the center of the action, can you?"

Feeling a bit poleaxed by that, Alaric could not help but chuckle. "I suppose not. I hope you'll forgive the intrusion."

"Would it matter if I didn't?" She had the glass back to her eye and was peering behind the ship. Beside him, one of the lanterns was snuffed, then another. Alaric got it; her command had been to put out every light on the ship and to go forth in utter darkness.

"It would matter inasmuch as you, the mistress of this ship, could have me tossed overboard for my insolence," Alaric said. "I believe it would be uncomfortable to have such a sharp landing be my reproach for not knowing my place here."

He could have sworn he saw a slight motion of her shoulders. Perhaps a chuckle? But there was no hint of it seconds later, when she spoke, and she seemed resigned to his presence. "I suppose you are wondering what all the fuss is about."

"Dugras mentioned pirates," Alaric said, taking her pleasant reply as an invitation to step closer. "From Chaarland?"

"A rapacious nest of vipers if ever there was one," Mazirin said, and once more she removed the spyglass from her eye. "United, like Amatgarosa, but lacking our decency and ingenuity. Much of it is a frozen wasteland all the year 'round. Trading with them to the point where they developed airships was a mistake, and one I fear that we will long regret."

"Then you consider us to be...in danger?" Alaric asked.

She pondered this a moment, then offered him the tube. He took it up and curiously placed it to his own eye as he'd seen her do. At first, he saw nothing but darkness, deep and infinite. But then—

"Ah," he said. For there, in the dark, he saw it.

"You do not know what makes me sure it is a Chaarlandian pirate, do you?" Mazirin asked in that curious accent of hers.

"There are differences," Alaric said, squinting into the glass, "between it and the Amatgarosan vessels I have seen. More...curved. Less shovel-like."

"Be careful how you insult my ship," Mazirin said, and her voice was rent with a surprising amount of amusement. "For that, I might have you thrown overboard."

"I didn't mean it as insult," Alaric said, continuing his study of the shadow trailing them. "Merely the shaping of the thing. The hull glints in the dark—"

"Armored," Mazirin said. "Rather than timbers. A new innovation, at least for the Chaarlandians, and an ominous one."

Alaric swept his gaze to the side, to the place on the rail where a cannon smaller than his arm sat mounted on some sort of swiveling hinge. "Your weapons are as ineffectual against their steel as a bullet against my armor?"

"Correct," Mazirin said. "The only cannons I possess are these, bow and stern chasers. Eight pounders, and fairly accurate. Against an all-wood ship, we could do reasonable damage. Against a metal one, these are a pin dart trying to puncture a pangolin's skin."

"From the way you speak of it, I can only assume that is a creature with some armor," Alaric said, and saw her nod out of the corner of his eye. "What is to be done, then?"

"First, we would hope they haven't seen us," Mazirin said. "If that fails...we try to outrun them. Which is what we are doing now." She turned to look forward; at the wheel, one of the crew was hard at work, hands fixed upon it. "It now becomes a game of engine power, and steely determination."

"Your determination?" Alaric asked. "Or theirs?"

"Both," Mazirin said, her black braid stirring around her in the cool night wind. "For I am bound by duty to run, but also bound by the limits of my engines. Whereas he," and here she inclined her head toward the distant, steely ship glinting in the faint moonlight, "must decide whether a freighter our size is worth a day or more of pursuit. Especially once he realizes that I am willing to run my engines closer to the breaking point than many captains."

"I certainly do not doubt your determination," Alaric said. "Or your courage." A shadow passed across Mazirin's features.

"You don't care for my assessment?"

"The style of communication in your land is very different from my own," Mazirin said. "You are so...expressive. I find it distracting."

"How is it different from your language?" Alaric asked.

"It lacks subtlety," Mazirin said. "Yours is direct, like a broadside of cannons. Amatgarosans are an understated people, our language allows for more nuance. Openness of the kind your people express regularly is as an emotional hemorrhage to us."

"Sorry if I have ever 'hemorrhaged' upon you," Alaric said, though he couldn't recall if he ever had.

"You don't seem much the type," she said, regarding him coolly. "You are open, but in an honest way, not in the way of gushing feelings, as some are." Now she looked down. "I admire the manner in which you handle your crew. You have authority and respect, but not through anger, and threats. They follow because they genuinely believe you will lead them somewhere great."

"Well," Alaric said, "at the risk of 'hemorrhaging'...I have clearly not done so." He stared into the distance, where the Chaarlandian ship was beyond his sight on the horizon. "Even now."

This seemed to stir Mazirin back to the task at hand. "I do not know what sort of engines that ship possesses. Spyglass?"

Holding out her hand, he realized she wanted the tube, and he gave it to her. She placed it back to her eye, then breathed a word, deep, earthy, and under her breath; to Alaric's untrained ears, it had the aura of a curse. Barking two quick commands to the helmsman at the wheel, she then said, "They follow."

"Will they catch us?" Alaric asked.

"I am unsure," Mazirin said, and kept the spyglass honed on the ship, "but if so, it will be many hours." She looked at him, and with surprising gentleness given the situation, said, "My men are not fighters by nature. This is a cargo ship. If it comes to battle, we are unlikely to repel them without some significant help."

"You have my sword," Alaric said, "for whatever that is worth."

"I do not know how much it will be worth," she said, "only that if it comes to a fight, we will indeed need it. Between then and now...you should rest." She barked another order. Alaric started to speak up, but she held up a hand to stay him. "How long has it been since last you slept?"

Alaric wanted to argue, but the truth was...it had been some considerable time. Adrenaline seemed to fuel him, but its effects were waning, even now. "I will do what I can," he said. "What about you?"

"I need to calculate how long it will be before they catch us," she said, back to the spyglass. "Then I can decide my own course."

Somehow, he doubted she would sleep until this crisis was over, though he suspected confronting her on it would be a poor idea. "I will do as you say, Captain," Alaric said instead, for it seemed the wisest course. He came off the quarterdeck, watching her for some sign, strangely, as he walked away. But she remained fixed to the rail, glass up to her eye...and he had a feeling she would be for quite some time.

CHAPTER 23

Vara

"This was a terrible mistake," Isabelle said as the choking clouds descended once more upon them, blotting out the sky, and leaving them alone with raging flames on either side, buffeting them back and forth like meat upon a slowly-turning spit.

Vara could not find it in her to disagree. The mystical steel of her armor was beginning to warm, and her within it. In her armpits, in her lower back, and across her chest, she could feel the beads of sweat coursing, filling the cloth of her underclothes with an unremitting dampness. Beneath her helm, stinging droplets threatened to course over her brow and blind her even worse than the heat was already doing.

"We've lost the ship," Isabelle said, "we're in an unfamiliar city–"

"How are you unfamiliar with this city?" Vara asked, perhaps a bit less kindly than she might have had she been cooler, her tongue been less parched and desirous of a drink. "I've been gone a thousand years; what's your excuse?"

"That Reikonos is a cesspool run by a dictator," Isabelle said. "No elf with any wits comes here. Which is, I suppose, how I ended up coming here with you." She blanched against a heat that blew out at them as if fed by a steady pumping of a blacksmith's bellows. "I don't know what I was thinking. We should have stayed in Termina."

"I was thinking I made a foolish mistake leaving my husband in this horrid place to check on you, safe in blissful Termina," Vara said. "As it turned out, I was right – though how right, I might not have known until that spell blotted out all life in the city and turned the place over to Enflaga's own tender ministrations."

"Enflaga is quite dead, thanks to your husband. And in Termina, the match that lights the ready tinder has yet to be struck," Isabelle said cryptically. "So compared to this, it is bliss, I suppose." She looked at the sky with its choking smoke pouring out of every flaming building nearby, seeping skyward like water flowing upside down. "Where do we even go from here? If we knew the city better–"

"But we do know the city," Vara said, a thought lodging in her mind like a sword stuck blade-first in the ground.

"It's been over five hundred years since I've been here," Isabelle said. "I know nothing of this place compared to what I might have before Longwell – I'm sorry, Malpravus – took over. Humans have finite lifespans. Things have changed–"

"But not the big things," Vara said, taking hold of Isabelle's wrist. "Come. Get ready to run."

Isabelle stared blankly at her, tears glinting on her cheeks from the heat. "Run...where, exactly?"

"Straight ahead. Come."

Vara seized her and sprinted, not daring to let go. She knew Isabelle had a hand on Amoran, just as she did on Ferocis, and it helped. Helped keep the pain from the flames at bay as they charged up the middle of the road. Helped aid their passage, allowing them great strides through the worst of the heat.

After a hundred yards or so, it subsided, at least a bit, and they found themselves at a five-point corner. In the middle of that road stood a carriage with six horses dead, still in harness.

Vara did not dare look inside the carriage, and pushed aside the cold, pale corpse of the driver. She tried to get high enough to see through the haze of smoke that hung over everything.

And for a moment, she did.

"Yes," she exulted.

"Did you see the ship?" Isabelle asked, turning loose a terrible cough, racking and dry. She placed a hand over her chest, where her thin neck met her body.

Vara knew the feeling that made her do that. It was a scratchy sensation deep within her throat, as though someone had poured desert sand in her mouth while she slept. She looked left, then right, crouched atop the carriage.

"A-ha!" she pronounced, then grabbed Isabelle's hand as she descended, hurrying across the road to the entry of a building that was not quite as engulfed in orange blaze as the rest. Out front was a hitching post with which to tie up horses, as well as–

"Gods, yes," Isabelle said, and threw herself forward headfirst into the trough.

Vara joined her, and they both drank greedily from the filthy water, neither giving a single damn that it was water for horses, and had an appalling smell about it.

When they'd slaked their thirst, Vara gave Isabelle a look. "Finished?"

Isabelle looked as though she might never drink again. "For now. Why?"

Vara did not answer, instead jumping in as if the trough

were a coffin. After a few seconds of immersion she popped back out, dripping furiously upon the dirty cobblestones.

"Ah," Isabelle said, and then stepped in herself. She immersed herself as if in a bathtub, keeping her dignity about her, and when she came back out, blond locks all turned dark with wetness and stray pieces of hay stuck in her hair, she asked, "And now...?"

"And now, this," Vara said, tugging her sister's wrist as she stepped out of the trough. They headed back north, through the center of the five-point intersection. Ahead was smoky, uncertain–

Yet Vara was very certain she knew where she was going.

It was merely a matter of whether the flames would be light enough that she might find her way there before the burning city became utterly impassable.

CHAPTER 24

Cyrus

"Just like old times," Cyrus said, gathering his balance. Niamh was to his side, cowering in the face of Terian Lepos, who stood looking almost the same as ever, his carriage upright and axe held before him. "You trying to kill me – again."

"I assure you I've never tried to kill you before," Terian said, circling him, his weapon at his side. "I'd remember."

"Pinrade," Cyrus said, matching his circling movement. The sound of booted feet rushing all around him gave him the feeling he was being encircled, a concerning development. "I think that was the name of the little village in northern Luukessia, wasn't it? Where you slit Windrider's throat and left me for the scourge?"

"Congratulations," Terian said, his dark hair flashing in the firelight cast by the burning axe. More heavy footfalls, more shouts from the dark elves filling the docking tower's entry. "You've studied the history of Cyrus Davidon."

"I've lived it, you pile of dragon scat," Cyrus said, keeping his grip tight on both Rodanthar and Epalette. "Wait, that wasn't the first time you tried to kill me. You left me to fight that damned dwarven mercenary alone, too. What was his name? Former Guildmaster of The Daring? Partus!" If he'd had a hand free, he'd have snapped his fingers, clanked his mailed fingers together. As it was, he pointed Epalette at Terian. "Oh, and let us not forget–"

"Enough of this dry history." Terian swung at him, coming in with his axe in a wide arc low. It was a move suited to taking an opponent's feet away, to making him leap and, perhaps, lose balance or even a leg, depending.

Cyrus merely took a step back, for with Epalette and Rodanthar together, Terian moved especially slowly. He batted the axe down as he did so, sending the Sovereign of Saekaj and Sovar off balance himself. "You never were as good as me, Terian. It used to eat you alive. Does it still? Is that why you're exercised about my sudden appearance here?"

Terian's eyes flashed anger as they parted ways, standing off once more. "If I'm at all exercised, it's because another Cyrus Davidon impersonator has shown himself. True enough, you've done well to acquire a weapon, and the armor. If you surrender, and tell me where you found it all, I might even let you die quickly."

"I found it on myself," Cyrus said. "Because I've been wearing it all the whole time. Kind of like you with Alaric's armor." He saw the flash again in Terian's eyes, denial turned to hot rage. "What is it in you that makes you so angry at the possibility of me living?"

"You're an insult to his memory," Terian said. "I knew Cyrus Davidon, and you are no–" He swung once more.

Cyrus didn't bother to dodge, didn't bother to step away. He leaned into the swing, lifting Rodanthar to block it. The weapons clanged together, and Cyrus pointed Epalette at the center of Terian's chest, muttering the spell—

The force blast hit Terian squarely in the legs. Weakened as it was, it still took his legs from beneath him. The Sovereign fell for the ground, axe before him, and Cyrus caught it – and him with a twist of the wrist. The dagger came up and found its way into the gorget that waited for him there.

A gasp arose around them, and finally Cyrus looked.

There were a hundred or more dark elves, guards, dock workers, and sailors, all clustered around in a tightening circle. Niamh lingered close to Cyrus's legs, cowering against him in a ring of deep hostility. The smell of sweat and body odor was oppressive even with doors open on all sides and a light breeze blowing through over the platforms.

"Has the syphilis finally run its course in your brain?" Cyrus asked. Just behind him, he could see the face of Baynvyn, staring out at him from within the crowd of stunned onlookers. They wouldn't remain stunned for long, Cyrus knew. "You told me when last I saw you that you'd follow me anywhere." He maintained his grip, Terian's life the only thread he held to save his own, lest the mob loose itself on him. "But I come back and the only adventure you want to send me on is the final one, beyond death, where it looks to me like you don't care to follow." He ratcheted Terian's face closer to his with the point of his dagger and the strength of his arm. "You cling to life like a spider to its web, bereft of reason and without an ounce of recognition for one who was once a friend." With a twist he worked the elbow, eliciting a grunt from Terian, and Noctus clanked to the ground. "What happened to you, Terian, that's made you forget my face? And how shall I make you remember, if not by reason? Pain?"

Terian's breath was labored, and he grunted. "You cannot be Cyrus Davidon. Because Cyrus Davidon was my friend, and the hero of Arkaria." The lines around his eyes grew tighter and more lined as his scowl turned fierce, and the hatred dripped out of his lips across his words. "And if you have seen Arkaria, then you would know...Cyrus Davidon would not have stood aside and let these events merely proceed."

"I didn't see it happen," Cyrus said. "I wasn't *here*." He lifted himself up a bit more, and Terian's armor creaked as the joints pressed together tightly in a way they were not meant to. "It isn't as though I chose not to act and let things go straight toward the hellish."

Terian stared up at him. "You look...different. If you are Cyrus Davidon, in fact."

"I am," Cyrus said. "And I am here to warn you, Terian..." He released the Sovereign from his grasp. "...Malpravus has risen again, and he's destroyed Reikonos. He is on the move, and sure to come wherever there is life."

Terian stood upright, adjusting his helm, then his armor. With a look toward Baynvyn, and – to Cyrus's mild surprise – Hongren, he asked, "Is this true?"

"It is," Baynvyn said. Hongren merely nodded, stiffly.

The Sovereign stood there for a long moment, then stooped, bones popping in his back, to retrieve his axe, the fire now doused. Cyrus kept careful watch upon him, but he made no offensive move. He appeared deep in thought, then, finally, spoke.

"Come along, then," Terian said, taking in Cyrus with a long, sweeping look. "We have much to discuss, it seems." Raising his voice, he added, "Back to the work, the rest of you. What, have you never seen a fight before? Go on."

"We truly do have much to discuss," Cyrus said above the hushed chatter of the crowd. He nodded at Niamh, who mewled, but fell in beside him as he stepped forward to follow Terian into the dark of the center tower.

Terian, for the first time, seemed to take notice of Niamh as he led the way to a mighty platform in the center. "What...what the hells is this?"

He felt very on-the-edge with Terian already, as if teetering at a brink, and hesitated to answer. "A certain druid of our mutual acquaintance, who died shortly before we killed Mortus." He stepped onto the platform, and it let a hellacious groan at his weight. Baynvyn and Hongren followed, as if tied to them somehow now.

Terian gave the Niamh-scourge but a glance as the platform beneath their feet squeaked, and gears began to turn above them, reminding Cyrus very much of the same mechanism in the Citadel back in Reikonos. "That's not funny."

Cyrus kept his eyes on the Sovereign, still not daring to trust that he wouldn't still offer him a dagger in the back – or an axe stroke across the neck. "No, it's not," Cyrus said. "Though I imagine it's even less so for her." The squeak of the wheels turning occupied him as the darkness grew to surround him and he disappeared into the earth surrounded by people he found he trusted barely at all.

CHAPTER 25

Alaric

The room they had been assigned felt like a disused storage, small as a closet, with three silken hammocks draped across. The smell of feet and sweat mingled with some sour fruit Alaric had never sampled. The wood creaked in the walls as the ship moved, the engine thrummed, and the porridge that he'd been served in a small, wooden bowl an hour ago, his only meal for the last days, still lingered upon his tongue.

Guy snored softly in the middle hammock, a rumbling noise that projected from his nose but seemed to come from deep in his throat. The swaying of the ship should have lulled Alaric to sleep, but his eyes remained open, the darkness near-complete save for the orange of a lantern shining beneath the door, flickering as the flame danced and shed its silent light.

Alaric sighed; sleeping here felt impossible. Not because it was uncomfortable. He'd slept many worse places over the years, and with louder companions. Even sleeping in the chamber to which he'd become confined by Bellarum had been infinitely worse than this, and unspeakably less luxurious.

It was the worry. That much was the same between that chamber and this; the wondering of what would happen to the people he cared about. Of course...many of them might well already be dead. Curatio certainly was.

But what of Vara, who had fled the city in the days before? What of Vaste, who had been closer to the wall? And Cyrus, who had gone deep into the midst of Reikonos to rescue his son? What of Hiressam, of Shirri, Pamyra? Surely they had not all died in the red flare of spell-light that had killed Reikonos?

And what if they had? Well, that was on him. He had trusted Malpravus for too long, had enabled him to begin his long march of destruction when first he'd allied Sanctuary with Goliath. It had been a start for the necromancer, and enough of one to give Alaric great regret now.

"Where do I go?" Alaric muttered. "What do I do?"

"I wish I knew," Edouard said, whispering to match him.

Alaric lifted his head; the former executioner was opposite him, swaying in his own hammock, Guy between them snoring prodigiously. "Can you not sleep, my friend?"

Edouard shook his head. "I can't get off my mind what we saw back there. Every time I close my eyes I see red, I see...the end of all things."

"Certainly the end of many lives," Alaric said.

"But you say that was the Lord Protector," Edouard said. "But you see, I came to Reikonos to live under the Lord Protector. Came from the Northern Confederation across the Perda, for Reikonos is a place where one can claw up, if one is willing to serve. Well, I was willing, and I did all that was asked of me and more." He turned his face away. "I did things...things I cannot rightly justify in the cold light of that red spell. And I did it for what I thought was the good of Reikonos. To maintain that city, to keep it back from the edge where it perched."

"Malpravus has long been a prince of lies," Alaric said. "There were days when I trusted him myself, and he showed ever so much more of himself then than he presented to you. He showed you a fair face, did he not?"

"I thought he was Lord Longwell," Edouard said. "The savior of Reikonos. That he was working for our good, to give us a place where we could be, crowded as it was, dirty as it was, isolated as – well, you know. We thought it was the place where Arkarian humans could rise again, to become what we had the right to be, strong and prosperous."

"Part of leaving your past behind," Alaric said, "is learning to forgive yourself for past failings, while resolving never to make the same mistake again. Redemption is a struggle, and one you must bear for the rest of your days, for to simply declare yourself finished with it is not possible. You must take action to right the wrong, as best you can."

"I wonder if I ever can leave my past behind me?" Edouard asked. "Truly, I mean? I was an executioner for a man, for a system, that executed everyone in the end. All my so-called 'good works' in the name of Reikonos? They count for nothing." He lowered his head and seemed to be trying not to cry, though a tear coursed down his cheek anyway. "I was the headsman, and I took so many heads on behalf of that demon. People who might have stopped him. People who couldn't have hoped to stop him, who only breathed a word of opposition. He even pushed me into that fight at the docks, though I did not want to go. I am a headsman, and a coward, I suppose...and I did all that." He looked right at Alaric. "Does that make me evil?"

"What you did in the service of evil is doubtless evil," Alaric said. "But that is your past, and it does not own your future unless you let it." Alaric turned uncomfortably upon the hammock, his armor an impediment to that aim, the jutting edges constantly catching on the bound ropes. "And I would not suggest you do so."

CHAPTER 26

Vaste

"You showed your great courage again."

Qualleron's voice boomed in the forest some half hour after they'd made their escape from the humans. Ahead, the trees were thinning, giving way to sunlight and fields, leaving the shadows made by thick boughs overhead behind. The air was not as close now, a breeze seemed to stir to life, swaying the branches above and sending pine needles tickling down upon Vaste's head occasionally.

"I showed my irritation, nothing more," Vaste said. He kept a hurried pace, half hoping he might leave the larger troll behind. He could join those angry humans, perhaps get himself a job cutting his way through their enemies.

It seemed not to be, though, for Qualleron's heavy footfalls persisted in following a mere pace or two behind him, so close that he imagined he could stop and feel the bigger troll's sword hilt poke him in the back. Or something.

"This is how it is here, I have heard." Qualleron's voice was quiet, measured. "The men and elves, at each other's throats, always vying for advantage. But it seems to have advanced of late; I had heard nothing of base slaughters such as that."

"I saw women in there," Vaste said, hesitating. "In the dead, I mean. Besides the one we talked to."

"Villagers, I imagine," Qualleron said. "Some were dressed as farmers. Or at least, as you people dress as farmers."

"You think I dress as a farmer?" Vaste did not bother glaring at him. "Do you imagine this is a milk maid's frock?"

"You people," Qualleron said, giving him a vague wave as he came alongside. "Meaning Arkarians. You lamentable souls of this backward land."

"Forsaken," Vaste said. "I like 'forsaken' for this land. It fits."

"It does," Qualleron said with a nod. "Still, I suppose that wars like this are not so uncommon. Nations of Firoba still see such conflict. So does Bithrindel, and Coricuanthi. Not Amatgarosa, of course–"

"I don't know any of these names and I don't give a fig."

Qualleron's broad face bore a frown. "What is this...fig?"

Vaste fought the desire of his eyes to roll, but not very hard nor very long. "It's a fruit. Grows in the south, near – well, what was Taymor." That pricked his face into a frown of his own. "I don't know if they even grow at all, anymore. The scourge might have wiped them out." His staff bumped the earth as the last trees gave way and he found himself walking toward the top of a sun-drenched hill, the dirt road wending its way up the slope. "Along with everything else east of the Perda." He grunted. "What a time to be alive."

"It is good," Qualleron said, agreeing without, apparently, realizing the sarcasm of the statement. "Truly, in spite of our setbacks, we are blessed by the hand of fate."

This time, there was no attempt to control his eyeroll. "Yes. How good is our fortune, to stumble in here at the worst of times, when the humans and elves are killing each other in numbers. How fortuitous. I am the luckiest troll alive."

"Well, you did survive Reikonos," Qualleron loosed a small puff of exertion as they neared the crest of the hill. "That does, I suppose, make you lucky indeed."

Vaste's eye twitched. "There really is no end to your sunny disposition, is there?"

"Why would there be, while I still draw breath?" Qualleron breathed loudly, then let it out just as zestfully. "We lived when so many did not. We were ferried here, to this land, where there are troubles, true – but they are not ours, and we have extricated ourselves from them." He craned his neck, looking around with great enthusiasm. "We are on the path once again, the wind is at our backs, and the road is ahead. Why should we not be jubilant?"

"I can think of a few reasons," Vaste said sourly as they reached the crest of the hill, a switchback path curving up the last thirty feet or so of the steep incline.

But they fled his mind when he made it to the top, for there, below him, was a sight of untrammeled splendor after the long night and the dark of the woods–

A city, gleaming white, lay down in a valley of green, with fields leading up to it and woods spanning the edges of the hills that hemmed it in. Even from this distance, Vaste could see movement in its walls; fires burning, smoke curling out of the chimneys, carts moving along the roads toward the city gates. Along one side, curving in toward the town, lay a curious stitching of wood laid under metal lines, stretching off in the distance. He started to ask Qualleron about them, but the bigger troll spoke first.

"You see?" Qualleron slapped him on the back. "Our luck continues, my friend! Come, let us see if an airship is due anytime soon. If we are lucky, we can be on the winds to Firoba by night. Oh, the things you will see there! I almost envy you, especially if we happen to get to Vicienne."

"Yes, the place of dough, troll-loving women, and gnomes who have no regard for their own health and safety," Vaste said, but Qualleron was not listening. Already he was in motion, ambling down the hill, humming some unfamiliar tune.

And for some reason – perhaps because he had nowhere else to go, no friends left in the world, and nothing but trouble bubbling up behind him – Vaste followed the happy mercenary toward the sun-drenched city with its minarets and white walls, wondering what further trouble he could expect therein.

CHAPTER 27

Shirri

Calene's apartment was upon the twentieth floor of a carved tree tower, with a cranking, creaking mechanical elevator at its center. They rode it up in relative silence after a short walk into the bustling downtown area, and when Calene opened the door Shirri found herself stepping into an environ she imagined would have been better suited to a shack out on the Gradsden Savannah or in the isolated reaches of the Heia Mountains than in the midst of the great city of Amti.

Immense furs from the colossal savannah animals draped the walls; stuffed heads jutted out in the gaps, fearsome and angry, probably at being decapitated. There was also more prosaic decor including a traditionally stuffed elven couch and finely-made elven furniture, with tables populated by the occasional piece of fine statuary.

"Come in, relax, I'm guessing you've had a hard journey," Calene said, hanging her bow upon the cloak rack just inside.

She next shed her burned cloak, draping it beside the ornate bow.

"Can I ask about that?" Hiressam nodded at the weapon. "It's beautiful...and it has the aura of a weapon of the gods."

Calene let her eyes run across the weapon – but briefly, only. "It is Vita, the Bow of Life. I went into her realm after her death with a couple old friends and picked it up."

"Curious," Hiressam said. "But weren't you given the Claws of Lightning in the war against the gods?"

Calene cocked her head at him. "You're well-informed."

"Well studied, more like." Hiressam blushed, ever-so-slightly. "As in I've studied every bit of Sanctuary minutiae I could."

Calene nodded slowly. "Yes, I was handed the Claws by Cyrus Davidon himself. But to be honest, they never quite fit my style of fighting. So about a year after the last battle in the Realm of War, I started asking myself...'Whatever happened to Vidara's weapon?' She betrayed us in that fight, you know." She smirked, and it held an aura of danger. "Of course you know."

"So you went in and helped yourself," Hiressam said. "Not that I'm judging." He made a face. "Hell, I wish I'd thought of that myself. I could have used a godly weapon, especially lately."

"Tell me all about it, then," Calene said, settling herself upon one of the lush couches. She perched on the edge, though, coiled as if ready to spring. "All of it, leave nothing out."

Hiressam launched into the story – of the Machine, of the faux Longwell at the top of the tower, the battle and the escape on the airship. "...and while Cyrus was off trying to rescue his son, we fought a valiant defense of the shipyards," Hiressam said, gliding to his conclusion. "Unfortunately, a red light appeared above the Citadel–"

"And with that, magical death swept over the entire city," Calene said, fingers playing over the scars 'round her lips. "Yes, I've seen that particular trick from Malpravus before, the leprous skeleton."

"You have to have skin to be leprous," Hiressam said with the trace of a smile. "I don't believe that pile of bones does, at least not any of his own."

Calene turned her focus upon Shirri. "And you? What's your part in all this?"

"I...was in trouble with the Machine," Shirri managed to stutter out. She inclined her head toward Pamyra. "My mother and I, both. Cyrus, the others...they helped get us out of a sticky situation." She wished desperately to leave it at that.

"I am the daughter of Andren, the healer," Pamyra said, her chin rising. "Perhaps you knew him?"

"Hard man to forget, that one," Calene said. "Dangerous when he was drinking. Arguably more dangerous still when he was finally sober."

"I...I don't take your meaning," Pamyra said.

"He was a bit quick to get distracted and miss a healing spell," Calene said. "But what I really mean is...oh, forget it. Doesn't matter at this point." She looked back to Shirri. "So...I understand how you got in the door with Sanctuary. But...why stay, if your problems were resolved?"

"I don't know," Pamyra said, and there was a bracing dose of honesty in her reply.

"Because of Alaric," Shirri said, giving her an ireful look. "The way he spoke, the way he asked us to follow him. It was like nothing I'd ever heard in my life."

"And you never will again," Pamyra said. "We were fools to buy what he sold us. Utter fools, taken by the words of a smooth man, a smooth operator–"

"'Taken in?'" Shirri felt herself stand. "As though we were wandering through a market and found ourselves standing before a huckster selling foolishness?" She shook her head slowly. "We were standing before legends, Mother, people who fought with Grandfather for the betterment of the world. I was not *taken in*." Shirri drew herself up to her full height, which was still less than commanding. "I found something to believe in. Something to fight for." She took a deep breath. "And I will fight still, for Malpravus is coming...though I expect I may be alone in this."

"You're not alone," Hiressam said, rising to his own feet and putting his hands upon the hilt of his sword. "For I, too, keep the faith. What happened in Reikonos must not be repeated. I am with you."

Calene watched them both, then nodded once. "If it is as you say...you can count me in." She cracked her knuckles. "I've had a pleasant thousand-year reprieve from fighting Malpravus, but I never expected to survive him, truth be told." She lowered her voice to a whisper. "It's been a good run, but...well. I'm in, let's leave it at that."

The three of them looked at Pamyra, who stared at each in turn, then slowly shook her head. "You're all mad. We watched a city be destroyed. We should be boarding the nearest airship for Firoba, and from there, behind the walls of Amatgarosa if possible. Azwill if not. As far from here as possible, that should be our heading."

"I will no longer run and hide from danger," Shirri said, chin up. "I said as much after the Machine...and I meant it. I will no longer live in fear for my life."

"Then you'll lose it," Pamyra said.

"Better to lose it in battle against the great evil of our time," Shirri said, "then milk it for all my days and die in bed, clinging to cowardly thoughts as I expire from old age, with half the world or better in ruin around me." She stared her mother down. "If you mean to spare your own life, you should go, Mother, and swiftly. Find an airship to some distant land, and simply...begone." Shirri turned away from Pamyra. "But I cannot forget what I have seen, and I will not run and hide in the face of such murderous evil. I will look it in its shining skull...and find some way to jab a dagger in there."

"Brassy," Hiressam announced. "One would think you were ready to take up a sword and start hacking away at whatever trouble Malpravus brings next."

Pamyra sunk back into the couch, deflated. "Fine. Have it your way, then. I will stay." But the implication was there, in her eyes – *for now*.

Calene nodded. "Right, well, that's decided, then. Except..." and she looked tentatively, "...What exactly are we going to do about it?"

CHAPTER 28

Vara

"We have to hurry," Vara said, looking skyward once more in hopes that the near-magical airship would reappear and solve her dilemma for her.

But there was no airship, and the sky was blackening with thick bands of smoke. The buildings on either side of this arterial road through the heart of Reikonos were catching fire with great intensity. The sound of glass shattering provided background noise for the crackling of flames and the roar of the wind as it took up smoke and cinders.

Vara blanched as embers caught her on the back of the neck, sneaking their way through the links of her chainmail. It was only to get worse, especially as the water she'd soaked up in the trough seemed to be evaporating from her armor, from her underthings, from everywhere – and swiftly, at that. It was leaving behind a dry, uncomfortable, chafing feeling that she had little time to deal with save by the occasional muttering of a healing spell.

"I'm not trying to drag feet, you know," Isabelle said, holding her hand as tightly as she held Isabelle's. Isabelle was, though, a step behind, letting Vara lead through the smoke and heat. "I'm as keen to get out of here as you are, neither wanting to dry gradually like cured meat or be burnt to a crisp quickly."

"Why not the return spell, then?" Vara asked, holding up as they reached a small square. A small break in the black clouds from the buildings burning all around them revealed hints of blue sky above. Not much, but it was there, buried beneath the unending smoke.

Isabelle, hair matted to her head by the dunk in the trough, looked at her with flat blue eyes, her skin tinged orange by the blazing buildings at every compass point and nearly all points between, save for the road, which was covered over in the deepest black smoke. "Return, as a spell, is quite spotty these days, and best used over short distances. Were I to try it now, this far from where I'm bound in Termina, well...I should not wish to risk it, especially not with the two of us."

"Then teleport is similarly out?"

Isabelle's mouth twisted at a corner. "I am...not excellent at that branch of magic, having been educated in the time before heresy became commonplace. I'm not sure I can recall those spells at this point, in fact, as teleportation ceased to be reliable some two hundred years ago. It was well known to be potentially fatal to try."

"Very well, let's keep that one in your robe pocket, then," Vara said, and tugged her forward again. The smoke had cleared just enough that she could see the Citadel once more, only a few blocks away now. "We proceed on foot."

"You think the Citadel will offer us safety?" Isabelle asked, letting herself be led. Vara could barely hear the sound of her boots upon the cobblestones over the roar of the flames.

"No," Vara said, "for in truth and in spite of the escape of the red light at the end of that spell, I am unsure whether Malpravus remains in the tower, and I would not care to chance an encounter with his bony arse." She shook her head. "Up is a fool's errand, I fear. No, it's down for us, I would think. Down into—"

"Into the old city beneath?" Isabelle asked, stifling a dry cough. "The space of the ancients, where the portal is?"

Vara nodded. "I think I can recall the old spell to dissolve that wall, the one Curatio used all those years ago."

"Marvelous," Isabelle said through a great, racking cough.

They plunged forth into another blinding cloud of smoke, nearly a wall of it. Vara kept her grip tightly upon her sister's hand, and shuffled her way through the flames, eyes burning and wet. Sooner or later, surely she would run out of liquid in her body. And what then? Would she be dried out, as wrung completely of dampness as she currently seemed to be of feeling? Would her eyes tear no more, would there be no blurring and stinging?

Or would that come long after death, after she'd fallen to her knees with that same racking cough as Isabelle, her very chest filled with the black smoke that filled the air?

Forward. Whatever the answer to that question, she needed to go forward so as not to discover it firsthand.

She nearly tripped over a pile of corpses that she could not even see, a pile that was higher than one, higher than two, and thicker than three or four or five. With her hand clenching Isabelle's, she shouted, "There are bodies in the road."

Isabelle did not answer, but she was coughing as well. The buildings on either side of them were not visible, save as glows of orange in the haze of smoke where the flames licked out of their windows or through their crumbling facades.

There was surely a way, though. Vara tried to let the heat be her guide, let the feel of the flames on either side be balanced, to let her know that perhaps she was equidistant from each burning side of the street. She was stumbling blindly now, forward, forward, ever forward, in hopes that they were close to breaking through. For there had to be a square ahead, some respite from burning buildings on either side.

The smell of cooking meat was becoming more pronounced now, and Vara knew what that augured a moment after she detected it.

Bodies on fire. Horrifying as that prospect was, she felt an uncontrollable shudder in her belly. "Forward," she whispered, trying to shut out the smells, clenching her eyes against the smoky, burning feeling gouging at them. Her fingers were clenched on Isabelle's wrist, and she would not let go, not through the fire, not through the smoke, not through—

An explosion rocked the street, flinging Vara through the air. She smacked wetly into something, felt the splatter of ichor and the stink of something vile. The smoke faded for a moment, and she realized she'd hit the street and rolled, rolled through something terrible—

Bodies. She'd rolled through bodies, and struck with such force as to tear one of them up. Her pauldron glistened with dark red, and her sleeve beneath was slick with it. No searing pain presented itself at her side, either, no wound to explain it. She brushed a chunk of bone from the silvery armor and grimaced, almost tempted to apologize to whomever's corpse she had made her soft landing on, but—

But she was alone. She lifted her hands, and they were empty.

"Isabelle?" She called. Orange blazed brightly in front of her, and she put together what had happened.

A building had exploded and flung her through the air. Now here she was, on a knee, fire burning bright behind and in front of her, her sense of direction utterly fouled—

And her sister...was missing.

CHAPTER 29

Cyrus

The clank and clatter of the machinery rattled in the wide, empty space at the center of the tower above Saekaj Sovar. It had seemed to extend above the ground for a mile or more, a lonely, black flower blooming in a dead land. Now Cyrus was at the center of it, Terian, Baynvyn, and Shipmaster Hongren around him, blooms of suspicion around him at the center, as well.

"You haven't been here in a thousand years," Terian said, pulling off his helm and tucking it under his arm. His eyes glinted in the dark, barely more than his hair. "Last time you were here, it was just a walk through an open cave."

"The time before that it was a rubble-strewn blockage because of Goliath," Cyrus said, watching for the attack, the knife, because he sensed the tension in Terian's speech.

"Hm." A small chuckle, almost pained, escaped the Sovereign. "The treachery of Malpravus knows no bounds."

"He certainly hasn't changed in that regard," Cyrus said. "Terian—"

But Terian held up a mailed palm to stay him. "Not here," he said as the elevator slowed in its descent. Around the periphery, and in the darkness, Cyrus saw movement. The whispered effort of an Eagle Eye spell granted him only a slight reprieve from the shadows dancing at the edge of his vision. Shapes were there, shapes of men and women and other creatures; spiders the size of trolley carts with their black legs the size of timbers. Seeing them skittering in the dark ran a shiver through Cyrus's whole body.

Apparently Niamh did not care for them either; she made a whimpering sound and bumped against Cyrus's greaves.

"It's all right," Cyrus whispered, stooping to brush a hand across her broad, wrinkled back. "I won't let them hurt you."

He caught the twist of Terian's lips, disdain and disgust all in one, but the Sovereign said nothing save for, "This way," and led him forth.

Cyrus recognized the place as the great entry square of Saekaj and Sovar, a cavernous chamber with rock walls that looked like shadowy lines in the far distance, behind stacks of crates and carriages of spiders. The smell of waste from men and vek'tag was strong and pungent, and a carriage rattled by that took the rank scent with it, leaving only traces lingering behind.

Terian caught him looking. "We can't waste anything, even our own filth, you know."

"No, I didn't," Cyrus said, trying to cover his nose with his hand to stifle the smell. It didn't work, giving him only a thin aura of dirt from when he'd been driven to the ground while fighting scourge as bare cover for the stink.

Terian's head rose just a millimeter or so. "Of course you didn't. It'd be too much to ask for the great Cyrus Davidon to spare a thought of how we meager dark elves are getting along."

Cyrus almost swung spitefully back at that obvious bait, but instead checked his back. Baynvyn and Hongren were both there, just out of swinging reach, as though waiting for an opportunity to knock him down and leave him in the dirt. "After you," he said, stepping aside for them.

Hongren looked quite ready to protest, but Baynvyn shoved him along. "Fine," his son said, and Cyrus followed them, Niamh in tow.

"You don't mind a walk, do you, Cyrus?" Terian called back. "I quite enjoy a good constitutional these days, at least any time I'm able to leave business behind and get out of the palace."

"Not having ever had a palace," Cyrus said, "I'm quite fine with walking."

"Not accustomed to taking your horse?" Terian asked. "What was it called again, back when I knew you?"

"Windrider," Cyrus said absently, distracted by his surroundings. When last he'd been in this place, the path out of the square had been but a tunnel leading down into the further depths of Saekaj Sover. But now...

...Now it was like a city street with no sun overhead, no break to the lines of the buildings. Store fronts peeked out from either side of the path, with scratched signs in the open windows, no glass separating them from the street. Ragged, filthy children played here, the gutters running with excrement and urine that made Cyrus cough in the dark, then gag. It stretched before him, lining either side, and the crowds of bedraggled urchins paused to stare at him, then jeer in their own language.

"Do you know what they're saying?" Baynvyn asked.

"I sucked enough at Elvish," Cyrus said, still holding his nose, "I don't think I ever picked up more than five words of Dark Elven."

"They're calling you an imposter," Terian said, leading their little parade. "But in a much less friendly way."

Cyrus looked into the shadowed face of one of the children; the jeering was apparent. "Of course they are." With a whispered word, he produced a small flame in the darkness, emanating from his palm like a torch in the dark.

That shut them up.

Terian chuckled. "Remember when things like what you just did would have been considered the realm of petty tricksters?"

"Almost as well as I remember you walking funny out of the whorehouse in Scylax," Cyrus said. "What was it that woman did to you that made you walk bowlegged?"

"I almost don't remember." Terian stared pleasantly ahead. "Almost."

They went onward, the scenery becoming somehow more wretched. The dark elves he saw were clothed in burlap and canvas, rough clothing for a rough people, encased in dirt and filth. Cyrus let the flame in his hand die, and his eyes adjusted back to the darkness. Eyes peered back at him, whispers raced ahead, and the questions the watching souls asked were as obvious to him in their own language as they would have been in his own.

Is that Cyrus Davidon?

The real Cyrus Davidon?

"Tell me you didn't make a religion out of me after I left, Terian," Cyrus said tightly, the pressure and weight of all those eyes, all those people upon him. "Not like they did in Reikonos."

"Would you rather I made a savior out of myself?" Terian asked, not looking back. "Like the last occupant of my seat? Hmph." The scoffing noise came from deep within his throat, leavened with disgust. "Besides, I had little to do with it other than to ride the tide of your popularity by tying myself to you. The rest of Arkaria made you an infallible hero. I just stood in the shadow of your greatness."

Terian paused next to a silver-helmed guard, the metal's sheen barely visible to Cyrus's eyes. He whispered something in the man's ear, got a nod in response, and then the guard hustled off down the slope at a steady run, armor clanking as he went.

"I take it by your guard uniforms you don't have many of those newfangled pistols floating around down here," Cyrus said.

Terian gave him a withering look. "They're expensive, and Saekaj Sovar is just about the poorest place on the planet, last I checked. So no...we do not have very many rifles and pistols just lying around. It's just all I can do to get enough food in here to keep people from starving."

Cyrus thought about that for a moment. "Baynvyn said that you only built the tower ten years ago. How did you feed everyone before that?"

"We didn't," he answered quietly. "Come on."

They continued down the slope for some ways, the reek of the place seeming to grow stronger with each step. Baynvyn fell into step beside Cyrus, looking at him sidelong. "Place has changed, hasn't it?"

"It wasn't like this when you grew up here, was it?" Cyrus asked, making a vague wave at a nearby shop that had mushrooms for sale. So very many mushrooms. Next door was some kind of bakery, and the scent of the bread was...off-putting, to say the least. The next shop had some sort of giant stew pot out front, and the smell emitted was nearly worse than the urine running through the gutters. A spider-drawn wagon laden with a dozen crates rattled past along the cobbled stones of the avenue.

"All this was expansion after the scourge," Baynvyn said, watching the people watching them. "We had to close up the entrance, couldn't farm the top land any longer. We were reliant on mushrooms and roots and spider herds. None of the fancy things you're used to."

Cyrus avoided rolling his eyes, but only just. "What I was used to, son, ranged from the finest beef all the way down to stews of water and rabbit bones." He fixed Baynvyn with a hard stare. "Don't look at the high points of my life and think it was always wonderful. I grew up in tough conditions, and by the end of Sanctuary, we were mostly eating conjured food."

"Made by the Sorceress," Terian piped up. "Who could turn dreck and shit into fruit pies and side of beef."

"Doesn't change my time at the Society of Arms," Cyrus said, "where I didn't taste beef for a decade, not even the damned hooves. It was horsemeat, mostly. The occasional chicken at best."

"I feel great tears welling up for your most pitiful of tales," Terian said. They walked on, the crowd falling into silence before them, whispers preceding them. The street turned ahead, into a wider cavern, and beyond–

Cyrus's first glimpse of the upper chamber of Saekaj in a thousand years nearly took his breath away; he only managed to keep it at the last through great effort.

Where once had stood a series of manors and townhomes, fine as anything in Reikonos, now the old buildings still stood, hewn out of the same stone as the caves, given style and finery by the endless efforts of craftsmen, but...

...every one of them looked filled to overflowing. Staircases were carved into the upper levels of the facades, spiraling higher in the chamber than ever had been built before. People stood upon these upper levels, and in great numbers, staring down into the cavern below.

Cyrus turned to Terian, who caught him looking. A smile, laced with malicious satisfaction waited on his lips. "That's right. This is the upper chamber."

"This was the place your wealthy hung their hats," Cyrus said. Children hung out of windows, and immense crowds thronged the streets. Where before Cyrus had remembered peaceful streets, now there was no placidity, only a riot of noise and color of the sort he would normally have associated with the lower chamber, Sovar. "Your elite lived here, lording it over the lowers."

"Oh, they still do – sort of," Terian said. "But our population has grown in your long absence. And all our digging into side tunnels, all our efforts at expansion – why, we've tunneled under half the continent, Cyrus." There was a gleam of peculiar triumph in his eye. "Gone all the way to the river Perda with our efforts – thrice – though that didn't turn out well for us any time. We even tried to reach Reikonos, but there's a vein of hard stone in the way that refuses to be reduced, though we keep trying. Probably will call it quits now, though I'd been told we were a mere two, three years from finishing that project. I was a bit torn on it, honestly." His eyes were cool. "A direct path into that city might have been a problem, see. Importing troubles with the foodstuffs."

"I would say so," Cyrus said. "You knew who was running the place?"

A flicker in Terian's eyes told Cyrus it was so, but the Sovereign merely said. "Come along. We have things to discuss," and swept forward through the crowd, who barely put effort into parting for their Sovereign, but had eyes and worshipful looks aplenty for Cyrus as he passed.

CHAPTER 30

Vaste

He found what he had half-expected, natives with their eyes narrowed in suspicion at the approach of two trolls to their gates. Vaste trudged, his legs tired of bearing his frame, his stomach rumbling at having no food since...well, hell if he could recall...and at every indignity visited upon him since arriving in this place. Birissa, he suspected, lay near the top of that list, if not at the very top.

"Not a very friendly place," Qualleron muttered, slowing his pace when they drew near to the city gates. The white city looked a bit more dirty up close, the stone having a weathered appearance. Vaste estimated it had been here since his day, and it even looked familiar with the minarets. As he drew closer, he saw elves, elves, and more elves in the stalls at the entry, in the elaborate armor that had not changed since his day, with its sculpted breastplates and winged helms, with shields of the most intricate metalwork, finer than any sculpture the trolls had produced, ever.

"Well, you said they're in conflict with the humans in this land," Vaste said, drawing his own conclusions quite rapidly. "Men are short-lived, and came here a thousand years ago seeking escape from the scourge, I imagine. They also have many, many children. Elves are ridiculously long-lived, and have...well, they had no children, at least in my remembrance."

Qualleron had a very strange look upon his face. "That must be a very unsatisfying life."

"I'm not sure which thing you're referring to there," Vaste said, catching a suspicious look from an elf guard, who was probably overhearing him, "the lack of children in their lives, or the lack of doing the thing that causes children."

"Both," Qualleron said, his brow a dark, thick cloud. "My children have been the greatest joy of my life. As was my lifemate, in both our bed and out of it."

"Lucky you," Vaste said, trying to keep from sneering. "She didn't turn out to be a figment of some ancient power's imagination, I take it?"

Qualleron stared into the distance. "No. But she did die during the last upheaval."

"I don't give a fig for your tale of woe right now," Vaste said spicily. "I have my own woes, thank you very much." Catching the solid and unflinching glare of the guards ahead, he turned his attention to them. "What do you want?"

The head guard shook his head slowly. "Always the foreigners come here with no conception of how to speak our language," he said to his fellows, in elvish. "They expect us to be the ones to bend, to speak that filthy human tongue."

"I do expect you have a filthy tongue," Vaste said, in elvish, prompting eyebrows to raise among all the guards, "but that's more down to where you've been putting it." He stopped before them, drawing himself up to his full height; he was taller than any of them by a solid foot. "May I pass, or do I need to take a language test first? Because my elvish is admittedly a bit rusty; it's been a while since I've been to Pharesia or Termina."

The guard seemed to regain his composure. "Is that where you learned to speak our language?"

"No, I learned your language from the stalls of public toilets in Reikonos," Vaste said. "Now...is this a formal blockade? Or are you just drawn together as arseholes are to an outhouse? Which clearly, your city is." He eyed the dirty stone walls.

The guards seemed still too gobsmacked by his command of their language to take affront to his constant stream of insults. "You may pass," the guard said uncertainly. "You're not a human, after all."

"At least your eyes work," Vaste said, plowing on through, and sending a couple of them scrambling to get out of his way. "Which is more than I can say for your brains, you knobs."

"Sorry," Qualleron said, following behind, but in the human language. "He's had a bit of a day."

"Don't pretend you know what I said to them," Vaste said. "You don't speak this language. You're not even from here."

"I speak the human one, and I'm not from here," Qualleron said. "But you're quite right, I have no idea what you said. But I know you how you said it, and it leaves little doubt as to the content."

Vaste did not argue, for why would he? Qualleron was right, of course.

Now they passed into the city, and if the outside had been a vision of a place gone to seed, the inside was little better. The market stalls lining the entry boulevard were old and battered, the bright awnings faded from years of sunlight, some so badly frayed that they seemed in danger of coming apart into threads entirely.

The smells of the city were old elven spices that Vaste knew mingled with new ones he might have scented in Reikonos over the last days. He knew the names of none of them, but they were pungent, and he thrust his wrist over his nose, the smell of his days-worn and unlaundered sleeve blotting them out rather unfavorably.

"It smells like home," Qualleron said, inhaling deeply and savoring the scent.

"Like a toilet, then," Vaste said. Qualleron did not seem to take notice.

The city was smallish; soon enough they were at a crossroads, and the market square. Little was to be found here, though – bakers, butchers, vegetable carts. A stand nearby had the aura of fried, greasy food emanating from it. From his height, Vaste could see some sort of meat wrapped in parchment paper, the oils darkening it and seeping through.

His stomach thundered at the smell. Far from the stink of the foreign spices, this had an agreeable aroma, especially to a someone who'd not eaten a full meal for some time.

"Food?" The elf manning the stand asked in the human tongue. His raised eyebrows and hopeful look suggested he was not nearly as affronted by speaking the language as the guards at the gate had been.

Vaste checked his belt, hoping to find his coinpurse. It was, unfortunately, not filled. It had been rather empty, in fact, since he'd tossed his fortunes in with the rest of the Sanctuary band's when they'd needed to purchase the grain to feed Reikonos. "What a waste," he muttered, coming up with his sad purse, giving it a shake for good measure. "All that gold meant for grain and not a mouth to be fed by it."

"I'll take ten," Qualleron said, shoving his way past Vaste and plunking good gold down in front of the merchant. The merchant's eyes widened, and he hurried to work gathering up wads of parchment paper and greasy, fried meat.

"Yes, well, enjoy your meal," Vaste said, turning quickly away from that spectacle.

Qualleron landed a hand upon his shoulder. When Vaste turned, he found the larger troll extending five of the parcels to him. "These are for you." He chuckled. "Did you think I could eat ten myself?"

"I don't wish to put anything beyond you," Vaste said, taking up the load of meat. It was enough that it took up all the space from his wrist to elbow, and he cradled it like a babe.

"Except yourself, perhaps?" Qualleron chuckled again, collecting some silver and bronze back from the merchant, who seemed quite pleased with the transaction, grinning broadly, almost dancing behind his stand. "Come. Let us still our hunger."

They ate with great gusto, in blessed silence, the sound of their teeth tearing into delicious fried meat. Oil ran down Vaste's stubbly chin, and he did not care, even as it soaked its way down the front of his robe. He might regret it later, but he had no regrets in the moment, filling his belly with...

He paused, thinking as he took another bite. The consistency of the meat was strange. Not quite as rich as beef, nor as dry as chicken. It seemed heavier than pork, though...

Qualleron caught him looking, about to open his mouth. "Don't."

"Don't what?" Vaste frowned at him, caught before he could sling his question at the merchant.

"Don't ask what it is," Qualleron said, shaking his head slowly.

"Oh, no," Vaste said, almost choking on his current bite. "It's human, isn't it?"

Qualleron let out a hearty, bellowing laugh. "No, you fool." He wiped the thick layer of grease off his mouth. "It's horse. That's why it's fried. The meat lacks fat of its own, so this adds it, gives it a bit more flavor, makes it more palatable."

Vaste turned; a butcher's stall stood not ten paces away, and sure enough, there were obvious cuts of one or two horses hanging there behind him as he worked. A section of stringy meat lay before him, and he chopped away at it with a cleaver, making meat for stew, his attention entirely upon it.

"This is a land on the brink of war," Qualleron said. "The cattle have been slaughtered or stolen, the chickens too, by the armies vying for this place. Harvests traded back and forth, fire for fire, for a decade now. Starvation, famine...these are the weapons of a people who hate each other deeply enough to drag one another into perdition." He chewed slowly, grease dripping down his chin. "I'm amazed they had the rendered fat to cook this in. But, then, it's probably been used for quite some time." With a shrug, he polished off another parcel of meat and balled it up.

"Have you been here before?" Vaste asked, his own thoughts suddenly a bit more...picky. He'd eaten horsemeat before, but it was not exactly a preference.

"To this land? I don't think so," Qualleron said, chewing. "It is a pattern I have seen in other places, though. Other wars. I've seen more wars than I've had children – and I've got many children." There was a glint in his eyes with a small amount of triumph, as if surviving wars and fathering children were the only joys he had. Other than being insufferable, of course.

Vaste chewed on that thought, ignoring the meat for a few minutes. Then, his hunger got the better of him and he attacked it once more, going through three packages before he found himself satiated enough that he could handle not one more bite of the oily, stringy meat. "You want the rest?"

Qualleron took it, wordlessly, watching the street before them. With care, he folded it up and tucked it under his arm. "Hopefully I'll eat it later."

"Full?" Vaste asked.

Then he looked around, and realized...no. Qualleron was likely not full, though it was possible. More probable, though, he'd noticed the band of large, aggressive-looking elven men who'd crept in around them while they'd been eating. Their eyes were sullen, weary, resentful. The eyes of men who'd seen much war, and rather than being merely tired of it, were thirsty for it the way a drunkard wanted his wine.

"Oh, wonderful," Vaste murmured, wiping the grease from his fingers upon his robes in preparation for what was surely about to come. "More friendly faces."

"Friendlier than yours," came a voice to his side. He looked, and realized the elves had crept in even closer than he'd realized. This one was mere steps away, though he looked surprisingly less hostile than the others. "You have a sour mien, especially for one who just ate in minutes as much as any man in this village would in a week."

"I'm not a man," Vaste said, clutching Letum tightly to hand. "Not a human one, nor an elven one. I'm a troll, and a very angry troll, at that, simply looking to get on an airship and get away from this hellish land–"

"No airships land here," the man said, again, more judicious and restrained than the eyes of his comrades might suggest. He was tanned, for an elf, and his hair was long and dark, and in relatively good order. He had a handsome face, though it was clouded with concentration. "The nearest place for that is Termina, some three days' ride by horse."

"Well, I'm fresh out of things to ride," Vaste said, rising to his feet. The other elves took a step back, then another once Qualleron did the same. "Especially seeing as you've apparently slaughtered the horses of this town for food. Unless you're offering the services of your mother in that regard."

The man's tight lips broke wide into a mirthful smile. "I knew it was you when I heard the tales from the guards of a saucy troll, green as grass, and in command of a perfect tongue for elvish. How could such a being be, I wondered? No troll has spoken our language in a thousand years." He pointed toward the staff in Vaste's hands. "Of course...Letum is recognizable, and the answer in itself."

"Do I know you?" Vaste asked, peering at him. "Because I've met a few elves in my time, and the ones I remember? Are generally the ones I like. You? I don't think I like you."

"I don't think we've ever been properly introduced," the elf said. "Though we did have dealings – or at least, I did with your comrades, in the days of old. My name is Merrish," he said, and bowed his head, "and I was the lord of this land once." His gaze hardened. "But these days are hard, and now I am lord of nothing. So, welcome, troll of Sanctuary...for I know it is you," and he smiled, "welcome to my little patch of nothing."

CHAPTER 31

Alaric

Calls that made their way through the deck jarred Alaric out of a haze he hadn't realized he'd entered. It had been yawning, like himself, threatening to pull him within the depths of a sleep that he might not have willingly wakened from. When he did come out of it, it was to a gloomy room, hints of daylight creeping in from beneath the door.

"Whuzzat?" Guy mumbled, the ropes crying out from exertion as he twisted in his middle hammock, sword in scabbard clutched against his paunchy belly like some oversized figure entombed in marble.

"I believe it is the call to arms," Alaric said, swiftly dumping himself out the side of his hammock, boots thumping upon the ground. Edouard was absent, already gone perhaps in the night, and Alaric took up Aterum, grasping the hilt in his mailed fist, and charged out the door and up to the deck.

Sunlight blazed above, and a cloudless sky provided no

barrier between them and its heat. Gray earth was visible off the edge of the ship, stretching to the horizon on the two sides Alaric could see upon entering the deck. Edouard stopped him as he reached the top of the stairs; he had been waiting beside the rail. "They are catching us," he said.

"Did you sleep at all?" Alaric asked, pausing to take stock. He had been in many battles in his life; being well-rested was an occasional edge, and one he'd seen pay off a time or two. In one battle he recalled the fatigue of men so great that some laid upon the ground, surrendering their weapons in hopes that things would end more swiftly.

"A bit," Edouard said, fidgeting with his hands against his black gambeson. "I woke in the night, and came up to watch."

"Watch what?" Guy asked, emerging, rubbing his eyes against the assailing sky. A few days' stubble did not make him more presentable. He glanced along the side of the ship, and then said, "Oh."

For now it was more visible in the light, the iron-clad airship trailing them. Cutting through the clouds with a hull of smooth curves, and a deck that gleamed in the sun, was the Chaarlandian vessel. Its rotors caught glints of reflected light in its steady spin and parted a small cloud formation as it sailed through as if upon the smoothest seas.

"They have gained on us quite a bit while we were sleeping," Alaric said.

"One of the crew told me they'll be in range of the stern chasers in minutes," Edouard said.

"I should consult with the captain," Alaric said. "Get an update on what the next few hours might look like."

"Yeah," Guy said with great, dripping sarcasm, "I'm sure that's all you'll be talking about. Nuffin' else."

Alaric cocked his head quizzically at the smaller man, but did not feel obliged to press.

The wind was blowing heavier up on the quarterdeck. Alaric

nodded at the helmsman, who nodded back, his eyes fluttering, threatening to close. Making his way past a small knot of Mazirin's officers, he approached the captain, who stiffened slightly as he drew near, though she did not turn. "I hope you slept well," she said.

"Surprisingly," Alaric said, the fog of sleep already gone. "I did not think I would, given the circumstances."

She lowered the spyglass, rolling it in her hands as she turned her head but not her body. "It is good that you are rested. We have quite the chase before us today."

Alaric stepped beside her at the rail, feeling the wind channel through the cracks in his armor. "What will that look like?"

"I don't know," she said. No spyglass was necessary to see the ship clearly now, though the crew upon its deck looked smaller than ants to him. "If they catch us – and I don't know that they will, but we give way and allow them to board without battle? We are at their mercy, but they are unlikely to damage the ship. If we do not stop, though..."

Alaric let that hang a moment. "What would their response be?"

"Once they catch us, they will match our speed and use the cannons along their sides to deliver broadside after broadside until we either stop or crash," Mazirin said.

Alaric peered at the ship, looking for cannons. He could not see any, just the smooth sides of the vessel, and started to say as much when Mazirin proffered the spyglass. He took it, steadied it on the chasing vessel and its gray sides, and saw– "Ah."

"Yes, they conceal their cannons when not in use," she said.

"That makes sense. How many cannons do they have?"

"I estimate thirty-two per side. It's a sixty-four gun frigate." She sounded very calm as she said all this. "They would destroy the *Yuutshee* and force a crash landing within two or three broadsides. Assuming their aim is fair."

"And is that what they'll try and do?" Alaric asked. "Crash us?"

Mazirin pondered this a moment. "Unlikely. They'll want whatever goods they think we have in the hold. Little do they know we have none. But they would be quite content with the proceeds from our last trip, which were paid in gold. And then..." Her voice drifted off, and stray, black hairs whipped around her face.

"Yes?"

"They do not want Amatgarosa to know what is happening here. Therefore..." She pursed her lips. "...they will take us back to Chaarland in chains as slaves and sell the *Yuutshee* there as part of their spoils. Chaarland is a savage place, the worst on the globe, led by the most dark-hearted men you might imagine. It is the only place where slavery is still enshrined in law, the only place where human flesh is in market – along with anything else that can be stolen or sold."

"It sounds appalling," Alaric said, handing back the spyglass, which caught the light with a glint. "Not a place I wish to visit if avoidable." He clenched his jaw. "That Arkaria is held so low in esteem, and Chaarland somehow rates below it..."

"Your land is not filled with terrible people, it is just...backward. It is as though some great force above held you back while everyone else leapt forward into a world of airships, steam, and technology. Even your long-lived elves seem to lack foresight and wisdom, still engaging in penny-ante civil wars more violent than the squabbles of Firoba, which is a backward place as well."

"Then your homeland, Amatgarosa," Alaric said, "are they the world leader in what you would consider 'advancement'?"

This prompted a very slight smile. "Amatgarosa is the world leader in almost everything. The only closer competitor are the nation-states of Coricuanthi, but they lack unity, though they are more felicitous than the squabbling ones in Firoba." A hint of darkness crossed her face. "Though tension has been on the rise there, too, I still hope they will work their problems out before much comes of it." She turned her gaze back to the steel ship. "Chaarland, though...problems will come from them, and soon. It has been a long time since Amatgarosa has been forced to put its foot down in this part of the world."

"You patrol these lanes of commerce, then?" Alaric asked. When she gave him a questioning look, he added, "We are following a preset path."

She nodded. "Around nightfall we will reach the old, crumbling, stony sky tower. It is the second marker, the one we use to confirm our compass heading. We'll make a slight adjustment, and soon enough we will be over the water, mere hours from the Amatgarosan outpost at Xiaoshani. If all else proceeds as it is, we should make Xiaoshani before they catch us."

"Then they will not catch us?"

"I said 'if all else proceeds as it is,'" Mazirin said with a faint smile.

"What might interrupt the current proceedings?" Alaric asked.

A boom in the distance was followed by a whistling as something flashed about thirty feet before them and the deck rail. A puff of smoke wafted from the front of the great, steely ship, and Mazirin peered at it, squinting her off-eye shut. "That. A ranging shot, only," she declared a moment later, pulling back the spyglass. "They're making adjustments, and–"

Another boom echoed, and this time the whistling was louder, more pronounced, and suddenly–

To Alaric's left, the backmost corner of the ship exploded in a hurricane of splinters, and he put himself swiftly between the explosion and Mazirin. It rang across his armor like tiny, pealing bells, and rang in his ears for moments thereafter.

He turned to Mazirin. "Are you all right?"

She was brushing a few splinter shards and a prodigious

amount of dust off her cloak. "Yes, but none of us may be for long. That may have been a lucky shot, but they have us in range of the chasers now, and they will continue to pound us." She took two swift steps over to where the blast had landed; there was a hole the size of Alaric's helm in the deck. After a moment's study, she shook her head. "This is the way it's going to be until they catch us, and unleash the big guns..." Another distant boom, and then – blessedly – a miss, as the cannonball whistled past them to the left. "...or we surrender."

CHAPTER 32

Cyrus

The throne room was not what Cyrus remembered, not from when Yartraak had set his immense gray arse upon the throne that was the size of a small building, nor what it was a thousand years before when Cyrus had trod the immaculate, varnished wood floors of these halls and a smaller throne had sat upon a dais for Terian to look just slightly down upon whoever came to address him.

Flakes of wood left the floors with a speckled appearance, seams of rot running their way through, chipped and gouged from steely boots walking paths across it and leaving their toll. Once again, Terian caught him looking at the imperfections; now his smile was pride and malice. "Importing wood to replace them hasn't been a priority."

"Did I say anything to indicate I judged you for the keep of your hall?" Cyrus asked, feeling quite needled by the continued unpleasant conversation. "I don't give a damn if you tore the whole thing up and made a mushroom patch."

"That could be arranged," Terian said. "We certainly have need, though I must warn you – they're beds of shit and corpses."

"That there are immense beds of shit is hardly surprising in a kingdom you run," Cyrus said, taking a stab of his own.

It didn't land as he might have thought it would; for a moment, even, the old Terian seemed to be back as he cracked a smile. But it faded quickly, and he trod the last steps to reach his throne, sitting upon it and shucking off the helm once more. He held it out and an attendant – female, young, thin, robed in a brightly-colored garment, her head low in respect – rushed out to take it, then retreated into the shadows. "You know, when I heard there was another Cyrus Davidon impersonator treading the streets of Reikonos – not one of the hollow ones, you understand, the religious sorts who preach the gospel of the undying warrior, but a real, true usurper – I sent Baynvyn to collect him."

"Oh, so he wasn't trying to kill me on the command of Malpravus?" Cyrus asked, giving his son a wary eye.

"You should show more respect to your host," Hongren said with a rush of passion. He'd separated himself from Baynvyn and Cyrus, inching his way toward Terian's dais in a move that reminded Cyrus of a scorpion crab-walking toward prey. "You are a guest in these halls."

"I was kidnapped and brought here against my will," Cyrus said. "That does not make me a guest but rather an abductee, and one that would happily go elsewhere given the slightly uncharitable reaction I've found thus far."

"I saved your life," Baynvyn said quietly.

"You hardly walked off our ship as a prisoner," Hongren cut in.

"Because I freed myself when the airship crashed, you utter

jackspoon," Cyrus said, giving the shipmaster a daggered look. "If it were up to you, I'd still be clapped in irons."

Terian laughed mirthlessly. "He brings a point both steely and sharp, Shipmaster." His laughter faded, and the cool chill of the look that replaced it brought Cyrus a moment's relief, only. "You are a prisoner here, lack of chains to the contrary."

"So I can't just leave?" Cyrus asked, taking the opportunity to glance around. The room was so expansive, the shadows gathered at the edges could have held an army. The sounds in the dark were little more than the echo of their conversation, and perhaps the distant drip of water from the cave ceilings.

"You can leave at any time," Terian said.

"But would you enjoy crossing the endless miles of scourge to get anywhere else?" Hongren asked with undisguised smugness.

"Oh, I don't know," Cyrus said, taking the opportunity to give Niamh a small pat behind the ears, "I get along better with scourge sometimes than I do with people who may want me dead but lack the balls to flatly say it."

"You're not an impersonator," Terian said languidly. "I don't want you dead." But there was something in his eyes that made Cyrus wonder.

"Is that what you did to my impersonators?" Cyrus asked.

"Seldom," Terian said, leaning against the high back of his chair. "But occasionally, when they were too mad to recant their belief that they were you."

"Who made you the sole arbiter of me?" Cyrus asked. "What right do you have to kill lunatics that profess to be me?" A true heat burned in Cyrus's blood. "How dare you do such a thing in my name."

"Many terrible things have been done in your name since you left," Terian said. "Longwell – the real one – took power in your name, gliding to control of Reikonos when the scourge came rolling across the land."

"My Sovereign," Baynvyn said, and Cyrus saw out of the corner of his eye that his son looked as though he had a chicken bone stuck in his throat. "About Reikonos—"

"It's been destroyed by Malpravus, yes," Terian said. He met Cyrus's eyes. "We saw a great red light on the horizon, and I was summoned up. I saw but the end of it, but of course...when you've seen it once..."

"You remembered," Cyrus said.

"I could hardly forget that day at the temple in the Waking Woods," Terian said. "We watched some ten thousand die before our eyes. People we hated, certainly...but so many as to leave a sure mark in mind, nonetheless." He leaned forward in his seat. "What I want to know, though...is how he did it." With a flick of his wrist, Terian lit a small flame in his palm. "For this is all I can manage these days, like yourself, but enough to set a dried leaf aflame. Yet Malpravus—"

"So you did know," Cyrus said. "Before, I mean."

Terian's head cocked to the side. "Of course I knew. Reikonos is our closest trading partner. Half our ship traffic comes from them. How much a fool do you think me, to miss so large a detail?"

Even Niamh made a small growl at that. "It's less about how you might miss a detail," Cyrus said slowly, his hand still upon the hilt of Rodanthar, though Epalette remained in his belt, "and more about how corrupted you've become to be willing to treat with—"

"I'd like to see you run this city with Reikonos against you," Terian said, coming to his feet with a real, crackling anger. "We cannot all go around Arkaria leaving immense messes for our friends to clean up after we leave the land."

"That stings true," Cyrus said, putting on a pale facade of a smile. "How long have you been waiting to say that? A thousand years?"

"No," Terian said, bereft of humor, "for the last thousand

years I thought you were dead, for how could the great Cyrus Davidon, hero of Arkaria, possibly leave us to this fate?" He leaned forward. "We were in the dark, of course, the great gates closed and locked and buried as best we could beneath rock and stone, barred to close the way to the scourge. And here we sat for near a thousand years in the darkness, no light save for by fires, suffocating chambers of heat lit constantly to keep the chimneys too hot for any scourge to creep into them. How could you have left us like that? The answer was obvious – you were dead, somewhere, bones mouldering in that old black armor, swords at your side." He looked Cyrus over once. "Rodanthar. But you didn't have that last time I saw it. You gave it to Zarnn. You had–"

"Ferocis and Praelior," Cyrus said. "Well, I don't have them anymore. Vara took Ferocis–"

"Vara is dead," Terian said, leaning forward, eyes blazing.

"So we thought," Cyrus said. "But it was not so. Nor was Alaric or Curatio." He lowered his voice. "I think Curatio might be, now, though."

Terian's eyes smoked, but his voice stayed smooth, if strained. "Tell me how, then."

"Sanctuary was the Ark," Cyrus said. "It lived – and Vara was saved by it. It was the source of Alaric's ability to be the ghost, and it had...absorbed Curatio during our war with the dragons, taking him into the ether."

Terian started to open his mouth, some riposte threatening to spring forth, but it faded, and so did his ire, as his countenance settled into a peculiar peace. "You know...that's such a ludicrous assertion it has just the ring of truth to it. But if Sanctuary survives, as you say–"

"I think," Cyrus said, "though I was not there to see it...that Sanctuary was the reason Malpravus was able to cast his spell. I believe he drained it as Bellarum drained the God of Evil, and thus–"

"Vek'tag shits," Terian said, rising from his seat. "You handed him the means to destroy us."

"Illuminating, isn't it?" Cyrus caught the horrified look from Shipmaster Hongren, the sidelong glance from Baynvyn. "All that time, the reason Malpravus came to the Temple in Waking Woods was that he planned to make his next stop Sanctuary. I think it was why he was after our guildhall all along. He sensed the power, coveted it, was hungry for it on an almost subconscious level."

"And you handed it to him," Terian said, standing, chest puffed out. "You've as good as sealed our fates."

"Nothing is sealed – yet," Cyrus said. "But he is out there, and more powerful than ever. And we need to stop–"

"You pull out the cork, turn the bottle sideways, watch the wine spill out, and complain that we all need to do something to stop it?" Terian's voice hit highs, echoing off the unseen walls of the dark chamber. "Fool! This is the same shit a thousand years later; you kill Mortus, and all is ruined in two lands. You break the power of the gods, and there's no one to stop the scourge. Goodness knows we couldn't count on you to stick around–"

"Blame me for all your woes if you wish," Cyrus said. "But you might toss out the small question when you're done – why not apportion some blame to Mortus for capturing dead souls like hers in the first place?" He made a gesture to Niamh. "Trapped, gone mad, enraged at the living – does he not bear some small responsibility for what he did? Because you can throw the thunderous anger of righteous indignation at me, if you like, but I was not the one who set the gears in motion any more than anything that happened after the death of Yartraak was wholly your fault."

Terian looked down, a quicksilver smile flashed across his face. "Do you remember our expedition to the caves of Vaeretrau?"

Cyrus pondered it a moment. "After Narstron died...?"

"Just before the Kalam raid," Terian nodded. "So you do recall."

"I remember a dark cave," Cyrus said, glancing about. "The pores of the rock weeping constantly."

"As though the very walls slithered," Terian said. "I think about that day...constantly."

Cyrus froze; there was sound behind him, someone moving in the chamber, short steps, a light weight, but still present, quiet...

...Familiar.

He turned and found a small figure at his back, in striking distance. Niamh at his side whimpered, pushing up to interpose herself between him and the tiny, frail dark elf standing before him, her face wrinkled by the ravages of time but known to him nonetheless. Her hair was still pale white, and she wore silken tunics that clung tightly to her thin figure. By human years, she might have been in her fifties, but she still looked reasonably good, and her eyes held a dangerous mischief.

"So you are still alive," Cyrus said, trying to keep his shock firmly in check.

She raised Epalette, which he had not seen nor felt her take, and tossed it, gently, to her son, who caught it with only mild surprise. "You never did see me coming."

"That's because you always faked it with me," Cyrus said. "And that wasn't the only thing I never saw coming from you." Cyrus said, looking sidelong at Baynvyn...their son. "Aisling. I'd say it's lovely to see you again...but I think there have been enough lies between us for twenty lifetimes."

CHAPTER 33

Vaste

"Your name was Crass-tay?" Formerly-Lord Merrish asked, his handsome face showing barely a hint of age, his long, dark hair flowing back over his shoulders.

The smell of grease had settled on Vaste's chin. There was some regret rumbling his belly now for having devoured such a volume of food after a long fast, but it paled in comparison to his regret for not having simply detoured around the dirty white city in favor of some place with something other than horsemeat and old lords who recognized him when he wanted to remain anonymous. "My name is Vaste," he said crossly. "Voss-tay," he pronounced with exaggerated emphasis, as though this former lord was a moron. "And I'm pleased that you remember me. For my part, I barely recall your name. Something about involving yourself in the overthrow of the kingdom, turning itself into the alliance."

"Quite so," Merrish said, folding his hands one above the

other. "I did help overthrow the kingdom of old in favor of an alliance. Helped usher out the old caste system in order to bring about an equality between my people. And for a few years it worked swimmingly."

His gaze hardened as if an old memory stirred him to anger. "Then the scourge came, and with them, the humans. They flooded over the northern Perda, the southern Perda, until we destroyed the bridges as the first scourge were mere steps away. We tried to live together, but fell to acrimony as they became unwilling to be governed under our covenants—"

"How exciting that must have been for you, rebel that you are," Vaste said.

Merrish went on as though Vaste hadn't spoken. "—so we carved a refuge for them, a new human state that encompassed the land from a line just north of Elintany all the way to Termina." His face darkened. "My own city, Traegon, was given over, and I welcomed it at the time. But the years have passed and I watched Emerald at the south and their new Confederation of the North become united in a singular desire to crush and subsume us—"

"Oh, my, I've never heard of such tension and conquest before," Vaste said with excessive dryness. "Why, this is unprecedented, neighbors turning on one another, vying for land, slaughtering each other. I bet it was quite the surprise."

Merrish's face hardened. "You mock."

"Always, yes. It's what I do."

"This much is true," Qualleron said. "I have seen it so."

"We stand on the precipice of war," Merrish said.

"So, things haven't changed much since I left, it seems," Vaste said. "I mean, obviously we set things 'right' in the sense of ending all those pesky wars, but clearly they didn't hold. I heard about the trolls, of course—"

"That was the humans," Merrish said, a little too quickly.

"I'm sure it was," Vaste said. "I'm certain they have done all the wrong and none of the right in this back and forth between your peoples."

"You speak true in that," Merrish said. "We have received more provocation than we can bear, an unending string of offenses perpetually hurled in our faces." He straightened. "So...what brings you to our grounds of conflict, Master Vaste?"

"I was thrown bodily from an airship after escaping Reikonos," Vaste said. "By a dirty, surly group of sailors who took great umbrage at my very person being present upon their deck. I am fairly certain it was because I was bringing an element of cleanliness and beauty into their dingy, disgusting, filthy and ugly lives."

Merrish's eyelids fluttered. "You are certain of this...how?"

"Some things you just know, Merrish," Vaste said. "Like that you're lying about the humans being solely responsible for the extermination of the Arkarian trolls, and that you're lying about the humans doing all the wrong in your 'relationship.'"

Merrish bristled. "You have no reason other than mere suspicion to think—"

"Other than the piles of human corpses we ran across on the walk across the forest out there," Vaste said, gesturing in the direction from whence they'd come. "Farmers and field hands, women. Not warriors. Not soldiers."

Merrish's face fell. "We have been provoked—"

"So you've said."

"Are you sure this is wise?" Qualleron said softly.

"No, but I don't care," Vaste said, plowing right on through. "Let me say that again, Merrish: I don't care." The elf blinked. "I don't care that you're killing humans, that they're killing you, that you're getting along about as well as a savannah cat and a plains wolf." Vaste stood, feeling the creak of his bones as his weight shifted, and watching Merrish lift his head up, up, and up to look him in the eye. "I don't give a fig for your little war, or your many and numerous sorrows, because I have an overabundance of my own to choke on. And as soon as an airship passes through this place, I will leave it, you, and your unending troubles behind me in favor of...well, I don't know. Death, I expect, sooner or later."

Merrish looked quite caught up for a moment. "What...what happened to Reikonos? We have heard but rumors." Behind him, Vaste could see merchants watching, seemingly straining at the bounds of an invisible barrier, their eyes flitting to him and Qualleron. So, the horsemeat merchant had told his friends where the money was today.

"The Lord Protector turned out to be Malpravus, of Goliath," Vaste said. "In disguise, rather cunningly. Anyway, he cast a spell that drained the entire city."

Merrish seemed to take that on board slowly. "Then...he lives?"

"Unfortunately."

Merrish chewed this over for some time before speaking again. Other merchants were crowding around, hoping to get a bit of Qualleron's gold. A boy no older than ten had sauntered casually up to Qualleron and was thrusting beads at him. By his eyes and his grin, it seemed obvious he expected a payment of some stripe. Qualleron, for his part, was studiously ignoring the lad, focusing on Merrish.

"That sounds truly terrible and you have my apologies for your loss, whoever your friends might have been," Merrish said. "I would like to help, but there is little I can do. We are, of course, tied up in our own problems."

"Of course," Vaste said. "Those humans aren't going to slaughter themselves. But hey – Malpravus might do it for you. Of course, he'll also be taking your lives, but that's clearly a small price to pay for killing those pesky humans, am I right?"

"Well...you are not entirely wrong," Merrish said, "in that we are trading lives right now, until such time as one of us gains enough advantage to–"

"Wipe out the other, yes, I understand how a war works." Vaste clapped both his hands onto Letum and thumped it against the ground, causing the boy with the beads to squawk and jump away, startled. "Well, I'd love to help you about as much as you'd like to help me, so I suppose we'll be finding the airship docks and getting on our way—"

Merrish shook his head slowly. "There is no airship dock here. This is but a small village."

"Bloody hell," Vaste sighed.

"However," Merrish said, and he turned to point down the eastern direction of the crossroads, "as I told you before, Termina is in that direction, and it has airships aplenty moving through constantly."

Vaste sagged, feeling the weariness upon his mighty frame. "How many days in that direction?"

"Walking? Some five," Merrish said. "Perhaps three, if your stride is long and your pace is quick."

"My stride is long but my pace is 'near dead,'" Vaste said with a sigh, "I'm tired."

Merrish watched him for a moment, then seemed to come to a decision. "I could offer you a ride, if you'd like."

"Oh? And what would this ride cost me?" Vaste stared at him suspiciously. "And please, tell me it's not on your mother."

Merrish chuckled. "No, and nothing. It would be my small contribution to *your* war, for I assume you will be fighting this Malpravus."

"Sure," Vaste said, not nearly so certain he would be. *A fight? It'd be a slaughter as things currently stand, me against a necromancer – no, a sorcerer, now – who has lived over a thousand years and has a deep command of magic, a thing I can barely muster enough of to heal a bloody nose at present.*

"Then you may hitch a ride upon our supply train, which will be leaving within the hour," Merrish said. "And it will bear you to Termina by nightfall. Come – I will show you to the depot." His smile suggested he would not soon forget this particular kindness, and it gave Vaste a dirty feeling of obligation. "Remember me to your friends when the day comes that you have settled this Malpravus's accounts favorably, and have time to expand your view of the world to encompass us smaller people and our tiny problems again."

Vaste merely nodded at that, for when would he ever have time to repay this obligation? *We'll all be dead soon enough*, he mused darkly, following the former elven lord down the dusty street of the forgotten town, hoping vaguely that death would find him, in one form or another, before he might be forced to settle this particular account.

CHAPTER 34

Shirri

"I don't really understand what I'm supposed to be doing here," Shirri said nervously. "Nor why I'm the one here rather than Hiressam or my mother."

They sat in a wooden waiting room carved into the trunk of one of the oldest trees in Amti. The name out front, in elvish, had been Narr'omn. They'd threaded their way up the ramp-like corkscrew through the center of the open-air trunk, wider in circumference than almost any building in Reikonos, and now they sat outside an office carved into the thick trunk.

"Who else was I supposed to bring?" Calene asked. Her calloused hands rested upon the armrests of the finely carved wood chair. "Hiressam? Been known as a madman for years, flitting from city to city, preaching the gospel of Sanctuary. Or maybe your mother, who has all the conviction for this fight of a woods mouse that's just seen a savannah cat?"

"You may have some small point there," Shirri said, "but I still don't know what you expect me to do."

Calene huffed loudly enough that the secretary in front of the office door looked at them both quite irefully in her modern, conservative tunic. "What kind of fight did you think you were asking for here? Did you think when you committed to action you were just going to line up and charge into battle like days of yore? Send yourself running across the field against Malpravus with armies between you?"

"I...don't know, actually," Shirri said. "I just sort of imagined that maybe it'd be like the fight at the shipyards, or perhaps like the one at the Machine's headquarters."

"Yeah, well, darlin', those sound like a real barrel of spiced rum," Calene said, "but what you've got here is something entirely different. Malpravus is the worst of the worst, a sorcerer of the kind we have not seen in nearing a thousand years. The humans of Reikonos or Emerald? I'm not sure they're mentally prepared to deal with that. Hell, the elves might not be, either. Certainly not in Pharesia, those hidebound fools."

She leaned closer to Shirri, intensity aglow in her eyes. "Here...if you pick the perfect arrow and wait until the wind's just right, you may actually have a shot."

"Oh...okay," Shirri said, putting her fingers tightly back onto the carved arms of the chair. She pressed against them, feeling the damp of her fingertips and palms against the intricate carvings. "Who are we seeing here?"

"The man who hired me," Calene said. "He goes back a ways with Sanctuary, too, so–"

The door to the inner office swept open, and a man in a dress tunic of finest silk stood waiting there, a bowler hat on his head looking jaunty, but unable to hide his elvish ears. "So don't hesitate to mention that, because Calene knows I have a soft spot in my heart for anything and anyone Sanctuary." The man had dark hair laced with gray, and a bitter trace of a smile. "For

I was there, you see, on the day when Cyrus Davidon and his lot saved Amti from the titans. And I was also there on the day we stormed into the Realm of War and took the fight to Bellarum to free us all from their yoke – forever."

"This is Gareth," Calene said, already on her feet. "He used to be a ranger, like me," and she gave him a once-over with her eye, "before he gave up on nature and all to help run this city."

CHAPTER 35

Vara

"Isabelle!" Vara called again, rising to her feet. Her face was stuck in a perpetual cloud of smoke deathly thick, and she sunk back to her knees, coughing furiously. Trying again a few seconds later, she could feel none of the breeze that had threatened to clear the air before, to show her the sky, if only for a brief few seconds.

Now it was only smoky blackness, unfathomably heavy, and daring to sink into her lungs like leaden weights with every breath she took.

There was a temptation, there, on her knees, to give up. For what was there to do? Chance to cast a return spell, see herself torn apart in misery as the magic tried to carry her somewhere that no longer existed, for Sanctuary was gone. Perhaps that would be a more graceful end than this, crawling about on her hands and knees, no longer able to so much as stand, nosing around in the flames and smoke and dirt for her sister.

"This is my fault," she whispered, for it was true, and all the more miserable for it. If she'd stayed with Cyrus, not lost her head in foolishness, perhaps she'd have been here for the spell that devoured Reikonos instead of rooting around in the newly made ashes, at hazard of burning to death. Isabelle would still be safely in Termina, and not lost on a smoke-covered street.

But there was no going back now, and all that was left for it was to go ahead, somehow, to find her sister in the bleakness and either carry her out or hunker down and embrace death together.

"I did not live a thousand years in the bloody ether to go out like this," she whispered, and the decision was made.

She'd been holding Isabelle's hand when the explosion had torn through the street. Judging with an impartial eye, Isabelle was lighter than her, therefore she must have been flung farther assuming the two of them were hit with roughly the same strength of the boom, and at roughly the same place.

Well, she knew where the explosion had originated, for there was a convenient, bright glow of orange where the building had become utterly consumed, the facade torn off by the blast. It pierced the veil of smoky darkness, a wall of flame in the inky haze.

She had scarcely moved from where she'd landed, too, so that was a known factor. Putting her back to the burning orange glow in the smoke, Vara eased forward, reaching out far and wide, trying to feel her way in the smoke-filled street. Like a canyon of black death, it hemmed her in on either side of the billowing plumes. She hugged the earth, almost kissing the cobblestones as the thick, choking smoke forced itself down on her. "I will not lose...my sister..."

Her rage carried her through the blackening haze curling around the edges of her vision. She crawled forward, coughing furiously, in the direction she supposed Isabelle must have flown. She clanked her gauntlet against the ground, trying to feel for softness of flesh, for a body, for bone and joint and maybe a grunt of pain at the thump of her metal-encased hand at her touch, which was rapid and pitiless, hurried and seeking.

Wave after wave of murderous heat came from all around, cooking her slowly in her armor like an oven just for her. She felt around against the cobbles, rustling against cloth, thumping against bone.

Someone moaned, very nearby. Vara thumped her gauntlet against cloth and flesh, and the moan was louder, more pained. She seized an ankle, hauling a body in her direction–

Vara pulled Isabelle to her, and Isabelle grasped at her arm, weakly. Her grip failed, but Vara's did not, dragging her over the cobblestones and corpses, into the center of the valley of fire. When they were as safe as they could be given the burning heat all around, she paused long enough to draw Isabelle close, her sister's pale cheeks marred with black ash, her hair aglow with embers that Vara worked to snuff quickly, before they could make things worse.

"I don't think..." Isabelle choked out through a series of weak coughs, "...we're going to make it to the Citadel."

Vara looked in the direction they'd been heading. The explosion had set things mightily aglow ahead, orange searing through the smoke clouds and blotting the sky utterly.

"Not that way," she agreed, casting looks about. The way behind them looked marginally darker, less aflame, but surely it wouldn't for long. "We need to go."

Isabelle nodded slowly, stupidly. Vara cast another healing spell, and her eyes cleared – a bit. "Yes," she said, voice a little stronger, "we should hurry, shouldn't we?"

"Perhaps we can find a way around?" Vara said. "But we'll have to crawl – and you'll need to go first. Are you ready?"

Isabelle nodded again, and in spite of the tears on her

cheeks, Vara knew she was as ready as she would be for this. "Yes," Isabelle said, sitting upright, and then putting her hands down, crawling forth, smoke all around them, like it was hiding them from the devouring flames that were coming, inevitably. "I am as ready as I am going to get." Vara followed her into the choking black.

CHAPTER 36

Alaric

The big ship's bow chasers thundered at a maddening, steady rate. Every other shot seemed to impact the *Yuutshee*, sending splinters of wood flying through the air and screams floating to the heavens when one would land close to one of the crew.

Mazirin tore loose in her own language, and Alaric listened, trying to make sense of anything she said. There was an intensity in her eyes, upon her face. One of the crew that Alaric did not know lay bleeding upon the main deck, a dozen tiny pinpricks of blood sponging through his white clothing. Crew scrambled, hurrying to collect him, as another distant boom rang out. Alaric listened for it, trying to see–

The *Yuutshee* shuddered, moving to the side just slightly, and the cannonball whistled past.

"Is this to be it, then?" Alaric asked, catching Mazirin's attention when she turned back. "The bite of a thousand flies until they can train their large guns upon us?"

"No, they are trying to hit the propellers." She gestured to the blades turning above them like silver moons.

"Will that cause us to crash?"

"Not immediately. But striking one will force us to divert engine power from propulsion to keeping us aloft. That would be a win for them, cut things shorter." She glanced back. "Either this captain is in a hurry or he doesn't care about taking the *Yuutshee* as a prize when he's done."

"Or he doesn't believe he can," Alaric said.

"That could be," Mazirin said. "Most ships would probably surrender by now, hoping for mercy."

"But you don't?" Alaric asked. "Hope for mercy, I mean?"

A bitter smile crept across Mazirin's lips, but only for a second. "Perhaps it's because I've spent time in Chaarland, but...no. I wouldn't expect mercy from these pirates."

"Is it possible you could be wrong?" Alaric asked.

"Take a look," she said, and handed him the glass.

He took it and peered at the Chaarlandian vessel. It seemed so large now, so clear, with men now visible upon the deck. Another puff of smoke from the bow, and here came another cannonball whistling in. It hit somewhere forward, and no shouts followed, so Alaric put the glass back to his eye. He scanned the enemy's deck, and–

"Do you see the man in the fur hat?" Mazirin asked. "With the smooth jacket?"

"That's quite the emphasis on his fashion," Alaric said, "and yes, I see him. Tall fellow. Both axe and pistol on him."

"That is the captain," she said.

"Hm," Alaric said, staring at him. The pirate captain lifted his own spyglass at the same moment, and it glinted as it shone, catching the sun. He seemed to be looking right at Alaric, and he bore a toothy grin, tufts of long black hair wild and hanging behind him, stirred by the airship blades. It was not a friendly smile. "How can you tell that's the captain?"

"He's the one with the spyglass."

"I'm holding the spyglass on this ship," Alaric said, giving Mazirin a sly look. "Does that mean that I am currently the captain of the *Yuutshee*?"

She almost smiled, he thought. "I have been watching, no one else on that ship has held up a spyglass, and I doubt they have an honored observer such as yourself onboard. Speaking, though, of his fashion – did you take note of his jacket?"

Alaric looked again; smooth leather covered over the Chaarlandian captain, a barely-brown shade of the stuff formed into a waist-length coat. "I see it's some sort of leather. Chaarlandian tanners don't produce very fine work, do they?"

"What they produce is somewhat more flawed material than what you're perhaps used to," Mazirin said. "It's human leather."

Alaric found himself nearly choking on his own spittle. Sticking the spyglass back to his eye, he looked again. "Is this your object lesson for me on the mercy of Chaarlandian pirates?"

"Yes," Mazirin said. "They have none." She took a step closer to him, lowering her voice, presumably so the crew could not hear. "If we are taken alive, none of us will have an easy life or death from here on out. Chaarland is a savage place, and the tales of those who escape are horrifying. They view all as inferior to them and their imperial needs. If they catch us...well, I am considering letting them down the ship when they get close, just to deny them our lives and our suffering."

"Let us hope it does not come to that," Alaric said, taking the spyglass from his eye. Having looked at their captain, he felt an urge to shudder. Anyone who wore the skins of their enemies into battle was...concerning.

"Soon they will be in range of our stern chasers," Mazirin said, looking to the two small cannons at either corner of the quarterdeck. "Though I do not expect we will be able to do much to stop them, perhaps we can slow them down with a well-placed shot at their props. It is a faint hope, though. Grasping at threads of silk."

"I have done much with thin threads of hope in my time," Alaric said, trying to smile faintly.

Mazirin seemed to lose the tightness around her eyes for a moment. "You have been in many battles?"

"Even one is too many in my view," Alaric said, hand brushing Aterum. "But yes...I have been in many."

"I watched you during the fight in the dockyard," she said. "You fight so differently from our army, save for the cavalry."

"Those small cannons that the warriors of these days all carry," Alaric said, "they change things. I don't know whether it requires more courage or less to fight with one of those in hand."

"I don't know, either," she said, and drew back her long coat, revealing a browned leather holster, and a pistol hanging from her belt, "but it is not just our warriors who carry them."

He took this in with a glance, and found himself unable to pry his eyes away from her shapeliness, so often cloaked by her overcoat. "Oh, you are a warrior, whatever other profession you may officially hold. I would stake my honor on that."

That almost-smile came back again, and she seemed amused for a moment. "I have been in a few battles, but only in passing. I have not stood on the line and watched the charge of the enemy come at me, nor have I ever wanted to. I have fought when needed, to protect my crew, but I prefer to surprise my enemy, to not let them see me coming when I must dispatch them, for to be seen as a threat is often to lose immediately."

She took a step closer, and seemed to be only inches from him, which made Alaric stiffen up in his armor. She placed both palms upon the deck rail, and, whispered, "If you have been in many battles, surely you have lost one or two?"

"I've lost more than that in battle," Alaric said.

"Then let me ask you, leader to leader," and her voice affected the softest crack before she steadied it again, "how do you prepare your people for that sort of death and defeat?"

The pop of a cannon firing on the Chaarlandian ship was followed by a clear whistle as the ball missed again, high. It seemed to punctuate their conversation.

"I once stood behind a wall of magic in a city that was being razed to the ground as the power of the barrier's caster began to fade," Alaric said. "We survived that. On another occasion, I was ambushed by a titan – those creatures as large as–"

"I know what they are," she said. "We have our own, in Amatgarosa. They are vital subjects of the Empire."

"Oh," Alaric said. "Well, ours were at war with us, and crossed the mountains in a war party to kill me. He very nearly succeeded. And he did succeed in killing my wife."

"I am sorry," Mazirin said.

"It was a long time ago," Alaric said, as though that were some worthy explanation. "And he did eventually receive vengeance, paid in full. But the point is...I never thought of those moments as being hopeless."

"Perhaps because the threat of being skinned alive and having it turned to leather was not an option on the table?" she asked.

"No," Alaric said. "My enemies over the years, though perhaps less savage, were no less desperate to kill me, or my friends, my armies. I have faced the old gods of Arkaria with nothing but a sword and some spellcraft, and but a thin hope to survive." He looked out over the narrowing gulf between the *Yuutshee* and its pursuer with the iron sides. "I do not know much about ships, or the battles that take place in your world. But I know I have stood many times in a place where I was sure there was no escape, no survival...and I survived."

"We all run out of time eventually," she said softly.

"Yes," he said, feeling that quite deeply. With the possible loss of Cyrus, of Vaste, of Curatio – he felt that quite keenly. For over ten thousand years he'd had the aid of Sanctuary to fight his battles.

Now, though, as he looked across at the gray ship, he had only his sword, Guy, the crew of the *Yuutshee*, and, possibly, Edouard. Though the last three were questionable.

"And perhaps today is our day," Alaric said, though a shout from the forecastle made him turn, lifting the spyglass.

In the distance before the bow of the ship, he could see a small, dark line jutting from a bank of clouds. "That is the second marker," Mazirin said. "Where we would turn. The crumbling tower."

"Vernadam," Alaric said, recalling Cyrus's tales of the sky tower, built on a mound and stretching to the clouds. In his day it had been smaller, a mere keep, though named the same.

"I didn't know it had a name," Mazirin said. "If we could hold them off we could be to Xiaoshani by nightfall."

"And help waits at this Xiaoshani?"

She nodded. "A squadron is based there – destroyers, frigates, cruisers, perhaps even a dreadnought or two if we're lucky. More than a match for that pirate."

Alaric looked once again at the mouldering tower jutting out of the thin layer of clouds ahead. It appeared like a dark beacon of hope in the distance. "Then our day is not over yet," he said, and for a moment it felt as though Mazirin grew just a little taller in his sight.

CHAPTER 37

Vara

They crawled back a block and cut over to their right – the west, Vara felt certain, coughing as she went, and finding the next street less enflamed and without any explosions, at least presently. They choked their way through the black, enveloping smoke that poured off every building, out of every window, and searched for exit in the sky and found not nearly enough egress.

Sparks of ash glared out at Vara like tiny embers on Isabelle's back, and not for the first time. Vara reached up, slapping her sister just below the ribs on the right.

Isabelle bucked, jerking at the strike. "What are you doing?" she looked back accusingly, face half-hidden in the haze.

"Trying to keep you from catching fire," Vara said. All hints of moisture they'd picked up in the horse trough had long since vanished, and her hair felt as dry as the sagebrush of the Inculta desert. With an idle thought, she wondered if that place even still existed.

"Do it a bit more gently next time," Isabelle said, her face growing more and more soot-stained every time Vara saw her. "Or better yet, let me know. Watch."

With a twirl of her fingers, a small stream of water coursed from Isabelle's hand, soaking her robe along the back and dousing all the bright embers that had been raining down on her. She turned it up to her hair and gave it a quick once-over before looking at Vara, grinning impishly, and covering her over.

Vara's armor hissed as the water ran down it, steam mingling with the toxic black fumes. She had felt the heat rising in the mystical steel, of course, but there was naught she could do about it. Besides, its protection – along with the padding inside – had kept it from bothering her more than the oven-like heat coming from every direction. Her very pores felt in danger of combustion the longer she stayed in this place, and in her head she stopped, trying to concentrate on what lay ahead.

When Isabelle finished dousing them both, Vara said, "I think we want to take a left about three blocks ahead."

Isabelle's brow rose weakly. "Are you sure?"

"No, I'm not bloody sure," Vara said. "It's been a thousand years since I've prowled this section of the city, I'm doing it blind with fire and thick smoke all around me, all whilst crawling on my knees like a beast. I have to hope that Malpravus did not wholesale demolish this section of the city, because I'm gauging as best I can by blocks where we need to go."

"And where are we going?" Isabelle asked, turning her water spell loose once more, this time on her tongue. She made a gesture as if to offer it to Vara, who happily accepted.

The answer waited until she'd finished. "Recall, if you will, how we used to access the portal beneath the Citadel."

Isabelle frowned. "Ah," she said after a moment's pause, in which her mind must have been working to overcome the heat, the fatigue, or perhaps the thousand-year interregnum since last she'd been beneath the Citadel. "The tunnel entrance."

"Indeed," Vara said, nodding her forward. "Let us hope that it remains as open as in days of old."

"Let us also hope," Isabelle said, "that your memory and the streets of Reikonos have remained constant as well."

"Yes," Vara said, "let us hope." And she dared to do just that, because the alternative was nothing less than the absolute depths of despair, and the wanton desire to give up.

CHAPTER 38

Cyrus

"Considering it's been roughly twenty human lifetimes since last we saw each other," Aisling said with her old, puckishness, "doesn't that mean we're due for a fresh slate of lies?"

"So this is him, then?" Terian asked. "In your opinion?"

Her eyes narrowed as she looked up at the Sovereign. "Of course it's him. Have your eyes grown blinder than mine? I thought I was the one who'd grown old." She reached up, taking hold of Cyrus's jaw – lacking some gentleness – and pushed his chin toward Terian. "Look at his face. How can you forget this chiseled jaw? That pronounced nose?"

"I guess I didn't pay as much attention to those things as you did," Terian muttered.

"The longness of my arse, then," Cyrus said, jerking his chin away from Aisling's grip, feeling much abused and irritated by this whole process.

Terian cocked his head, looking at Cyrus's backside, which was partially turned toward him as a result of his shaking off Aisling's hand upon him. "Hmmm," the Sovereign pronounced thoughtfully. "Yes. Yes, now I see it."

"That is what you take as proof of my identity?" Cyrus asked. "Not my commanding height, not the shade of my eyes or the lines of my face, but the—"

"The oblong nature of your arse, yes," Terian said, waving him off. "It's more distinctive than the other things."

With a look at Aisling, he received a shrug in reply. "It is long," she said simply.

He glanced at Baynvyn, who was struggling to look over his shoulder at his own arse, which, to Cyrus's eye, did appear rather...tall. "So that's where it came from," Baynvyn muttered.

"Enough of this frivolity," Terian announced. "I am weary, and I'm sure you are, too." He looked at Cyrus. "You'll be shown to quarters – not of the prison variety – and we'll reconvene tomorrow."

Cyrus felt the touch of weariness, but did not care to say so. "We don't have time to rest, Terian. Malpravus is out there, he's unleashed...and he's coming."

"And we'll deal with him if he comes this way," Terian said coolly. "But we do ourselves no favors by grinding ourselves into nothingness while waiting." He stood, and Cyrus could see for the first time, truly...

...Terian had grown old. Not perhaps in the flesh, for he was unwrinkled, and unbowed. But there was a weariness that had settled on his bones, a weight that dragged down his shoulders, that settled like bags beneath the eyes, but upon his spirit.

Sensing he would get himself nowhere by argument, Cyrus turned to the Niamh-scourge and said, "Come on." And she did, following him toward the exit of the mighty throne room.

"Cyrus," Terian called back at him. "If what you say is true...about Vara, and Alaric, and Vaste..."

He felt the prickle of worry at the back of his neck. "Vara's in Termina," Cyrus said.

"Then I'll send word for my agents in the city to look out for her," Terian said. "For all of them."

"Thank you," Cyrus said, and left the throne room with none but Niamh at his side. Listening to their quiet whispers continue as he left, he got the distinct feeling that he might have little indeed to be thankful to Terian for.

CHAPTER 39

Alaric

The booming of cannons was a constant now; not only from the Chaarlandian pirate, but also the *Yuutshee's* own stern chasers, firing every minute or so, being frantically reloaded by the small crews of four, re-aimed, then fired again. Puffs of smoke clouded the deck, and the strong smell of burnt powder was acidic in Alaric's nose.

"Slowly but surely," Guy said, leaning over the rail, "they're catching up."

Edouard had seemed distant, but at this he spoke. "Do you know much of the Chaarlandians?"

"Only the same legends as you, mate," Guy said. "When they're not engaging in their favorite pastime of chasing down people for meals and servitude, they do a fair bit of dancing, and enjoy playing haunting music on instruments made of human bone." When he caught Alaric looking at him, he deigned to add,

"Because human bone is the material most abundant in supply in that endless wintery hell."

"I do not care for the sound of these Chaarlandians," Alaric said. "Though I am sure there is humanity beneath their leather made of human flesh–"

"Oh, it's not just human," Guy said. "They make it out of dwarf, gnome, elf – they are not particular. One time, the King of Gilitonga in Coricuanthi tried to invade them, and when he died at the head of his army halfway across the frozen tundra – middle of bloody winter, the daft prick – they skinned him and turned him into a stuffed display item still sitting in one of their palaces. They say he's got glass eyes and is a footstool for the kings."

"Be that as it may," Alaric said, "there must surely be some wellspring of humanity beneath their cruelty. Still and all – I do not care to be their captive, for it seems they offer little quarter."

"No, we'll all be their slaves or food," Edouard said. "Out of certain death into certain hell, that's what it feels my life has become." And he wrung his hands.

"Indeed," Alaric said. "Few on this ship seem to be fighters, or skilled with a sword. Fewer still have a pistol or rifle of any sort. The cannons appear to be of limited utility," the booming of one seemed to underscore his point, "and must eventually run out of fodder. Which means the captain will either let us go down to the broadsides of those pirates, or–"

"We'll be boarded," Guy said, "and either surrender, or fight man to man. Or man to savage, as the case may be. Seems a waste to just scuttle us. Plus, they'd be leaving evidence of their deeds behind for the Amatgarosan navy to find. Hard to hide the wreck of a ship on this near-empty continent."

"But they may just think it crashed," Edouard said. "If the Amatgarosans find it. How could they prove otherwise?"

"Right," Guy said. "You could blame the missing crew on the scourge eating 'em, and who would argue?"

"True enough," Alaric said. "Regardless, I will fight. So long as there is breath in me, I cannot allow myself to surrender to these savages."

"Pleased to see you've still got it in you after what we went through back there," Guy said. "More than one man's probably been laid dumb by that ordeal, spell crawling toward us while we're trying to skitter away. All that fight for nothing, you know? Tends to leave a man bereft of hope."

"Are you hopeless?" Alaric asked.

Guy's hand fell to the hilt of Praelior. "No. Not anymore."

"I have seen lands die in the past," Alaric said, "and the fall of Reikonos...well, that's a thing I will carry to my grave. But that grave will not be one I lie in alone if these Chaarlandians have their way. And it will not be the only grave if I cannot find a way to put a cork in the plans of Malpravus, and whatever evil he intends."

"You can count me in for the fights, Alaric," Guy said. "For whatever good it does, I am with you all the way. I'd rather die nasty now than slave away the rest of my days in some hut in the north, a whip lashing the fat off my back, and the good right hand of some northy peasant always slapping the shit out of my arse."

Alaric gave him a nod of approval, then looked to Edouard. "And you, my friend?"

Edouard wrung his hands. "I was an executioner. A headsman, not a soldier. I swung my sword on unresisting souls. Perhaps I might have to wrangle a struggling, bound inmate from time to time, but that's not a field of battle." He looked over the edge of the ship. "When the Lord Protector sent me to the army to help take the dockyards...it was maybe the most frightening thing I was ever commanded to do."

"And I thought *I* was a coward," Guy said. "In my past life, you know. I'm a bloody lion now, especially compared to you."

"I...I..." Edouard said.

"There was never a greater coward than I," Alaric said, "in the days before I became a warrior. I was a dilettante, and a would-be king who'd only ever lifted a sword to practice with men who dared not hit me. I have been enslaved, and it was to masters considerably more charitable than ones who would make leather and meals of their subjects." He shook his head slowly. "Not every man is destined for the fight, Edouard. It is better that you know yourself than to find yourself looking in the eyes of some skin-wearing savage and then realize you have not the heart for the fight." He paused. "Still...I choose to believe there is more in you than you know, if you would only decide to reach deep and find it in you."

"Actually," Guy said, "while I am in for the fight, I cannot guarantee I will not feel a trickle of piss running down my trouser leg thinking I might be looking in the eyes of one of those Chaarlandian beasts. Thinking about what they'll do, you know?"

"I thank you for understanding," Edouard said. "Few would, I think."

"I understand all too well," Alaric said, thinking of those early battles in the arena in Sennshann, when he'd died and died, and then died again, before Jena had taken pity on him. "But I tell you this, too – courage is a choice, made in spite of fear, in spite of despair, if not because of it. A man is not brave when he feels fearless, when there is no threat. He is only brave when forced to dig down into his soul, to stand fast against certain death. For we all face death at some point, soon or late, and we have little control over the hour of its arrival. Our brush, I think, comes soon," he said, as the cannons of the Chaarlandian vessel boomed again in the distance. This one whistled closer, and came low, and–

The deck some twenty feet from them exploded as a ball landed upon it. A spray of splinters reduced a nearby crewman to screams, his left leg and arm turned crimson. He writhed upon the deck in a lively dance, and blood seasoned his white robe as onions seasoned a stew. It was everywhere, and Alaric rushed to his side.

When he reached the side of the bleeding man, he noticed the wide gouge in the man's throat. The crimson pumped in great flows, but already the spurts were fading. "Hold on," Alaric said, breathing a healing spell in hope.

The light twinkled and faded, and a great gush of blood poured out the hole, nearly unaffected by his effort. Another casting, another spurt, only marginally smaller than the last. The man's eyes were beginning to loll, staring at the sky above.

"Please," Alaric said, and cast again, feeling weakness from the ebb of his magic leaving him. "Remain here. Remain–"

But the blood stopped, and the man's eyes went still, staring heavenward. The white light on Alaric's hand died, and he slumped back on his haunches.

A black humor descended upon him, for he stared at the dead man and realized how little his magic truly counted for in these days. And if he had no magic, and no ether to fall back on...

...what, truly, was left that he could do?

CHAPTER 40

Vaste

"This was not the conveyance I had in mind when Merrish said 'supply train,'" Vaste said, the world clattering around him, metal clanking as the vehicle in which he sat rattled its way down the curious lines of metal and wood that he'd seen coming into the town.

"It is called a train," Qualleron said, sitting beside him in the boxlike car, piled with but a little straw and a few stringy, unhealthy horses that were probably fated to end up in the dinner pail of the people of the village were they not sent away. "They are a preferred means of conveyance within lands, and are wonderful for moving cargo and people over the shorter distances that make airships inefficient."

"A lovely explanation for my primitive mind, thank you," Vaste said. "But you didn't answer my actual question, unstated, which is – why is it so damned clangy?" The train seemed to bump once more, and shuddered left to right, leaving Vaste to thump against the wooden side of the car.

"It runs upon metal tracks," Qualleron said. "Balance shifts, and it hits upon either track, moving back and forth like a cat battering a ball of yarn before it."

"See, now that was a much better explanation," Vaste said with a frown. "Albeit discomfiting. Tremendously discomfiting."

The world rattled around him, and out a high window on the other side of the cart came plumes of smoke from the engine up front drifted in with a burning smell. Soon the rattle seemed to become part of Vaste's very body, and he was able to ignore all but the most severe clanks and pitches of the car.

The pungent scent of horse piss permeated his nose, mingling with the straw. He saw it drifting in puddles underneath the thin layer, staining the wood, as one of the horses unleashed a mighty spray across from him. Covering his nose with his sleeve, he turned to see Qualleron, whose eyes were closed. "How can you sleep at a time like this?"

Qualleron did not open his eyes. "An old soldier's trick. You must learn to grab rest whenever it can be had, because what comes next is uncertain. You could be ambushed in mere minutes, and spend days in battle. Better to be ready for that, and thus…"

A frowned pricked at the corners of Vaste's mouth. He'd slept on the airship, but it had been hours since then, and he was tired. Outside the window he could see the shadows lengthening in the distance, the trees acquiring the orange tinge of late afternoon.

And he'd walked many miles this day. The red storm of spell-magic over Reikonos seemed a lifetime ago, though they were less than a day separated from those events.

Still, his eyelids drooped not at all, and Vaste kept them open, eyeing the horses, hoping he would not get hungry enough to eat their ilk again anytime soon. "You know," he said, words slurring a bit as fatigue did set in like frost on a morning field in winter, "I was a knight with a manor in Termina once upon a time."

"Oh?" Qualleron's eyelids did not so much as stir.

"Sir Vaste the Wry, dubbed by the last king's own hand," Vaste said. "I had a manor house in Termina, high on Ilanar Hill. I even stayed there for a spell, just before Cyrus and I rode to Sanctuary for the last time, leaving behind...well...everything."

"You may tell me the tale if it soothes your heart," Qualleron said with great indifference.

That prompted a frown. "I'm not telling you my tale when you could clearly not give a single shit about it. Sleep if you want to, you bastard." He paused. "Also, I say this grudgingly...thank you. You have been a steadfast companion on this–"

"You need not explain," Qualleron said, and here he opened his eye just a slice. "What you have been through in this day...I have not seen its like in my many years of war. I have made countless widows, more than a few widowers, sundered many a family. I have seen cities destroyed, of course, through bomb and cannon and siege." Now his lips curled in anger, and his upper teeth were bared. "What was done to Reikonos, not in war, and by its own leader...this I cannot countenance. And what happened to you beside–"

"We need not tread the ground of my foolishness again, thank you."

"I refer to your comrades being lost," Qualleron said. "Anything else...well, many a person has been taken in by a lover who is not what they appear at first blush."

"That makes me feel a bit better," Vaste said. "I suppose that's true, yes. Which means maybe I'm not the largest fool in all the world. I merely got taken in by a more capable hustler than most." His chest puffed a bit. "Why, in fact, I'm not half the fool–"

A squeal of the rails produced a sudden shudder through the train, and it rattled as it began to slow.

"What's that?" Vaste sat upright.

Qualleron matched him, eyes springing open. The straw moved, and the piss shifted the direction of its roll. "The train is stopping. Perhaps for a town?"

Vaste stood, picking his way over the straw, and stuck his head out the small window. The track curved so he could see all the way up the engine with its puffing black cloud coming out of the chimney atop it. Beyond there were green fields, tilled and planted. "I don't see any towns ahead. Wait..."

His eyes picked out something beyond the engine some several hundred paces, and he squinted. A blockage sat athwart the tracks, bundles of wood and metal. And it was on fire.

Qualleron pushed against him from behind, shoving his own head out the window as well. "Hmm...that is probably not good."

The train squealed once more, and shuddered as it slowed.

"That's not a naturally occurring thing, is it?" Vaste asked. "Fiery blockages upon the tracks?" Qualleron shook his head, prompting Vaste to sigh deeply. "Of course not. Because by no means could we be allowed to simply make it to Termina, safe and sound and untroubled." He clutched Letum tight in his hand...because he was suddenly quite certain he was going to need it.

CHAPTER 41

Vara

They crawled on their hands and knees for eighteen city blocks that Vara counted carefully. She could not see the street signs posted on the corners, for the smoke was too thick and choking. Neither could she tell if things had changed, for the buildings themselves were not visible save as eyes of orange fire peering down on them out of the dark mist on either side, flames bursting from the easiest point of the facade – the windows. She tried to ignore them except in general, focusing instead on the gaps where they did not exist as such, denoting the cross streets as they crawled forward, threading the needle between flaming eyes on either side, watchful.

"This...is it, I think," Vara gasped. Her knees ached, her chest ached, and the less said about the pains in her back, the better. She pointed to a faint glow in the darkness to their left, the hint of recess between those flaming eyes leering down at them that signaled an intersection. "Isabelle?"

"Yes," her sister said, turning back to look at her. Now her face was darker than ever, and not just because of soot. There were rings beneath her eyes that showed the fatigue, and her coughs were more and more dry and pained, constant and racking. The tears had smudged her cheeks, and her robes were dark instead of white. She tilted her head in the direction Vara had suggested, looking a bit like a horse whose reins had been tugged. "I understand."

They crawled onward, and Vara followed. The glow was bright, unspeakably so, and even if blinded she could have followed the coughing of her sister. But the flaming eyes of the buildings of Reikonos glared down at her, casting heat at them both, and Isabelle's pace had gradually slowed. Vara had been about to say something when a shiny wetness on the cobblestones caught her eye.

"Hold," Vara commanded, and Isabelle trudged to a stop. Ash covered everything, everywhere, coating the streets. She had felt it at the tips of her gauntlets for some time, piling up on her back in light layers, the bitter taste of it upon her tongue.

But something had changed, and the glow had revealed it.

Wetness. Streaks of liquid on the street, bunching the ash together in thin trails leading forward.

Vara crawled up alongside her sister, ignoring the buffeting heat from her left as she drew closer to the burning buildings at that side of the street. She traced the wet trail and stopped alongside Isabelle. Checking forward, she found it ended before her sister – as she suspected.

"You're bleeding," Vara said, grasping at her sister's robes. Sure enough, beneath the ashy black she found wetness at the knees, where large holes had been torn in the garment. Checking Isabelle's hands yielded light spotting there, as well, where the constant contact with the rough street had slivered her palms. Wet, dark spots welled from each amid the stain of ash.

"Yes," Isabelle said wearily, looking as though she might collapse just there. "I believe I may be wearing down."

"Not yet," Vara said, casting another healing spell, her hand on Ferocis to draw aid from the sword. "We have things that must be done before you rest, sister. We need to achieve safety."

Isabelle stared dully into her eyes. "I am not sure we will find safety anywhere in this fallen city."

"We shall," Vara announced, suddenly more certain simply by speaking the words. "Two blocks. That is all, and then we shall be at the entry to the old catacombs. Come on, chop chop."

Isabelle nodded slowly, and began to crawl once more. Vara knew the bloodletting would begin again anew, for there was simply no protection against the streets for her. Windows had burst at the heat, covering the street in steaming glass, and even absent them the friction against the cobblestones was enough to slowly tear the skin from knee and palm. Now she rather wished for the old days of dirt roads, when perhaps they might have escaped with mere grains embedded in their skins and a rough set of new callouses. Progress, indeed.

"One more block," Vara announced as they crossed the next intersection, the fiery eyes abating, withdrawing into the smoke to their left and right. She was near certain they hadn't changed things, at least not too much. New buildings, sure. Roads paved with cobblestones? Absolutely.

But razing the city to the ground and building all new roads? Of course Malpravus would not have done that. Not with the city walled off and surviving on rations brought in daily. There were too many other things to worry about for him to waste his time with such trivialities.

Or so she told herself as they crawled what she deemed to be the last yards. The gate would be there, just as it had been some thousand years before, alone by itself in the recess of the hillside. Why, she could already feel the tilt of the landscape as she crawled along the heated path, beset on either side by the breath of hell.

"And...right about...here," she whispered, trying to judge where it would be. The old one had sat mid-block, in the midst of emptiness, a neglected reminder of the city's past. Buildings sat upon the corners, sure, but not here, not in the middle–

But there was pause to the fire-glowing eyes, the windows that glared down upon them like enemies about to destroy them. Only ahead, at the end of a block, did she see the glow's pause. There, at the corner, and they sat equidistant between them.

A sharp pain hit Vara in the heart. She'd been so sure, and now that certainty fell away like scales from the eyes.

There was no gap in the buildings here.

The space where the entrance to the Reikonos underground – their safety, their haven, their survival – should be...

...Was not here.

CHAPTER 42

Vaste

The train ground to a halt, the torturous squeals of metal as it slowed like screams of some primitive animal in Vaste's ears. The stink of the burning smoke out of the engine's chimney made him want to pull his head inside; but fear of what might be coming for him from somewhere out there kept him from doing so.

This land was green and verdant, with rolling hills and fields interrupted by the occasional woods. There was one just ahead, in fact, quite close to the blockage on the tracks, and the mere sight of it filled Vaste with a sort of dull dread, as though he'd already lived this moment once today.

"Right," Vaste said, already thinking ahead, "so the train stops and we're swarmed from the woods by whoever is doing the stopping, yes?"

"That seems the most likely course of events," Qualleron said.

"Great," Vaste said. "So we explain that we have nothing to do with the elves or their ilk, we're merely taking a ride to the nearest airship docks, and hopefully we are on our way within a matter of minutes."

Qualleron shook his head. "That blockage upon the tracks will not be easily cleared."

Vaste groaned. "I don't even care that much about getting to Termina, specifically. I really just want to get out of this land. Rather like being sat naked upon a hill of flame ants; you don't much care where you go next, you just want your arse to be anywhere but in those sands."

"Few live their lives here unscathed by this conflict," Qualleron said.

"I would like to be one of them," Vaste said. "Except for, you know, the 'living here' part."

The train ground to a final halt, the metal squealing and the whistle blowing loudly from the engine car. A plume of smoke burst out, black, swirling to the heavens, and as soon as it died it was replaced by another noise, more familiar to him from his own time—

Angry voices, shouting their war cry.

Humans clad in similar garb to the ones he'd seen this morning burst from the trees like specters from between gravestones. They howled with what might have been unearthly fury, a strange trilling cry ululating from their throats as they swarmed onto the train like a wave breaking upon the rocks. They entered the forward carriages at speed, the occasional blast of a pistol heralding either warning of violence or the act itself, and Vaste could see little of what happened there, though the screams suggested nothing good was afoot.

"What's up there?" Vaste asked, nodding at the forward cars.

"Passenger carriages," Qualleron said.

Vaste felt the line across his brow twist. "Wait...there are carriages for passengers? People? And Merrish stuck us—"

"In a livestock car, yes," Qualleron said with a very amused smile. "But be not offended; the seats in the passenger areas are meant for elves and smaller beings."

"I give no figs for that," Vaste said. "I'm feeling quite insulted here that I was accommodated with the damned livestock!"

"So curious," Qualleron said, frowning. "Are these figs of yours often a medium of exchange? I should like to try one, the way you keep talking about them."

The shouts were echoing closer now, and Vaste peered out the window, not daring to stick his head out now. Doors were being unlatched and pulled just up the train, now; it seemed a thorough search was being undertaken, and would surely reach them in mere moments–

A clang of the pin holding closed the door heralded the arrival of the raiders; a moment more and the door rattled open and light flooded into the car as a trio of shadows were silhouetted against the waning sunlight. One of them was long-haired, and female, and tall for her kind–

"You!" she hissed, pointing her pistol right at Vaste. It was, naturally, the woman from the woods.

"Why does everyone shout 'YOU!' at me so accusingly?" Vaste asked. "As though it were some sort of crime to be me?" He pointed a thick finger at her. "Let me tell YOU something – were I in charge, it would be a crime to be all the rest of you." He waved Letum to indicate them, and the world. "The penalty would be death, of course, for I have begun to think it is the only way I can get any peace from YOU!" And he pointed at her.

She hoisted herself up into the car, never once lowering the pistol from pointing at him. "Explain yourself."

"Well, I'm complex yet slightly fruity. Like a young vintage, really–"

She poked him in the belly with her weapon. "You jest."

"Again, you make it sound like a crime," Vaste said. "As though I'm the one out robbing trains and accosting strangers walking in the woods. I am merely trying to get to the nearest airship, which I am informed is in Termina." He gestured wildly toward the front of the train. "Where was this train bound before you stopped it?"

She looked at him through thinly slitted eyes. "Termina." Crooking her arm, she pulled back her weapon and let it point in the air. "So it is mere coincidence you are traveling on an elven train that we happened to rob?"

"I don't know about that," Vaste said. "How many elven trains passing through here do you rob?"

She let the pistol sink to pointing at the wooden floor. "Every one we get a chance to."

"Well, then my odds were absolutely marvelous, weren't they?" He threw his arms up in resignation. "Take what you want. The horses aren't ours, and neither is the straw. Though I think you'll find it quite soiled, you are welcome to it."

She still regarded him with clear suspicion. "By you or the horses?"

"Honestly, it could go either way, this day I'm having," Vaste said. "But take what you wish and leave us be, please." He shrank back against the wall. "I just want to get out of this accursed land."

Sliding back her cloak, she holstered her pistol. "You won't find that easy riding this train."

"Of course I won't," he said, tossing a look of pure exasperation to Qualleron, who seemed much more sanguine about this whole series of events. "Between you and Merrish, I seem positively destined to be batted back and forth–"

"How do you know Merrish?" Her weapon was in her hand again, though not pointed at him.

"I barely know the man at all," Vaste said, "he's an acquaintance from a thousand years ago."

Her eyes slitted more deeply. "Trolls do not live a thousand years, not even trelves."

Vaste felt an odd prickle run through him. "Is a 'trelve' what it sounds like?" He glanced at Qualleron, who was nodding. "Well...good for those fellows, I suppose. I must admit, I pity the elven women who had to birth them–"

The woman spat on the straw, making...really no more mess than had already been made. "I have no pity for elves, past or present, and you should not either."

"Let me make this extremely clear to you," and Vaste leaned closer so he could look her in the eye. "I give no figs about your war. Not for your side, not for the elves you wish to kill. I want to get out of here."

She pushed the pistol to his chin. "A dangerous sentiment to express here, troll, when it is us against them."

"Be against them all you like," Vaste said. "You cannot force me to hate the people you hate, you can only kill me, and then at least one of us will have all our problems solved."

She stared him in the eyes, her own brown and glistening with a sort of rage Vaste had seen mostly upon the battlefields of a thousand years ago. For a moment he felt sure she would let the weapon boom, but after a moment she looked down, holstered her pistol again, and turned from him. "Bring the horses," she said to the men with her, and they sprung to do just that.

"Sure you don't want the straw, too?" Vaste asked.

"Your tongue is acid," she said, hopping down from the car but giving him a look back. "You should take more care with it in the future, to ensure it does not needlessly get you killed."

"I refuse to be a mealy-mouth in these times of woe," Vaste said. "Let others whimper and whine; if death comes for me, I almost welcome it. Certainly more than I welcome muttering some disingenuous sentiment simply because you'd like to hear it. Say, something probably along the lines of 'Skin all the elves!'"

"They are much more agreeable without their skins," she said.

"I'm sure they'd say the same about you," Vaste said.

"And to them, I certainly would be," she said as the horses were led down on planks she placed for them. Still, she looked at Vaste as the work was done around her, not moving off to converse with others or issue orders. The hubbub was dying down, the raid nearing its end. "Do you have a name, insolent troll?"

"My name is Vaste," he said, because he had no strength nor inclination to lie.

"Vaste," she said, rolling the word over in her mouth. "It has a familiarity to it, your name."

"I promise you, other than this morning, we have never before met."

"Yet fate has chosen to draw us together twice this day," she said, and there was a certain gleam in her eye.

Qualleron made an auspicious grunting sound which Vaste ignored. "Sure, fate," Vaste said. "Or, alternatively, the fact that you were searching out dead villagers that I stumbled on by accident, and you decided to rob the train I was on, a feat you admit you do often. But, yeah, other than that, yes, the hand of fate is working madly to push us together."

"Here is fate for you, then," she said with ripe amusement. "This track will not be repaired nor this train move along it for days to come."

"Well, shit," Vaste said.

"But my band and I are making our way to Termina even now," she said with a gleam of triumph in her eye. "If you come with us, you will be there within the day. Or you may wait...however long that may be."

"Our adventure does not seem to be threatening to get any less interesting," Qualleron rumbled.

"That's all you have to say about this turn of events?" Vaste asked, wheeling on him.

The mercenary shrugged. "As she says...the hand of fate does as it wishes."

"I wish the hand of fate would give me a happy ending already," Vaste said irritably. "Fate did not choose her destination. She did. The fact she's going where we are...well, I imagine Termina is the biggest city in the area by some margin."

"Correct," the woman said. "And the only city still jointly controlled by both human and elf – though that arrangement frays by the day."

"Of course it does," Vaste said, and he buried a head in his palm, for what else was there to say to that?

Wait here for the track to be repaired, assuming the train would linger where it had just been attacked?

Or strike out on their own, following the tracks, walking for days through territory at war? They would likely meet another party like this one, or the elven equivalent, and they, perhaps, might not be nearly as agreeable as this woman, for all her prickly difficulty.

"Fine!" Vaste said, at last, and she almost laughed at him, the mirth evident on her face. "But I don't travel well with strangers, and I've yet to hear so much as your name either of the times you've tried to hijack me."

Her eyes were laughing now. "My name is Aemma, and that is all you need to know for now. Come," she said, and slapped her hand once upon the side of the car, rattling it heavily. "We leave at once."

CHAPTER 43

Alaric

He found Mazirin on the quarterdeck, the wind rushing through her hair, which was loose, and her eyes fixed ahead, even as the pirate cannons seemed to find a target with every firing. The *Yuutshee's* response was muted by comparison, the small chasers raged in turns, and Alaric watched the subtle whistle of the metal projectiles through the sky as best he could, the reaction when they hit the ironclad always underwhelming.

Mazirin had a scent about her when he drew closer, a hint of wine, perhaps, barely detectable. Looking ahead as she was, the wind whipping at her hair and knee-length coat, she cut a very fine figure, he thought. Though it was a thought he'd had before, certainly. "Our time draws low in the hourglass," she said.

Alaric nodded and joined her to stand by her side. Ahead was the tower, Vernadam, with a very slight lean. The topmost turret roof had rotted away, leaving nothing but the stone jutting up above the clouds.

"I find it odd," she said, nodding at the only object near in sight. "This marker...it signifies nothing, and yet it has swollen to become my whole world, as if by reaching it we somehow win this race and all our troubles are over."

"In times of great strain, the mind needs things to fixate on," Alaric says. "I once saw a man decide in the moments before a battle that this was the perfect time to arrange his collection of dried leaves. Admittedly, it seemed less than ideal timing to me, but to him it was perfectly reasonable."

She stared straight ahead. "Did you have him killed for his cowardice?"

"No," Alaric said. "He fought, and fought well, though he had to be prodded some. His mind was struggling with what was to come, though, and needed some small measure of release before the moment. He was not the greatest fighter, but neither did he break and run like so many." He lowered his voice. "It is normal to contemplate other things in the moments before catastrophe."

Mazirin looked at him sidelong, slowly. "It would be easier if there were something I could do other than stand here while the engines race and the cannons thud almost uselessly." One went off behind her and she barely blanched. It struck him that this was, perhaps, the most open he'd ever seen her, though there was no hint of despair upon her face. As a captain, she was simply too buttoned up for that, even in this moment.

"I would say the waiting before battle is the hardest part, but it would be a lie," Alaric said. "Battle is often terrible, with severed limbs and sundered skulls, and hearts laid open to bleed. But the waiting is no peach, either, when armageddon looms."

She took a step closer to him, and her voice dropped. "My crew have, almost to a man, been raised in an Amatgarosa that has known nearly only peace, and have seen only shades of the brutality that awaits beyond our shores."

"But you've seen it," Alaric said, for he knew by her eyes.

She nodded once. "I went to Chaarland in my youth, when I traveled the world. My government knew I was there, and accorded me status as an observer, so the Chaarlandians did not dare to touch me without provocation. I went among their villages, saw their reavers come back from their raids, from other lands. They invited in me, and grinned, and skinned a woman alive in front of me, then cooked her for dinner while they made leather of her flesh, pillows of her hair, and implements of her bone."

Alaric felt a clammy shudder down his back and fixed his eye on the tower in the distance, trying to forget what he'd just been told. At least the ancients never resorted to eating people. "It seems a terrible fate awaits us if we fail."

"And I do not see how we do not fail," Mazirin said. "Even if we make it to the coast before they catch us and cut the *Yuutshee* to pieces, I do not see them stopping. But perhaps there is enough fear of Amatgarosa's response, concern that the dragon will wake and turn them to ash, that they would stop when we reach the sea. But I do not think so, for our escape would bode particularly ill for them when I report to Xiaoshani."

"Will your people respond?" Alaric asked. "If you tell them what happened here?"

"I don't know," Mazirin said. "The empire...it is not what it was when I was young." She waved a hand in his face when he opened his mouth to protest that she was still young. "We have no time for foolish games. I am forty summers old, Alaric, and youth is not prized in my culture the way it is among, say, your elves. Wisdom and experience are valued in Amatgarosa, so I wear my gray hairs with pride. But the point remains – we are not what we used to be. We stopped climbing the mountain and now sit where we are upon what we perceive to be the peak, and the wolves...they are coming."

"Someone is always trying to catch hold of the brightest star," Alaric said. "To steal their luster."

"If I were running the fleet," Mazirin said, "I would dispatch ten squadrons to sweep over the continent of Chaarland, destroying every airship field and factory, burning their pockets of industry. They are not a people to be trusted with the skies." Her expression hardened. "But I am not in charge of anything but the *Yuutshee*." Another whistling cannonball found home at the front of the ship, crashing into the forecastle along the side. "We are fortunate indeed they have not hit the engines or props yet, but it is only a matter of time."

Alaric took this all in with a steady ear, and looked once more to the tower, growing closer with every minute. It had a pronounced tilt, and an idea occurred to him. "You have cannons at the forecastle, yes?"

"Of course. Why?"

"Have they any effectiveness on stone? And do they operate at distance enough to pick at the tower?"

She cocked her head, thinking. "A small effect, but...perhaps. Perhaps. That is a dangerous game you propose."

"More dangerous than being caught and flayed alive, then made into supper?"

"Dugras?" Mazirin called after only a moment's thought. The dwarf appeared on the quarterdeck; had he been there all along? "Man the bow chasers, and make them ready." She hardened her gaze. "I want to drop the tower on that ship."

CHAPTER 44

Shirri

The smell of Calene – rough, that of grass and dirt, of honey and bread from her place – gave way to the smooth, perfumed scent of Gareth and his soft hand as he shook with Shirri, that strangest of human customs that had made its way across even elvendom. "Pleasure to meet you, Shirri," he said once the introductions had been made, and beckoned them into his office.

A floor to ceiling window gave them a commanding view of the towering trees that had been turned into mighty buildings. Gareth's chair squeaked as he seated himself across from them in a desk carved right out of the tree itself that hung over his legs like a floating table. "So...what brings you here today?"

Shirri just about swallowed her tongue.

"Bit of a sticky thing," Calene said, slipping her bow off her shoulder and seating herself. A bit late in the game, to Shirri's mind; whereas Shirri had followed Gareth and gone right for the chair, Calene had taken her time sauntering in, as though stalking her prey across the office. "Have you heard any whispers about what's happened in Reikonos?"

"Just the things that come in on the morning airships," Gareth said airily. "Catastrophe. Fires raging through the city now, they say."

Shirri fought to hold her tongue. They had spent the eve in Calene's apartment after all, giving it a solid day for news to percolate through Amti. Was Reikonos now on fire? It probably was, given that there was no one left alive to tame them.

"Hardly the sort of thing that affects us greatly," Gareth said. "Not one of our key trading partners, after all. They bought from us some, of course. But not nearly as much as the dark elves, or Termina and Pharesia. Or Emerald. Or just about any of the chaos states in Firoba." He chuckled. "A tragedy, no doubt, whatever's happened there. But hardly our problem, and not our concern."

"It will be your concern shortly," Shirri said.

"Tell me, Gareth," Calene said, cutting over her sharply, "do you recall the name...Malpravus?"

Gareth's broad face twisted up, a far-off look as though trying to see prey in the distance. "Malpravus...rings a bell. But a quiet one, like one of those hand bells the children run around with."

"It's going to be a tolling temple one soon enough," Shirri said, for she could not help herself.

"Malpravus was the guild leader of Goliath," Calene said. "Do you remember them?"

Gareth's lips puckered in a small smile. "Wasn't that the lot that Sanctuary had a great rivalry with?"

"In that they tried to kill us and have us exiled from every land possible, yes," Calene said. "You could call it a rivalry. Their leader was a man named Malpravus. Well...'man' might be overstating it–"

"What does this have to do with us?" Gareth asked. "I thought you were on a contract right now, about to head out. Twenty bears from the mountains near old Kortran, and any drakes you can bring down."

"I don't hunt drakes, you know that," Calene said darkly. "And I was going to set out after the bears. However, I got a bit derailed. See...my associate here came in from Reikonos yesterday."

"You know, I do remember hearing another thing from Reikonos," Gareth said, sitting up in his chair, looking piercingly at Calene. "An old name I hadn't heard in any seriousness for some time...Cyrus Davidon. Certainly, you hear his name – 'the blessed Davidon be with you,' 'Davidon's fury be upon your enemies,' all that claptrap." Gareth's gaze really honed in on Calene. "But this was different. Someone told me–"

"That Cyrus Davidon had returned?" Calene asked. "Yes. I heard much the same. But that's neither here nor there."

"Just struck me as funny," Gareth said, and he plopped a perfectly shined, glossy black shoe upon the corner of the desk. "Cyrus Davidon rumored to return. And then you bring me this name from back when. Not to do with each other, are they?"

"Malpravus is more concerning than any rumors of Cyrus's return," Calene said. "Because Malpravus–"

"Now hold up a jot," Gareth said, and his smile said he was clearly enjoying the joke, "I can see by the way you're avoiding the subject you're trying to put me off, but I won't be fobbed off just because you wish to ride past the subject without comment, Calene. Cyrus Davidon is long dead. Surely you must know that."

Calene seemed to be warring with herself. "Why would you think that?"

"Because humans live and die in less of a time span than it takes an elf to grow to adulthood," Gareth said with clear amusement.

"How long have I known you, Gareth?" Calene asked.

His smile evaporated. "But you're different, Calene."

"How long?"

Gareth paused, swallowing visibly. "A thousand years, I think."

"And how am I different than my fellow humans?"

Again Gareth seemed stuck for words. "You are not the same as—"

"As Cyrus?" Calene asked. "No, I'm not. He had two swords, and had the skills of a mage. I can but pluck twine and send arrows a-flying; hide in the grass for many hours at a go. You want to ask me? Fine – have your answer. Cyrus Davidon has returned. I believe it. I know it. And along with him has come more trouble than we might have bargained for, and it will not stay confined to Reikonos."

Calene leaned forward. "Malpravus is a madman, Gareth. He's been posing as Longwell for hundreds of years. Surely you must have realized that if you've ever seen him. He doesn't even look like Longwell."

"I never knew the man all that well," Gareth said, "and it's irrelevant in any case—"

"He cast a spell of death upon Reikonos," Shirri said, moved to speak at last. "I was there. I saw it. A great, violent red light as though a lantern were shone through a ruby, and everyone in its path died."

"That sort of magic has not been possible for half a millennia," Gareth said.

"It's not possible for humans to live a thousand years, either," Calene said. "Yet here I sit. It's not possible for Cyrus Davidon to return. Not possible for magic to destroy Reikonos. I disabuse you of one assertion, and I'm telling you two more are wrong. Will you believe me?"

Gareth stared at her for a long, long moment before finally shaking his head. "No. No. I am sorry, Calene, but I do not.

Cities burn all the time. Why, we almost lost Kortri but a couple years back to a fire that got out of hand. And as to the Cyrus Davidon idea?" He shook his head again. "We've heard that one before. No. The age of Cyrus Davidon has passed, I'm afraid. No more gods, no more magic to speak of." He smiled, but the twinkle in his eyes seemed dulled to Shirri. "Just us now. So...the contract on the bears? Can I count on you? Or do I need to find a less...distracted hunter?"

Calene took hold of her cloak, burnt hem and all, and lifted herself out of the chair. "I'm telling you about something that will threaten the very existence of your nation...and all you can think about are the bloody bears."

"They're killing settlers, Calene," Gareth said, eyes darkly lidded. "This is my responsibility."

"If you think the bears are bad for that," Shirri said, "you should see what that spell of Malpravus's will do when he gets here." They left him then, shaking his head sadly in the lushly appointed office, as though they were the fools for not believing him.

CHAPTER 45

Cyrus

The soft, padding steps, barely audible beneath his own great footfalls, were his first clue that he'd not left the throne room alone, and he wanted to sigh. "Why are you following me?"

Aisling passed him with her still-dextrous steps. "Someone has to show you to your quarters. Would you prefer some silent guard, awestruck at the mere sight of Cyrus Davidon, do the task?" She turned just enough that he could see the mirth in her silhouette. "Or would you rather someone who knows you, so as to avoid a supplicant dogging your steps like an eager puppy?"

"Seems I already have one of those," Cyrus said, glancing at Niamh. She bumped her head into his thigh with enough force to make him miss a step and stagger sideways. "Or not."

Aisling's smile faded as she looked upon the scourge. "I

didn't want to ask about your follower, but I take it that is some soul you knew well?"

"Niamh," Cyrus said. "Did you hear our conversation but miss the name?"

"I didn't hear any of it," Aisling said, leading him down a dark tunneled hall. "I came from my manor as quickly as called by Terian, but it was a little distance and I was settled in for the night, hardly in a fit state to present myself at court. Though admittedly I care less about such things as I might have when I was young. Still, when you have a scourge not upon a chain, not throwing itself at every living thing in the room...well, the conclusion seemed easy enough."

"May I confirm one of my own with you?" Cyrus asked, and when Aisling nodded, he went on. "Terian's wife died some time back."

"Indeed," Aisling said. "About a century, it was. The entire nation was thrown into mourning for almost a decade, and he's not been the same since." She paused, catching his eye. "They never had children, you know."

"How would I know that?" Cyrus asked. "I just got off a ship not an hour ago, and before that I was a little busy fighting a fruitless revolution in Reikonos. Well...not fruitless, I suppose. It did bear the bitterest fruit."

"Try not to become Mopey Cyrus over it, whatever it was," Aisling said. "It's never useful, and it's damned unappealing. Still, to Terian – Kahlee told me that he always blamed himself. Because of the whoring in his youth, you know? Picked up a few diseases that linger with him even now, and he feared that while his axe kept him from feeling them, they passed to her and–"

"Ravaged her ability to carry life within?" Cyrus blanched. "That would explain the rather deep tinge of bitterness Terian carries with him."

"It should explain more than that," Aisling said, looking at him with great significance. "Baynvyn will be in there, even now, consulting. Probably even after he's sent Hongren away, that old fool."

"Isn't Hongren just a ship captain?" Cyrus asked.

"Do you know how few ships the dark elves have?" Aisling asked.

"Going to make like you and take a stab in the dark – ten."

Her smile was laced with good humor at his jibe. "Few enough that Shipmaster is a high title indeed. Hongren is one of the inner circle."

"Are you?"

Her smile dimmed. "I was, once." She stepped closer and he saw again now the lines of her face. Holding Epalette for all the years she had before surrendering it had perhaps postponed her aging, but it had not halted it. "But I grew weary of it, especially after all the many lean years when the gates were shut and it was just us in here, tunneling and digging and turning upon ourselves. There is little civil about civil wars, and we fought with astounding regularity until we built the tower."

"How did you build the tower?" Cyrus asked. "I saw the swarming hordes of Scourge impaling themselves on those needlepoint defenses, but how did you get it upright without being completely overwhelmed by–"

"Shhh," Aisling said with a shake of her head. "It's a story that would require explanation, and a reasonable bit of it to make sense. To rush it might leave you with misapprehensions, but suffice to say...an old friend helped us in a way that we would not have expected possible before we saw it ourselves."

"That just leaves me with more questions," Cyrus said, frown prickling at his brow.

"Good," Aisling said, "for I suspect Terian looks forward to telling you that one himself, given the tower is one of the few triumphs in the last thousand years that didn't involve a great tragedy for our people."

Cyrus nodded slowly. "Very well, then. I suppose it doesn't matter just now. But what about—"

She placed a hand upon his cheek, and her touch felt cold as she brushed his skin in a way that reminded him of the old days when she'd done the same with a much different intent. This felt maternal, or like the care of a friend. "You must be tired."

"Oddly...no," Cyrus said. He hadn't slept well or long for days, and his last bout of unconsciousness had been when Baynvyn had clubbed him insensate. Still, the blood pumped in his veins, and all he could think of was Malpravus. "I fear what is coming, Aisling. We need to—"

"There is nothing to be done tonight." Her voice became a soothing whisper, different than when she'd been his lover. It made him wonder if this was the sound Baynvyn had heard when she'd soothed their son in his raising. He had a feeling it was exactly the same. "Rest. Refresh yourself as best you can, for you should well know by now that defeating Malpravus will not be an endeavor for the bone weary."

"You speak an annoying amount of sense," Cyrus said, giving a hearty sigh. "But I like it none the better for the truth it brings."

"Truth is often annoying," Aisling said, pushing open an ornate door in the hallway. Darkness waited within, but by the Eagle Eye spell he could see the shape of a bed and other furnishings. "But indispensable nonetheless."

"Very well," Cyrus said, conceding the field. "I will take your advice and rest...if I can."

"Barricade the door if you must," Aisling said, with a bit of her old impishness. Not much; just a tinge, as though that part of her might have been almost irreparably severed to leave behind the world-weary figure that remained. "If you fear Terian coming for you in the night."

"There's probably a secret passage in the back of the room in case he needs to do that," Cyrus muttered. He would not be sleeping soundly this eve, he suspected. Or day. Since entering the earth, he found he'd already lost track of time.

"So you see enemies in every shadow," she said. "Good. You learned from the days of old. In any case, though, you will need to trust him eventually, if you intend to receive his help against these troubles you say are coming."

"I'll try," Cyrus said, and slipped into the room. With a flash of her still-white hair, she turned and was gone.

Niamh had trudged past him in the quiet, and now boosted herself up to the bed, the supports beneath squeaking at her ascent.

"No offense, but we never shared a bed in life and I don't care to start after your death," Cyrus said, but caught a dark, twinkling glare from the scourge that made him sigh. "It's your first time in a bed in a thousand years, isn't it?" With a quick glance around, he found a single upright chair with a not-unreasonable amount of padding. With a squeak of his armor, he gave it a try and found the back just high enough to catch his neck should he lay it back. "Fine," he said, adjusting his scabbard from where it had caught upon the upholstery, "the lady gets the bed."

Niamh settled her head down, lying like an over-sized dog upon the covers. She made a sound so unlike anything Cyrus had heard from a scourge before that he lifted his head up to make sure it was her that had made it, and not some other creature that had been here since before they'd opened the door.

She was...purring, almost, her gray head resting now upon the silken bedspread. The sound of breathing, usually coarse, had settled into a steady, albeit strange rhythm, and her big, black eyes had closed.

"At least one of us should enjoy Terian's hospitality," Cyrus said, leaning his head back against the seat back. He certainly didn't feel much like sleep, and listened to the sound of Niamh's breathing as he stared up at the cave ceiling, waiting for an attack from Terian that he didn't even feel sure was coming, while worrying about the one from Malpravus that he knew for certain was.

CHAPTER 46

Vara

Everything she had been working toward, been crawling toward, for what felt like hours and days, was now lost. Vara stared at the flaming windows in the thick black smoke, glaring down at her like the hellish eyes of angry gods now dead, and the heat battered at her skin, baking the last drops of moisture from it.

But the hope she'd held seemed to have gone up in a blaze, burnt out in the fires that surrounded her and Isabelle in nearly every direction, growing stronger with each passing second as they consumed the city of Reikonos in total. The waves of scorching hotness buffeted her, and she coughed, her throat dry as death.

"Where is it?" Isabelle asked, numbly. She was bleeding again, the drips of red reflecting bright orange by the flames on either side of them. It was valleys of fire, really, and glass and hard cobblestones lay beneath their knees and knuckles, though

Vara's were shielded by her greaves and gauntlets. Her sister had no such luck; her once-white robes were now nearly black from ash, her golden hair a shade of ebony laced with gray and lit by the ochre fire-light.

Vara took a breath, and choked upon it. The air was miserably hot, like sucking straight from an oven, and the burnt taste covered her tongue like she'd licked dry charcoal. The dry rasp in the back of her throat was an uncontrollable tickle that she wondered if she'd ever be able to dispense with, even if she somehow miraculously lived to five thousand years of age.

That, however, was looking improbable, for the entrance to the underground tunnels of Reikonos – that ancient conveyance path of the Protanian Empire – was not where she thought it was.

Or, worse – she was not where she thought she was.

"Where is it?" Isabelle asked, collapsing to her chest, flat against the road. The cobblestones to either side of them seemed to be smoking, and Vara wondered how hot indeed it was here, now.

"I don't know," she said, and the words sounded like death knell to her ears. To have survived all this only to come to such an end, in such a place...

Her bleary yet somehow scorchingly dried eyes probed at the place where the entry should have been. Bright, burning orange windows stretched one, two, three, four stories up from the street. A building was here, the glass shattered and spewing hot fire skyward, belching smoke into the heavens like burnt offerings. The whole city was a sacrificial altar, though, wasn't it? Not to the old gods, though.

Rather, to the new one: Malpravus.

Well, it looked like he'd get one more sacrifice, though he wouldn't receive the advantage of it, at least. Two, she supposed, heart sinking at the sight of Isabelle laid out before her, as if sprawled on a couch almost facedown.

"It should have been here," she said, thinking back. The five-point crossroad, she'd been so sure she'd known. Then they went north...

It should have been here, she thought as she reached the end of her mental count, staring once more at the angry, flaming windows looking down upon her in her defeat. Graceless, they were, unpitying. And she could have used some pity right now. But no, they just leered down from the upper floors down to–

But wait.

They did leer down from the upper floors. And from either side, as well. But in the middle...

In the middle there was a gap. Quite a large one, too, shrouded in the smoke, but too large for a simple entryway. And there were basement windows afire, too, but only on the sides of the building, not just before them.

Vara stared at it, and an idea presented itself. "Isabelle...I think we are here, we just can't see it."

"How...what are we to do, then...?" Isabelle asked. "We cannot...stumble closer." She fanned herself, for all the good that would do. "Vara...it's too hot. We cannot stay here. We are dying."

That much was certain. "We need to see," Vara said, trying to peer into that gap of space. She eased toward it, crawling her way in that direction, trying to shield her face from the heat beating down like the angriest sun imaginable. Three body lengths, she made it, and then retreated, her armor hot as a boiling kettle.

"What was there?" Isabelle asked as she drew close again.

"I can't...I can't," Vara said, shaking her head. Her helm felt as though it weighed tons, and part of her wanted to take it off, stifling as it was. "It's too hot over there. The fire is..." She gestured uselessly, hand barely able to move beneath the weight of her gauntlets. She felt about five hard seconds from collapsing like her sister.

Isabelle stared into the fiery death that awaited her, then nodded. She had a look of concentration, then raised her hand, which glowed white–

Vara looked back to where the shadows reigned, where the entry should be, and saw the smoke rise as a wind whipped through – and up. The flames coming out of the windows above raged in the presence of new air, crawling up the building's facade, licking like great tongues up the brick. The black smoke flew into the sky, clearing a small space in front of them–

And Vara saw it, in the firelight, in the gap of smoke, under the brewing, hot-burning fires above.

A staircase up to one door, which was already glowing, its handle like a blacksmith's iron, dull compared to the blazing flames above, and framed with embers threatening to burn through the door.

And then, down a separate staircase, she could see it. It wasn't what it used to be, a gate to keep the children and mischief-makers out. That would have been a simple thing.

No, instead it was a slab of pure stone, and when she hauled herself over, it was cool to the touch in a way that nothing had been in this whole city since she'd got back. It stretched to the edges of what had once been a small tunnel, a very old thing perfectly meeting the newly constructed stones and brick of the building, a small change in the architecture that might not even be noticed unless one were looking for it.

She'd found the entry to the underground.

And it was blocked by solid stone, sealed off in such a way that she had no hope of moving it.

CHAPTER 47

Alaric

The cannons boomed forward and Alaric stood at the forecastle, looking out over the green and gray landscape where nothing large enough lived to move. Perhaps blades of grass swayed in the wind down there, but they were too small to see, and not a tree stood upon the plains of dirt, blighted of any life by the scourge.

Ahead, the tower showed signs of a hit. A plume of dust rose at the edge of the structure where the cannon ball, which Alaric had seen were about the size of his clenched, mailed fist, had struck home. It made a small impact, minimal upon the face of the tower of stone.

"Going to be a long day, chipping away like that," Guy said, then turned to glance at the Chaarlandian ship trailing them. It had grown closer. "Or maybe not."

"We seize upon narrow chances because sometimes they are all we have," Alaric said as the cannons rang out once more. The tower was nearing, and showed no sign of swaying, but stone chips blew out in another powdery billow of dust.

"Let's hope we seize something," Guy said, keeping his focus on the ironclad, "and that it's them, by the short and curlies."

Movement on the deck caught Alaric's eye. Dugras emerged from the hatch, as swiftly as his small legs could carry him, though he paused when he saw Alaric, changing directions to climb the forecastle step. "Any luck?" Dugras asked. When no one answered, he seemed to get his answer from the tower, still standing tall and unmoved. "This your idea?"

"Indeed," Alaric said. "How did you guess?"

"Because it's not one a seasoned captain would come up with," he said with a thin, knowing smile. "And not one she would accept from...oh, anyone else onboard."

Alaric cocked his head. "I'm afraid you're going to have to explain your meaning."

"The captain is not well-disposed to suggestions," Dugras said, and suddenly he seemed quite antsy to get up to the top deck – or perhaps merely away from this conversation. "Especially ones that have no chance of working. The timing required..." he shook his head slowly.

"We have no alternatives, by my reckoning." Alaric turned once more to look upon the ironclad. Strange lettering upon a panel fastened to the curved bow suggested, to him, a ship name. "Unless I am missing something."

"You're not missing anything," Dugras said, "other than perhaps the last minutes of your life, if you're not paying close attention." One of the stern chasers fired into the rising belly of the ironclad, and with a sound like a ringing bell, the cannonball bounced off the under armor. "Because that's the end of our being able to damage them, really."

Now Alaric saw it; by bringing the ship up, higher than the *Yuutshee*, it had presented its under armor to them. Even lifting the cannons up to their maximum extension on the hinge –

which they were – would produce nothing but more of those bell-ringers as a result.

The pirate ship was now, for lack of a better strategy, nigh invincible.

"Your captain saw this coming, then?" Alaric asked.

"Undoubtedly," Dugras said. "I could redirect engine power to bring us up to their height, but I'd take it from the propulsion, and they'd catch us for sure, then." He flashed a wolfish smile. "Which is why the captain hasn't bothered to issue said order. She still hopes to reach the coast, and by doing so, convince them to abandon pursuit."

Alaric looked up; upon the iron deck of the Chaarlandian ship, he could see the captain once more, and closer now, staring down at them like some ancient slavedriver in Sennshann, about to turn loose his whip. It made Alaric's blood pump; he saw the wicked grin, and knew the man's expectation.

Blood and flesh. Both would be his soon, along with whatever remained of the *Yuutshee*.

"Still and all," Dugras said, "congratulations on getting the captain to accept your suggestion, long shot though it might be." He grimaced. "Better than nothing."

Alaric paused. "I can't tell if you were being serious or not."

Dugras chuckled. "I was being serious, though after spending some time with your friends I can see why you'd struggle to tell."

"I see," Alaric said. "I don't wish to detain you any longer. I'm sure the captain waits to hear from you." Another boom, and he turned, watching small clouds of dust once more strike the tower, which was now just ahead, and closing fast.

"I'm still hoping your plan works," Dugras said. "Even a faint hope is better than none." And he walked away, leaving Alaric puzzling over one small piece of what he said: the bit about how the captain did not take suggestions...yet had, for some reason, done so with his.

CHAPTER 48

Vaste

"This has been the worst day since, oh, I don't know – yesterday," Vaste announced after trudging in near silence for almost an hour through wood and field. Only occasional hushed whispers were spoken among the column of raiders.

"What happened yesterday?" Aemma asked rather genially. She seemed unbothered by his outburst, or the sound it made echoing over the quiet northern fields and woods.

"I had a front seat for the destruction of Reikonos," Vaste said, tromping lightly through the underbrush. They seemed to Vaste on a parallel path to the train tracks, heading east, though it was hard to tell because the sun was low in the sky and the woods were thick around them. He cast the Eagle Eye spell upon himself, and it helped – a bit. Less than it would have before the slow death of magic.

"Truly?" Aemma raised an eyebrow. "Reikonos was destroyed?"

"I mean, the city is still standing," Vaste said, "but the people within – quite dead."

Aemma's nose wrinkled. "How does something like that happen?"

Vaste sighed. "I will tell you, but I doubt you will believe me: magic."

Qualleron snorted; he was walking some rows back, and engaged in quiet conversation with at least three of the human raiders. They seemed quite mirthful, swapping war stories that he caught snatches of here and there. Whether his noise was at Vaste's comment or one of the tales being passed between them back there, Vaste did not know.

"Magic, you say?" Aemma cast a skeptical eye upon him.

He found it curious, having to look down not nearly so much upon her as with most women of the non-troll variety. Why, she was taller than most of the men with her. "Yes, magic. Though I doubt a thoroughly modern woman such as yourself places much stock in such things."

She cocked her head at him. "'Thoroughly modern?' Do women not fight in wars where you come from, Vaste?"

"Oh, the women I grew up with *fight*. Like hell itself unleashed them, in fact," Vaste said. "No, when I said 'thoroughly modern,' I meant in relation to your probable beliefs about the existence of magic."

"Hm." She seemed to give that some thought, then said, "It's true, I don't put much stock in ideas of magic. I find them rather quaint. Like the notions of the old gods of Arkaria, or the worship of Cyrus Davidon – all myths of little use and better left in the past."

"Well, at least we can agree about not worshipping Cyrus," Vaste said. "Though that may be the extent of our concordance."

"Cyrus Davidon was never even a real person," Aemma said.

"The latest evidence suggests he was instead, perhaps, a composite of several people of that age. We look for heroes wherever we can, seeking the best attributes and wishing to pile them on one person." She lowered her voice and looked around. "Not a popular sentiment among my people, naturally. They're all Davidon worshippers, and view me as little more than a heretic."

"Having been an actual heretic, I doubt they treat you the way we were treated that year," Vaste said, prompting quizzical look from Aemma. "Still, I take your point about standing out in a crowd because of what you believe." He coughed. "Though you're quite wrong about Cyrus. I certainly wish you weren't, sometimes, but..." He shook his head in mild annoyance. "...he existed. Exists, still, maybe."

"Then you believe in Davidon though you don't worship him?" Aemma asked. "And you're a troll. Who believes in magic?" She laughed, and it was silvery. "You are simply filled with contradictions, aren't you?"

"Hey, you're the one who just cited some mystical evidence about Cyrus Davidon not being a real person," Vaste said. "As though people still living didn't meet the man."

"When I talk of Cyrus Davidon's not being real, I speak of human evidence, of course." Aemma's voice crackled, carrying through the woods. "The elves are to be trusted in nothing, especially not matters of human faith. I would no sooner believe one of them telling me stories of the Great Davidon's life," her voice took on a mocking quality, "than I would believe them if they offered me food freely claiming it was devoid of poison."

"I suppose my experience with elves has been less embittering than yours," Vaste said slowly. He thought of Vara. She had gone to Termina, had she not? Perhaps he could find her there, though he did not look forward to telling her about Reikonos...or Cyrus. He pictured the flash in her cold blue eyes at news such as this, and a bottomless dread prickled in the pit of his stomach.

"I imagine so," Aemma said. "They destroyed my village when I was five. Plundered it, burned it...did everything you might imagine they would do to a hated enemy. I heard the screams until the last of them ceased, and escaped only by hiding in the fields, even as they set them aflame." She pulled off her glove, and in the dark, Vaste could see the ripples of burns long healed to scars coursing up her wrist to beneath her sleeve. "So yes...I have a good reason for my hate of the elves." She glanced over at him as she slid her glove back on. "What experience have you had with them?"

"Oh, let's see...I was schooled at one of their academies until they refused to teach me any further," Vaste said. "Then I encountered a group of misfits who finished my training, and several of them were elves. Several were humans. Also, dark elves. A smattering of dwarves, gnomes – whatever, you get the point–"

"You are not from this land, clearly," Aemma said with a wistful smile.

"What makes you say that?"

"Because those peoples have not gotten along in a thousand years."

"Perhaps I'm just very old," Vaste said, feeling every bit of it now.

"I did hear you say something about a thousand years ago, didn't I?" She gave him a curiously regarding look. "You said it in relation to your acquaintance with Merrish." Her eyes flashed hate now. "If you knew him a thousand years ago, tell me how he was then."

"I didn't know him well," Vaste said, "but he was a firebrand lord back then. Of Traegon, if I recall?"

Aemma let out a snort of derision. "Traegon. A hateful name

the elves still use for a city that hasn't been theirs by right since time immemorial."

"I am quite confident that many of them still remember living there," Vaste said carefully. Her hate was twisting her up, that much was obvious. "Assuming your people didn't wipe them out."

"We did not 'wipe them out,'" she said. "Our ancestors crossed the river when the scourge came. They welcomed us – at first. Then they turned on us, piling us into ghettos in the towns and cities while they lived in their great manors on hills, looking down upon us and cossetted in their mighty estates, far from the stench of any human save for the few they brought on as their servants."

"So...everyone got along very well, it sounds like."

"They would have been happy for us to starve in that first hundred years," Aemma said, her voice taking on a ghostly quality, the darkness coming with the last rays of day shining through the forest. "To see all their former lands cleansed of us, returned to the pristine, unused state. But we seized our place, tilled the land, broke it to our will, made them see us a force rather than mere servants here only for their pleasure. We broke free of the plague-ridden ghettos–"

"And ripped their land away from them," Vaste said.

"This is the only land – the only home – we have ever known," Aemma said. "For us, anywhere our ancestors lived before this is beyond memory. Our fathers and grandfathers and all remembered before that lived only here. This is all we have."

"Look, no one understands better than I do having nowhere to go," Vaste said, feeling the strangest, dimmest awakening of compassion twitching within his heart. It was an odd sensation, and one he was fully prepared to hate. Somehow, he didn't, though. "Still and all, given the historical back and forth, perhaps a sort of compromise might be reached in which both parties are left equally incensed and angry about how much they've lost?"

"I'm sure that would resolve things marvelously," Aemma said with tightly laced sarcasm. "More bitterness is always a soothing balm for festering resentments."

"I only mean," Vaste said, "that it would seem preferable to lose some of what you think to be yours rather than lose many or all of those you hold dear. As wars tend to – obviously. If you see a path to peace, you might want to take it, before things get even worse."

"The only path to peace I see," Aemma said, holding her chin up, eyes gleaming defiantly in the last light of day, "is over their dead bodies."

"And if they feel the same about you?" Vaste asked.

That gleam in her eyes barely diminished at all, and she was, he realized, so sure of herself that she would not be dissuaded. "Then I suppose we'll see who comes out on top, won't we? Excuse me – I need to speak with the others." And she lessened her pace, falling back to speak with a human man with a series of scars across his forehead.

"You might not like who does," he muttered under his breath. But even if he'd said it fully to her face, he doubted it would have made the slightest difference.

CHAPTER 49

Cyrus
One Thousand Years Ago

"This is the wonder of Vaeretru," Terian said, voice infused with wild enthusiasm as the small party of adventurers slipped into the gaping entrance of the cave. It had started just beneath the curve of a box canyon carved into the landscape of spare weeds and the occasional tree girdling the lands south of the Inculta desert but just north of the bandit lands and the jungle beneath. The temperate air carried great moisture, and Cyrus had begun sweating the moment they'd appeared at the portal outside the human city of Taymor.

That had been two days ago, and he hadn't really stopped since.

"There had better not be any bloody temples on this expedition," Vaste proclaimed, not for the first time. "If I see so much as an altar to one of the gods with anything approximating a seal, I shall be casting the Return spell swifter than you can say 'Discount Brothel.'"

"If you do it faster than he could last in one, that'd be especially quick," Niamh said, her green eyes dancing. There was a wicked smile upon her full lips, and her red hair was aglow in the last light from the canyon.

"You wound me so, you bastards," Terian said, his enthusiasm not dimmed one jot, "but you won't stop me from enjoying this day. You know why?"

"Because you're properly drunk?" Andren asked, scruffy beard laying flat over his dirty white robe, his healers' vestments as grungy as the rest of his attire. He had a flask in hand, slightly drained, an amber liquid within. "As one should be on an expedition of this character and type."

Cyrus felt the urge to chuckle but resisted it. He hadn't laughed much in these last months. Not since Narstron had died. "Because he's excited to get out of the guildhall and be among friends – rather than accompanied by the likes of Orion and Brevis."

"That's part of it," Terian said, holding up a single finger, mailed in that dark armor of his, spiked and vicious-looking. "For I do grow so tired of the carping of children. But only a part, you see, for we have things to do, and ambitions to fulfill, and for Vaeretru–"

And with a flourish, he lit a glowing Nessalima's Light spell that cast brightness upon the interior chamber, illuminating white serrated columns of stalagmites and stalactites, a steady drip beating a maddening tempo.

"I feel a bit too much at home," J'anda Aimant said, the quiet enchanter loosing a breath only a step or two behind Cyrus. "Why must it so often be caverns?" With a wave of his hand, Cyrus saw a glow of magic, and then his vision filled out around the edges. A spell – Eagle Eye, he'd heard it called.

Cyrus gave him a glance, thinking at once of the depths of

Enterra, the place of tragedy that he'd seen only months before. "It's not all grimness in caves. I met Orion, Seleven, Vara, and Niamh in a cave, after all. Without them, I wouldn't be here." That brought a twinge, too, though; for if he hadn't, Narstron might still be alive.

"Point taken," Terian said. "Still – consider the riches in this one," and he waved a hand about. "And try and forget that we might occasionally pick up stragglers of such little worth that we're forced to drag them places against their will, like barnacles on a ship."

"Hey, we're hardly barnacles," Andren said. "More like that young human lass you pick up at the bar on a late evening, the one who's had her fill of workaday men and city guards, and is looking for something a bit more exotic? But after that night, she just wants to follow you about as though your efforts into the chamber pot smell like freshly baked bread?"

"I don't know quite what you mean by most of that," Vaste said. "But I do agree, all my contributions into a chamber pot smell like freshly baked bread with a hint of cinnamon tossed in for good measure."

"You've never taken advantage of young human women, jaded by their own kind?" Terian asked.

"They're just too intimidated by my stunning good looks, obviously," Vaste said. "They go running away to the less manly specimens that are more in their realm of attainability – like you two."

"J'anda, surely you know what I mean?" Terian said, looking to the enchanter.

"We should probably focus on the task at hand," J'anda said, his face a mask of discomfort that passed as quickly.

"I just want it to be said, for the ages, that you boys are swine taking advantage of young, impressionable human women like that," Niamh said, wagging her finger, blazing hair brighter than any color in the cavern. She spared a finger wag for Terian, then Andren, and finally turned to Cyrus, who blinked.

"Wait, why did I get included in this?" Cyrus asked.

"Because you're probably one of the men that helped jade those poor girls so much they would go running for comfort and excitement to these two lowlifes," she said, sending a reproachful glare back at Terian and Andren.

"Yes, when I think of 'comfort and excitement,' I think immediately of Terian," Vaste said, looking exaggeratedly at the dark knight's armor. "Especially the excitement that comes from being accidentally impaled, and the comfort that death would bring after bedding him."

"Did anyone hear that?" J'anda asked, cocking his head. "Or am I the only one paying any attention?"

"I hear the sound of a troll that needs to be solidly thumped with his own stave," Terian said, the playful edge still present in his voice.

"I heard something," Niamh said. "Hard-pressed to tell you what it is, though, especially under that drip. Like a scraping noise, rocks scratching against something."

"Not like footfalls," Andren said. "Or even the flap of wings. Those are distinctive."

Cyrus heard it too, suddenly. More like a rustling in the dark.

"I thought there were goblins in this cave?" Niamh asked.

"No, it was supposed to be imps," Terian said, He brought his axe up to a defensive posture. "Imps with treasure aplenty."

"This doesn't sound like an imp," Vaste said. "Or even a group of them. What would you call a group of imps, anyway? I vote for 'plague.'"

"I often hope for a plague when I adventure with you boys," Niamh said. "In some ways, I feel it would be more merciful."

Andren looked down at the tunnel. "Say, does anyone notice

a sort of distinctive track in these cave floors? Like the sand is arrayed in a bit of a moon-shape...?"

Cyrus looked, and he saw the pattern in the sand, seemingly cutting a curve into the dirt on the cavern floor. At the far end of the room in the cave depths, he could hear something drawing closer over the drip, a noise like sand running between fingers.

Then, from out of the depths of the far cave burst a snake so large as to make Cyrus think at first that it was a dragon, head huge enough to swallow a man whole. It turned its neck, and there, split from the first like a branch from a tree, was a second neck, and another head, just the same size.

"Isn't it marvelous?" Vaste asked. "We found something that can eat all of us in just three easy bites."

CHAPTER 50

Vara

"It's shut," Vara whispered, more to herself than Isabelle. She lay against the stone blocking the entry to the underground of Reikonos. Whoever had placed it here, they'd done a marvelous job. She doubted even the tenants of the building realized what had been buried here.

But it was here, and it was sealed, and with a thump against the stone she knew that doom had found them at last, that her hopes had indeed come to their natural conclusion.

Fires raged in every direction. They were held at bay by the wind that Isabelle had conjured, blowing the smoke away so Vara could see this – their end, in stony form. The end of their road, at least, and that meant their end. Their very own tomb, and yet they could not enter.

The air was hot and dry and full of the relentless malice of a city on fire. It meant to kill them, the last living things here, and Vara could see no way to deprive it of its demanded toll.

She rapped the stone, and it was hard and thick, feet of depth hinted at in the richness of the tone it made against her gauntlet. Tons of weight, her chances of moving it, dislodging it, pulling it out now, while she felt weaker than a newborn gnome – well, they were none.

This was it, then. With a hand on Ferocis, she gave it another rap with her knuckles, and it made not even a chip in the stone.

"What...what is it?" Isabelle called from the street. The white light that had surrounded her hand now glowed red, and the wind that had whipped around Vara was waning. Soon, her sister would run out of strength and the flames, fed by the winds, would reach their licking tongues down upon them, and it would be done.

"It's blocked," Vara rasped. Her throat felt so ill-used by all the smoke that she wondered if she could speak normally ever again – if by some miracle she lived.

"So open it."

"Would that I had such powers at my disposal," she mused, putting her cheek against the stone. It felt surprisingly cool, as though something other than heat, fire, and death waited beyond it. Life might be lived behind it, but she was on the wrong side of it. And soon, perhaps, on the wrong side of life, too.

"Break...through," Isabelle said.

Vara felt so enervated she wondered if she could find it in herself to walk at this point, even absent the flame. "How would I...?" She stared into the smoky dark, knowing her sister was there in the haze, her mind churning perhaps even slower than Vara's.

Break a stone? How would one even go about that?

Sure, in days of old it was possible. Strength – which she didn't have – could have been put to it. With sword work, maybe, it could be done.

Vara brushed her hand against Ferocis, and felt–

Well, a little strength remained, at least.

Drawing the blade, she lifted it up. The sword of Bellarum, the Warblade. She'd done a poor job of taking it to war, at least thus far. Now she was in a war for her very survival.

But there was strength in the blade, and she felt it, and somehow drew a breath that felt like hope.

Getting to one knee, she lifted the sword. Pulling it back, she brought it forth in a great stabbing motion. The tip of the blade, pushed weakly, for her, for it, still found purchase in the stony block.

The stone cracked, and the blade slid in almost an inch.

Vara breathed, and did not choke as much as usual. The wind was fading, and so was her time, but it was not over.

Not yet.

"I have been in direr straits," she whispered, mostly to herself. "I lay near death in Purgatory, a blade wound through my guts, thanks to Archenous." This was a story she told herself, and it seemed to give her strength, like having Ferocis in hand. She drew back the sword again, swung it forward in another stabbing motion—

It clinked, shattering chips of rock against her armor, and she turned her face down as they pinged off her helm. "And we all know what happened to him, that basta—"

She froze, the tip of the sword planted squarely in the stone. She peered at it; it was in a good, three, four inches.

With another breath – growing more choking all the time, she would need to hurry – she swung it back and stabbed once more, putting all her strength into it. She would need to be a bit deeper for it to work, and—

Now the blade was in six inches or so. A real six inches, a woman's-gauged six inches, not that estimated by a man. She held it steady there, and closed her eyes. "Isabelle?"

"...Yes?" the call was weak. Her sister was fading. The light was red, and she needed to ignore it.

"Cover your face. I'm about to make a mess."

With that, Vara cast a spell she'd cast more times than she could count, and put everything into it.

Force blast.

She felt it well within her body, placing all the desperation and fear and anger at what had happened to her, to Isabelle, to Sanctuary – and yes, maybe even to Cyrus – into it and felt it flow through her like the fire running through Reikonos–

It shuddered its way through Ferocis, perhaps picking up some small fragment of the power put there by a god, and it ran its way into the depths of that damned, impassable stone–

And the world exploded around Vara.

Rock and stone rang out across her body, finding the gaps in her armor and pattering her chainmail like rain on a metal roof. She was flung back again, but she kept her grip on her sword, and rattled as she landed a few feet away.

"Vara?" Isabelle's gasping, desperate call cried out to her from only a few feet away.

She crawled, crawled to Isabelle, using the strength of the sword. Finding her, she patted her on the side, got alongside her sister's face, and–

"Good gods," she said, finding a face that had aged ten years in human terms. Red light glowed from Isabelle's fingertips, and Vara knew there was no time to spare.

Seizing her sister around the waist, and keeping her weapon firmly in hand, she rose to her feet and charged forth as the last of Isabelle's spell-light died in her hand, and her body went limp in Vara's grasp. The wind fell away, and the flames that had been howling up turned–

Vara leapt like she had in days of old, using that glow of heated iron as her guide. If she was wrong, she would be jumping straight into a stony wall, and would shatter her sister upon it.

But the fire was raging down now, and she had seconds only

before it would consume the building whole and block the entry she hoped she'd just made.

They slid into a growing blackness, and the heat around them gave way to something cool, something stale, something old but not fiery–

And they flew into the darkness and hit hard, rolling as the desperate, hungry flames came searing down behind them, and the building collapsed, cutting off the tongues of fire and leaving them alone, gasping, in the dark.

CHAPTER 51

Alaric

The tower was nearing now, the *Yuutshee* approaching swiftly. The pirate ship paced them, a few hundred feet back to their left, high above, the iron hull glinting in the sun.

Puffs of smoke on the bow yielded puffs of dust from the tower. Alaric practically leapt up the three steps to the forecastle, finding the bow chaser crews still in constant operation. They were reloading frantically, a boom every dozen seconds the reward for their hard labor.

This, then, was the end; only one more shot was possible, and it was made with the crack of thunder. One ball struck the right side of the tower, stirring dust and stone. The tower creaked, barely audible beneath the sound of the airship, and then the *Yuutshee* was almost there, the tower a hundred feet ahead or less.

Mazirin's voice boomed over the deck. She shouted something first in her own language, then, "Brace yourselves!"

Alaric did not hesitate, throwing himself against the deck and swiftly grabbing hold of one of the metal handles embedded every few feet. The ship creaked sideways–

The *Yuutshee* seemed to thump against the tower. A rippling cloud moved up the tower's side as though the masonry were expelling dust, then–

It began to fall. Alaric looked up, and there was its terminus, so high in the air, tilting just so, toward the ironclad, dropping sideways–

It arced toward the ship, and the captain of the Chaarlandian vessel was shouting something. The tower crumbled, blocking Alaric's view and then...

...he was gone, dust billowing out, enshrouding the *Yuutshee* in a wave. It bloomed into Alaric's nose, down his throat, coating his tongue, spasming into a cough. He hung tight to his hold on the deck, the noise a roar, the dust like a cloud surrounding him.

Movement at his side betrayed the arrival of someone, and he turned to find Mazirin there, kneeling beside him on the leaning deck. "Did we get them?"

The dust was too much. Something crashed in the distance, the last pieces of the tower falling down somewhere behind them. "I think so," Alaric said. He raised his head; the sky was gray all before him now, residual dust trailing behind them, stirred by the *Yuutshee's* rotors.

But as the gray began to fade, the blue skies starting to peer through, and the outline of something large trailing close at behind them peeked like a shadow...

And as it cleared, Alaric could see the Chaarlandian captain's toothy grin, his leathers dusty, the ship covered in a thin layer of gray but still there, inching ever closer to catching them.

CHAPTER 52

Vaste

The hike was long and arduous and carried them well into the night. Vaste was left to wonder how far they'd come, how far they had still to go, and yet he didn't see a friendly face to ask. Aemma had vanished within the depths of their little army, and he daren't seek her out.

Qualleron, for his part, continued his engagement with the humans. The occasional laugh crackled over the quiet formation, hushed whispers as they crossed wood and hill, breaking here and there out into the open for long stretches under soft moonlight.

When day was coming and Vaste thought his feet could take no more, they made camp in a wood. No fires, it was ordered, and cold, greasy horsemeat was his meal, proffered by Qualleron, in dripping paper. The humans eyed it enviously, possessed only of small rations of jerky or minuscule wheels of cheese themselves. Tempted as he was to offer what he had to some other, instead he ate it silently, the bites sliding down his throat in a wet lump.

For a time, he slept, the sun streaming down above him through the leaves and boughs as day broke. The rustle of the trees coupled with not-so-gentle snoring from a few of the humans – and Qualleron, though his was mild compared to some of theirs – left him fitful. Whichever way he turned, he seemed to find a small stone in his back, and every time he rid himself of one another seemed to spring from the earth and find his back. When paired with the drenching sun fighting its way through in a mad attempt to pierce his eyelids, he found little rest in the copse, and turned restlessly for some time.

"Wake up." Someone kicked his boot close to nightfall, the sky peeking above the breaches in the canopy now orange with strains of purple. Sitting upright, he watched the human who'd kicked him awake move on to the next in the row and deliver similar treatment. If anything, it might have been less gentle, as though his waker had been afraid Vaste would murder him for dinner.

Tempting, Vaste thought. But he looked almost as thin and stringy as the horsemeat.

They began their walk minutes later, a quiet shuffle as the tired band broke their minimal camp and moved on, crunching their way through the woods. When they emerged onto a wide-open field, the howls of wolves in the distance seemed to echo under the rising quarter moon.

Far, far in the distance, he could see light on the horizon in the direction they were moving. Orange pinpricks in the distance, that was what he saw, and the shade cast on the clouds above as lantern light reflected against a nearby wall. The city itself was shrouded, over a dozen hills, off in the misty distance.

"It's Termina," Aemma said, for she had made her way to his side. "Have you ever been there?"

"I lived there for a short time," Vaste said, listening to the low rumble of Qualleron's laughter some two dozen paces or more behind him. Louder than anyone else in the band, that was certain. "In a manor house, on Ilanar Hill."

Aemma chuckled. "A fine jest."

"I'm not jesting," Vaste said. "I had a manor there."

Aemma's face was quite blank as she looked up at him. "Well...those manors are not sold, so if that were true, you would still have a manor there."

"I rather doubt it," Vaste said, and steeled himself for her reaction as he prepared to deal her another truth she would likely scorn: "It was a thousand years ago."

"Ah, yes," Aemma said, "this chestnut again."

"I can avoid this 'chestnut' in our future conversations if you like," Vaste said. "Since I very much doubt you believe it."

"I truly don't," Aemma said. "But I appreciate that you have the awareness to know I don't." She chuckled again. "Though as our guest, how about I humor you? Pray tell, how have you survived a thousand years?"

The whole sordid story flashed through his mind – Sanctuary, Cyrus Davidon, and the ether. "You know what? I don't think you'd believe a word of that, either."

"Too fanciful?"

"By many miles, yes," Vaste said. "If I were to set the story of my life down in verse, it would be regarded as the most improbable sort of fiction, the kind of tale you offer to that misbehaving child you wish would shape up."

"Full of imagination and of a cautionary nature?" Aemma seemed to be quite enjoying this.

"Well, I've certainly made enough serious errors of judgment and suffered enough for my mistakes that I would hope some caution emerged," Vaste said. "But mostly it's because of the magical elements and how much derided they are for you people these days."

"Why would I believe in magic?" Aemma asked, offering

another of her silvery laughs. "There is not a speck of proof that it exists."

"So if I did some form of magic right here, now, in front of you, you would say...?"

"Everyone has seen the tricks of street conjurers," Aemma said. "Fires in the palm of one's hand. A spray of water from out of the air. When pressed about the magic of ages past, they all say the same: some great hindering has come upon their craft. That they are not what they once were." She shook her head with a knowing smile pasted upon her lips. "It all sounds very much of a piece to me with the child who claims that he had naught to do with the disappearance of the sweets."

"I'm sorry you feel that way," Vaste said, "but I understand your skepticism." He cast Nessalima's Light, and let the faint orb glow from above his hand, hovering inches above his palm. "Magic is certainly not as easy as it used to be, and but a fraction as helpful."

Aemma's eyes caught the glow of the orb, and she reached out a hand to sweep her fingers through it. They passed neatly through the center of the illumination, casting shadows where her hand blocked the light. She played with it for a few moments, a childlike amusement on her face, until she stopped. "A pretty trick, but nothing more."

"How about fire?" Vaste snuffed the light and then cast a fire spell in his palm. Small, contained, he felt could maintain even this for some time without much effort. "As good as a street magician?"

"Better," she said, her face warmed by the orange glow. She almost missed a step as she passed her fingers through this one, then looked up in startlement. "It's hot!"

"It's...fire," Vaste said, regarding her as though she might be a simpleton. Then he threw the fireball away, snuffing it into the trunk of a nearby tree where it glowed for a few seconds before passing to embers that gradually lost their glow. "Did you expect it to be cold?"

"I assumed it was a trick of mirrors," she said, "though I see now it's probably a thing of gunpowder and flint."

"No, it's a thing of magic and me," Vaste said. "Though I see how your mind might interpret it more easily that way."

"My 'thoroughly modern' mind?" she asked with great amusement.

"Indeed," Vaste said. They were coming up on a hilltop now, and his body was straining, the ache of several days unmitigated by the soothing effect the ether had seemed to have on his bones. All sorts of magic were well missed now.

"Riddle me this, then," Aemma said. "If you have magic at your command, tell me what spell you have – not fire, not light – that would make a modern woman such as myself leave her practiced skepticism behind. For surely, if you have the craft of wizards from ages past at your disposal, even in some lessened state, you must have a spell that would amaze even me."

Vaste thought it over. He'd never been much good with enchantments, a branch of magic so convoluted and complex that even the most stunningly adept spellcasters he'd met, such as Curatio, seemed to eschew it, leaving it for only experts like J'anda. Druid spells were easy enough to cast, and crossed over quite a bit with the offerings of wizards, save the druidic branches that delved into animal control and wind in ways wizards did not bother. Similarly, paladins and dark knights had their own offerings, things he'd never troubled himself to learn once they'd become heretics.

There was that one thing, though, that Vara had taught him. It had taken a few dozen snorts of impatience, a fair amount of scoffing, and more than a few times she'd lost her temper, but that was to be expected for anything involving Vara.

"I do have this...particular spell," Vaste said, when he was able to pull his mind from Termina ahead, and Vara being there, hopefully, somewhere. "Could you pick up a stone?"

Aemma looked perplexed for but a moment, then lowered her gaze, sweeping the moonlit ground before them. They were treading through a dusty field, the hilltop just ahead, and she soon pronounced, "Ah ha!" and stooped, picking one up without missing so much as a step.

"Hold it flat on your palm," Vaste said. "Hand open."

She did just that, the stone perched in the middle of her hand, the moon shining down on it.

Vaste concentrated, trying to remember the words. They weren't important, really; behind them was a deeper construct, the ability, the faith and the trigger that let one access magic, in much the same way one pulled at a memory buried deep in the mind. It was only a small strain for him, and then–

Aemma let out a short, sharp scream as her hand was jerked to the side, the stone shooting off across the field with a WHUMP! as his Force Blast hit her. It was not nearly as refined as anything Vara could have produced, but it had some small effect, especially considering he was standing almost six feet away from her when he'd cast it, and had not drawn so much as an inch closer.

"How did you do it?" Aemma asked, shaking out her now-empty hand. She clenched her fist, as if testing to see if the stone were somehow still there and she was merely missing it with her eyes.

"I ran over there and slapped it out of your hand faster than your eye could follow," Vaste said.

She blinked. "Truly?"

"No, it was magic."

"Hm," she said, looking once again at her empty hand. "You may make a believer out of me yet...unless I can work out for myself how you did that."

"Well, good luck with that," Vaste said. "Because once you

eliminate magic as a possibility, any answer you come up with is destined to be...wrong..."

His words trailed off as he crested the hill and found the others in the band who had made it up before him stalled in their progress. Far ahead, the lights of Termina were clearer now, the mists subsiding in the moonlight, and the orange glare infinitely brighter.

Because it was not mere pinpricks in the dark night, but rather a glow in sections of the city.

Fires raged.

"I have seen these sights before in many a city," Qualleron said, standing tall upon the hilltop next to Vaste, speaking into the quiet unbroken by their human travel companions, who looked upon the destruction in silence. "It is never a good sight."

"It is the best sign of all," Aemma said, her voice full of awe. When Vaste looked up at her, he saw tears forming in the corners of her eyes, and one sliding slowly down her cheek in the sun. She looked at him, eyes gleaming, and in a voice of pure joy, she said:

"The revolution has begun."

CHAPTER 53

Shirri

They cut across the marketplace, Shirri trailing a step behind Calene, who walked with purpose and anger, but said nothing as she steamed like a train through the booths and stalls of ornate baubles and fine silks.

Walking past a fish stall and blanching at the smell, Shirri decided her feet had reached their limitations. "Can we slow a bit, please?" Her shoes were worn down, the first holes beginning to appear in them. It was surprising it hadn't happened sooner; after all, she'd been poor for a very long time. When had she even bought this pair of boots? Or had her mother made them? Shirri couldn't even recall that, anymore.

Calene slowed her pace. "Sorry," she said, voice tight, jaw a set line. "I know that probably didn't go as you hoped—"

"No, it did not," Shirri said. "But it might have gone about as I expected."

Calene's trim shoulders slouched. "Yes. About as well as I

expected, too." She turned her head to the fishmonger hawking his wares. "You can't say the name 'Cyrus Davidon' and the word 'return' in the same sentence and expect very many people – except the faithful, maybe – to do anything but roll their eyes."

"Oh, I know," Shirri said. "You must keep in mind – I'm the one who summoned them back, saw them first, and I didn't even believe it was truly them for...well, quite some time. Bit hackneyed, isn't it? Cyrus Davidon returning in our hour of need?"

Calene hesitated. "In truth...it's a moment I've long awaited. Though perhaps I didn't believe it ever would come. I thought as Gareth did, really. That he'd just...died somewhere, a thousand years ago. Because if he was alive..." A torrent of emotions began to play just beneath the surface of her scarred face. "...how could he have just let the scourge have their way with Arkaria unanswered?"

"He was with Sanctuary, and blind to it," Shirri said. "They all were."

"What did he...what was he like when you saw him?" Calene asked with a trace of hope. "It's been long, I just...I don't even know if I remember what he looks like anymore."

"Oh," Shirri said. "Well...not like his statues."

"I do recall that being the case," Calene said. "They're quite monstrous, those. A bit too handsome, as I recall?"

"Yes, he's no beauty," Shirri said. "That might have been one of the reasons I didn't believe it was him at first. He's tall, true – stunningly so, even. But not very handsome. The scar around his neck is particularly horrifying–"

"Mmmmm," Calene nodded, arms crossed over her lithe body. "I remember when he got that one. It was Luukessia where that happened. We'd just come back from the north, where we first encountered the scourge and – well, never mind." She blushed upon her swarthy cheeks, though it was hard to see it save in the lines of the scars. "The point is...I remember a little better now, thank you. He wasn't handsome but he was...magnetic, I suppose."

"Aye, there was a zest from him that transcended his mere looks," Shirri said. "At least once Alaric talked him out of his desperation."

"Oh, you met Mopey Cyrus, too," Calene said. "But he did...?"

"Come out of it? Yes," Shirri said. "Quite well, in fact. He was in motion, in action, all the way up to the end, I think. Even after the revelation of his son, and Vara leaving him—"

"His...son?" Calene asked.

"With some dark elven woman," Shirri said. "He called her 'eyes' or something of that—"

Calene's own eyes lit up. "'Ais?' As in 'Aisling?'"

"That sounds right, yes. Of course you'd know her, being of that—"

"Oh!" Calene made a pained face. "Oh. Ohhhhhhh." It became steadily more pained with each spoken addition. "Yes. I bet Vara was furious. Madder than even getting killed probably did to her."

"None of this talk matters, I suppose," Shirri said. "What should we do, now that we've spent ourselves trying to convince your friend and failed?"

Calene stood still and considered. "Well, that's not my only in with the Amti government. I have others, and we can go see one of them right now, it's just..." and here she looked almost pained, "...this next one, while perhaps a more useful fellow than Gareth, is young, and it will be a bit more of a stretch to get him to believe..."

CHAPTER 54

Cyrus

Waking from the dream of the caves, of the two-headed snake, was a less gentle thing than Cyrus might have hoped for. It came with a prickling whisper in the back of his head, the dim remembrance of the day itself, when they had gone to Vaeretru.

"They were better in my memory than my nightmare," Cyrus muttered, sitting upright in the chair, parked in the corner of his room in the palace of Saekaj. The cool, slightly wet cave air made him feel sweaty, and the sound of Niamh breathing on the bed only increased his feeling surreal unease. Her gray, pallid flesh was almost a nightmare of its own.

How had she become this...this thing, so far removed from what she'd been in life? He felt vaguely sick at the sight of her, wrinkled skin and terrible smell.

And whose fault was that?

Cyrus froze; the thought leapt out at him, almost foreign, a whisper in his mind that came in a voice that was unlike his own.

Only a fool could look at all I've done and not have a twinge of regret, Cyrus thought. *Could look at all my choices and not wonder how things might have gone better if I'd done the exact opposite of what I decided. Vara – gone, and who can blame her? My friends – dead nearly to the last,* and here he looked at Niamh – *or perhaps wishing they were. And Arkaria?*

He looked around the cavern walls, saw the sheen of perspiration on them, the cavern sweating.

Do you always ponder your failures in your sleep? a voice seemed to whisper at him.

Shaking the thought away, Cyrus stared at the creases in the stone of the far wall. How could he not, though? There were so many.

Cyrus, the whisper came again, that same voice, but louder.

He sat up straighter in the chair; on the bed, Niamh stirred, lifting her great, gray head. Her black eyes lolled around to him questioningly.

"Did you hear that?" he asked, and the hiss echoed through the chamber once more.

Cyrus...

This time, though, he recognized it.

"Malpravus."

CHAPTER 55

Vara

"Well, now what the hell do we do?"

The question rang out in the empty crypt of the tunnels, silent and foreboding. Beyond the fallen sections of stone and building that had collapsed, covering the entrance they'd used, there was a faint crackling of fire working its way through wood and cloth, burning through the fuel that had been the city of Reikonos.

Vara had asked the question mostly to herself, but it had popped out aloud. A part of her wondered if maybe she hadn't merely wanted to say it, to see what Isabelle thought about it all.

She was not answered at first, and when she cast Nessalima's Light, she found her sister's eyes closed, and her chest moving slowly up and down.

"Damn," Vara whispered.

"Just give me a moment," Isabelle said slowly. There were lines at the corners of her eyes, a warning about overexerting one's self in these days of weakened magic. She stirred, but only feebly. "I think I might have poured out a few thousand years of life just now in keeping that fire off us."

Vara held back a sobering reply about how losing a thousand was probably better than the potential nearly twelve thousand they had between them, but it was glib and snide and stupid at a moment when Isabelle had literally given a part of her life for Vara's idiocy, and so she held her tongue. Instead, taking hold of Ferocis by the hilt, she rose, sliding a look left, then right, trying to peer into the darkness.

There was little to see; the catacombs below Reikonos had not changed in a thousand years. The old patterns and colors were still present from the days of the ancients ten thousand – no, eleven thousand, now – years ago. It seemed unlikely they would change much still in the time hence, outlasting the city that had been built above them twice. If the land above became populated again – and surely it would, given enough time – it was entirely probable that those settlers would eventually find these dark and empty places beneath their streets.

The only question on Vara's mind was whether they'd find the two elves sheltering beneath them or not, still here.

"We can wait a few days for the fires to burn out," Vara announced, pacing ten yards down the tunnel, listening for anything other than the sounds of a civilization falling into ash behind her. "Subsist upon conjured bread and water, which surely we shall be able to make happen between the two of us. Then we'll emerge once the flames have subsided, and find a ship passing over." She nodded once to herself, decided. "Yes. That's what we'll do."

"Don't...be so sure about the conjured supplies," Isabelle said, her voice dragging as though she were about to drift off. "Have you tried casting that spell since arriving here?"

"No," Vara said, looking down at her gauntlet, suddenly a bit worried. "Do you wish to tell me something about it, seeing as I have nearly exhausted myself merely on two force blast spells?"

"Like so many other spells, it doesn't work particularly well these days," Isabelle said. "Instead of conjuring a loaf of bread, you spend all your magical energy for a few crumbs...and then you're too weary to regenerate."

"Bloody hell, this age is a nightmare," Vara said.

"Even before Malpravus unleashed the most powerful spell seen in over a thousand years, yes," Isabelle said. "Never should have–"

To this, Vara rolled her eyes. "Come back. Yes, I know. But you did, and I did, and here we are stuck trying to find our way to survive."

"Well, I very much doubt anything in these tunnels will sustain us," Isabelle said with what was probably an attempt at a great, harrumphing sigh. It came out pathetic, as though she were already on death's door, which – hopefully – she was not.

"There is still, beneath the Citadel, a place for us to go," Vara said. "Several realms lie through that portal, places of power–"

"Which Malpravus has surely been serially draining for a thousand years," Isabelle said, looking up at her, her eyes snapping into focus. "I am sure it is not lost on you that this was undoubtedly one of the reasons for his selection of Reikonos as his headquarters?"

"It was mentioned," Vara said, fairly certain it had been discussed after they'd discovered Malpravus's identity. "But surely you don't think he's–"

"Left them all withered and consumed?" Isabelle asked. "I have no idea. I would not put it past him."

"The gods drank from those places for ten thousand years," Vara scoffed. "You cannot believe that Malpravus, fractionally powerful and practiced as any of them, could have drained them dry in a mere thousand?"

"I have no idea," Isabelle said, pushing herself to a sitting position, her dirty, ashen robes hanging limply from her, her knees coated in freshly scabbed blood. "The rules of magic have changed, sister mine. I would not care to speculate how much or how little he might have done in that time."

"Well," Vara said, offering her a hand, "there is only one way to be sure, and it is not sitting here, speculating in the darkness."

Isabelle's eyes reflected the tiredness that had fallen on her, perhaps even before things had gone so wrong above. She sighed and somehow pushed to her feet. A wave of her hand brought a white light that turned suddenly red, and she shuddered, coughing once more, but perhaps a bit more clearly for the healing spell. "Very well, then." And she held Vara's arm as if she were an old woman, ready to be escorted along. "Let us see for ourselves."

CHAPTER 56

Alaric

"How far to the coast?" Alaric asked, though he felt sure he already knew. The Chaarlandian ship was cutting through the last of the dust cloud, looming over them like a lion in mid-leap over its prey.

"An hour or so," Mazirin said, stricken, standing at his side. Her coat was gray from the dust, and it highlighted her raven hair.

The Chaarlandian shouted something. "He speaks your language?" Alaric asked.

"Almost everyone does," Mazirin said. "At least well enough to be understood."

Another shout from above. The Chaarlandian ship seemed to have lost some distance on them in the fall of the tower, but it was gaining again, slowly.

"It was a worthy effort," Alaric said, almost as much to himself as to her.

"I think we can make the southern coast before they catch us," Mazirin said. "They may still be persuaded to remove themselves from the chase then."

Alaric stared at the captain above and behind. The grin was too feral, too cocksure. "Perhaps," he said, though he did not believe it.

Another shout above, and Alaric waited. This one sounded different.

"I have to go," Mazirin said, and turned to the quarterdeck, clearly looking to return.

"What did he say?" Alaric asked, and she hesitated.

The Chaarlandian bow chaser boomed again, and a cannonball arced down onto the *Yuutshee*, an easier shot than any they'd made before. It struck the quarterdeck, and the port stern chaser exploded along with the rail, and a hailstorm of splinters swallowed the quarterdeck.

Alaric, hand upon Aterum, grabbed Mazirin and threw her down, putting his armored form atop her as the hail of wood motes dinged across his helm, across his armor. Two tiny pinpricks in the vicinity of his neck told him some got through, though they were small enough not to be bothered about. They stung and little else, trickles of blood welling at his neck.

The quarterdeck was smoking, dust hanging in the air. With one hand, Alaric pulled Mazirin to her feet. She caught herself unsteadily, as though afraid the deck might shift at any moment. Peering into the gloom, Alaric stared–

The wheel was unmanned, and there were bodies scattered upon the quarterdeck.

As he watched, the wheel began to turn, and the *Yuutshee* began to tack directly toward the pirate ship.

CHAPTER 57

Vaste

Their pace quickened after the sight of Termina burning greeted them on that hilltop. Not a word was spoken to hasten them, but hastened they were, nonetheless.

Aemma led the way, hustling them through valley and over hilltop, the others following behind. Scarcely a breath was drawn where some sunny statement was not made that was kin to: "I hope we're showing those damned elves properly," or, "I bet we've got them about driven out of the city by now."

Qualleron held his tongue and his laughter, and Vaste did too, and probably for the same reason.

Their night walk became a march, and a much more forceful one than Vaste could recall from most of his endeavors with Sanctuary. Sure, they'd done the odd walk to Gren or some place too difficult to reach by horse, but mostly they rode or used a teleportation spell. Even an airship or a train would have been a welcome change now.

But he walked on through the night, not daring to complain. And with each hilltop they crested they grew closer to the fires, though no clearer picture emerged of what was happening in the burning city.

The moon had reached its zenith and begun its long path to setting when they came over the final hilltop and found themselves looking down into the city proper. Houses and farmsteads spread before them in a sprawl, but the city walls were lit by the moon and the fires, and the largest buildings visible from here, obvious to the eye.

"The Chancel," someone said. "It's burning."

"Damn," Vaste muttered. The Chancel had been the holiest building in the city, the center of Vidara worship for at least Termina, and possibly for every place north of Pharesia's influence. It was certainly burning, too; the grand dome in its center looked as though it might have caved in – again. It had happened in the dark elven sack, and seeing it thus had been quite disheartening even to Vaste, who cared little for the goddess but was mightily impressed by the architecture.

"I told you it had begun, didn't I?" Aemma turned her back, hurrying down the hill. Her pace quickened yet more, boots treading swiftly on the well-worn path.

Soon they reached houses, and with it, a road; their progress over open fields and hills was at end, and they passed houses with the windows covered and a grim pall prevailing in the early morn. "Let us keep as quiet as possible," Aemma announced when they found themselves on a main avenue into the burning heart of the city.

"Whatever is going on seems to be confined to the city proper," Vaste said, taking a long, sweeping look around. Every house was boarded up, the windows shut against troubles. "Though this I find interesting."

"What's that?" Aemma asked. He was keeping pace with her easily; or at least keeping up to a step or two behind her, not wanting to walk abreast and see the demonic glow from her excitement over something that was undoubtedly causing the death of many.

"The windows being boarded," Vaste said. "That's not a simple thing, you know. Not everyone keeps them on hand, yet I've seen perhaps one house out of the twenty or thirty we've passed that is uncovered. This suggests a certain amount of planning, does it not? Preparation, at least."

"This has been brewing for some time," she said. "The writing was on the wall – and in ten-foot flaming letters, no less."

"Yes, I understand tensions and boiling points and all those convenient metaphors for describing the horrors of war," Vaste said. "My point is merely – is this town well mixed?"

This puckered her brow. "What do you mean?"

"Humans and elves. Do they live next door to one another, as neighbors?"

Aemma gave that silvery laugh, a mark of the absurdity of his question. "Good heavens, no."

"Is this an elven area or a human one?"

"Elven," she said. And the first glimmer of uncertainty appeared with her then, and he knew she'd taken his meaning.

"Then they were ready for this," Vaste said.

"As I said, it's been building for some time," Aemma said, and turned away from him.

They went on. The fires drew ever closer, but not, seemingly, to them. The buildings grew taller as they walked, and here and there, on an upper floor, Vaste saw faces peering down. No words were spoken, though the noise grew as they proceeded into the city proper and could smell the smoke on the wind.

"What's burning?" one of the men asked as they reached a cross street. The fine stone buildings of the outskirts had given way to grander and grander constructions. Ahead, Vaste could see the government center. It stood like a silent, unpleasant, blocky sentinel in the middle of a square. The road curved its way to it, and behind it...

...A whole section of the city burned.

"That's Var'eton," Aemma said, a tone of disbelief infusing her words. "That's...a human area."

"Var'eton...and the Chancel," Vaste said, still seem the orange glow upon a ceiling of smoke that covered the city. There was a haze in the air, but the wind was pushing it east, over the river and to the scourge-covered wastes of Eastern Arkaria.

"What is happening here?" Aemma whispered as they hurried down the street.

"If I might suggest?" Vaste seized her by the arm and held her back. The others of her band surged past, flowing around them, and he looked down into her eyes, finding them again misty with tears, but for a different reason. The men were grunting, curses under their breath florid and filled with heat.

None of that was present in Aemma. She merely stared at him, joy turned to sorrow. "What?" she asked, but much of the life had gone out of her now.

"I think your people might have started a fight at the Chancel," Vaste said. "Maybe even...destroyed it?"

She looked down, then nodded. "It was a symbol of elvendom in a way their dreadful government building was not. The square is thrice the size of that there," and she waved a hand around the tiny – by comparison – governmental center ahead. "Yes. Any sort of revolt...it would start there, not here."

"Then something happened," Vaste said. "They were ready."

"They couldn't be," she said, and now she looked up, tears coursing down her face. "How–"

"You said yourself it's been building for a while," Vaste said. Qualleron stopped beside him and was listening; the other men were still hurrying up the street, paying the laggardly three no mind, and Vaste was in no hurry to catch them as they charged ahead. "The people in the elven quarters have boarded their windows. You don't do that for no reason. Trouble was expected – and when trouble started, they were ready."

Aemma turned her eyes slowly to the governmental center, silhouetted as it was by the fires burning behind in the Var'eton. The Lowers; that was what Var'eton meant.

"Perhaps," Aemma said, finally, reluctantly. "Perhaps there is truth to what you say. Perhaps they were ready and–"

Shouts down the street silenced her, and Vaste snapped his head 'round to look. The men of their band had run for four blocks while he'd talked to Aemma, and now they were hemmed in, suddenly blocked by figures with silvery armor glinting in the firelight, winged helms catching the sheen of orange, the fire's glow making them look like devils in the night.

"The Termina Guard," Vaste said, watching them swoop in from the streets on either side like falcons upon a field mouse. The guard blocked their sight of the human men, and the glint of metal by firelight was all Vaste could see, swords and spears rising and falling, thrusting and–

"No – NO!" Aemma shouted, and started forth.

Vaste seized her around the waist and hauled her back. There were a hundred, two hundred elven soldiers, armored, ready, falling upon thirty or less unarmored humans. A few shots rang out, a few cries echoed down the street, and then gave way to grunts and screams, and the sound of stabbing weapons.

"This fight is over," Qualleron said.

"Agreed," Vaste said, and dragged Aemma back the way they came.

The screams did not last long, and by the time they stopped, the three of them were already down an alleyway and out of sight of the street.

CHAPTER 58

Cyrus

"Where the hell are you, you pile of bones?" Cyrus asked, looking around. It wasn't as though he expected the necromancer to be here, actually here, in his room. He half expected an animal skull mounted on the wall to be the means of transmission for Malpravus's bile. Upon the bed, Niamh twitched, her black eyes gleaming in the darkness. She, perhaps could feel the disquiet brought by the disembodied speech.

"I am here," Malpravus whispered, "and there. And everywhere you look. I am in the colors of the rainbow that bends across the sky, in the rustle of the leaves in the park in Termina. The crash of the sea upon the shores of the Emerald Coast – I am everywhere, Cyrus, thanks to you and your friends."

"Wonderful," Cyrus said, slowly getting to his knees to look under the bed. There were no odd shapes beneath it, no skulls waiting. With a whisper of breath, he cast Nessalima's Light and watched the soft, white glow confirm that beneath was merely, a flat, chiseled cave surface and nothing more. "That's what we've needed all this time, a power-mad lunatic with a god complex to be watching our every move."

"I will do my very best not to catch you on the chamber pot," Malpravus said. "But I make no promises."

Cyrus lifted his hand, shedding light across the walls. A few blankets of shiny silk hung upon one wall; the other had a relief carved into the very rock, a sculpture of a battle scene imbued with great – surprisingly great – detail. After peering at it for a moment, he actually recognized it. "What the...?"

"A pitiful reproduction, no?" Malpravus's voice leaked from somewhere within the sculpture.

Cyrus leaned in, looking closer. The action upon the relief was questionable, a wall carving of heroes and soldiers in poses that looked nothing like his remembrance of the event, and yet there, in the center, was a tall warrior wearing his armor, fighting against Kalam the dragon. Far, far behind him stood a skeletal figure in robes: Malpravus. "At least I look better in this one than you do."

"History is written by the victors," Malpravus said, "but keep in mind that victory is a temporary condition – as was defeat, for each of us, truly. What matters is power, and the final victory. Cyrus..."

"I thought we were past this," Cyrus said, pushing back from the relief, the cold stone wall. "You did try and kill me. Repeatedly. Recently."

"Yet you survived," Malpravus said. "Which compels me to look once more at you, to question myself because of my failure, however temporary. Your will to live, to succeed, it matches my own. Imagine what we might accomplish united, for once."

"You'd have to really alter your plans for that to happen," Cyrus said, mind moving swiftly. "Because you know I'm not on board for destroying cities."

"Sometimes I feel you don't listen to me at all," Malpravus said, the disembodied voice presenting a definite sigh. "Power, lad. Power is what gives you the chance to survive my machinations. Power is what gives you the uncanny ability to halt me in my tracks. I always considered it curious how you were drawn to such weak people. Defending them, partnering with them. Yet still you persisted in this deranged strategy. But I see it now; it was a strategy, after all. To draw power from the crowds, loyalty, love, even. Not a thing I'd ever considered–"

"You've never known love? Color me shocked."

"–Yet you opened my eyes to the possibility that people had something worth contributing to the quest for power beyond the ability to demagogue them," Malpravus said. "Of course I refined your strategy a bit." A light cackle echoed through the room, making Niamh twitch once more. "What do you think of my implementation?"

"I think you're deranged," Cyrus said. "I think you've had nothing on your mind but power for so long that you don't see a dead city is an empty place to spend your endless life."

"It isn't as though I see no value in any people at all," Malpravus said. "But even you must admit that the vast majority of those chattering animals you work so hard to protect, to channel your efforts into pleasing and saving – they are little more than herd creatures, fit for eating in an emergency, and with all the thinking power of a cow or a pig."

"I hear pigs are quite bright, actually," Cyrus said; he'd realized at the last the voice was not disembodied at all. It was coming from behind the chair where he'd been sitting. "And that you've determined that living people are little more than grist for your magical mill is a reflection of you, Malpravus, of your ruthless utilitarian approach to life, your smug belief that you are superior, that all else should sit below you in the hierarchy of your need and desire." He approached the chair slowly, drawing his sword. "It is a cheerful elitism, and your lack of pretense is, I suppose, refreshing after a fashion given the thinly disguised and more sneering version of it I saw from such luminaries as the gods and Pretnam Urides."

"I am elite because I am, in fact, better than any of these so-called people you seem to love," Malpravus said. "Do you not see the emptiness in their eyes as they toil about doing little and accomplishing even less? They have no power, no thoughts of their own. Prey for the hunters, that's all they are. There are no thoughts behind the mask of their eyes, only the dull look one might expect from an insect buzzing about its business. Why should I concern myself with the feelings of the swarm?"

"If you have no foundation for seeing living beings as having some inherent worth...if their thoughts, however great or small carry no value for you, then there is nothing I can say that will allow you to see things differently," Cyrus said. "Your determination is made; all are less than you, all beneath your feet, and you'll act accordingly to put them in their place. Or worse – beneath the ground."

"You are already beneath the ground, Cyrus, but your point is taken," Malpravus said. "It's a grave you're in, all right. A grave I feel a need to dig you out of, give you one last chance to present yourself with the unvarnished truth – that some are better than others. Some are more powerful than others. Smarter than others. And that gives them the right and the duty to rule, and, if needed, to take from those weak and inadequate souls to make a truly better world for those who matter." A sigh of discontent rippled through the room. "It grieves me, but I don't see this including you."

"I'm relieved to hear that," Cyrus said, reaching behind the chair and coming up with an old animal skull, something that looked to be from ages past. "I would not wish to live in a world that includes only those chosen by you to inhabit it, for it would be sad and small, and empty of all but a very few indeed."

The door behind him clicked, and Cyrus turned. Niamh

leapt off the bed, interposing herself between the door and him, though it did little good—

Terian was inside in a moment, axe in hand, and brushed Niamh aside. He pointed the blade at Cyrus, and his eyes were narrowed in his helm. "Who were you talking to?" Hongren was a step behind him, the shipmaster's face all malicious triumph; he had some part of this, Cyrus was sure.

"Me, of course," Malpravus's voice sounded in the room.

The animal skull rattled, and Cyrus crushed it in his gauntlet, sending bone chips raining over the floor. "Boring conversation anyway," Cyrus said.

Terian's eyes narrowed further; he did not appear in a believing mood. "Of course." And with a look at Cyrus, accusing, he pointed his axe once more. "Come with me. Now."

CHAPTER 59

Vara

The tunnels were dark, and the light was needed the deeper they went. Vara had not realized how the faint, seeping glow and residual heat had made their way through the collapsed entry, but they had been present there. Now, the deeper they went, the more reliant even their elven eyes were upon the Nessalima's Light spell Vara had projecting from her fingertips, a mere sliver of what it had been a thousand years ago.

Still, it was enough. And the turns and twists that led them through the subterranean labyrinth were familiar, still, perhaps more to her than Isabelle, who leaned against her and sighed every few steps in exhaustion. Her sister had not fared well above, and in spite of several healing spells, there was little to be done for the wheezing cough she'd acquired in the flames.

For her part, Vara could still feel that poison in her chest. It felt tight, constricted, and the coughing was prodigious.

Still, there was nothing to be done for it, so she went on, shouldering as much of her sister's weight as she could carry – which was nearly all – and kept them moving onward. The stale air sustained her, returning a portion of her strength sapped by the smoke outside.

The tunnel opened into a wide chamber soon enough, and here there was a faint glow that allowed her to douse that draining spell and go by what they could see naturally. In the center of the cavernous, ovoid room was the thing that Vara had hoped to find–

The portal.

And it was aglow! Orange light flared out of its middle, enough degrees off the color of firelight not to unsettle her.

With care, she set Isabelle down and approached slowly. "What do you suppose it's set for?" Vara asked.

"Probably some miserable place that Malpravus has made his own," Isabelle said, collapsing onto her back. "The Realm of Storms, maybe? Winter?"

"I have never seen either," Vara said, looking at the orange swirls in the center of the portal. They looked like ripples on the water, and oh, how she wanted a drink.

"Ask your husband about them when next you see him," Isabelle said. "He destroyed them both."

"I thought you said he was dead?" For this, Vara managed both a mischievous smile and a slight turn of her head so her sister could see.

"He assuredly is," Isabelle said without moving. "I assume we will be joining him shortly. Ask him then."

"Hmph," Vara said, turning her attention back to the portal. "If he destroyed them, there is likely not easy transit to and from them any longer. So...I think not. If we are to voyage in, I think it would be best if we visited somewhere a bit less likely to kill us." The idea occurred, of course. "Somewhere...perhaps a bit familiar."

"To who? You?" Isabelle asked. "Because I'm familiar with all these places. Realm of Fire, of Air, Earth, Water. I've been to all, seen all, ventured – oh, you didn't mean those, though, did you?" Through clear great effort, she sat up. "You mean one you've been to."

"Indeed," Vara said. "I was thinking of Vidara's realm."

Isabelle's mouth was a dour line. "You know she betrayed us, yes? Before the end?"

"I do dimly recall hearing something of it," Vara said, inspecting the runes at the edge of the portal.

"Didn't you also have a terrible experience in her realm when last she was gone?"

"Why, yes, I did," Vara said, tracing her fingers over the runes in the stone. The patterns were intricate, like something out of elven craftsmanship. "Why do you ask?"

"Because given that," Isabelle said, propped on her elbow, "Why would you choose to retreat there? Into a land of vicious, uncontrolled winter and devilish beasts?"

"We don't know that it'll be like that when we arrive," Vara said, her inspection of the runes at an end. They were lines, they were symbols, and to her they meant precisely nothing. "Last time they were that way because the Goddess had been kidnapped, and Yartraak's fell influence had come over the place."

"Yes," Isabelle said with more than a little sarcasm, "it's the realm of a goddess dead, who breathed her last betraying your husband and friends. How can it be anything but wild and untrammeled, filled with things that mirror the desire of the Goddess herself before her end?"

"Well, what are our other options?" Vara asked. "Would you care to step into the Realm of Fire? Surely we'll find sustenance there – if you fancy eating lava on rocks. Speaking of – how about the barren tunnels of the Realm of Earth, that delight dwarves and no one else? No? Air, then? Should be a lark, seeing as we are no longer capable of casting the Falcon's Essence spell. I wonder if we'll merely plummet forever, or if there is some sort of natural ground below that we would eventually smash into."

"Your points are annoying," Isabelle said, "but taken."

"Can you imagine what the Realm of Fire would look like in a corrupted state?" Vara asked. "I cannot imagine it would possess something even so docile as angry, soul-blackened chipmunks. Fire elementals and rock giants with a spirit of destruction? I shudder to imagine. It might well make Reikonos just now look like a pleasant oasis by comparison."

"Fine," Isabelle sighed. "In this battle of ideas, I feel I must submit and allow you to lead me somewhere so much worse than my present circumstances – again."

"Now, now," Vara said, offering her a hand, "where's your sense of hope? Of optimism?"

"I think I left it either in Termina or on the airship." Her eyebrows, blackened with soot, were turned down. "Or perhaps it was burned out of me at the sight of that great spell destroying the city above."

Vara paused after lifting her to her feet and shouldering some of her sister's weight. "This is not the end."

"No," Isabelle said wryly, "as I said before, I expect things will get much worse before the actual end."

"What a downer you've become in your old age," Vara muttered. "All right – speak the words of the spell, and I'll cast it."

"It's not that easy," Isabelle said, sighing once more. "I'll do it."

"No, you will not," Vara said. "You've lost a minimum of a thousand years of life today. Say the words, I'll take them up and cast it. There's no need for you to start looking like an elven priestess on the far side of the Turn for a simple spell like this."

"You win again," Isabelle said. *"Eleni, iliara, eyalastar."*

Vara spoke the words allowed, concentrating all her energy on them.

The ripples in the center of the portal subtly changed, as did its shading, becoming a deep and vibrant green, like grass in summer.

Vara braced her sister against her. "Very well. Are you ready?"

"Almost certainly not," Isabelle said, and her voice still scratched with the deep-seated smoke that had taken their breaths away. "But as that has been true all day, I don't see why I should use it on this occasion as a reason to stand athwart our next step into oblivion."

"Yes, onward into oblivion," Vara said, drawing Ferocis in her free hand and moving into the portal, leaving the dark tunnels and slow death behind them in favor of an uncertain future.

CHAPTER 60

Alaric

Mazirin leapt out of Alaric's grasp. "There's no one at the helm!" she shouted, sprinting for the quarterdeck.

The *Yuutshee* was drifting in a slow turn toward the Chaarlandian pirate, threatening to cut beneath her. No good could come of that, at least in Alaric's estimation; while they might have been out of the line of fire, other possibilities loomed. The Chaarlandian ship could, for instance, decrease its altitude and crush them like a horse's hoof upon a gnome.

He pounded up the stairs with Mazirin, finding naught but carnage for his trouble. The helmsman was a shredded mess, and the port stern chaser and the rail were both gone for ten feet around the back corner. Blood and strings of meat remained as the sole evidence the gun crew had ever been there.

Mazirin seized the helm and righted the ship with a jerk, pulling hard on the spoked wheel and sending them slewing to the right. Pieces of debris slid off the back of the *Yuutshee* to join that graveyard of detritus below. The stump of Vernadam's tower was barely visible behind them, shrinking by the moment as they crawled forward across the dusty sky.

"That was not good," Mazirin said through clenched teeth as she manhandled the wheel with great effort. A backward glance confirmed that, yes, the Chaarlandians were still behind them and above, the unexpected turn having given them some ground.

"Captain!" Dugras's head appeared just below the quarterdeck railing. "We've got some kind of problem with shaft one. Propulsion is down to one half."

Alaric looked to Mazirin for guidance, but all he saw was the strain in her face as she wrestled the wheel for control of the ship. "Fix it," she said, but it was less an order and more a cry for help.

Dugras merely shook his head. "Whatever happened...it's on the outside, probably debris against the propeller from that last hit. I can't fix it from within. Had to shut it down."

"Then go over the back and fix it!" Mazirin shouted.

Alaric shook his head and hurried toward the back rail, which ended about halfway across the quarterdeck. With care, he tested it at the end. It was still anchored well just before it ceased, so he put his weight upon it, leaning over the back of the ship–

There. Twin propeller shafts jutted from the back of the *Yuutshee*, and one of them had a tangled fragment of the quarterdeck and railing resting upon it, clearly having simply fallen during the last cannonade. Careful not to overextend himself, Alaric took careful aim. Whispering words he'd long ago committed to memory, the Force Blast spell leapt from his palm and stirred the debris.

Stirred, but did not drop it.

He grunted, and took a breath, steadying his aim. He whispered the words again, and loosed another–

This one hit hard against the edge, unbalancing it. It creaked, leaning right, and while it did so, he cast again, adjusting his aim to the side. The debris unbalanced and shattered, falling piecemeal off the shaft and safely away from the ship.

"Nicely done." Dugras was beside him, taking care to lean over without putting any weight upon the damaged rail. "That ought to do it. I'll go get the engine restarted." And he scampered away.

"For now," Alaric said, and he looked up.

For the Chaarlandian ship was still there, and closer than when last he'd looked, and it did not seem it would ever get farther away.

CHAPTER 61

Vaste

Aemma stopped struggling against Vaste once they were off the main avenue. They dodged down an alley, then down another, hurrying into the dark, no lamplight leaking out of the windows or barred doors to speed them along. Vaste had cast Eagle Eye upon them, though it seemed much reduced in its usefulness.

The distant shouts and cries were directionless now, lost in the warren of alleys they wove their way through. Vaste was moving, consciously, toward higher ground, a plan in his mind even as he gently prodded Aemma forward on numb legs. She made no noise, simply moved as he directed, rudderless in a way he had not seen her in their brief acquaintance.

Smoke wafted past like mist, and they reached a main thoroughfare. Pausing momentarily to look either way, Vaste shoved her gently to the right and they followed the curve of the hill upward, ever upward.

"You seem to know this city well," Qualleron said.

"It hasn't changed in a thousand years," Vaste said. "Which is fortunate for us." A shout some distance behind him made them all swivel, but it was a shadowy figure running across the street several blocks down. He was swarmed and overwhelmed by several shiny, armor-clad figures with winged helms, and once more the swords rose and fell in a clear slaughter. "On the other hand...maybe it has changed a bit."

"Where are we going?" Aemma asked through a scratchy voice.

"Remember how I mentioned I had a manor on Ilanar Hill, and you said they wouldn't have sold it?" A shout behind him made Vaste pause; it was far down the avenue, and the armored figures were moving farther away, taking no note of them here, scurrying through the darkness. "Well, we're about to test that assumption."

"What if they have sold it?" Qualleron asked.

"Then we're no worse off than we are now," Vaste said, and kept moving.

The path up Ilanar Hill was a steep curve. Tall walls partitioned off the manors once given by the king to the heroes of Sanctuary. The gates were closed, bound tightly shut, and Vaste was left to wonder if indeed they would find themselves boxed in when they reached his own house – if it was, indeed, his own any longer.

He reached the gate and it was unlocked, to his surprise; the drive wended across a beautifully-manicured lawn and up to a blocky house built in the exquisite elven style, with a colonnade and a portico, cobblestone path wending its way to the entry. The glow of a lamp burned in the window beside the front door, and Vaste led them up, feeling the weariness of the last several days' travel afflicting him. With a hammering hand upon the door, he paused and stood back, waiting to see if anyone would answer.

CHAPTER 62

Shirri

There was a park in the center of the great wooden city, fields open wide and green in the midst of the towering former trees. Lush, empty grass fields were framed by stretches of surviving jungle vegetation, a reminder of what this place had once been. The scent of plants came with the warm breeze out of the west, rustling Shirri's robes.

"Who are we going to see?" Shirri asked. The grass crunched beneath her feet, short enough that goats or cows must have kept it low.

"An old friend," Calene said. "Someone who operates on the margins of Amti's society – sort of." She must have caught a questioning look from Shirri, because she added, "Do you know anything about the southern elves' law keepers?"

"Just that they have one. I forget the name of the group. Brotherhood of...something?"

Calene nodded. "They trace their heritage back a thousand

years, to a group of exiles that came here after the fall of Sanctuary. They're revered in this place, and membership is very selective." She raised a finger to point across the sunny, open ground to a distant collection of lightly armored men standing in a formation...atop the largest creatures Shirri had ever seen. "They're known as the Brotherhood of the Savannah Cat."

They certainly seemed aptly named. The riders ranged from extremely tall and bulky, for elves, to...only rather tall and bulky, for elves. And many of them seemed to have a green tinge to their skin.

"They're Trelves," Calene said, reducing the volume of her voice. "Descendants of the original trolls of Sanctuary that came here and comprised the membership. A lot of them lost their lives in extermination in the northern swamps." She stared off into the distance. "That was a hard time."

"Were you there?" Shirri asked.

Calene nodded slowly. "Aye. I went with Zarrn and the others to try and fight a last ditch defense, but we were just no match for them. Only the quick action of a spellcasting friend saved me, otherwise I might have died there." Sticking a finger into her collar, she traced the line of a scar that ran along the side of her neck. "Picked up this one there. Only reason my friend was able to get me out, for if I'd been on my feet I'd have likely fought to the bitter end." A flash of hatred came over her face. "I saw the worst of people that day. Not for the first time, nor the last, but...truly, it was ghastly."

"I'm sorry to hear that," Shirri said.

Calene held out an arm to stop her. "A word about my friend." She made a show of glancing over her shoulder toward the cats, now parading around the grounds in formation. "Trelves can vary greatly in their looks depending on what generation they are. They don't marry amongst their own very often. Which is odd considering they're rather outcast here."

"But you said the Brotherhood of the Savannah Cat is revered...?"

"They are," Calene said, "which makes marriage offers possible. But socially...they've never been truly accepted."

"That...that makes little sense to me."

"To me as well," Calene said with a heavy sigh. "Look, it's like this – an elder elf who's, say, three thousand years old, originally from Pharesia, because there's a bunch here of that sort? He'd marry his daughter to a trelf, but he wouldn't become a business associate with him, wouldn't become *covekan* – that's like a close friend – or consider him welcome in his home for anything other than the most perfunctory, required sort of occasions."

"Even though married to his daughter?" Shirri frowned. "I don't understand."

"Elves are insular people," Calene said. "They don't trust easily. Things are a bit different here with the newer generations, but the old are constantly flooding in from the north given the situation there. They bring their old ways with them, and it causes problems. Point is – if my friend has a bit of an attitude, that's from whence it springs."

"So I should probably avoid mentioning that my mother is an elf?"

"Probably that'd be wise," Calene said, then beckoned her forward.

One of the savannah cats broke from the parade formation, and trotted across the field toward them. Shirri had to draw upon every reserve of courage to keep from screaming and running. The savannah cat was mammoth, nearly the size of a horseless carriage. The man upon it, though, seemed well matched to his mount.

Exceptionally tall, with dark hair that stood at great contrast to the pure-bred elves that Shirri had known, the Trelf loomed over her even after he dismounted athletically from the savannah cat. He had a spring in his step, his armor was silvery and formal, and looked as though it had never seen battle. Which was impossible, because if there was one thing Shirri had heard about the Brotherhood of the Savannah Cat, it was that they were perpetually in combat of some kind. Whether dealing with livestock rustlers or garden-variety criminals, they were the first line of defense for southern elvendom.

"I am Birstis, son of Fuertan," the man declared, chin stuck out proudly as if daring Shirri to strike at it. He looked straight into Shirri's eyes, as if challenging her, and then his gaze fell to her ears, and she felt a rush of discomfort as he evinced the slightest curling at the corner of his mouth.

"I am Calene, daughter of...well, no one really remembers anymore," Calene said with an endearing half-smirk. "Good to see you again, Birstis. How fare you?"

"Well," Birstis said, looking once again at Shirri as if assessing her for a threat. "It is odd to see you in the city when there is hunting to be done."

"Even I need a break from slinking through the tall grass every now and again," Calene said. "Besides...events are in motion."

Birstis greeted that with a faint grunt. His skin was a more golden shade than a usual elf, maybe a tinge of green coloring it. "Your friend has the aroma of death about her. Did she come from Reikonos?"

That made Shirri raise an eyebrow. "Yes," she answered, before Calene could do it for her.

"I have heard that the city is burning," Birstis said, looking at the ground. His silvery breastplate was hard to look at in this sun, and smaller than the ones Cyrus or Vara or Alaric wore, as if it were ceremonial. "You have my regrets if you are from there."

"I am and thank you," Shirri said, wondering how to broach this. The second discussion with an utter stranger she'd had on the subject, and she still didn't know quite how to say it. "That's part of why we're here—"

"There's a bit more to the Reikonos story than you've perhaps heard," Calene said. "It wasn't a simple fire."

Birstis's eyebrow raised to that. "Do go on."

Calene looked to Shirri, and suddenly there was a great pressure in her chest, in her heart. Or perhaps on her shoulders. "There was a sorcerer there," Shirri said, her voice wavering. "He cast a great red spell that encompassed the whole of the city. Airships were fleeing the yards in every direction, and it crackled through the town, killing all it touched until it finally pulled back and nothing but silence and fire were left to reign."

Birstis was quiet for a long moment, then finally a small nod escaped him. "I have heard rumor of this. It circulates in the streets, behind closed doors. Hushed whispers from mouths that know but ears that fear to hear it." He fixed his gaze in the distance, at the formation of savannah cats practicing their pounce. "You bring this to me for what reason?"

"Because you might actually do something with it," Calene said. "The Brotherhood is tasked to the defense of the south. You could—"

"I must stop you there," Birstis said, and he held a mailed hand before him like defense from her words. "You overestimate my influence. I am the weapon in the hands of the Council. They point me in a direction, I go. A train robbery happens outside Kortri, I am sent with my troop. I do not decide my course; I am the arrow fired from their bow. You need to make this case to the hand that wields it."

"Perhaps you could help us get an audience there," Shirri said, seeing the light flicker and die in Calene's eyes.

There was something behind Birstis's too, words unspoken that she had a feeling were understood by Calene, by Birstis, but that she was an outsider and not privy to. "There is nothing I can do," Birstis said simply, and inclined his head in a bow to her, then Calene, in turn. "If you are still in town two days hence, come back in the morning. We are having a parade of the Brotherhood to commemorate Liberation Day and the fall of the titans. It is a great holiday here. The children seem to enjoy it. Perhaps you might as well."

Shirri wanted to argue, to state her case plain: someone needed to do something.

But she feared her words would fall on deaf ears, and she stayed as silent as Calene as they watched the tall trelf saunter back to his cat, his shoulders considerably more slumped than when he'd approached, and somehow Shirri knew there was a weight upon them that she had not put there.

CHAPTER 63

Cyrus

Cyrus was led to the throne room in silence, a cold chill infusing the passages of the palace of Saekaj. It was a damp quiet, and one that left Cyrus uneasy as he marched, the footfalls achieving a cadence that reminded him of a funeral procession as he walked.

"What is this about?" Baynvyn asked, falling in behind him, darting in front of the dozen or more guards that had all tightly circled around Cyrus along the walk.

"Malpravus was whispering to in me in my sleep," Cyrus said.

"You were giving aid and comfort to the enemy," Terian said, at Cyrus's back.

"And you've been trading with him for years," Cyrus said, "and sent my son, your servant, to his service in order to have me killed. Interesting that only now you find it a problem for me to have a conversation with him. And in your own city, no less."

"If he's here it's because you brought him here," Terian said as they marched into the throne room. He slipped up the dais, throwing only accusing looks behind him like spears in a battle line. "Because you elevated him halfway to godhood."

"I had little to do with it," Cyrus said, folding his arms in front of him, the armor clanking enough that Niamh, standing at his side, twitched again. "I was busy saving Baynvyn at the time. You know, the man you put in servitude to this heinous villain that you now accuse me of serving?"

"This seems rather absurd," Baynvyn said. Epalette was prominently back in his scabbard, and a pistol was again mounted upon his belt. "You did put me directly at Malpravus's service. I don't think Cyrus, for all his faults, would willingly collaborate with the man. He's notoriously good at worming his way into places he shouldn't have any sway at all."

"He's never reached us here before," Terian said. "Tell me what has changed, other than taking Cyrus into our halls?"

"Reikonos and Sanctuary being drained to nothingness upon the altar of his apotheosis?" Cyrus asked dryly. "Oh – and also, you have a new haircut. I've just realized. Seems important to make mention of it since it has about as much to do with Malpravus talking to me here in your halls as I do."

"You put the flintlock in his hand, Cyrus," Terian said.

"No," Cyrus said. "I had a flintlock, he broke into my home while I was out saving Baynvyn, he stole it, shot someone with it, and is now holding it at all of our heads. Quite a difference."

Terian shook his head slowly. "You still talk about these things as though you had nothing to do with them, as though you were as innocent as a shepherd asleep at home when the lion comes for the flock."

"Do you have lions and flocks in Saekaj Sovar?" Cyrus asked, looking around. He could feel the absurd press of Terian's anger. "I would have assumed it was more about spiders and fish around here to hear you all talk about it."

"There aren't many fish anymore," Baynvyn said. "The Great Sea went fallow of them long ago."

"This has nothing to do with that–" Terian started.

"It has at least a little to do with that," Cyrus said, taking a step forward. Every guardsman about him raised their weapons, metal clinking. He rested a wary eye upon them but moved no more. "You have been sitting here in this place, shut off from the world for the better part of a thousand years, Terian. Stewing in your own considerable resentments...apparently mostly at me. Why you would choose me, I can only imagine–"

"Can you?" Terian asked, rising from his throne, spittle flecking out of his lips. "If you can't, I assure you it's the fault of your imagination, because it only needs a little vigor to construct a reason why I might resent you. You, who did such damage to this world and left, left us to be–"

"What would you have had me do, Terian?" Cyrus asked.

"Stay!" Terian's voice boomed pure fury over the throne room. "Stay and help us put right what wrongs you did by killing the gods!" His voice softened only a little. "Stay and stop the scourge from flowing over the land, turning it to ash and gray dirt as far the eye can see. Keep Malpravus from having his way with Reikonos, from the letting the elves descend into madness. Can't you see?" Genuine pain waited in his eyes. "Nothing's been good since you left. Arkaria is a ruin, the worst place in this world we've barely any part in. The only thing saving us from being torn to pieces by our neighbors is that no one would want this land of ash and bones." He lifted a finger to point at Cyrus. "And it's because of you. We're weak because of you, the things you did, the choices you made, the ruin you left when you decided you could no longer bear the consequences of your own decisions."

"It would take a man of unspeakable arrogance to listen to

you just now and say, 'I had nothing to do with any of this,'" Cyrus said, bowing his head. "Because I had much to do with all of it. I walked the path that Bellarum put before me, so caught in the threads of ambition he wove I didn't stop to ask what seeking that power would do to me, to others. I threw myself against the machinations of evil people, evil gods – Malpravus, Mortus, Yartraak – and I didn't always ask myself what every consequence would be – for I had no idea."

Cyrus felt his spine straighten, his shoulders square back. "Every terrible thing that happened because of my choices, I bear some responsibility for. But that you, my friend, would put the blame entirely on me and not on those who conspired to enslave and milk Arkaria and the dead of our land for their own power and benefit? Well, hells, Terian...I have shame for my part in all this. Have you none? None for accusing me of bearing all this weight of blame while apportioning none to the sins of Yartraak in what he did here? To Mortus for capturing the dead, driving them mad, drinking them for his own benefit until they were mad and uncontrollable? For Bellarum, who planned to tear the whole creaking edifice down for his own benefit? Or Malpravus, who waited in the wings, hoping to shape himself into a successor god?"

He leaned closer, afraid to violate the angry circle of weapon-toting dark elves, seemingly ready to strike him down at the merest sign of a threat. "Have you only spite for me, your once-friend, for destroying the threats without a perfect plan to assume the empty throne? Do you mean only to indict me for my failings, for my self-indulgence when I thought my wife died? For becoming mopey Cyrus and failing here and there, for laying sacrifice after sacrifice of our friends, our family, upon the altar of the old gods as we labored to bring them down to give the people of Arkaria some chance to breathe free? Has familiarity bred only contempt in you for me, Terian? Blinded you to any good I tried to do? Clouded over your old anger at those who did wrong before, replacing them in your sight with me, and only me?"

"It wasn't so bad before," Terian said. "You remember."

"We were as slaves to them, Terian," Cyrus said. "They would kill us as soon as brook the slightest disagreement. Look what they did to the Protanians. Look what Mortus did to us, with the blessing or benign neglect of the other gods! We were nothing to them – just like we are to Malpravus. Less than insects; a means to an end." Though he didn't dare step forward, he did raise a hand and point right at the Sovereign. "And what an end Malpravus has planned for us. Do you not see it?"

"Tell me," Terian said. "What does your old friend have planned for me and mine?"

"Weren't you listening at the door?" Cyrus asked mockingly. "He called this place a grave, or near to one." He caught a horrified look from Baynvyn out of the corner of his eye. "Doesn't it become obvious when put like that?

"He means to make Saekaj Sovar his next target," Cyrus said, not letting up in the force of his words. "The next pyre, the next offering on his path to godhood. Every body in this place laid to rest here, their souls ripped from their forms by that red spell of devilry."

Terian was quiet for a long moment. "Because of you."

Cyrus closed his eyes, and at his side, he felt the jerk of Niamh as she twitched once more. "Yes, blame me, if you need to. Don't give Malpravus a moment's condemnation, but slap me with all of it." He opened his eyes again, peering at the Sovereign of Saekaj and Sovar. "But at least prepare yourself to do something about, for he is coming, and whatever fight you might present, I suggest you get to work preparing."

"Do you remember Vaeretru?" Terian asked, looking right at Cyrus.

"I do," Cyrus said. "I was even dreaming about it before Malpravus woke me with his bullshit."

Terian's face cracked into a very small, satisfied smile. "Do you know why I brought it up?"

Cyrus let out a small, impossibly small, breath. "I have a suspicion."

"It was before you killed Ashan'agar," Terian said. "Before you left and began recruiting for Sanctuary, before you dragged all those people into our halls – hell, before I was even pushed out that first time–"

"You quit, you muttonhead," Cyrus said with a sigh.

Terian smiled. "Yes. I suppose I did. But it was before all that, you see. Before you took the first steps to your destiny. Do you remember? Because there was a moment–"

It occurred to Cyrus at last exactly what he was talking about, and he closed his eyes. "You bastard."

"I'm not the one–" Terian started.

"You're a bastard, Terian," Cyrus said, as the memory came back to him, vivid and alive, the stuff of his nightmare, and he remembered the feel of the cave, a thousand years before, and knew the moment that the once-dark-knight spoke of.

CHAPTER 64

Vara

There was a sensation as though walking into water, thick and viscous the world became around her. The weight of Isabelle was suddenly weightless, and then she took another step and–

They came out in a pristine field, under a bright sun, the heat a pleasant change after the chill of the catacombs. The smell of fresh grass was in the breeze, and bright yellow blowball flowers swayed to its rhythm. A sweetness was in the air, like faint honey, and the rush of a distant brook tickled her ears.

"Well," Vara said, taking a look around and finding none of the harsh night or brutal hedgerows, chill of winter, or frightening creatures that had evidenced themselves last time she'd been here. "I was so primed for oblivion, I begin to wonder if I even recognize true danger anymore."

"Yes, it is what we left behind outside the tunnels," Isabelle said, "and very possibly what waits ahead – somewhere." Her eyes searched tiredly along the horizon, which was hemmed in by thickets and bushes and forest. "Surely the creations of Vidara are still here, somewhere, waiting to attack our genitals."

Vara turned her head to give her sister a questioning look. "How did you know about that?"

Isabelle merely shrugged. "Vaste was never reticent to share his experiences."

"Ah, yes," Vara said, and spared a thought for the troll. Had he escaped with Cyrus?

Had Cyrus escaped?

Had anyone?

"I saw that," Isabelle said, watching her carefully under the bright sun.

"Saw what?"

"You had a moment of doubt," Isabelle said, "possibly in relation to your trollish friend."

"He can take care of himself," Vara said, and snugged Isabelle's arm around her, ready to move forward.

"They all can," Isabelle said, "but there are limits, you must acknowledge. Your husband is a hearty fellow – but he cannot stand against the spell Malpravus cast–"

"Ah, but you forget," Vara said, hobbling with Isabelle beside her like a particularly weighty bundle, "we have, in fact, survived that spell once before."

"With the help of his mother, the Sorceress," Isabelle said with an air of impatience. "As I watched her die, I know she was not about this time to aid him. Which leads me to believe he is, in fact, dead now–"

"He is not dead," Vara said hotly. It came from out of nowhere, that insistence, welling from somewhere deep within.

"And how did he survive?" Isabelle asked, taking up a little of her own weight.

The crunch of a foot upon grass ahead drew them both up short. Vara froze, looking immediately in the direction of the footstep. Another followed, and she traced its origin to a thicket of bushes to her right, one of many that was scattered over the grassy plain.

"Someone comes," Vara said, "can you stand on your own?"

"I will try," Isabelle said, and attempted to take up her own weight. She failed, and landed on a knee, but braced there, waving Vara off with one hand and lifting Amoran in the other. "You will need to be loose of me if you wish to fight."

"I don't wish to fight at all," Vara muttered, taking up Ferocis with both hands on the hilt in a front guard. "But my wishes are not being much taken into consideration by the universe of late." She raised her voice. "I don't know who you are, but I can hear you! My sister and I are seeking refuge in this place, and we are not looking for a fight. Still, if you force us, I will give you one such as you have not tasted in a thousand years – assuming you've lived that long. And if you have, I also assure you – you won't live another day if you cross me."

A rustle was heard in the bushes, and then a wild man burst out of them in a blur of speed, a spear taller than him held high over his head and a beard longer than his chest dark and untamed, flowing freely below where his belt would have been, had he been wearing one. His tunic was earthen and faded, his trousers a similar color.

With dizzying speed he struck, and Vara turned his blow aside only at the last moment, with a hard strike from Ferocis. He shouted with no coherence and struck at her again. Footwork saved her, and she parried, turning the blow aside. His eyes were wild, bright brown and filled with fury–

And in that moment, she recognized him.

"Longwell?" She batted aside the spear's elaborate tip once more, taking a step back and holding her sword before her. "Samwen Longwell?"

He was barely recognizable; gone was the armor that the dragoon had worn, and the spear in his hand was something more ornate by far than the one he'd carried when last she'd seen him. Beneath the beard and the long hair, though, there was something of the man she'd known before, the man of Luukessia and Sanctuary, a somewhat solemn fellow after his land had fallen, but hardly wild and mad, like here.

Longwell twirled his weapon about his head, bringing it overhead, taking her in with but a look, yet said nothing.

Instead, he charged, bellowing to the sun-drenched sky and bringing his weapon forward as though he meant to see her dead.

CHAPTER 65

Alaric

The shadow of the Chaarlandian ironclad lay upon them, blotting out the hot sun above. A breath of life had come back to the engine, and it rattled behind and beneath them as Alaric stood alone with Mazirin upon the quarterdeck. An occasional cheer from above and behind them worked on Alaric's nerves. Mazirin's knuckles were pale with exertion; she seemed to be struggling to keep the wheel from turning over, but had denied him when he'd asked if he could help. "I think your help will be needed elsewhere very shortly," she said, beads of sweat popping out on her forehead.

"Still think they might stop at the shore?" Alaric asked.

Mazirin slowly shook her head. "He's too deep into this now." She stole a look above and behind. There, the Chaarlandian captain waited with his wolf's grin. "He would pursue us right into the teeth of the squadron. He smells blood."

"Never a wise choice to fail to realize when you've been beat," Alaric said, then caught exactly what he'd said. "I meant–"

"I know what you meant," Mazirin said with wry amusement. "But I also know what you said, and the two are not compatible." She was still for a moment. "In all your days, have you ever been as hopeless as this?"

That was an easy question. "I was once a prisoner of a particularly dedicated enemy of mine," Alaric said. "For years his servant tortured me in the most unbelievable ways. Every wound he left, he would heal another, then repeat the process."

"That must have been a difficult time," Mazirin said. "How did you escape?"

"With help from a friend or two."

"If only you had a friend or two in close attendance now," Mazirin said.

Alaric cast his gaze out over the deck. Sure enough, Guy and Edouard were still there, still watching. "You may be surprised. I still have a few close at hand."

"I don't think they're going to be enough."

"We don't ever really know until the moment comes," Alaric said. "You, though...you don't seem to believe in last-minute rescues."

"I suppose I've had enough friends go missing over the years," Mazirin said, straining at the wheel, "I don't hold out hope to believe every ship always comes home, every time. This is the life, you see. Sometimes...this is the way it ends."

"I hope you're wrong," Alaric said. "I don't believe we've come all this way just to see the end. I refuse to despair; I find there is always hope–"

A pop echoed from above. At first Alaric thought it was a pistol, but it was quieter somehow. Something whizzed toward them and struck amidships. No bang, no explosion, no hail of splinters this time, though. Something hit the deck and stuck there–

"Got some sort of grappling hook!" Guy shouted, sticking his head up above the end of the quarterdeck. "Heavy rope leading back to the other ship!"

Another pop was followed by more; they came in a steady rhythm now, a cavalcade of fire. "Another one – uh, lots more!"

"What is this?" Alaric asked.

Mazirin's face showed clear strain. And the ship strained, too, as the ropes began to pull tight, the Chaarlandian pirate tautening the lines now binding them together. "They're about to board us."

CHAPTER 66

Vaste

"Gods damn you, answer the bloody door!" Vaste said, clubbing once again with thunderous effort. He felt as though it rattled upon the hinges, and loudly enough that it could surely be heard echoing down Ilanar Hill, down to where the elven army were doing their bloody work. Knock loud and long enough and he felt sure they'd hear before any soul inside.

Fortunately, with the squeak of a small hinge, he was proven wrong.

Vaste turned and saw a small, square port open at face level, and within its depths, eyes peered out at him sunk in a slightly doughy face. They flashed with recognition, then the little port shut, a lock clicked – rather loudly – and the big door swung open to reveal–

"Master Vaste!" the steward declared, sounding genuinely pleased, "At last you've come back!"

"Much more to my surprise than yours, apparently," Vaste

said, shoving Aemma past the steward, who moved immediately out of the way for her, then Vaste, and finally Qualleron before shutting the door and bolting it tight.

"Indeed, I have been waiting," the steward said. What was his name? Vaste struggled with his memory for a moment – Glaven! Yes, that was it. He peered at Vaste. "Why, master – you haven't aged a day since last I saw you!"

"I am fairly certain I have aged years in the last days," Vaste said, looking around the foyer as though some armored member of the Termina Guard might leap out at him from behind the tasteful statuary, "but I thank you for your obsequious compliment nonetheless." He focused in on Glaven. "Did you expect me?"

"Well, I certainly hoped!" Glaven said with an enthusiasm that could not be feigned, though Vaste was unsure how that was possible. "Rumors swirled, you see," and here Glaven adopted a conspiratorial air, "that mere days ago, Lady Vara returned to us, and that Cyrus Davidon had come back to Reikonos." With a flourish of a chubby hand, Glaven indicated the door and all that lay beyond. "So I left the gate open for you in hopes you might return. A bit worrisome considering what's going on out there and all, but...well," he chuckled, "this is Ilanar Hill. If you can't leave your gate open here–"

"You should probably close it now," Vaste said. "I don't think things are getting much quieter out there."

"Certainly, good sir, certainly," Glaven said, and out he went.

Vaste turned to find Aemma looking at him with dull eyes. "What?"

"'Haven't aged a day?'" she parroted dully. "In a thousand years? Casual mentions of Cyrus Davidon? An elven steward happily at your service?"

"I said to you that you wouldn't believe me if I told you about my life," Vaste said without a single ounce of guilt; still, he did feel a slight pang at the look of vague betrayal upon Aemma's face.

Glaven burst back inside moments later, before anyone had a chance to break that silence. He was huffing, his silken tunic heaving up and down with the effort of his chest. "Well, that's done!" His cheer was boundless, and he bolted the door, looking straight at Vaste. "So, good sir...are you hungry?"

"Famished," Vaste said. "Do you have anything to eat?"

"Quite so," Glaven said, waving him forward. "Your estate is endowed amply, and plenty is included for provisioning."

"But he hasn't been here in a thousand years?" Aemma asked.

"Yes, I recall well the last time I saw Master Vaste," Glaven pronounced cheerfully. "We'd just received a messenger from Lord Davidon's manor. Master Vaste read the missive with some interest, then flushed a much darker shade of green and said, 'Get me my staff, Glaven, and saddle my horse! I'm going out! And also, pick up more of those cheese wheels from the market while I'm gone, for I shall surely be hungry when I return.'"

Vaste blinked at the exact accounting of his last words in the house. "Those *were* good cheese wheels. Very properly sharp."

"I have kept several on hand continuously since," Glaven announced with pride as they entered the kitchen. It was possessed of white marble floors and the typical, incredibly intricate elven cabinetry. Glaven led them to a door on the far wall and threw it open, waving a hand inside to reveal a well-stocked pantry, cheese wheels in the front.

"With a servant such as this, I am hard-pressed to see why you left this place," Qualleron rumbled, though he had to lower his head to see into the pantry.

"I assure you, it was not Glaven who caused me to leave," Vaste said, helping himself to one of the wheels and breaking it in half, handing the other to Qualleron. Offering a piece of his own to Aemma, he received a shake of the head in reply; not hungry, he guessed, and set about attacking it as though he hadn't eaten anything good in days. Which he hadn't.

"This city was a bit difficult for the master, you see," Glaven said, busying himself in the pantry. "Please, be seated, I'll bring you whatever you like," and he pointed to a small, circular table in the corner of the kitchen. "These were the days before humans were here in great numbers. Termina wasn't ready for anything approaching social equity with a troll." He bustled out with a cutting board of bread and put it on the table between them. "Especially so soon after the war."

"Which war was this?" Aemma asked, her eyes moving lazily from Vaste to Glaven and back again.

"The great one, of course," Glaven said. "The Sanctuary war."

"That's what they ended up calling it?" Vaste asked around a mouthful of cheese. "That's terrible."

"The elves call it that," Glaven said. "The humans call it something different – the Davidon war, I think?"

"In Emerald they do," Aemma said. "In the north we called it 'The Second War of the Gods.'" She sniffed. "Or they did."

"Not believing in any gods, what did you call it?" Vaste asked.

Her eyes, slightly resentful, slid over him and his cheese. "I didn't really think about it. Had other things on my mind, you see."

"Were the rumors true, Master Vaste?" Glaven asked, hovering at his elbow. "Did Lady Vara return with you?"

"She did," Vaste said, still struggling to speak around the mouthful of cheese. It was delicious, and he found himself unable and unwilling to stop long enough to answer.

"And Lord Davidon as well?" Glaven's voice rose higher. "I heard from a banker–"

"Yes, him too," Vaste said, and stopped eating the cheese. "We were all there, in Reikonos." He swallowed an oversized bite. "Before it was destroyed."

"So it has been destroyed?" Glaven asked with fluttery hand upon his silken breast. "I thought that was human propaganda!"

"...What?" Qualleron asked.

"Well, you know, they have long been seeking for a reason to light this particular powderkeg," Glaven said, favoring Aemma with an apologetic look that she did not seem to notice. "I just assumed that tales of Reikonos were lies, an excuse to begin the thing. Then, when they burned the Chancel, the Termina Guard had their reason and moved in–"

"Slaughtering them all," Vaste said. "Var'eton is burning."

Glaven nodded sadly. "Things have not been easy these last years, between humans and elves. But many do not care for what is happening now. Woe be to all who have lived to see these terrible days."

"I am fairly wishing I had not come back to witness them," Vaste said. "Among other things."

"So...where have you been in these intervening years, master?" Glaven asked. "As I say, you look quite good for your age. Why, I might not have believed it possible had I not already heard of Cyrus Davidon coming back, and Lady Vara, too...but when I did, I thought...why, anything may be possible for those of old Sanctuary!"

With a slow blink, Aemma turned her head to him. "Old Sanctuary?" She merely mouthed the words, and he ignored her.

"I might have almost believed that myself a few days ago," Vaste said. His belly full, he started to feel sluggish.

"You have journeyed far if you've come from Reikonos," Glaven said brightly. "You look tired, good sir. Beds are made upstairs, plenty enough for you and your companions."

"Perhaps I will...enjoy my bed," Vaste said, rising from the table. "It's certainly been long enough."

"I wouldn't mind one of those as well," Qualleron said. "Do you happen to have one that would fit me? I wouldn't wish to break your furniture."

"Such manners! All the good sir's furniture is fit for the troll form," Glaven said brightly. "I will happily show you to a room." He glanced at Aemma. "And you as well, miss, if you'd like?"

"Sure," Aemma said. "Why not." It was not a question.

Vaste barely made it upstairs, with the first hints of sunrise peeking through the sheer white curtains covering the great windows of the estate, his legs dragging with every step. Glaven showed him to a bed, words muted and muddled in Vaste's hearing. He collapsed on a soft mattress, and was out before he heard another word.

CHAPTER 67

Cyrus
One Thousand Years Ago
Vaeretru

"That is, in fact, a giant, two-headed snake," Vaste announced as though it were some great pronouncement, on the level of an annunciation by one of the gods. "Why, it's half the size of the Citadel, I believe."

"J'anda..." Terian said with a clear rise in alarm in his voice.

"I am trying," the enchanter said with great strain, "but it is resisting me. Its mind may be too different to bring under my control."

The rattle of a hiss seemed to echo through the caverns, and Cyrus turned his face away as the snake made a noise more akin to that of a dragon than any serpent he'd encountered. It rang through his armor like a light bell, making him turn his head away cringing. He reached for his sword, drawing it swiftly and defensively.

"Where the hell do we even attack that thing?" Terian asked.

"I suggest from within the guts," Vaste said. "Hurl yourself in there and don't even worry about your own health, I will definitely be casting healing spells...for as long as my spell can reach you, anyway. It may be hampered by both my distance from you as I run away and the obstruction of the snake's own skin, but do not let that diminish your courage one single bit, for I am behind you. Way, way behind you, but still."

"I know I won't let it diminish my courage," Andren said, tipping up a metal flash that he didn't even bother to hide beneath the sleeves of his robe. "For I'm going to diminish it myself, and swiftly if we remain here. Well?" He looked right at Cyrus. "Get after it, eh?"

Cyrus looked up at the snake, whose two heads were, to him, at the height of a four-story building of the like he might have seen in Reikonos. "Uh...how?"

"People kill dragons, so this should be easy," Niamh said, but there was a catch in her voice. "It can't fly or, uhm...hop." Her brow furrowed. "...Can it?"

The snake, having apparently had quite enough of their chatter, made the first move, lurching forward and slithering toward them with great alacrity. Its sides heaved with life, shining in the low light of the cavern as he lunged right at them at a speed not unlike a galloping horse.

Terian dove out of the way just in time; as did the others.

Cyrus...did not.

It caught him in one set of its jaws, snatching him as fangs the size of his upper arms buried themselves in his chain mail, pressing through and into his stomach, where they drew blood. Cyrus gasped, and his sword nearly slipped out of his hands.

"Cyrus!" Niamh's voice echoed in the dark as, with a lurch of motion, the snake wheeled about, and clasped in the jaws, Cyrus felt it turn to spirit him away.

CHAPTER 68

Vara

Samwen Longwell, clad in ragged clothes and brandishing a spear that was utterly unlike the one Vara had last seen him with, charged at her in fury. He lunged with the pointy end, stabbing forth with the haft, intending to skewer her like a piece of meat.

His speed was beyond quick; the weapon was godly, and in an instant she knew its provenance. Amnis, the Spear of Water.

But she held Ferocis, and had little patience for this, or Longwell's apparent madness.

"Samwen!" she shouted to garner his attention, even as she stepped to the side, letting him stab the empty space where she had just been. "I am not your enemy, Longwell!" She brought her blade up beside her face in a high guard. "But if you persist in this, you will make me one, and I will be forced to stab you squarely in the liver – and then perhaps consider healing you afterward. But only perhaps."

He stumbled but regained his footing, and looked back at her as if seeing her for the first time. "Who are you?" His gaze hardened again. "No – I know who you're meant to be, but she's dead." He lifted the tip of the spear and pointed it at her.

"She's not dead, Longwell," Isabelle said, still on one knee, and brandishing Amoran. "Though we thought certain you were."

Longwell cast a look back at Isabelle, and for a brief, fearful moment, Vara thought he might attack her while she was down.

He did not. Instead, he shuffled to the side, suspicious eyes on both of them, putting each at the corners of a triangle he completed himself. "...Isabelle?"

"What's left of her, anyway," Isabelle said, collapsing onto her haunches. "I haven't seen you since..."

Longwell lifted the spear almost imperceptibly, and Vara read it as a breakthrough of sorts. "The Realm of War."

Isabelle nodded slowly. "Indeed. A hard day."

"Yes," Longwell said, then looked again at Vara, anger flashing in eyes. "The day we avenged her. The day we saved Arkaria."

"I can say by what I've found since I returned," Vara said, dripping irony, "you lot did a poor job at both, unless you think that scourge covering the land from the Sea of Carmas to the river Perda constitutes saving Arkaria, and striking down Bellarum even though he failed to completely kill me constitutes 'vengeance.'"

"You died with Sanctuary," Longwell said, and the point came back to alignment with Vara's face.

"Yes," Vara said, "except Sanctuary did not die, and neither did I, for Sanctuary was the Ark all along."

"The...ark?" Longwell's eyes moved back and forth. "Then...Cyrus?"

"He is alive," Vara said.

"Oh, he's dead," Isabelle said, then, catching Vara's rageful look, amended, "but he was alive until yesterday or so. He died with Reikonos."

"He is not dead," Vara said.

"How did Reikonos die?" Longwell said, and now the spear fell from pointing at Vara.

"Malpravus, of course," Vara said, lowering her own blade. "In his guise as you."

"You know about that?" Longwell thumped the haft of his spear into the dirt, clutching it just below the ornate tip. He looked away, his beard bushy and falling over his belt. "I had a feeling he'd be the end of this city, I just..." He did not look up at them.

"How long have you been here?" Vara asked.

His eyes seemed sunken, though he did not appear malnourished. Instead, he had a bit of a hollow sense about him, as though something had been emptied out from within him. "I don't know."

"Well, it should be simple enough to figure," Vara said. "When did you arrive?"

Longwell's eyes flitted back and forth. "I...chased across the sea to find Baraghosa. I was gone for a time, seeing the world, and when I came back I was at Emerald Fields for a spell. Then, news reached my ears of my triumphant return to Reikonos..."

"Except it wasn't you, was it?" Vara asked.

He shook his head slowly. "I went to confront whoever it was. And...it didn't go well." He looked away again, and she sensed the matter was closed. He looked back up. "But you...how did you survive? I don't understand. You said Sanctuary was–"

"The Ark," Vara said. "Repository of hope? Gift of the God of Good?"

Longwell blinked at that. "Rubbish."

"Much is rubbish," Vara said, "like the streets of Reikonos, now. But the Ark was real, and it was Sanctuary. Cyrus, Alaric,

Curatio, Vaste and I have been within it, in the ether, for the last thousand years. We returned mere days ago, responding to a call for help from someone in need in Reikonos—"

"But Sanctuary was in the Plains of Perdamun," Longwell said, his eyes clouded with confusion.

"Gods! It can move, Longwell," Vara said. "Because it's the Ark. It's the reason why Alaric could disappear at will. Ether-magic, you see."

"Show me," Longwell said, looking at her again with great suspicion.

"Two days ago I could have," Vara said, lifting a hand. "But this morning, as Isabelle and I approached Reikonos, I felt a shuddering tear within me as something happened to Sanctuary. Then, the sky went red, like the time we were at the temple in the Waking Woods, and Malpravus sacrificed his army—"

"How do you know about that?" Longwell asked, squinting. He looked to Isabelle. "And you – you remember the last time we met. The actual one."

"Because I'm me," Isabelle said weakly. "And she is her."

"Not some artifice of Malpravus's construction?" Longwell peered at Vara. "I have long expected him to come for me. Why, I barely made it here alive. But finally someone comes to me and it's...impossible." He shook his head slowly. "And yet...I think you are...you? Not a ghost, not some illusion, but the real Vara...except you were dead. And you come bearing stories of Cyrus and Alaric and Vaste and Curatio, all of whom – they were gone." His eyes looked haunted, dancing in the bright, sun-drenched day. "You were all gone, and the world without you...it was not the same. Never."

"It is I, Samwen," Vara said. "Ask me some question that Malpravus could not know."

Longwell's eyes flashed, and the corner of his lip quirked. "Calene once told me she walked in on you and Cyrus naked in your quarters."

Vara felt a steely twist in her gut, and she sighed. "Yes, that's true. I recall well the look on her face – before she hid it."

"What did she see in that moment?" Longwell pressed. He looked so sure and full of himself. "And what did she say about it?"

"She said," Vara dragged on this, for it pained her, almost, to say it aloud, "...that she pitied me."

"Why?" Longwell asked, pressing further, as though leaning ahead.

"Yes, why?" Isabelle asked. She, too, seemed to be leaning in anticipation of the answer.

"You're going to make me say it, aren't you?" Vara huffed. "Because I stole the sheet to cover myself, and Cyrus was left...unclad. And thus Calene saw...him...all of him...and...gods, why of all the questions you could have asked? The Temple of the Mler? My slaughter of Yartraak. The battle we waged in Amti. Hell, anything from the last year before I 'died' to Bellarum, when we were outcasts and heretics, even something about the shape of his arse being long – yet this is what you ask?" She drew a deep breath. "She pitied me because...she did not see how I could possibly comfortably–"

"Vara," Longwell said, and there was a strange relish. He threw aside his weapon, and charged her in what was, to her eyes, impossible slowness.

She did not stop him, for she felt his intent before he reached her, and he wrapped his arms around her as if they were bosom friends that had not seen each other in forever. Which was at least half true. "It is good to see you, Samwen," she said, feeling the pressure of his arms holding her tight, his breaths coming raggedly. "It's good to see you."

CHAPTER 69

Alaric

They came sliding down the ropes, their howls in the wind and a stink of sweat and blood riding along with them. The first hit the deck not far from Guy, and he swung, cutting the man down and turning his brown furs red with slick blood that spattered in a line along the wooden deck.

Alaric leapt into the fray, because they were coming now. A knot of four Chaarlandians, all attired in furs and leather and reeking of death, had landed near the rail, and Alaric cast the Force Blast spell, some simmering resentment in him boiling over. The spell bowled them all over the rail. Their screams trailed off as they fell out of sight.

Alaric struck swiftly at the rope that was, even now, bringing more of them to the deck. It was stiff, a chain, but he shattered it with one good overhand blow, and it snapped away. More screams; he looked up as it rattled, slipping over the side, six

Chaarlandian savages riding it straight down between the *Yuutshee* and their vessel, eyes wide and limbs flailing.

"'ey, you lot!" Guy bowled over two of the pirates, like a tiny figure against their hulking physiques. He delivered a coup de grace to one, then brought his own sword down, shattering another chain. It, too, snaked over the side, dragged by the weight of its riders, and another six Chaarlandians were delivered to the land of Luukessia, screaming into the wind.

This, however, did not appear to be a sizable enough difference to sway the battle.

There were dozens of Chaarlandians upon the *Yuutshee's* deck now, screaming in a battle frenzy, clutching pistols and hand axes and daggers. One of them buried a blade in a crewman, turning his robes red and impaling the man up to the pirate's wrist. Then the pirate yanked him close and buried his face in the crewman's neck; blood spurts followed, the crewman screamed, and when the pirate emerged again, his smile glistened with crimson and chunks of meat were stuck in his teeth.

"Aw, bloody hell," Guy said, crowning one pirate with a blow of Praelior's hilt and shattering his skull. He turned the blade edge against the next Chaarlandian to come his way, burying it in the man's chest.

But the pirate did not die. Blood oozed between his teeth, which were fixed in an angry rictus, and he pulled himself down the blade, head butting Guy, who was rocked back by the blow. He did not, however lose his grip on Praelior, and ripped it out as he fell.

A howl to Alaric's side made him turn; two pirates were circling him. One lifted a pistol and fired six times in rapid succession. They spanged off Alaric's armor with little impact but quite a bit of noise, the last bouncing off his helm.

"That's quite enough of that," Alaric said, and cast Force Blast – this time, a bit weaker – at the pirate, succeeding only in knocking him back a step and jarring the pistol from his hand.

Alaric attacked. There was no quarter here; not from these savages, and so he offered none in return. He slashed leather and cut down the first pirate with a hacking slash that cleaved his chest open just beneath the armpit. Bone was rent asunder, chest laid open, and the man fell backward, his viscera laid open for the world to see.

With a strong elbow, Alaric knocked him out of the way to die, but found four more had seemingly sprung up in his wake. Just ahead of him, two more chains and grappling hooks were delivering pirates to the *Yuutshee's* deck.

A Force Blast spell rocked them back a step, and Alaric moved in, Aterum cutting its way through their numbers. He gave a slash here across the face, destroying the skull, a stab there through the throat, severing the spine. It was a messy business, but it got him to the nearest chain just as a Chaarlandian reaver was sliding down.

Alaric chopped the chain with a rattling blow, inadvertently sinking to one knee. It broke; more screams, a snap as it snaked away at high speed, taking the legs from beneath one of the pirates as it did so. He saw shadowed figures fall as if raining from the deck above as they dropped, but it seemed to make no difference.

He swung at one of the pirates and the move brought him off balance, back to one knee. While down there he could see under the steps leading up to the quarterdeck, a pair of eyes peering out at him, wide and fearful.

"Edouard!" he called, recognizing the man immediately. "Take up a weapon and join us!" With a wild swing, Alaric ended another pirate, though it seemed little to matter, for there were so many. He got a shake of the head for his troubles, and the headsman did nothing but creep deeper into the shadows, clearly desperate to remain unseen.

"I think we might be losing this one, Alaric," Guy called from close to the forecastle. He was a blur of motion, but it was clear the rhythm of his swings was much reduced, the little man breathing heavily. The pirates were moving out of the way now, and even with the gift of Praelior's speed, he seemed to struggle to marshal enough alacrity to hit them, landing a blow only once in three swings. And even then, some were glancing. The pirates were laughing at him.

Another hook plowed into the deck mere feet from him, and Alaric diverted to snap the chain. A pirate swung in on him then, burying a dagger into his chainmail and stinging him greatly, though it did not break skin. Alaric whipped around, bludgeoning the man in the skull. The deck beneath him was slick, and pirates were charging him.

Fury dawned as Guy's words struck home, and his heart swelled with anger. He lifted his blade at the coming pirates and shouted his anger, casting his spell as he did so. A dozen were blown off their feet, sent spiraling over the rail of the *Yuutshee*.

"Alaric!"

A shout from the quarterdeck drew his attention, and Alaric turned. What he saw there made him halt, blood chilling like an ice spell had been cast on his veins.

For standing there, with Mazirin snugged against him, her neck trapped in the crook of his elbow, stood the Chaarlandian captain, grinning evilly, a blade to her skull, and the meaning plain even without words–

Surrender.

CHAPTER 70

Vara

"Then Arkaria burns," Longwell said, fingers slipping through his dark, tangled beard. His eyes were pointed ahead, deep in consideration, after having listened to the story – whole and complete – that Vara had offered him. She had covered everything, in her estimation, between the fight with Bellarum in the Council chambers up to now, giving him all the events of the days since their return – with only a little eliding over the events around her departure.

Isabelle sat against a tall stone, taller than all of them put together. There was a circle of them in the midst of a meadow with short grass and hills surrounding it. It was, Vara knew, the old seat of Vidara herself, though there was nowhere to sit but the ground, which was pleasant enough after the hard cobblestone streets of Reikonos and unyielding stone floor of the catacombs. Isabelle rested her head, eyes half-closed, just listening. "It burns," she agreed.

"But you burst through the block wall at the old entrance?" Longwell asked. His spear was leaned against the stone nearest him.

"With spell and sword, yes," Vara said. Honeycombs lay out on series of leaves before them, and they had eaten their fill, followed by all they could drink from a nearby stream. "Though it has collapsed behind us, I am hopeful that once the fires run their course, I can perhaps clear the way for us there."

Longwell nodded. "I have, on occasion, gone out to try and see. But that block has been there the last dozen or so times I gathered my courage up, thwarting me. So I return here, and..." He waved a hand around. "...Stay."

"And you have been here for nearly a thousand years?" Isabelle asked. Her color had improved since their arrival, but she still looked weathered enough that Vara nearly blanched to look upon her.

"I suppose, if you say so," Longwell said. "To me it is a never-ending succession of days in which I practice with my spear or hunt the realm's game, or lie out in the sun and soak up the warmth." He shrugged. "I can scarcely believe it has been as long as you say."

"It has," Vara said. "Once you were out, though, the first time, before the block – why not try and escape the city?"

Longwell chuckled dryly. "The only escape was the docks, and – well, I tried. But Malpravus had guards posted at every approach to the shoreline, and there were posters everywhere with my face upon them declaring me traitor and imposter. The guards were numerous, everywhere, a sign of the changing city under his rule. By then, nearly all who had known me in Reikonos from days before had passed, or simply left. In any case, I could barely get close enough to hear the ocean."

Shoreline. Of course. They hadn't had airships when Longwell had arrived here. "It's a shame," Vara said. "If you could have gotten free–"

"That's the thing that kept me here," Longwell said softly. "If I'd gotten free...then what?" He leaned forward, suddenly animated. "Sanctuary had been gone and dead for a hundred years by that point. What could I have done? Rallied the few of us left? Gathered Calene and Ryin and Zarnn and...who else?" He looked at each of them in turn. "You were gone, Cyrus was gone, Alaric – we did all we could when the scourge poured over the northern mountains, but it was the last gasp of what was left of Sanctuary. Terian and Mendicant closed up their gates and disappeared into the earth; Scuddar led his countrymen into the desert to defend their places, none ever to be seen again." He drummed fingers against his dirty trousers. "I thought about it a thousand times, for every waking night. The gods broke Sanctuary; the scourge just finished the job."

There was a breath of silence, then he spoke again. "We all met up again – those of us left – on the front lines when the scourge came through. It was like Luukessia all over again." He stared off into the distance. "We all had godly weapons and we still couldn't stop them."

Isabelle stirred. "I remember those days."

Longwell looked up. "You were there?"

She nodded. "I fought with Burnt Offerings and Endeavor one last time, trying to protect the coastal front. It was a bloody slog through the Riverlands, and by the time we had retreated to the Gnomish Dominions..."

Longwell winced. "I heard things got ugly there. I was on the northern line, at the coast of the Torrid – errr, Placid Sea. It went about as well as you might have heard."

"Everyone failed and many died," Vara said abruptly. "Then you hit on the idea of digging out a great moat around Reikonos. Well done."

"It was all I could manage at the time," Longwell said. "I regret it now, of course; they'd talked about evacuating the city. Better that than what happened with Malpravus." He shook his head slowly. "Nothing in Arkaria has been right since Sanctuary broke. Anyway, like I said – I thought about what I'd do if I got out for a thousand – maybe a million nights, at this point. But I'm a realist now. Have been since I lost two lands to the scourge. There was nothing to be done against Malpravus if I'd gotten free." Once again, he set his sights on a point in the distance and spoke to it rather than them. "So I stayed here...waiting to die."

"You'll be a long time waiting with that in your hand," Vara said, nodding at Amnis.

"I can't get rid of it," Longwell said, giving it a glance. "I put it down for half my time here. See what good that's done me."

"I think whatever effect the weapon has, it has something to do with the bonding with the holder," Isabelle said, stirring. "I put Amoran away, not wearing or carrying it for months at a time, but it doesn't seem to have much effect. We are still the masters of these weapons, until someone else takes them up."

"Why would it matter if you put yours down, though?" Longwell asked. "You're an elf."

"I still age," she said. "Though admittedly a bit more rapidly in the last hours than usual."

"Do you feel your magic returning?" Vara asked.

"Slowly," Isabelle said. "But I don't know what good that does for us. We are stuck here until the fires fade."

"Until the fires fade," Longwell said slowly, as if trying that out. "You mean, after that...we might leave?"

"We *are* going to leave," Vara said, and for her, that was that. It was merely a matter of days, and all her thoughts were already on the surface, and wondering when the heat would die away and the smoke would fade, so she could leave this empty paradise behind and go seek out rescue.

Because, eventually...she still needed to find Cyrus.

CHAPTER 71

Vaste

"Sir Vaste?"

Glaven's soft voice echoed through the cavernous bedroom, stirring Vaste out of a deep slumber, one in which he'd dreamed of nothing, experiencing a jarring passage of time and coming out of his slumber to bright light shining in through the curtains like a fire burning in front of his face on the darkest night.

"Mmmm?" His mouth was cottony, his tongue three sizes too large for it, and the pillows felt attached to his face, sirens calling him to keep his cheek right there, upon them, forever. His head, being full of rocks and quite weighty, was agreeable to this proposal.

"Good sir, there is a lord at the door," Glaven said, standing at the door.

Sleep was a tempting mistress, daring him to come into her

verdant and inviting bosom. That thought reminded him of Birissa, and Sanctuary, and jarred him rudely out of sleep and off his pillow. He sat upright in the cushy bed, the light streaming in the windows through the white sheers, and asked, "How long have I been asleep?"

"A day and a night, and now it is just after daybreak again," Glaven said. He was perched in the half-open door, head barely inserted, as though to come any farther would be to violate Vaste's privacy. Or get his own head bitten off. It was a good instinct, and had he been more awake, he might have praised Glaven for it.

"Must have been tired," Vaste said, his stomach emitting the most worrisome growl. "A lord at the door, you say?"

"Merrish, his name is," Glaven said.

"I thought elves didn't hold to that whole lords and titles bit anymore." Vaste rubbed his eyes, regarding his attire; he'd fallen asleep in his robe and it looked it. His bladder made plaintive noises, and he caught sight of the toileting room, door wide open just across the way.

"It's ceremonial more than anything, now, yes," Glaven said. "Old habits are hard to break, you know."

"Excuse me," Vaste said, propelling himself out of bed. "I will be with his whatevership in a moment. Inform him I have been sleeping for some time and will greet him as soon as I can vacate my bowels, which I place infinitely higher on my priority list than him."

"I will probably withhold that information, my good sir."

"No, no, make sure to tell him," Vaste said, thumping heavily on the cold marble as he made his way to the toilet. "I want him to know with certainty exactly where he fits in my day."

"As you wish," Glaven said, with clear pains about what he was being asked to do.

Vaste did not care, especially once he reached the toilet. Having held it all in for over a day, his relief was immense.

And with a properly civilized toilet, no less, a thing he had not seen since...well, before he had left Sanctuary. He took his time, and washed in the basin sink afterward, splashing his face with cold water and looking at himself in the cloudy mirror. Even in the blurred reflection of the imperfect glass, he looked...tired.

But there was little time to contemplate that now. Taking up Letum, he headed downstairs into the foyer, where Merrish stood waiting, watching his descent with only a thin veneer of patience.

"I was worried about you," Merrish called when he was about halfway down, fingers dragging the smooth, artfully crafted banister. "After the train was attacked. But I see I had no call for concern."

"It little profits you to concern yourself about me, Merrish," Vaste said as he reached the grand foyer. "For I am always getting into the trouble, and I would hate to see you take years off your life worrying about me."

Merrish, his dark hair pulled up, loosed a wary sigh. "You escaped the humans, then?"

"I didn't have to work very hard at it," Vaste said, hewing as close to the truth as he felt comfortable doing. "They offered to escort me here, since this was the direction they were heading. Coming into town, they walked into a trap near Var'eton and were slaughtered in the street like gnomes released in a wolf den."

Merrish's forehead puckered. "A curious analogy."

"Not that curious if you'd seen what the Termina Guard did to them."

"But you escaped?"

"*I* didn't walk into the trap," Vaste said. "I stopped several blocks up to pause, to consider. Then, when I witnessed the entire thing, I was left in a perfect position from which to slip away unnoticed and come here."

"Skulking through the streets?" Merrish asked with a note of accusation.

"I suppose I could have trumpeted my way through," Vaste said, "but I have a suspicion I would have been murdered by those vengeful elves you call allies. Between you and me, they didn't seem particularly discrete in who they killed. One might have mistaken them for an angry mob, in fact."

Merrish stared at him for a few uninterrupted seconds, then broke away his gaze abruptly. "There is anger enough, that is certain." He looked up again, his fury renewed. "But had you been through what we have this last millennia, with the countless grievances, slights, insults, and murders–"

"Yes, the trolls have no complaints in that department," Vaste said. "Always treated so equitably by everyone. Which is to say ignored by all, you know, now that they're all dead, save me."

"It is hardly the same thing."

"It is exactly the same thing," Vaste said coldly. "People make war on one another. Some are conquered. Sometimes the conquered go on to be conquerors later, and the wheel continues to turn. Perhaps I have the advantage of being outside this conflict and able to see it in a way you can't."

"And what do you see?"

"I see two sides scrapping over land, the same as ever," Vaste said. "You have the advantage now, and you press it, to the death of them all. Very well, you are the conquerors, nay, the slaughterers, and you can do so – for now. But what next?"

Merrish blinked. "What do you mean?"

"Well, I imagine by now you've almost wiped out the humans of Termina, which was no small feat," Vaste said. "So...what next? Are you going to take this war to the Northern Confederation? South to Emerald Fields? Those are the two human powers that squeeze you like a pincer, are they not?"

"Perhaps both," Merrish said coolly. "Perhaps neither."

"Wherever your rage leads you, then," Vaste said. "But you

will not see the true destination until it is upon you – death. For the humans, much as you hate them, hate the very thought of them, of surrendering an inch of land to them, of listening to them one more second – they are nothing compared to what is coming for you, Merrish. A conqueror who does not want you dead so you will leave them alone," and here Vaste felt a puckish smile spring upon him, "but one who wants you dead so he can use your very souls to fuel his magic."

"I am glad you have survived your encounter with the humans," Merrish said, drawing himself up; Vaste got the sense he was suddenly in some hurry to conclude this conversation so he could leave. "And I hope you find much peace in your stay in Termin – uh...?"

He stopped speaking and had cast his eyes to the balcony above, frowning as he stared upward. Vaste looked up to follow his gaze and found a bleary Aemma shuffling up there, rubbing her eyes. She blinked a few times as she looked down, and her face twisted to utter horror as she saw Merrish.

"YOU!" Merrish shouted, pure rage twisting his statuesque features. He reached for the flintlock pistol on his belt.

Vaste lashed out with Letum, and with unerring accuracy cracked him across the knuckles. He cried out in pain, and his hand fell away. Grabbing for it with his other, he turned his hateful eyes upon Vaste. "You did not tell me you were harboring a human!"

"This feeds into my thesis that one can always tell someone's quite peeved when they say 'You!' in that accusing tone," Vaste said. "It seems now you think being human is a crime."

Merrish's eyes burned. "I am warning you, as a courtesy. Let me take her from here so as to circumvent the troubles you will experience if you do not relinquish her."

"Put plainly," Vaste said, "if I don't give her to you, you're going to return with a mob, aren't you? Burn my manor down, beat us to death, hang our bodies as examples to the rest of the city? Something on that order?"

Merrish's teeth showed, an even row of pleasant, perfect white at odds with the dark flush of hate that disfigured his face. "Something on that order and maybe worse. You should know when you are beat, Vaste. You can force me out now, if you like, but you cannot resist against the rage of all the elves in Termina."

"Yes, the best societies are run by unruly mobs," Vaste said. "The most accomplished, too, surely, for I find the height of civilization is to conduct yourself as close as possible to the behavior of a pack of ravening wolves. Take your rage and thrust it up your arse, Merrish." Vaste smacked him across the backside with Letum, driving him toward the door. "And remember this: you threaten a man of Sanctuary."

"Sanctuary is no more," Merrish said coldly. "You are like a rifle that has no powder for the bullet, for your guild has seen its day vanish, and magic has run its course. Even a godly weapon will not stand you in good enough stead to protect you against the crashing waves of elven sentiment in this place."

"If you believe that, then come back, you and all your friends," Vaste said, iron coursing through his blood. "And we'll see what life still lies in the heart and ideals of Sanctuary. Glaven–" And Vaste started, because the servant was already there, and opening the front door for him, so he delivered another rap to Merrish's arse that ushered him out under the portico.

"If I have to come back for her," Merrish said, "it will be with more than you can stand, and you will not survive this."

"You better come back with a metric buttload, then," Vaste said, "and they all best be prepared to die." He flourished Letum, whipping it beneath Merrish's nose with the approximate velocity of a bullet. "For I will not go quietly – I am a man of Sanctuary, through and through, and you had better be prepared for the fight you will receive, for it will be the sort you have not seen for a thousand years. Glaven, if you please?"

And the servant slammed the door on Merrish's outraged face, rage stippling across his features, the gauntlet properly thrown, and Vaste knew in that moment—

The elf would surely be back, just as he promised.

CHAPTER 72

Shirri

"No one wants to believe us," Shirri said, pouring out her feelings in the apartment as she paced, Pamyra and Hiressam watching from the couch before her, and Calene shuffling around in the kitchen at the far side of the room. "And if one of them did, as I think Birstis might, he did not profess any power to make aid."

"This puts us in a tricky situation," Hiressam said, forehead puckered in concentration. "Without assistance, I don't see how we move forward."

"Yes, it would be remarkably grim to see Malpravus approaching the city and find it's only the four of us out on the plains standing before him," Pamyra said. "One might even call that suicidal, by virtue of us having little ability to stop him, but great ability to die at his hand."

"I don't think it's quite as bad as that," Hiressam said.

With a clank, Calene sat four glasses on the table before

them. She had a bottle in hand, and pulled the cork with little effort, splashing a hearty portion in each of the glasses and then picking up her own. Downing hers, she returned the glass empty and said, "It's as bad as that, if not worse."

Hiressam frowned. "Explain."

"Shirri already did," Calene said, pouring herself another. This one she did not knock back in one go, instead sipping it as she strolled to the commanding windows looking over Amti. The lights in the old tree trunks were mostly out, only a few lit at this time of night, giving the city a strange, dark quality. "Influence is crucial to avoiding the scenario Pamyra just set out for you of us standing in a field by ourselves as a storm of red magic crawls across the savannah while we wait to die, a city of useless screamers at our back." Now she downed the rest of the glass. "Problem is: we have no influence. None."

"But we must get some," Shirri said.

"Yeah, I'll pick some up at the corner store next time I'm out," Calene said, pouring again. She eyed the rest of the glasses on the table. "Well, come on. They aren't going to drink themselves."

"This is hardly the time–" Hiressam started.

"This is the perfect time." Pamyra picked up the glass nearest her and gave it a sip. Then she made a face; Shirri could tell between that and the scent wafting off the liquid that it was not a gentle liqueur. It smelled as though it might be used to strip varnish from the countless wooden surfaces found in the city. "It's good," she announced. "Strong, though."

"The weak stuff is ill suited to the purpose of forgetting the problems at hand," Calene said. "And I don't know about the rest of you, but I look to forget what's happened here today, and as swiftly as possible."

"But we need a plan," Shirri said. She looked to her left; Hiressam seemed stricken. Pamyra, meanwhile, had taken another strong sip, and made much less of a face this time round.

"There's no plan to be had," Calene said, her glass in hand, strolling toward the windows. "See, we took our best chance, the one where we speak reasonably to people who are willing to hear us as such. Now, you can escalate, sure, try to throw yourself in the path of a council member, maybe. What are you going to say to them in thirty seconds before they run off that'll get through the shell of complacency that's built around them, and likely thicker than the one around Gareth?"

"We tell them what's coming," Shirri said. "We tell them—"

"That Cyrus Davidon has returned?" Calene asked. "Talk about a message that carries about as much weight as a dry field mouse. You might as well call 'Dragon!' and see what happens. Nothing, by the way. That's what happens, because there are no dragons foolish enough to come to Amti, and no one believes Cyrus Davidon will actually return save for the fanatics."

"Therefore," Hiressam said, "no one will believe that Malpravus was sitting on the throne of Reikonos, and now comes to kill us all." His drink was now in hand, and he took it back in one good gulp. Setting it down before him, he picked up the bottle and refilled it himself, amber liquid sloshing within the glass bounds.

"Do you see the problem now, Shirri?" Calene asked. "The message we've got is hard to deliver without looking like a nutter. Yet it'd be impossible, or near to, to deliver any other message to get them to move. What would we even say? Firoba is coming, ready to invade through the southern tip?" She scoffed. "No one would believe it, Firoba's already about two seconds from dissolving into its own continental war, far too busy to be interested in us at present. And no one would believe Emerald would come over the northern mountains, either, being as they're focused on Pharesia at present." She shook her head slowly, and took a sip. "You can't even accuse the neighbors of warmongering and be believed, so what do you do?" Her voice fell. "What do you even do?"

"You don't give up," Shirri said. This much she knew.

"I give up," Pamyra said, sipping from her glass once more.

"You weren't in the fight to begin with," Shirri said.

A hard hammering at the door stopped Pamyra's reply, and all four of them turned.

"Who'd be knocking on my door at this hour?" Calene muttered, setting down her glass and moving to answer it. When she opened it, waiting outside was not a messenger or a guest, but a guard, in garb slightly different than that of one of the Brotherhood.

He took them all in with a quick look, and said, in the voice of a herald trying to be heard in Amatgarosa, "You are summoned to give account before the Council of Amti."

Calene just stared out the open door. "What, tomorrow?"

He shook his head slowly, and with a wave of his hand beckoned them, the meaning obvious.

They were to see the council *now*.

CHAPTER 73

Cyrus

"You know why I think so often of that moment?" Terian asked, fixing his gaze, hard and spiteful, on Cyrus. There was a twinkle in his eye of smoldering anger, long papered over but now it burned through.

"Because you're thinking of how close you came to being well shut of me," Cyrus said. "Without even having to do the stabbing yourself, like you tried later."

Terian scoffed. "It has nothing to do with that." His gaze hardened. "It's because if you'd died in that moment, if the snake had just gotten away with you...none of this would have ever happened."

"You think you'd be living in some perfect paradise if I'd died that day, Terian?"

"Think about it," Terian said. "You'd never have started down the path of–"

"Remember Ashan'agar?" Cyrus asked. "His plan was to turn our cities to ash, including yours."

"We could have stopped him without you," Terian said.

"Dunce, you didn't even figure out it was him without me," Cyrus said.

"You give yourself too much credit," Terian said.

"And you give me none," Cyrus said. "The difference between us is that I'm clear-eyed about my numerous failings, whereas you can see *only* them. You're a historian of grievance with an axe to grind; your feelings influence the tale you tell about how things came to their present, unpleasant shape."

"The difference between us is that while you've been safely ensconced in the ether for a thousand years," Terian said with a cold and crackling anger, "I've been here, forced to live with the ruin you left behind."

A thump at the far end of the throne room drew the attention of all of them, and Cyrus turned. There was a breathless guard puffing his way toward the circled knot around Cyrus, and he threw himself to his knees just before Terian's dais. "Sov...Sovereign...on the horizon..." he said, barely able to get his words out.

"Yes?" Terian asked, his back arched, chest puffed out; he was every inch the Sovereign now, his petty bickering on hold.

Niamh twitched at Cyrus's feet, and he suddenly knew what was about to be said before it was said. "The scourge," Cyrus said, and the messenger looked over at him, nodding.

Terian met Cyrus's eyes, and, already filled with rage, they narrowed into tight, cold slits. "They're coming."

CHAPTER 74

Vara

Days passed in a crawl like a slow-moving worm wriggling across uneven blades of grass, and Vara felt them all. The sun hung in the same place in the sky until they were ready for sleep, and then it seemed to make its way down swiftly.

"It's always like that," Longwell said, as if apologizing for it. "I just figured...magic."

And it was magic indeed, much like the ever-replenishing foodstuffs – corn that seemed to spring off the stalk, grains that grew nightly to height, beans that waited to be picked up, nuts growing right out of vines in the earth. Animals that practically stood still waiting to be slaughtered.

And there was seemingly no end to any of them. The bounty of the realm was ever-replenishing, always waiting. Hell, Vara reckoned if she waited long enough between meals, a hare might waltz its way over and thrust its own leg into her mouth for her to eat.

She counted only by sundowns and sunups, and even then wondered if perhaps the realm was accommodating them rather than being truthfully reflective of the days of Arkaria. Impossible to tell, though, she determined, and stopped that war within her mind before it could run too rampant.

Mostly she thought of Cyrus, and occasionally of the others.

"I know your thoughts," Isabelle said once, catching her in a quiet moment. But she did not offer, and Isabelle did not press, and thus they both let it go.

Samwen was not nearly so restrained. For the first time in some great length of it, Vara estimated, he was perhaps feeling alive. He talked constantly, irrepressibly, and even when she separated herself from him and Isabelle by going for a solitary walk, she could hear him for some distance. Whether it was at the shores of a lake where once she and Cyrus had battled upon the ice with corrupted creatures of the realm, or into the deep woods nearby, there was no escaping the sound of Longwell anywhere in the realm.

At least not, she thought, until the seventh day, when she decided it was time to depart and check the Reikonos tunnels to see if the fires had run their course.

"Are you sure you want to go now?" Samwen scratched at his wrists, the ragged sleeve pulled up, his tufted beard looking perhaps a bit neater than when they'd arrived, though it was tough to be entirely certain.

"Oh, I do," Vara said, steeling herself as she walked back to the portal, Longwell at her side. Isabelle had deigned to remain behind. Though her condition had certainly improved, she seemed keen on not exerting herself overmuch. "I can honestly say that with the exception of Cyrus and perhaps a pair of leather shoes I once saw in a window in Pharesia, I have wanted little else in my life more than this."

Longwell squinted at her beneath the fierce light of the realm's day. "You cannot believe he is alive, still, though. Isabelle told me–"

"Isabelle does not know," she said. "I do. He is alive." That certainty stayed with her.

"But the entire city was destroyed," Longwell said, hurrying to keep up. "If not by spell, then by fire. You said as much yourself."

"Yes," Vara agreed, that sense of certainty unswayed by his argument. "Yet he lives. How, I am unsure. An airship, perhaps. A regular ship, maybe. Some spellcraft, even. I hardly know, though I will learn when I find him again. All I know for sure is...he is out there," she said as the portal appeared on the horizon. "And I must find my way back to him, so that we can begin the process of setting things right."

Longwell laughed, a hard rasp. "The world is not like some sculpture knocked off a shelf that you can merely pick back up and put back upon its pedestal unharmed. It is shattered and broken, and those pieces do not go back together."

"I don't believe that's wholly true," Vara said, her feet crunching in the green grass with every step. "While the world is in an unpleasant shape, I don't think it's a sculpture that's been shattered. I view it more as a canvas with a very unfavorable painting upon it, one that I hate deeply. Thus far Malpravus has been the painter, and we have let him. Well, no more. I mean to seize the brush, and add some colors I find more pleasing, until all the burnt orange and black death have been covered over with greens and blues, the shades of life."

Longwell lapsed into a silence, then, and it hardly mattered for they were already at the portal. "If he's out there..."

She did not need a translation to know who 'he' was. "He is not," Vara said. "He left after he leeched everything out of Reikonos that he wanted. Malpravus is on to the next vein, the next sparkling locus of power." She stared at the rippling portal.

"The ruin is ours alone – ours and whoever shows up to pick its bones." She steeled herself for the crossover.

"And you're going to...what? Rely on the charity of those strangers to convey you onward?" Longwell said. "To where? I have been beyond the sea, Vara. Yes, there are good people out there, but they have their own problems. And they have not the strength you would need to dislodge that sorcerer." He shook his head. "If Isabelle is to be believed–"

"I don't believe Isabelle anymore," Vara said.

To this, Longwell looked surprised. "She is older and wiser than you."

"She is jaded and cynical," Vara said. "Covered over in grief by the loss of her family, stuck in the prison of the possible. This I understand. But it closes her eyes to possibilities that I am still young and naïve enough not to write off. And in any case," Vara smiled ruefully, "if she is right, I lose nothing by striving to the ends of my leash. But accept her limitations, and, well...I'll be sitting here forever, in this green and verdant dungeon, trapped for all our long lives."

Longwell fell silent at that, and with nothing more to hold her back, Vara gave him the briefest of smiles and said, "I shall return," and with no more reason to wait, stepped into the swirling colors of the portal to return to the ruin of Reikonos, of the city she had left behind.

CHAPTER 75

Alaric

Mazirin was tight in the clutches of the Chaarlandian captain, clad in his fur hat and human leathers. His chest was exposed, and dark ink had been pattered across it beneath a crest of hair. He smirked, his blade pressed to the side of Mazirin's head.

"Do not yield to this cur, Alaric," Mazirin said, her teeth clenched. She bucked against him, but, small as she was, he pulled her back with a firm arm, locked around her head. She was barely up to his chest. "He will kill us all anyway."

The Chaarlandian's black grin gave way to a puckered brow, and he stared down at Alaric. "Arkaria?" he asked in a thick accent. "You...Arkaria?"

Battle sounds had given way, and Alaric looked swiftly around; the crew of the *Yuutshee*, having given barely any resistance, had yielded, their resistance broken at the sight of their captain held hostage. Guy was cornered, blade still chopping at the air, his back to the forecastle rail. His chest rose and fell with alarming speed; he was played out.

"Yes," Alaric said, feeling the pirates inching in around him. It was natural they would take advantage of this opportunity to cross the blood-slicked no man's land around him safely. "I am Arkarian, or near enough at this point."

The Chaarlandian captain laughed. "Ha! Arkarian. Savage." He tapped himself on the shoulder with his dagger. "You – give up. Or me – kill her. Hm? Bloody. Very pain."

"Don't listen to him," Mazirin said, and received a jerking around for her defiance. "He's going to kill me anyway."

"But more pain," the Chaarlandian said, then bared his teeth. "Eat alive. Much suffer." He stared down at Alaric. "You fight hard. But you not win." He made a gesture that seemed to suggest Alaric lay down his sword. "Fight...over."

There was a war within him, staring up at Mazirin, that hard defiance in her eyes, yet a flicker of worry behind it that he could recognize now. Even with a weapon at her head, a thin trail of blooding starting to trickle down through her dusty hair, she was resigned to a fate of death, of pain.

"Your fight...over," the Chaarlandian captain said again.

And what was left, truly? Push every last one of the Chaarlandians over the deck, or gut them, or cut their heads off? Even if Alaric could manage that feat, what would remain by then? Guy was cornered, his strength flagging by the second. Edouard was already surrendered. The pirates had surged belowdecks and were still coming aboard, sliding down the chains with a rattle, in less numbers now but still coming.

Could he fight on, alone, forever?

Perhaps.

But the pirates...they would kill Mazirin, kill Guy, kill Edouard and Dugras and every other crew member of the *Yuutshee* until it was him and them, and whoever won...

...the crew of the *Yuutshee* would already have lost.

"My fight is over," Alaric said, looking the Chaarlandian captain in the eyes.

He let Aterum slip from his grasp. It clanked and rattled upon the blood-soaked timbers of the deck.

For truly, it was done.

CHAPTER 76

Vaste

"He's gone," Glaven announced, peering out a foyer window, "beyond the gates, and at quite the trot." The servant fluttered the white sheers as he came away from the window, not a trace of worry on his face. "I don't imagine it'll take him long to summon a reasonable host to his side, good sir, not given what's been going on 'round here of late."

"Be a good fellow and lock the gate, will you?" Vaste asked. "No need to make it easy for them when they come back. And take care, in case he's lurking out there waiting for someone to do just that."

"Aye, master, I'm sorry it was open – I went to the market this morning," Glaven said, and he was out in the door in a flash, hurrying across the lawn toward the exterior wall. Vaste surveyed the wall and gate with grim apprehension; it would not hold back a mob, not for long.

"You didn't have to do that," Aemma said. She'd descended

the stairs silently, and was lingering by the banister, looking quite worn. "I invited this war."

"I recall you voicing sentiments of that sort, yes," Vaste said, keeping an eye on Glaven as he hurriedly shut the gates. Merrish did not leap out to ambush him, and he breathed a bit easier once Glaven was trotting his way back.

Aemma was now at his elbow. "Why not surrender me, then?" Her voice was delicate, and guilt racked her tanned features. "My people are dead. I earned this fate."

"Yes, well," Vaste said, opening the door for Glaven to scoot back inside, "we'll talk about that in a moment. How long do you reckon we have?" he asked Glaven.

Glaven shrugged. "No idea, really. Termina Guard are clearly still burning the human homes with them inside." He gestured to the window, where billows of smoke were visible beyond the bounds of the estate. "I was watching a bit ago from the southern balcony, before the elf came to the door."

"Wake Qualleron, would you? He deserves a chance to have a say in his fate here," Vaste said. "Now we are left with the choice of what to do next, though." Glaven hurried up the stairs to do just that.

"You could still give me up," Aemma said, seemingly resigned to any fate that came her way. "I would not protest. My friends, my countrymen – they're dead. My end, now, in this place...well, I would not be missed."

That sent a spike to Vaste's heart. "I know how you are feeling right now, because I have felt it myself, quite keenly, these last days." He seized her by the shoulders and gave her a gentle shake. "Being shuffled from place to place, not knowing if anyone I care for has survived the calamities behind me. It's a particular burden, knowing that you've had a hand in death and destruction, and a burden I'm afraid you're going to have to live with."

A tear snuck out of the corner of her eye. "How?"

Vaste hesitated. "I don't know other than by just bullishly taking the next step before you, no matter how idiotic or pointless it might seem. It's all I have done since I saw the wave of death sweep Reikonos, stagger forward another step even when it seemed absolutely moronic to do so, pointless to do so. I was betrayed so thoroughly that I cannot even properly describe my humiliation and my uselessness, in the face of what happened there."

He took a heavy breath. "Yet moving forward I somehow blundered my way into your conflict and now, *now* I see why I still stand, why I still walk, why I still plunge ahead in spite of clearly being up to my neck in a shit swamp of world events." He looked her right in the eye. "It's to help save you, because not another soul in this land could surely understand you now better than I do, having just freshly stepped in the exact same shit swamp you are now near-buried in."

Aemma laughed, somehow, in spite of all. "But you – surely you do not feel you brought about the destruction? That you warrant a terrible fate the way I do? I cheered for this war."

"We're all forever warranting our own destruction," Vaste said. "We are none of us perfect – not you, not me, certainly not Cyrus Davidon. We're stumbling through our lives as our worst selves and inviting all sorts of unpleasantness upon us. That doesn't mean we deserve death or any of the thousand other plagues that come our way."

"But they come," she said. "They come nonetheless."

"Aye, they do," Vaste said. "Sometimes. For I have seen innocents die, and Malpravus get little of what he deserves in recompense for the thousand merciless crimes he has committed. The only thing I can think is...when we see a chance to help a soul in need...well, maybe that's what Sanctuary truly is. Extending that grace, even unearned, if there's the slightest chance of aid to a soul that can be redeemed. For too long I've thought my mission was to punish those who erred even lightly in war and violence, but I see now – it's grace. Mercy, if you will. I wish I could give it to everyone suffering in this city, I can't. But this I can do, offer...well, Sanctuary, to you." He waved off her coming protest with his hand. "And don't tell me you don't deserve it. None of us miserable souls do. You get it anyway."

She looked overcome, but said, simply, "Thank you."

"That was as beautiful a display as I have seen of late," Qualleron's voice boomed from the upper level, Glaven a step behind him as he descended the stairs like an elephant coming down a hill. "I hear troubles are coming." He adjusted his armor. "What, then, shall we do?" He grinned. "Ready ourselves for a great and terrible final stand?"

"Oh, gods, no," Vaste said, shaking his head. "We should run like hell."

CHAPTER 77

Vara

She stepped through into the quiet below the Citadel, and it was exactly as she remembered it. None of the passages to above were opened, no signs were left of Malpravus returning to his old haunts. Even the air had that musty smell that the catacombs had held since the days of yore.

Vara took it as a positive sign, lit the spell to give her light, and began her jog through the passageways.

Her footsteps rang in the silence, rattling down the hallways and corridors of the subterranean ruin. Every corner she turned was filled with foreboding before she came to it, as though Malpravus himself might be lingering there to ambush her, to strike her down with a spell of deadly red light.

After two corners of that anxiety, Vara chuckled to herself. If Malpravus were about, it seemed unlikely he'd be here, down some random tunnel in the underground, which had been sealed off so long even rats did not exist in this place. It truly was a dead city down here, and as below, so, likely, above now.

It took forever and yet not that long to reach the ended passage where the rubble had crashed in, leaving naught but a dead end where she and Isabelle had taken their rest only a week heretofore. The smell of smoke lingered here, as it did lightly upon Isabelle's robes and Vara's own armor and underclothes, even after repeatedly drowning both in the lake of the Realm of Life. It seemed stubbornly thicker here, and Vara took heart in that. Perhaps it still seeped in through the gaps in the rubble.

To wit, those selfsame gaps appeared small to her eyes. Ash had poured in the cracks, settled between them and lay in piles on the floor, undisturbed where they rested due to the lack of air and wind in this place. Vara took the tip of Ferocis and traced the uneven patterns of the breaks between pieces, and found a veritable pile of rubble and stone that lacked any coherence or structure.

Still, there was nothing for it but to dig, and so she plunged her sword into the biggest crack she could and unleashed her spell.

The fury was unexpected but sudden, the response from an angry and unsympathetic tunnel filled with wreckage like a furious rebuke from an angry god. Stones and dust blew through the air, raining off the sides of the tunnel and clanging madly against her armor, battering her to and fro. Vara staggered back a dozen steps, pelted from each side by the hailstorm of stone and drowning in the clouds of thick, nearly impermeable dust she'd just kicked into the air.

Ten, twenty steps back she was forced to flee, coughing nearly that same racking cough as when she'd fled down here. The billowing cloud filled the air now, thick and heavy, like the streets with smoke only a week before. She held a gauntlet up to her face and retreated further until the worst of it seemed to settle, then approached the mouth of the tunnel where the wreckage lay.

Had that large mountain of stone been there before? She could have sworn not; it looked as though she had made no progress at all, that things had actually gotten worse, but perhaps it was the cloud abusing her memory. The air, at least, did not feel hot here, though a few embers remained sparked in the ashes that had come down, dying out even as she watched, plotting her next attack on the blocked tunnel.

Last time, the small fragments had blown off the walls and threatened to beat her senseless. But surely she had cleared most of those. This time, she tried to judge her position more carefully, shining Nessalima's Light into the gaps, seeking a place to lodge Ferocis that would not blow back a literal ton of stone upon her. When she thought she'd found it, she wedged the sword's tip into the spot, drew a deep breath, and breathed the words...

And the world seemed to collapse upon her, rock rumbling and sliding, crashing and weighing her down. Vara was bowled over and then covered over, ash forcing itself into her nose and mouth, choking her even as she felt crushed beneath a wall of death.

She lay there, scarcely able to breathe, covered in the darkness, waiting to die.

CHAPTER 78

Cyrus

"Should have known this would happen," Terian said, the rattling of the elevator carrying them up. The orders the Sovereign had issued had been short barks after the news was delivered: "Rally the army and assemble them in the courtyard. Start bringing regiments up the tower immediately, along with extra Dragon's Breath. And prepare me the fastest spider carriage we have." Then they'd mounted the carriage and been driven at mad speeds through the near-empty streets of Saekaj, up to the tunnel elevator.

"How?" Baynvyn asked as the elevator began to crank, machinery rattling as they were carried up into the tower.

"Because Malpravus can control death," Cyrus said, and Niamh loosed a long whimper beside him. "And the scourge? They're technically dead."

"You remember the time he recruited back to Saekaj?"

Terian asked. "After the battle with the scourge on the Endless Bridge?"

"What of it?" Cyrus asked, sensing perhaps a momentary thaw in their relations.

"How do you think he knew to be there in that exact moment, when the bridge fell, when you and I parted ways?" Terian asked. "He could sense the scourge coming like a dwarf can sense a vein of gold in the rock." A mask of anger fell over his face, and the moment of reprieve had passed. "He just didn't have enough power to take them in his thrall before, so...thanks for that."

"I didn't choose to come out of the ether at the time and place I did," Cyrus said, snapping. "I was summoned by someone in life-or-death trouble."

"And now we're all in life-or-death trouble," Terian said. "Well done." Turning his head, he looked to Baynvyn. "Where's your mother?"

"I assume at her home," Baynvyn said. "Why?"

Terian contemplated that for a moment, then turned to one of his guards. "You – carry a message to Aisling. Tell her to get down to the Great Sea immediately, to embark upon one of the fishing boats, and remain there, off the coast, until she receives word from me." When he received a nod of assent, Terian turned his attention back to Cyrus. "At least one of us will survive this lunacy."

"I thought your tower would protect you from the scourge?" Cyrus asked.

Terian gave him a crosswise look. "It will protect us against the mindless beasts such as the scourge have been up to now. But they aren't mindless anymore, are they? Now they're going to be a coordinated army linked to one mind, one general, who will be telling them exactly what to do. So, yes, I think they might find vulnerabilities in our defenses. I think they might overwhelm the climb points where scourge bodies tend to pile up, and then keep coming until they reach us."

The elevator rattled to its stop in the center of the loading area where he'd battled Terian earlier. Beyond the wide open doors, Cyrus could see the bare touch of the sun trying to squint through a blanket of clouds. It had the effect of almost winking at him in the haze of day's end.

"Not hard to guess where the trouble is coming from," Baynvyn said, slipping between Cyrus and Terian and heading for the far edge of one of the petals that made up the docks. A crowd of guards and dockworkers waited, peering into the distance.

"I find that with Malpravus," Cyrus said, "the trouble often comes from behind, in the form of a dagger between the ribs."

"He must have learned that from you," Terian said, shoving his way to the edge of the platform. "Make room for your Sovereign, you dogs!"

And make room they did, turning and seeing him, then scattering to allow Baynvyn, Terian, and Cyrus forward. The platform clanked gently against Cyrus's boots, producing a noise that was nearly lost beneath that of the crowd.

Cyrus looked below, to the second level and the mighty catapults braced with barrels loaded upon them, guards staring down at the gray cloud rolling across the edge of the horizon like locusts descending upon a field.

"That's...that's a lot of scourge," Baynvyn said.

"Is she going to be able to resist Malpravus's control?" Terian asked quietly, with but a look at Niamh.

"I don't know," Cyrus said, looking down at the gray-skinned, black-eyed creature at his feet. She twitched, and whimpered. "She's more conscious than any of them, so my hope would be that she'd be better able to resist his prodigious will, but...truthfully that is a hope, only."

"Niamh," Terian said, taking a knee before her. "Can you resist that pile of bones?"

She stared at him with her black eyes, then the big head came up and down once, solidly.

"Good enough for me," Terian said, back to his feet in a moment. He looked out at the gray wave rippling across the horizon. They were already stacked to the base of the tower, and now seemed to be piling up. Thousands of scourge, maybe hundreds of thousands, and they were all coming this way.

"Why haven't they come like this before now?" Cyrus asked.

Terian did not even look at him. "You know what direction they're coming from?"

Cyrus found he did not; the landscape was scarred, empty, bereft of grass and hints of life. "Reikonos?"

"No," Terian said, "that'll probably be the knife to the back you mentioned," and he pointed at a near ninety-degree angle to their right. "That way to Reikonos. These...they're coming from–"

"The Perda?" Cyrus asked.

Baynvyn nodded as Terian fell into a trance of concentration. "There's always a wall of them at the edge of the river, trying to get into eastern Arkaria. Termina has a team of divers they send out occasionally to clear their corpses after they fall into the water so as to keep them from piling up enough to create a bridge."

"Surprised that didn't happen in Reikonos," Cyrus said, contemplating what he saw, the battle ahead. It did not look promising to his eye.

"They had a team of divers as well," Baynvyn said. "Tubes and helmets to let them breathe underwater," he mimed lines running behind the head, "and they'd go down, pick up a scourge corpse, decapitate it, bring it up, and toss it straight into crematory ovens made just for the purpose."

"How lovely," Cyrus said.

"All that because of you," Terian said sourly. "You should be honored by all the changes that you've brought to our world, Lord Davidon." And he cast an ireful look at Cyrus.

Cyrus glanced round in a long circle. Of the many petals around the tower, only one was now occupied, and with Hongren's ship. "What's your plan for when they get here, Sovereign?"

"*My* plan?" Terian looked at him with an almost absurd sense of amusement. "It's to fight them with everything I have, naturally. Because I have to, in order to protect my people. Thanks to–"

"Me. Yes, you've made abundantly clear where you think the blame lies for this entire misbegotten series of events stretching back into antiquity," Cyrus said. "However, when you've finished blaming me for things that happened a thousand years ago – and perhaps even some of the ones that happened ten thousand years ago, for I'm sure you'll find some way to include me in those disasters – maybe we could talk for a moment about how best to defend your city now?"

"You're quite right," Terian said, looking out over the undulating waves on the horizon. "There are things that need to be done to protect this city immediately. Things that cannot wait."

And with one smooth motion, Terian drew his axe and swung it at Cyrus's head.

CHAPTER 79

Alaric

"You...weak," the Chaarlandian captain said. The crew were all lined up on the *Yuutshee's* deck, from Dugras to Mazirin, Guy to Edouard, and all the survivors between.

Alaric had some difficulty concentrating on what he was saying. Blooms of pain were running through his back, along one of his legs, stinging in the back of his head. He'd had his armor stripped from him by the Chaarlandians, and they had not been gentle during or after. He'd taken a pummeling, a dozen grins flashing over him, loosing exultant cries as they'd taken revenge for fallen comrades.

Blood trickled from his nose, the metallic taste flooding his mouth. One of his eyes threatened to swell shut, and he cast his healing spell sublingually, but it dampened the pain only a little.

The Chaarlandian captain stood before him and clapped him upon the head. "Never chance. You weak." He held Alaric's helm in his hand, and brought it down, rapping him again on the skull. It made lights flash in Alaric's eyes, the gong of bells suddenly omnipresent as he hit the deck, face stinging where he landed, slick and bloody and sticky. "Us...strong."

"The ship is spiraling down," Dugras's voice penetrated Alaric's consciousness. "We're losing engine power."

The Chaarlandian captain snapped his fingers. Alaric looked back; to his surprise one of the pirates seized hold of Dugras, and the captain announced, "You – fix."

Dugras looked mildly surprised. "Uh...sure. I can do that." He was hustled away by the Chaarlandian.

"You not fix?" the captain called after him, then mimed biting Alaric's helm. "Hm?"

"Yeah, I get it," Dugras said. "Fix it or you eat me. Thanks for the motivation. I needed it." He disappeared below deck, pushed by his Chaarlandian captors.

"Mm." The Chaarlandian captain looked well-satisfied with this. He considered Mazirin for a long moment, then licked her along the cheek. Her revulsion jibed with the flaring blood in Alaric's head and heart, pumping with rage. The captain noted Alaric's response, and dropped Mazirin, sidling back to Alaric.

Alaric kept his head down. He knew this type; dominant and keen to let everyone else know it. Anything he said defiantly would be a challenge, and rob him of an opportunity to later, perhaps, turn the tables.

"You...old," the captain said, breathing down the back of Alaric's neck. He prodded at Alaric's underclothes with a knife, the sharp blade nicking the skin at the back of Alaric's neck.

"I have seen a few years," Alaric said, feeling the hot, stinking breath upon his back.

"Up," the captain said, and Alaric complied. The captain circled him, the blade hovering around his chest. He slitted the front of Alaric's sweaty, bloody tunic, then pricked him with the knife in the chest. Not hard; but enough to draw a welling of scarlet from just below his nipple.

"Old," the captain said. "No good."

"I was good enough to beat many of your men," Alaric said, finding himself looking the larger man in the eye.

The captain seemed to ponder him a moment, then said, "Old meat." He smacked his lips distastefully. "Old flesh." He said a word in his own language, and seemed displeased with it. "No good. Even as slave."

Alaric felt the flare in his eyes, but it was halted by a quick slam to his gut by the captain, he grabbed him by the hair and dragged him from his feet across the deck. Alaric's cloth shoes were lost, and his tunic ripped, the tatters thrown to one of the Chaarlandians standing nearby. Another raced in and grabbed his trousers, tearing them free as Alaric kicked his legs, the pain at the roots of his hair from bearing his own weight.

"You fight well," the captain said, favoring him with a toothy grin as he let Alaric dangle, trying to get his feet beneath him. "Too well. Too old. I see...you be problem." His grin widened. "No problem, now."

And with a last jerk, the captain threw Alaric forward, into empty space. He watched the deck disappear beneath him, his feet and hands flailing into wide open space.

To either side, Alaric could see bridges extending from the ironclad to the edges of the *Yuutshee*, and the pirates shuttling back and forth with armloads of purloined goods. One of them carried his armor and sword, he noted as he plunged ahead, the ironclad's steel hull hanging before him.

A look back and he saw Mazirin with a horrified look upon her face, reaching out for him. But swiftly she was gone, and he hung there for a second, in the air, whipping his head around to see where he was going.

Down. Down was where he was going.

Green grass and dirt were beneath him, and he fell from the side of the ship, dropping into open space, with nothing to catch him but the swiftly rising ground.

CHAPTER 80

Shirri

They were taken across town in silence, under the strangely dark towers looming down like shadows in the night. It worked Shirri's nerves as she walked through the quiet city, the only noise coming from the marketplace. Shirri watched the guards watch them, eyes constantly on her small party of four, their helms ornate and ceremonial, only covering the tops of their heads and crowned with a point and bright red feathers flowing out. They lacked the craftsmanship and detail of the ones from Pharesia; more slapdash, in a hurry, as this whole city seemed to be.

Within one of the old tree-trunk buildings, the council waited, inside a cavernous room of purest wood, staring down from a wide bench, twenty-one across. An older woman sat in the middle peering down at them as if judging them upon their entry. Halfway down on the right, she saw Gareth peering down at her on high, shaking his head slightly as if in disappointment.

"You are called to account," the woman in the center announced. She looked very arch, her hair a silvery blond, the hints of wrinkles around her eyes indicating she was a very old elf indeed. The placard in front of her read *Arcaeny*. It sounded to Shirri's ears like a name rather than a title. "Shirri Gadden, Pamyra, Hiressam, and Calene Raverle."

"Oh, no," Calene said, slurring her words a bit. "I reckon I'm in real trouble now."

Arcaeny stared down at her, arching a lone eyebrow. "Indeed, you might be."

"Oh, well, shits, I've never been in trouble before," Calene drawled. "'Specially not with an angry government on me arse. Oh, wait – yeah, I have. Many times, and by more impressive ones than this lot." She thumbed her nose at Gareth. "Tattling me out to your council, Gareth? Manly move. And for what? Stringing words together in a sequence you didn't care for?"

"This is not about mere words," Gareth said seriously. "Amti is a place of business, and the business of Amti *is* business. Silly as that might sound to you, we have grown into one of the premier metropolises of the Arkarian continent. Rumors such as you are actively spreading might induce unneeded panic, and destroy the productivity of our populace."

"You know what else will destroy the productivity of your populace?" Calene took a staggering step forward, clearly a bit unsteady on her legs. "A great ruddy spell, red in coloration, encompassing the whole of the city and draining the lives of every one of your citizens. That'd probably put a kink in your business. Of business."

"Silence," said Arcaeny. "Your arguments are unpersuasive."

"It would seem you do not wish to be persuaded," Hiressam said, "given that you have not asked for any argument."

Arcaeny peered down at him with pursed lips. "No argument is necessary. We already know what you would say, for you have told the tale all over town. To Gareth, to the head of our Brotherhood. Do the details vary enough that you feel compelled to set the record straight now? Or would you like to alter your story? Make some wholesale changes to punch it up a bit, make it more frightening?"

That one struck Shirri right in the gut. "Do you think we crafted this out of whole cloth?" she asked, taking a step forward. "Made up a story about Reikonos being destroyed for – what reason, exactly?"

"No one doubts Reikonos is destroyed," Arcaeny said, her silvery hair reflecting in the yellowed electric light. "The issue is that Reikonos burns, uncontrolled. There is no spell, nor has there been any magic of substance for hundreds of years." She pursed her lips again in plain displeasure. "To say otherwise is to perpetrate a fraud upon the populace."

"You seem very concerned about what your populace might hear," Calene said.

"Silly frivolities waste their time," Arcaeny said. "They distract, make people chase their own tails."

"Oh, have the elves down here evolved tails now?" Shirri muttered under her breath. "Such advancements since you broke away from the Alliance, I can hardly keep track of them all."

Arcaeny gave her a dismissive wave. "You betray your hatred of us. Your words show you to be another Pharesian saboteur, jealous of our successes and the fact that we southerners have eclipsed the elves of old."

"Just to be clear – I don't care one way or another," Shirri said. "You, Pharesia, Termina – you all seem quite stuck in your own particular ways."

"You needn't try and hide your feelings about us," Arcaeny said. "We are quite used to the jealous scorn of northerners – until they come here and find out that every bit of life is better in Amti. Which is why thousands flock from Pharesia and Termina with each turning of the years. Some even manage to leave their petty jealousies behind. Rare is the occasion where they feel compelled not only to bring it along, but also to serially fabulate whilst here to cause us havoc. But then, that is the province of wreckers like you." She sniffed. "Tear down that which dares to stand tall."

"None of us want to tear down your city," Shirri said, looking around in alarm. "I have no grievance with you, or against you, and I do not speak false. I saw what happened in Reikonos, and it may be burning now, but it was not burning when I left it. A spell killed that city, a spell cast by its own Lord Protector."

A small wave of laughter broke through the council. "Why," Gareth asked, "would Lord Longwell, who has spent the better part of a thousand years building that city into a surprising powerhouse given the dearth of anything available to them, destroy it?" He chuckled. "Madness."

"Maybe because it wasn't Longwell," Calene said. "Maybe because it was the villain of old, Malprav–"

"This is speculative foolishness," Arcaeny announced. "Still more fiction for the masses who you wish to draw away from their labors and into some drama of your own creation."

"We neither created this drama nor did we wish for it," Shirri said; Hiressam had fallen silent, and both he and Pamyra looked greatly abashed. Calene's cheeks glowed red, but she was silent, contemptuous. For some reason, only Shirri seemed to have found her voice. "I, for one, wish I were still in Reikonos, whole and safe – especially now."

"But that wasn't really an option for you, was it?" Arcaeny said; there was a nasty flush in her cheeks to match the gleam in her eyes.

"I don't take your meaning," Shirri said.

"It is known to us," Arcaeny said, "that before you left Reikonos, you owed a considerable debt to the less savory elements of the city. That you came to be in their debt at all tells us all we need to know about your character."

"You think I'm lying because I was in debt to the Machine?" Shirri asked. "To people who kidnapped my mother, who killed others, tried to kill me – you take their word over mine?"

"I don't see any of them here telling me the world is about to end and inspiring those around me to revolt," she sniffed. "The word of one such as yourself, coupled with your clearly ailing mother, a known madman preacher of the gospel of Sanctuary and a woman whose sole function is to tame the wilds..." a nasty smile split her lips. "...you war with common sense and what is known...and you lose. Take it gracefully."

"That's all the good I am to you, then?" Calene asked. "Slaying the wild animals that threaten your frontier settlements."

"It is an arrangement that has benefitted us both for some time," Gareth said soothingly. "You have built up an account with us, and it is still in credit. Please...get back to work before you find your credibility in debit and we ask you to leave."

Calene seemed to bite her tongue, a bitter note of complaint waiting to escape by the look on her face.

"As for the rest of you," Arcaeny said, "you clearly have no place here, no task of use here, no function but to agitate. Passage will be booked for you on a transport tomorrow. You may choose your destination – Firoba, Termina, Pharesia. Within reason, of course – we shan't be sending you all the way to Azwill or Amatgarosa when better options are near at hand. But you will not return here." Her smile vanished. "Because as of tomorrow eve...you are unwelcome in Amti and all of southern elvendom."

CHAPTER 81

Cyrus

Terian's axe blade, glinting like black steel, came gliding through the air at Cyrus's head, aimed to separate him from his jaw and perhaps even head from neck, but Cyrus saw it coming.

And his hand was upon Rodanthar, so with a simple step back, he avoided the blade. "Terian, there is a dire threat to your city right now–" Cyrus began.

"You are the direst threat to my city right now," Terian said, coming at him with a great overhead swing. Cyrus had managed to get his sword up, and it clanged madly against Noctus, sending vibrations down Cyrus's hands, up his arms.

"I think the army of scourge might be slightly more disagreeable to your city's survival than little ole me," Cyrus said, taking a step back. Strong hands shoved at him, the Saekaj guardsmen giving him a push back toward Terian.

"No running away now," Terian said with a gleam of triumph

in his eyes as Cyrus came stumbling back toward him. The guards were going to function as a sort of wall to keep him in the fight, it seemed.

Cyrus rolled low under Terian's attack, his armor clanking as he threw himself forward. If he'd tried the same maneuver without Rodanthar in his hand, it would have surely ended awkwardly, with him landing face-first upon the deck. As it was, he sprang up and spun to face Terian's next attack, a little more room to maneuver with the guards a dozen paces away on this side of the circle.

"Sovereign, what are you doing?" one of the dock workers asked, horrified. "That is Lord Davidon!"

"He's an imposter," Terian said quickly, his eyes flashing with malice.

"I see you've become quite the politician in my absence, Terian," Cyrus said, staring him down over Rodanthar. "You've truly learned to lie."

"I knew how to lie long before you left," Terian said, so softly the others surely missed it.

"Not a white knight anymore, then," Cyrus said, letting Terian take another swing but this time throwing his blade up to meet it. The shock echoed down his arms, and stung.

Terian grimaced, clearly feeling the same nagging aftershocks. "Was I ever really a white knight? I may have become a paladin, Cyrus, but I was always gray at best. Filth of the kind I partook in doesn't ever wash away, really. Surely you realized that after I advised you in all the ways of fighting dirty against Reikonos, against the elves, and against Malpravus." He swung hard again, an overhand blow like he was chopping wood, and Cyrus was the unfortunate log upon his block.

Cyrus let the blow fly past, missing his right shoulder by inches, and took the opportunity to lunge in past Terian's guard, slamming his left pauldron into the Sovereign's chest and staggering him off balance. "Yes, I recall the substance of your advice in those days. 'Stab your enemies in the back.' That sort of thing." He felt his own face tighten in resolve. "Of course, you actually knew who your enemies were in those days."

"With a friend like you," Terian said, staggering, "why the hell do I need to fear Malpravus? He could not do a more complete job of destroying the world than you have."

"Stop this, both of you," Baynvyn said from the edge of the circle. Beside him, Cyrus could see Niamh, still whimpering. "We have little time for such foolishness. Malpravus is coming."

"You think we'll defeat Malpravus with this knife at our backs?" Terian asked, recovering his balance and finding himself at a good range for his axe. Cyrus had not exploited his advantage, and for good reason – being tossed off the tower by the angry mob after killing their Sovereign seemed a poor strategy. Trying to get Terian to come to his senses was starting to appear a thin hope, too, though.

"If you truly believe that," Cyrus said, taking his sword and delivering it back to his sheath with one violent motion, "then you'd best just kill me now, Terian." He threw his arms wide, for there was no way he saw out of this city if he won this battle. Kill Terian and he'd be forced to tear his way through the rest of the guards as well, perhaps hijack an airship. And what good would that do?

No, Cyrus figured. Better to end this now, one way or another.

"Giving up again, Cyrus?" Terian asked, holding his axe at a low guard, looking for the trap.

"Vara left me," Cyrus said. "When she found out about Baynvyn." He glanced at the son he'd never really known. "Alaric, Vaste, Curatio...all are dead, along with our other allies in Reikonos." He bowed his head. "Along with the city. And Malpravus is coming – I see you believe me on that, now. I have tried for this last day – what feels like this last succession of days – not to succumb to the wave of despair that trails me,

Terian, but it is a tidal wave." He looked the Sovereign in the eye. "Truly, I see what I have wrought. I have endeavored not to indulge in what you – my old friends – used to term 'Mopey Cyrus.' I have kept moving forward, trying to think of the next front on which to fight this war with Malpravus. And it comes! Even now. And I would fight to fix it, but at a certain point..."

Cyrus loosed a mighty sigh. "I can't fight it utterly alone. So if you think you're better off without me...well, go ahead. Take your vengeance for the thousand years you suffered without me. But do it quick, so you have time to pull the armor and sword from my body and give them to someone who can aid you in the battle to come."

Terian stared at him for a long moment, axe waiting. Consideration passed over his tight features, the thoughts of a man long stewing in anger.

Without his hand upon Rodanthar, Cyrus saw the decision only a moment before Terian moved – and far too late for him to put a hand upon his sword, or dodge out of the way...had he even wanted to.

"Okay, then," Terian said, and swung the axe for Cyrus's throat. It sailed in swift and true at the warrior's unprotected throat, and Cyrus did not even feel the wind as it came.

CHAPTER 82

Alaric

The ground was coming fast at Alaric, the wind rushing around his naked limbs and exposed flesh as he fell from the *Yuutshee* to Luukessia below. Patches of grass dotted the landscape here and there, dirt covered the vast majority of it, gray and ugly, as he came out of the sky toward the land of his birth.

A swift, instinctual casting of Falcon's Essence escaped his lips, and he stopped, hard, but not painfully, for just a moment. Then he fell again, as though rolling down a hill. Another whisper of the spell, this one causing a flare of pain, a flash of red in his vision, and he jerked, caught once more–

He landed with a thump on the earth, pain shooting along his elbow and wrist, then his knee. They spasmed with the agony, and it shot down the length of him, along his thigh, and snapped back his head. Alaric grunted at the impact, finding his face buried in the dirt.

Alaric was becoming used to the taste of blood in his mouth, dribbling over his chin, mingled with the hard grains of Luukessian sand that covered his sticky chin and tangled in his beard. The rush of the *Yuutshee's* engines roared above him, and, trying ignore the pain that ran the length of his body, he turned on the elbow that didn't hurt, and rolled over.

Already the ships were receding. They were matched in speed, joined together with crossover bridges, slowly rolling across the sky away from him. From here, the difference in the contest was comically obvious; the *Yuutshee* was a third the size or less of her relentless pursuer.

Alaric murmured a healing spell and saw the glowing red that indicated he'd burned a bit of his life. And for what? The pain subsided just a bit.

But the *Yuutshee* and the pirate vessel receded farther in the distance.

With grasping fingers, Alaric felt the length of himself. There was not a stitch of cloth left upon him; he'd been stripped of anything useful before being thrown overboard. Not a weapon was available, and getting back to the ships?

Impossible.

Then, at the lowest ebb, before he could even find it in himself to stand, he heard the sound of thudding paws over the fading of the airship engines.

Turning his head, Alaric already knew what he would see.

For there, in the distance, black eyes glowing in the midday sun–

Scourge.

Hungry, slobbering, and coming to finish what the pirates had begun.

CHAPTER 83

Vara

Her helm was still ringing in her ears from all the falling stones, and though her armor protected her chest from being crushed, there was still pressure along the sides where the plate did not extend, and a tightness as Vara tried to draw breath. There was nothing to draw in any case, or scarcely enough to matter, and she wheezed and coughed with every attempt, sucking in ash and dust, suffocating.

It was an impossible thing, breathing, and she wheezed at the inability. Choking followed, a struggle for breath that outran every fight she'd ever been in for the fear that was now stoked. It was a living thing, awake deep in her mind, panic lacing through, and she tried to flail free, but found nothing but stone atop her, and Ferocis nowhere in her grasp.

Her arms and legs would not move save for inches, and no struggle gained her any ground. The breath would not come, she realized as the panic set in deep, rippling through her like the pain from lack of breath. With every attempt, her chest felt more weighed down, more crushed beneath the weight of stone.

"Vara? Vara!" a voice in the back of her consciousness plucked dimly at her ears, but was drowned out by the pounding of blood through her heart, magnified and echoed through her whole body like vibrations through a tuning rod. Something shifted, and the weight upon her increased, crushing her left arm tighter to the ground; now it could not move at all.

Loud thumps around her head barely registered over the thunder of her heartbeat, out of control. Something shifted above her, was thrown, crashed against a wall, and the weight on her chest and left arm reduced a hair.

"Vara, hold on," came a deep voice from above, and for a moment she thought it might be Cyrus.

It wasn't, though. The beard dangled above her in the dust, and she recognized Longwell a moment later as the weight upon her breastplate lifted, and he threw aside a block of stone the size of a wooden chest.

With urgency, he grabbed at something to her side, and metal rattled behind them. Then he grasped her beneath the arms and dragged her, ignoring when her foot snagged on something; she heard the snap but it was nothing next to the panic of not being able to breathe, to die suffocating–

A few seconds and she was loose, coughing and able to suck in great breaths of life, the sticky dust in the air like nothing compared to what had been choking her when she was beneath the stone avalanche.

"How did that happen?" Longwell asked as her coughing subsided. He sat next to her and nudged Ferocis with his foot. It lay on the ground a short distance away, the clanging thing he'd thrown before freeing her from the landslide.

Vara stared at the rubble; everything she'd done had only made it worse. How like Arkaria, then, for all their efforts. Stone and dust and pebbles and all else had come crashing down into the hole, an entire building or more cascading into the entry to the catacombs by her efforts. Not even a hint of daylight shone for all she'd done, no suggestion that she'd made things anything but worse by miles.

And as that realization settled in, she could not form an answer that satisfied, or left her anything other than rattled and silent, for all the desperation it allowed to seep into her heart. Finally she gave up, and let that crushing feeling sink in, and drifted off to the sound of Longwell calling her name.

CHAPTER 84

Shirri

The night markets hummed in Amti, with stalls displaying everything from fresh fruit to wooden toys to hobnailed boots, all laid out in ordered rows. It wasn't far from Calene's apartment, a short hike in which Shirri blazed stubbornly forward through sparsely populated streets, moving toward the source of the only real noise in town. The trains were quiet, and the airship docks too, which left only the buzz of cicadas and the chatter at the markets, and she drew toward the latter while surrounded by the former.

She breezed past a stand that promised fresh drake hearts and another touting their elephant skins. The air was thick and humid and heavy with the stink of the city sewers. It smelled better than Reikonos...but not by much.

Yet Reikonos was destroyed. Even now fire must surely be ripping through it. There had been fires before, certainly, in the time she'd lived there. A persistent danger, with wood buildings and tinderbox fears. But now it would be tearing through everything, unconstrained, no seawater pumped in to control it, no men, sweating and smelly working to douse it.

It was a small dagger to her heart to feel that, really feel it, as though the heat and the fire were there, eating her alive. It was only her that it would be eating alive, after all – it was not as though there were anyone else alive there for it to devour.

"Azwillian fry bread!" someone shouted, only a few feet from her. Shirri flicked her gaze toward the speaker and realized he was talking to her, for she was the only one nearby. "Yes, you," he said, waving her over. "Come, come!"

He wore the leather vest and chaps of a horse lord of Azwill. A slight smile creased his face, and the paint upon his cheeks stood out against his darker complexion.

"I...I don't have any money to speak of," she said, figuring that would push the hawker to look elsewhere for prey.

"Then you are in an interesting place," he said in a deep voice. He wore a headdress of feathers, which Shirri knew was mostly done ceremonially at this point. Probably a bit of color to draw customers in. "Are you here to beg for food?"

"What? No," Shirri said, shaking her head. "I'm not destitute – well, not exactly. I just left the small amount of coin I have back...where I'm staying." He seemed to be trying to decide what to make of her. "I went for a walk, and I wandered here not paying attention, I suppose."

"I am called Tsawana," he said, and made a motion toward himself that she had seen before but never quite taken in; it seemed a very Azwillian thing, very foreign. "What is it you are called?"

"Shirri. Shirri Gadden."

"Matters of great weight must be on your mind if you wander unthinking, Shirri Gadden," the man said. "What clouds your thinking, frees your feet to wander?"

"I..." She didn't know what to say to that. A quick check

around her and she realized, indeed, they were alone. Few stalls stayed open this late, the foot traffic died down to near nothing. A few stalls away, a hawker barked jealously toward her about hoof paste that cured many maladies, but his cries were shrill and made her cringe. "...have you ever watched a great calamity coming and found yourself powerful to do nothing against it?"

The merchant nodded slowly. "My brother decided to marry a woman from Binngart who sifted heap piles." When Shirri stared at him blankly, he added. "Dung. She moved dung. Came home smelling of...what's your word for it? Shite. She smelled of shite. Always, because she would not find a different job, for it was a family trade, and she worked with her family. Came to Azwill specifically for it. Paid better than anything she could find in Firoba, I suppose."

Shirri felt a little flummoxed. "And it didn't work out?"

He laughed loudly enough to silence the hawker two stalls down. "How would it work out? She smelled like shite all the time. He thought he would get used to it, but he swore later it seemed to get worse with every passing year." He chuckled. "I feel there is much wisdom to be gleaned from his lesson."

"Oh?" Shirri asked. "What's that?"

"If you smell shite at the start, don't proceed to the finish," the merchant said, and then broke into a bout of deep guffaws. "Because it will not get any better."

"Oh – oh!" Shirri laughed. "That was a joke. I didn't realize."

"Well, it was and it wasn't," he said. Tsawana took a step back, seated himself on the stool in front of his kiosk. Some fine Azwillian leathercraft hung behind him. "He truly did it, against my advice, and he truly ended up parting from her later. But it is funny, no matter how badly my brother protests it is not. The smartest among us glean lessons from the failures of others, and I find the most humorous are those most likely to stick."

"I wish...I had a funny story to go with my conundrum,"

Shirri said, "but I'm afraid it's rather a tragedy, devoid of joy and thick with loss of life."

"Oh, yes, those sort of stories," he said. "Well, if you don't mind, keep that one to yourself. I was planning to close up in a few, and I'd like to end the day feeling good."

"I'd probably give you nightmares," Shirri said. "Best keep it to myself. It was nice to meet you, Tsawana." She turned to go.

"Wait," he said. "What kind of nightmares are we talking about? The sort where you awake gasping at a bad step, or the sort where you family is devoured by locusts as you watch?"

"That was cheerfully specific...but the latter, I'm afraid," she said. "Though perhaps worse, arguably."

"Oh, yeah, no, definitely keep those to yourself," he said. "I don't need any more of those in my life. I did my time in the Azwill army in my youth, back when we went through the consolidation, the civil war between the provinces. Those memories still cloud my dreams. I don't need any more of those."

"You are not alone in thinking that way," Shirri said sadly. "It seems no one in this land wishes this particular burden thrust upon them. And I am hardly the sort they would wish to receive it from in any case, being as I have no solution to present. I have only tears to give. The ruin of life, really, and little hope, for this is the only thing I carry with me."

"Should definitely at least bring your coin purse next time," Tsawana said with a wry smile. "Carrying all that other garbage without a piece of gold to weigh against it? You're real hell for a merchant just trying to make a living here."

"I'm sorry," Shirri said, and genuinely, she was.

"Ah, don't worry about it," he said. "No one's out shopping this time of night, anyway. But as to your problem – bad news is badly received. Just the way it is." He smiled sympathetically. "Sorry. No one goes looking for trouble that's not theirs. People have enough of their own."

"What if the problem I know is going to become their problem soon enough?" Shirri felt herself straighten. "What if I know about something that's destined to overflow out of my life and into that of others, like a river running over its banks?"

"That sounds like trouble," he said. "Of the sort people should hear about. But don't count on them to go looking for it. And you can count on them trying to down the telegrapher when they bring them that news. Just the way people are." He almost looked like he wanted to ask, but ended up shaking his head. "Good luck, Shirri Gadden. With whatever you're dealing with." And he turned to his kiosk and began packing up his wares.

Shirri almost told him, but held herself back. She watched him work for a few moments, then turned away, dejected, and wandered off through the market.

CHAPTER 85

Vara

"I am alive," she whispered as she sat up in the middle of a field of perfect green. She woke to the certainty; the breath hit her lungs freely, unencumbered by the hard soot and dust of the tunnel.

There was a rustling against the grass, and Longwell and Isabelle were there in seconds, hurrying from just over the hill. "What happened?" Isabelle asked, moving better now than she had since they'd arrived. "Are you all right?"

"I am," Vara said, breathing free air hungrily. She reached to her side and found Ferocis lying there in the grass. Snatching it up, she put it in her scabbard and stood, brushing the dust in layers off her breastplate. "How long have I been unconscious?"

"A day or so," Isabelle said. She drooped slowly to the ground, still suffering the languid price of their escape upon her. Longwell lingered behind, dust still coating his long beard.

"You were in terrible condition when he found you, Vara. It sounds as though he arrived just in time."

"In perfect time, yes," Vara agreed, brushing her breastplate off once more. Its sheen was diminished by the clinging ash and residue of broken stone dust. "Thank you for that."

"You are welcome," Longwell said. "So surely you see, now?" Beneath the beard, he looked most befuddled, and took a knee, as if all his energy had left him. "We must remain here. Where we are safe."

A most curious tingle ran across Vara's flesh, and the answer came immediately: "No."

That raised eyebrows – four of them, to be exact.

"Vara," Isabelle said, "I understand being concerned about your – our – friends, and mourning–"

"My friends will either be fine, or not," Vara said, pulling herself stiffly to her full height and dimly aware that it was less than either Longwell's or Isabelle's and little caring. They were both kneeling, after all, and thus lording over them took little effort. "I cannot affect their paths at this point, especially not from in here."

Longwell blinked a few times. "Then what do you hope to accomplish? Other than bringing down more rubble upon yourself?"

"That's where you miss it, Samwen," Vara said, sharply pointing a glinting yet dusty gauntlet finger at him. "You have been here for a thousand years and didn't even realize it. So concerned were you with preserving your days that it escaped your notice – or you simply let it slip your attention – that people suffered and died and lived in the gutters and terror of Malpravus's city above. So obsessed were you with hiding your face and staying out of things that you could not influence that you failed to realize even the most elementary truth."

He flushed red but did not say anything.

Isabelle did, but tiredly. "What truth is that, sister?"

"That this is not about us," Vara said, pouring her heart out. "That if I die beneath the wreckage of the buildings of Reikonos – fair enough. A terrible, almost pointless end, but – dammit – I would prefer it to sitting here for a thousand years, forgetting what it is to be under an actual sun, fighting an actual fight, doing something that actually matters to someone other than me."

"You're new here," Longwell said, looking away. "You'll think differently in time. Realize...it's not like you say it is."

"But it is," Vara said, slipping closer to him. "You lost sight of the mission, Samwen. The fundamental belief of Sanctuary. And I can hardly blame you for it. You fought the scourge to utter defeat twice. Lost your city to Malpravus. Confronted him yourself and were beaten. These are events that would steal the heart out of the strongest of us – and I know, because I lost hope, too." She looked to Isabelle. "I failed to keep going, too. I retreated in the face of desperation. I know what you went through in a smaller sense, truly I do.

"But I say to you now," she clenched a fist in front of her, "perhaps that passage is blocked for good. But there must surely be another way out of here, through spell or portal or some way available to us."

"Spellcraft might kill us," Isabelle said.

"Then let us make a death of it," Vara said. "I would rather go that way, swiftly, lost forever between points of teleportation than languish here for the umpteen thousand years I have remaining, hoping someone, someday will stagger their way down here. And what tales will they tell, hm? Of a skeletal dictator who sits on a throne of the world's bones, unopposed because no one would face him?" She shook her head. "Death before that. Anything before that."

"A meaningless death *against* that," Longwell said, shaking his own head.

"There is meaning in *that* death, Samwen," Vara said. "Even if we die to a spell on the way out of here – there's meaning there. In your heart, you know it's true, that every day that passes here you become less of the man you were, the dragoon of courage who charged into dark elves and scourge and put his very life in the hands of his comrades to save those of others, to save lands, to save people, to preserve – to fight, dammit!"

"But the world is ruined, Vara," Isabelle said. "Look what has happened."

"I see what has happened and truly, I cannot have conjured a greater hell than what Arkaria has become in our absence. But I know it will not be set right if we sit here and feast on honeycombs and go to sleep when the will strikes us and discuss – I don't even know, elven philosophy or something to pass the time. We must act!" And here she took a last, desperate breath, for she seemed to be running out of them. "We need to at least try get back into the fight, whatever fate comes from that." Her bit said, she let her shoulders slacken. "Even if the three of us are the only ones in said fight, I tell you now that it would be better for us to die trying to get to Malpravus to stop him than to live here all the rest of our innumerable days drenched in regret knowing that he is doing whatever he wishes to the world out there."

A brief silence followed that, and then Isabelle, quietly, said, "All right. I will go with you."

Vara looked at her, felt the stirrings of hope, and then turned to Longwell–

And felt it die.

"You don't know," Longwell said, his face turned sullenly to the ground. "Probably never will, if you decide to leave." He shook his head slowly. "There's nothing for you out there but death, and I can't stop you from going after it – but I don't want it." He ran fingers through his tangled hair, pulling it back. The once clean-shorn dragoon looked almost like a dwarf in his appearance, save for the height. "I'll leave you be, so you can plan for this – this madness." And he stood, lifting his spear.

"Samwen," Vara called after him, "this may be your last chance to decide whether you wish to fight like a man – or cower like a mouse down here." She watched him bristle, his back to her. "You have done great things, and I know what you are capable of – and it is more than this. Please, I beg you – blow on those fading embers of courage in your heart, and join us."

"I have no hope that you will succeed," Longwell said, not turning to face her, "and so I feel no cowardice for saying the obvious: you will die." He turned and looked her in the eye, and she saw he believed this, wholly, all the way to the back of his soul. "You will choose what you will choose – and I will mourn you when you are gone, and tell others of how you passed, should they ever reach this place." With that he turned and strode off, and she saw again that he had acted in accord with his belief, for there was no hesitation in his stride.

CHAPTER 86

Alaric

The ground was hard, the sky filled with the buzz of the receding airships, and on the ground in Luukessia lay Alaric. Pain racked his body, his healing spell constrained by whatever hobbled magic in this time. But through all the sound, and the warm sunshine, one thing became clear.

Growling scourge were coming, were now a hundred feet or less away, and he had no weapons, no armor, no clothing–

And no hope.

The steady droning of the engines faded as the thump of scourge footsteps drew closer. Alaric listened, whispered another healing spell, and then wondered why he bothered.

There was no stopping the pain, no pushing it back to an acceptable level. And even if he didn't hurt at all, there was not so much as a stick on the ground anywhere about him with which to defend himself. The scourge were but a scattered few, a half dozen, perhaps, but with his magic energy down to nearly nothing and no weapons, his chances of killing even one of them was as good as nil.

Watching the *Yuutshee* calmly recede was like watching his last hope slowly burn in a fire. Death waited for him here, and little better waited up there, and if somehow he survived all of that...

...Malpravus was out there, somewhere, waiting to destroy all he cared about that still survived.

Though, truly, the Chaarlandian captain would likely beat him to that. It seemed unlikely that Dugras – bright, clever Dugras – would survive his whims. Or that Guy, so newly reformed, would see much chance to walk that fabled path to redemption Alaric had promised.

Regrets clouded around him; what else was to be done?

The strangest pang, though, came when he thought of Mazirin. The once-prickly captain had so changed in the last days, hadn't Dugras said? From when he'd met her at the tower to them saving each other as Reikonos was destroyed...

Mazirin, with her raven hair and straitlaced disposition, her dark, inscrutable eyes looking into his...

And now she was in the not-so-tender clutches of the Chaarlandian captain, and however many days she had before her, they would not be easy.

But the *Yuutshee* moved on, mated to that gray ironclad, sailing away from him.

The scourge were close now, the growls overpowering the sound of the airship engines. Without weapon, without hope, what chance did he stand? His hand fell upon the sandy soil of Luukessia; he had come so far, only to die here. Fought so hard, and yet his legacy would be destruction. If only he could have fought on, perhaps...

Well, redemption was a path one walked every day, but his path had come to a distinct end.

No weapons.

No hope.

No chance.

No Sanctuary.

What had he said to Cyrus all those years ago, though?

...There is always hope.

The scourge drew nearer, and he felt a faint tingle in his fingertips.

Another faint whisper trickled into his mind like something in a dream. A memory, long gone, and it took him a moment to realize what it was.

The call of the ether, from beyond death.

He closed his eyes to the sun, and the light faded...

And suddenly he was in the darkness, stretched through the light.

The clank of machinery rattled, and he found himself standing upright, fog shrouding his legs. Dugras was standing feet away, flanked by two Chaarlandian pirates, all three staring at him open-mouthed. "Alaric?" Dugras managed to get out first. "How did you get down here?"

"Here?" Alaric looked around.

It was the engine compartment of the *Yuutshee*.

Then he smiled, his hand falling to his belt, where Aterum hung, waiting, over his armor.

Hope lived.

CHAPTER 87

Vaste

"I'm sorry, what?" Qualleron asked, his voice that same low rumble but adding in a veil of disbelief.

"Merrish is coming back with an angry mob comprised of, at least, Termina Guard with swords, shields, and possibly guns," Vaste said. "We should not be here when he arrives."

"I thought you said you were going to fight for me," Aemma said, her brow furrowed. "To offer me sanctuary."

"I'm perfectly willing to fight if I have to," Vaste said, looking her in the eye, "and die, if need be. But it's not my first choice, because you'll be following shortly after me. All of you would." He looked to Qualleron, then Glaven. "We need to leave. If I had an army, perhaps defending this manor would be possible. Given it's just the four of us, we're better off getting out of here before they storm the place. Assuming they don't just fling in burning casks of oil and barricade us so they can listen to our flesh crackling as they sashay about singing the Elven National Anthem."

"It is a beautiful tune," Glaven said, almost forlornly. "The one before it, though, when we had a king? Was better." He seemed to snap out of his reverie. "If you wish to flee, the swiftest and surest route is through the cellar. There is an entry down there, an old well, that leads into the storm tunnels to the river."

"Is it big enough for trolls, though?" Qualleron asked.

"Plenty so," Glaven said. "This manor was constructed thousands of years ago, and was meant to house an entire wing of servants. Correspondingly, the well is quite wide, and the tunnels beneath agreeably large, part of the expansion project King Danay put in place during the early part of his reign–"

"That's good enough for me," Vaste said. "Glaven – will you be coming with us?"

Glaven blinked a few times. "I was sworn to your service by King Danay, for the act of courage you performed in saving the people of our city from the sure annihilation we faced at the hands of the dark elves. I proudly spearheaded the rebuilding of this manor myself, and have been here all the years since." He looked around sadly. "But...I was never sworn to the manor." He looked to Vaste. "I was sworn to you. If you tell me to, I will come with you."

"If you stay here, they're unlikely to offer you mercy," Vaste said.

Glaven stuck his chin out proudly. "If you ask it, I will remain, and sell myself dear to ensure that as few survivors of their mob as possible continue after you."

"How will you do that?" Qualleron asked. "I do not wish to offend, you simply do not seem to have any weapons about."

Glaven raised an eyebrow; then, with a swift punch against the carefully carved doorframe, a secret compartment popped open and a very sophisticated-looking musket popped out.

Glaven caught it perfectly and swung it 'round, pointing it at the door in a swift and smooth motion. "King Danay recruited me for this position from his army, where I served with distinction for over a thousand years." Withdrawing his weapon to cross it against his chest, the elf stared down the troll. "I have fought trolls, dark elves, men – and now it seems I will be crossing swords, as it were, with my own people."

"Is that a Muceainean auto-rifle?" Qualleron asked, clearly impressed.

"It is," Glaven said. "The household food stipend was meant for a troll, and it comes whether it is used or not, so I have spent it over the years at my own discretion. Ways I thought perhaps the master might like."

"I approve," Vaste said. "Heartily, in fact. You're with us, then. Do you happen to have any such weapons for Aemma? It's her life on the line as much as ours."

"It should be only mine," Aemma said softly.

"But it will not be," Qualleron said, putting a large hand on her shoulder. "Forgive me...but I must regain my honor after being complicit in what happened in Reikonos. Keeping you alive will be only a small start, but I will take it as my charge."

Vaste looked to Glaven. "And you're all right with this?"

The servant made little change to his expression, save for one corner of his mouth to curl. "It has been a long thousand years of quiet. I should not mind a chance to exercise my old ways in your service, my good sir."

"Well, let's hope you don't get the chance," Vaste said. "From the river, where can we go? Where are the airship docks?"

"Just downriver," Glaven said, "of what used to be the southern span."

"I remember that bridge well," Vaste said. "The night I stood on the Grand Span with Cyrus was maybe the longest of my life...until I met Birissa. Hearing the shouts of Lord of Rockridge as he tore apart the dark elves is a memory I think will be with me forever. How far must we go along the bank?"

"A few miles," Glaven said. "Few are down there anymore because across the river is only–"

"The scourge, of course," Vaste said. "Well, that works to our advantage. Perhaps no one will be watching and we can skate right along, catch an airship, and be somewhere else in a few hours." He glanced at Aemma. "Somewhere safe for humans, trolls, and elves."

"Emerald would be best for you lot," Glaven said. "I should remain behind."

Vaste landed a heavy hand on Glaven's shoulder. "If you mean to stay, do not come back here. Merrish is sure to be furious with me for escaping with Aemma. Find a place to hide, or come with us."

"I will not spend my life stupidly," Glaven said, head held high. "I will find a place to keep my head low until the situation changes, and, if my good sir wishes, I can contact via telegraph, keep you apprised of the current state of things."

"I don't know what that is," Vaste said, looking to see if anyone was as mystified by this new word as he; they were not. "But all right. Help Aemma find a weapon?"

"Yes, my good sir," and Glaven snapped to it. He led Aemma swiftly up the stairs, though she kept a grateful eye on Vaste as she went.

"I worried about you, you know," Qualleron said. "That you felt entirely too disconnected from things as they unfolded, as if you were done with the world, that it had no more to offer you."

"I felt that way," Vaste admitted, watching Aemma disappear over the edge of the balcony. "But I suppose I got over it."

"Good," Qualleron said. "You may feel done with the world, but clearly the world is not done with you."

"Yes," Vaste said. "I'm now at peace with the fact you people will not leave me alone."

"Excellent," Qualleron rumbled, a twisting smile of mirth on his massive face. "It is improper for a champion such as yourself to hide himself away from the struggles of life – when there are so many battles yet in front of you."

"Let's concentrate on winning this one, shall we?" Vaste said. "Now come on. We need to go, so collect whatever you need, and let's get the bloody hell out before they come back with pitchforks and torches."

CHAPTER 88

Alaric

He killed them swiftly, before either could loose more than a cry that was lost in the noise of the engines. Blood spattered the clanking machines, and pipes popped and hissed as steam escaped from them.

"Last time I saw you," Dugras said, looking him over very skeptically, "you were stripped to almost nothing and seemed to be the object of that pirate captain's attention." He raised an eyebrow. "How did you manage to get your armor back on, rearm and get down here?"

"I had help," Alaric said, keeping Aterum in his grip. "Are there other pirates down here?"

"I think we passed five on the way down," Dugras said, turning to fiddle with a knob. "I have to get these engines back in balance." He furrowed his brow as he worked. "But there's a shipload more just across the way. Killing these two, killing the other five – it's not going to do anything, Alaric."

"How many others do you reckon are in the Chaarlandian vessel?"

"I don't know," Dugras said. "Dozens? Hundreds? It's not a small ship, and it's not going anywhere – though we will be, and right into the ground if I don't fix this thing." He sighed. "I swear, nothing's ever easy around here – ah, there." He seemed to relax, and wiped his brow, profuse with sweat. "That'll keep us steady for a while, anyway."

"Then might you be available to give me a hand?" Alaric asked.

"A hand at what?" Dugras asked. "Look, you know I admire you, and what your group does, but this fight – it's over, Alaric. They won. We lost. It would take a damned army to kill those Chaarlandians–"

"No," Alaric said, a steady calm falling over him, and beneath that, a trill of excitement. "But it might take a ghost."

CHAPTER 89

Shirri

"Shut up and fire your arrows," Calene muttered darkly, almost to herself as she unlocked the door of her apartment. When she opened the door, the smell of strong drink still infused the air as though they'd spilled it before leaving, but Shirri knew it wasn't so. It was just where they had left it, the cork off, glasses half-filled or drained and waiting for them to return. "They as good as said that to me, didn't they?"

"At least they didn't tell you that you had no place here," Hiressam said. "A madman, am I?" He hung his head. "I've heard that before, and it sounded more realistic to my ears before I saw Cyrus Davidon return with my own eyes." His voice shook, though, and Shirri could see something going on within the man.

"Your reputation precedes you, clearly," Pamyra said, helping herself to her glass. "As did ours all."

"They thought the worst of us, that's sure," Calene said,

resuming her place at the window, bottle in hand. "Troublemakers. Wreckers. Hmph." She took a swig. "Wouldn't want any of that 'round here, I suppose."

"So, then," Hiressam said after a pause. "Where shall we go?"

Calene was first to answer, swaying and slurring her words. "Well...seems to me you lot have about as much chance of talking them into what you're selling in Pharesia and Termina as here. Maybe slightly less than you'd have in Saekaj. So...reckon I'm just going to see you off tomorrow, pick up my bow...and get back to work."

Shirri stood there, stunned. "But...you said you were with us."

"Yeah," Calene said. "And I was. Still would be, too, if I saw much point in it."

"I don't understand," Shirri said, for she didn't.

"There is no more road," Pamyra said, and Shirri turned to her mother, who sat, icy calm, upon the edge of the sofa. "Do you not see it, daughter? No one will believe us, outside of Calene here, because no one but the mad wish to believe in a past of magic and danger and adventure over a comfortable present of churning cities and busy life, where food is comparatively abundant and war is out of mind. Who with their wits about them would choose to believe a madman with spell-magic is coming to claim their very souls when more joyful options are close at hand?"

"They can bury their heads in the sand like one of the tallbirds of Coricuanthi," Shirri said. "But that does not make me free of my obligation to at least say, 'Malpravus is coming. And death comes with him.'"

"Shirri," said Hiressam and she turned and her heart fell, for she knew she had lost him ere he even spoke his mind. "Take it from one who has wandered these cities for the better part of a thousand years trying to spread the principles of Sanctuary to all who might listen...none will be willing to hear this. They were barely willing to accept me, a man who knew Cyrus and the others before the fall of Reikonos. This message you bring of doom, this heraldic warning of ills to come..." He shook his head slowly. "...it will make you unwelcome in every place you dare to speak it, and the few who wish to hear your message will not be the sort you want to associate with."

Shirri looked at each of them in turn as though she were being attacked on all sides; Calene with her calloused hand around the neck of the bottle, Hiressam looking at her sadly, and her mother with an air of self-satisfaction. "I cannot believe this. You – you two," she stabbed a finger at Pamyra and Hiressam, "you saw with your own eyes what Malpravus did."

"Yes," Hiressam said, "and no one will take a word of that testimony on faith, Shirri. I'm sorry."

"I am leaving tomorrow, daughter," Pamyra said. "I will take whatever airship ticket they offer, and will go as far as they allow me, at which point I will buy a ticket that will take me as far as my own funds will carry me. There, I may start walking, or riding if there is a motorcoach, but I will get as far from this place, from Reikonos and Arkaria, as I can. There I will live out my days, trying my utmost not to think of these past weeks, and grateful for every breath I am given."

Shirri exhaled, and it felt like she spat fire. "Every breath I am given, in that place, will be at the great cost of the breaths of the people of Termina...and Pharesia...and Emerald...and eventually, Amti, yes, whether they want to see it or not." Her voice rose, echoing off the walls. "Leave, then, all of you. Cowards." And she went for the door, unable to tolerate this madness any longer, this cold and cruel denial of reality, of what was coming – what they all *knew* was coming.

"The only people that will believe you are in this room," Pamyra said.

"If you believed what you saw," Shirri said, giving her an icy glare, "you would not be able to stay silent, nor run and abdicate the responsibility given. Not after the oath we took, the words we spoke – the vow that Alaric took from us."

"No one could possibly stand against this," Pamyra said. "Including Alaric – clearly. A promise made to a dead man need not bind you the rest of your days."

"The way I see it," Shirri said, "I will be bound by this or I will be bound by self-loathing about my own cowardice as I watch the death of millions." The words seared as they came out. "I know which I choose to be bound with. Goodbye, mother." And she left without another word, leaving the craven behind her.

CHAPTER 90

Vaste

The empty well in the cellar was as big as Glaven had promised, wide enough around that even Qualleron did not struggle to descend into its depths, clutching the metal and rope ladder that the servant had unfolded, secreted into the corner, "Just in case!" he said brightly.

It seemed to Vaste that Glaven had a great many things planned for in his thousand-year wait. He had not been idle, or at least not idle as much as he could have. On his back he carried provisions, his auto-rifle slung so that he could descend with the rest of them, hanging on surprisingly well given his additional paunch.

The tunnels had a rough stink; mildew mixed with the rich iron of blood. Little rain had clearly come since the great murdering spree of the elves, for clotted red dotted the edges of the tide pools, and rust-colored stains marked places where blood had washed in with currents that had now diminished.

"A city under siege," Qualleron commented as they moved by the light of the Eagle Eye spell, following Glaven, who apparently knew his way. "A city come to ruin, ripe with slaughter."

"I'm sure you have stories about those," Vaste said. "You know, from other parts of the world."

"Indeed," Qualleron said. "Many. None that involve sewers, so this is a first."

"This is more of a storm drain," Glaven said. "The sewers smell much worse."

"I'm going to trust you on that," Vaste said, "because I don't desire to smell them for myself."

The tunnels spanned for some way, and the sound of water dripping was the strongest noise other than their footsteps on the stone. They reminded Vaste of the undercity beneath Reikonos, save for all the water rushing through between the pathways that hugged the walls.

Walking down here, he could hear the occasional conversation above, the sounds of voices speaking in elvish, horribly distorted by the echoes as they were projected through the storm drain openings to gutters above. Whenever they heard such sounds, they fell to silence. The tunnels seemed to follow the streets, and pinched, milky light broke in from above here and there where the drains opened to the street, but barely enough to keep from leaving them in the dark most of the time.

Through twist after turn, Glaven led them, his auto-rifle clutched in his hands, held before him with the barrel always pointed into the darkness, ready to fire at whatever trouble leapt out.

None did, thankfully, and soon a pinprick of light in the distance heralded the exit. It grew in size and brightness as they drew closer, a circular pipe that soon enough gave way to bright, gray fog. It waited beyond, and when they reached the egress Glaven was first to pop his head out, looking carefully in either direction.

"We seem to be clear," Glaven announced, and dropped a foot or so out of the drainage tunnel to the bank below.

Vaste followed after him, looking for himself. The riverbank below was a silty dirt edge spanning from the tunnel some ten feet or so to the river, which swirled on unhurriedly north, toward, eventually, the once-Torrid Sea. Mist and smoke blotted the far bank from sight and, indeed, made even the ruin of the central span look like it merely disappeared into the fog. Vaste could tell, barely, that it came to an abrupt end, though perhaps only because he was looking for the edge in the mist.

"You fought one of the great battles of your life upon that bridge?" Qualleron asked.

"I suppose," Vaste said, giving the broken span another look. It extended to about halfway across the river then stopped, the stone road bed simply tapering to an end, as though a titan had hacked it cleanly off there. Black smudges marked where the explosion of Dragon's Breath must have cut it. "It was one of so many, really, but definitely a memorable night."

"Tell me about the battle," Qualleron said as they began their hike along the bank. He was sufficiently quiet, almost whispering, such that Vaste felt little need to get exercised about his politest of inquiries. His boots crunched softly along the silty bank.

Vaste turned, keeping his voice down, and pointed where the span of the north bridge was not even visible in the mist. "The Termina Guard was to hold that one, while Sanctuary took up the center and southern spans. The Grand Span was the largest of the three to unite the banks of the river, and it went right into the heart of Santir, the human city across the Perda. The dark elves had marched in after cutting a brutal swath through the Human Confederation's southern edge. Prisoners were...they were not treated well, let's say that." He caught Aemma looking at him with a sort of doubt mingled with wonder in her eyes.

"It was as bad as anything you've seen here," Glaven said. "I was with the Termina Guard that night on the Northbridge." His eyes glistened in memory. "Few of us made it out alive, and those that did – well, it was all thanks to Sanctuary and our own Endrenshan, Odellan."

"An unsung hero, Odellan," Vaste said, feeling a twinge of regret. "He came to Sanctuary after that, you know?"

Glaven's eyes became even mistier. "Indeed. I considered following him myself, but duty compelled me to stay."

"He was a good man," Vaste said. "The day we lost him, at the temple in the Dragonlands..." He shook his head slowly. "...I think Cyrus still blames himself for that one, though he doesn't talk about it much. But regardless...Odellan did his best in the north, but the elves broke under the onslaught. They had no spellcasters to speak of–"

"None," Glaven said hoarsely, the memory clearly getting to him. "We did our best, some five thousand elves against a host a hundred thousand strong, but as daylight broke we were overrun and reached the edge of the city." He cast a last look back; the Northbridge was still invisible in the thick mist. "There was no regaining that ground."

"Sanctuary held the center, though it was difficult," Vaste said, nodding along with Glaven's story. "And the Southbridge, though it was defended by only two of our number, a rock giant and a healer – both dead now. Actually, that applies to nearly everyone who was there that night. But not Cyrus. Not Vara. And not me–"

"Yet," said a voice from above.

At the edge of the walkway that looked down over the bank, a familiar face peered at them, along with dozens of the winged helms of the Termina Guard.

And looking particularly cruel and self-satisfied at their center...was Merrish.

CHAPTER 91

Cyrus

"STOP!" The voice echoed over the crowd on the tower pylon. It rolled like thunder over hills, crackling over the sound of scourge somewhere far down the tower.

Terian's axe stood poised at Cyrus's throat, the edge of the blade barely kissing the gorget. The Sovereign was staring at him fiercely, his weapon hovering, motionless. "I stopped before you yelled. Might have disrupted my concentration, you know."

Cyrus turned his head; Baynvyn was inches away, reaching out with Epalette, but too far to be of use, and not the source of the shout in any case.

Behind him, the tiny figure wrapped in a cloak against the fiercely blowing wind...she was the source of the shout.

"I trust your concentration is strong in the face of mere yelling," Aisling said, her cowl rustled by the wind. It blew hard, out of the west, and the reek of death came with it. "I imagine it is nothing against getting your face slashed by a sword."

THE SCOURGE OF DESPAIR

"Or your head popped off by the Siren of Fire," Cyrus added.

"I could still take yours off from here, you know," Terian said, and grudgingly pulled the axe back. "But I won't." He brandished the weapon, pointing it at Cyrus. "Not because I think I'm wrong about you; you are a hazard, you left us behind–"

"Yes, you've made plain your feelings about all of this," Cyrus said.

"–But because with those things coming," Terian said, "I don't think I can spare your help."

"Sense at last," Baynvyn breathed.

"A rare finding in the councils of men," Aisling said, shoving her way up to them. "So...can you put aside your differences and win this battle?"

Terian looked to the horizon. He lowered his voice, and Cyrus barely heard him. "I'm not sure this battle is winnable." He sighed, his shoulders gently slumping. "But if it is..." And he looked to Cyrus. "...I imagine some help would be in order from one who has won such battles before. If that someone were still willing to help us."

"I am willing," Cyrus said, and offered his hand.

Terian looked at it for but a moment, then away, and said, "We have much to do and little time." And shouldered his way through the crowd of guards and workers, toward the edge of the dock landing pad.

"Always nice to have your leaders at each other's throats just before a battle where we all may die," Aisling said, suddenly at Cyrus's elbow.

He could not find it in himself to disagree, with the gray cloud rippling across the open fields toward them, a living sea of scourge coursing like a flood toward the lonely tower. Still, he said, "Better than having just taken each other's heads off, though," and moved to follow Terian.

"Marginally, perhaps," Aisling said, not moving to follow. "But only if you survive the scourge doing it for you."

CHAPTER 92

Vaste

Merrish leapt down and landed deftly on the soft soil in front of them, neatly interposing himself between them and the dockyards. He wore a leering sort of look, undeterred by Glaven raising his rifle to track the man, and keeping it pointed such that Merrish would surely catch the bullet in his sparkling, perfect teeth when the servant fired.

"Now, now," Merrish said, his guard leaping in behind and in front of them on the bank, their armor clanking upon the landing. The mist curled around them as the wind blew through, circlets of white smoke with the scent of fire upon the air. "This still doesn't have to end in absolute calamity."

"How did you know we'd be here?" Vaste asked, getting a rather sick feeling in his stomach. Qualleron probably hadn't sold them out, but he'd sent Glaven after Merrish to lock the gate. It would have been a simple thing for the servant to call out, offering him the simple knowledge that they'd run. It wasn't as though there were many safe places or paths in Termina for non-humans just now, after all.

"I have a guard on the front of your mansion as well," Merrish said with a smirk, "but you should know that a city like Termina has no secrets. The average age of the elven residents is three thousand. We all know about the tunnels, for we were there when they were constructed. So if you planned to run, what were your options? To scale the walls of your own manor into the one next to you, and then to the next?" He shook his head. "No, you would crawl like a rat, of course." His smile grew broader. "And now you are trapped like one."

"I suppose you think of yourself as the sort to deal with pestilence," Vaste said, "and humans are, to you, nothing but that – worthy of extinction."

Merrish flushed. "It was not always so, but now it is them or us. Not the choice I would have made, but the one they have cried out for." He looked hard at Aemma, who stood behind Vaste's shoulder. "You would know more than most, would you not? You sought this war, begged for it with your every prayer–"

"I don't pray," Aemma said. There was no give in her, and her chin was held high. She would go to death with her pride, Vaste had no question. But how to prevent that outcome...?

"You might want to start," Merrish said smugly. A few of his men had pistols of the flintlock variety, and with grips as ornately carved as anything else to be found in the land of elves. "I give you a chance to save yourself, Vaste, because you were an honored hero of Termina. You, the mercenary, and your servant may still walk free. Step away from the woman."

"Qualleron," Vaste said. "Glaven. You heard him."

Glaven did not remove the rifle from his shoulder, and it was still aimed squarely at Merrish's unblinking face. "Are you giving up, my good sir?" Qualleron did not speak, but Vaste could hear the larger troll behind him, breathing quietly and steadily, as if preparing himself.

"Me?" Vaste asked. "I've seen enough death to last ten lifetimes. But...I find I'd rather die myself than betray my ideals. You want to slaughter the human?" He gave Merrish a hard look. "You'll do it over my dead body, too."

Merrish barely blinked. "As you wish."

Glaven fired, but Merrish had already jerked, and a gash skimmed its way across his jaw, blood spraying out as the former lord grunted in pain. Two of the Termina guards in front of them raised their weapons, but Vaste leapt forward, Letum in hand, and bellowed a spell–

The Force Blast shot from the tip of his staff and bowled them over, smacking into Merrish and knocking him, bloody mess that he was, to the silty ground.

"Glaven, leap up and cover us!" Vaste shouted, then spun. Qualleron was swinging his sword at the five elven guards behind them, and spiked one of them into the river bank with the flat part of the blade. A bone-cracking crunch was followed by the ringing like a gong, and the guard fell over.

"Ah!" Glaven shouted; apparently he'd leapt for it just as instructed and found the Falcon's Essence spell that Vaste had cast upon him. His shoes scratched against the stone, and he fired the gun again, the bullet spanging off a guard, who shrieked out and fell atop one of his fellows, removing another one from Qualleron's opponents.

"How many are up there, Glaven?" Vaste asked. Aemma was beside him, flintlock pistol in her hand, drawing a bead on one of the guards, bearing it down to shoot him in the gap of his helmet. He brushed it aside before she could fire, then shook his head. Killing elves was not going to solve this.

"None, Sir Vaste!" Glaven shouted.

"Up you get," Vaste said, giving Aemma a light shove. She jumped, and her foot hung in the air for a second, causing her to cry out. Another simple step and she was on top of the seawall, leaving Vaste and Qualleron alone with the remaining guards.

"Leave them with me and leap up, Qualleron," Vaste said.

The bigger troll did just that, clearing the wall in one solid jump. "Hahahah!" he shouted, "you cannot beat the physical prowess of a Prenasian warrior!"

"Yes, I'm sure that's it," Vaste said, and blasted the remaining Termina Guards with a broad-based Force Blast that sent them all tumbling over. That done, he cast his own Falcon's Essence and leapt up, catching the edge of the seawall.

A clang followed, and he looked down; hanging just beside him was Merrish, a blade in his hand, a spiteful look on his bloody face. A gash was carved from his lip almost to his left earlobe, as though he'd gone after an unshelled oyster a bit too enthusiastically. "You cannot think this will stop me."

"Stop you? Why, my dear Merrish," Vaste said, thumping him on the fingers and making him grunt, then fall to the silty soil below with a plop. "I'm just trying to get away from you." With a sharp nod at the three others, he said, "Let's go," and they were off, sprinting down the riverfront.

CHAPTER 93

Cyrus

"That year we were in Luukessia, I truly started to believe I'd die facing these things," Terian said, standing upon the edge of the lowest petal of the great tower, looking down upon the coming flood of gray flesh. This new wave of scourge was nearly upon them.

"On the Endless Bridge, I started to feel exactly the same," Cyrus said.

"I've heard the tales, and just to put it out there, I never wanted to be in any of those places with either of you," Baynvyn said, looking along beside them. "I know some of my generation felt as though they were born too late, having missed the great events of the War Against the Gods, then the Scourge, but personally I always felt quite gratified that I didn't come of age until all that bloodshed was over. Not that I mind a good fight, I just prefer the struggles of small actions versus one or two or ten people over the big battles in which one can find himself overwhelmed and struck down from any angle."

It was a long way down, wind howling under the blanket of iron skies. "It had its moments," Terian said, glancing only briefly at Cyrus before turning back to the trouble coming their way.

"One thing I don't understand," Baynvyn said. "Why does Malpravus not just cast his spell and kill us all in the earth and be done with it? Why send the scourge at all?"

"The earth is the answer," Terian said. "It diffuses magical energy. His spell would stop but a few feet into the ground. No, if he wants to cast this spell, this brutally intensive and draining spell, he needs to have no earth between his intended victims and himself. Therefore–"

"He needs to be in the caves," Cyrus said. "That's why he's using the scourge to open his way."

"But then...Western Arkaria?" Baynvyn asked. "He could bypass us, move on to them–"

Terian chuckled. "We're the most populous state in the land, and not nearly so spread out as the humans in the west or the elves in the south. Why, we're the most succulent berry upon the vine, and he probably imagines us ripe for plucking." With a nod at the coming swarm, he turned to the nearest catapult. "Are they in range?"

"Nearly, sir," the operator said. He was clad in but a tunic and lacked for anything but a stone knife on his belt.

"Fire as your weapons come to bear, then," Terian said stiffly, and stood up straight, heaving his gaze over the battlefield as though he could predict where the first blow would land. "Let us see if we can hold these beasts off," and he lowered his voice, "or if we are about to become swept away under the coming wave."

CHAPTER 94

Shirri

"Come on."

Someone shook her awake, causing Shirri to open her eyes to brightness unanticipated, jolting her out of a dead sleep into the chill of the early morning.

When she opened her eyes, a guard stood over her, his helm glinting in the morning sun. "Come on," he said again, his youthful face a barrier through which no emotion escaped.

Shirri stirred. She'd fallen asleep on a bench on the edge of the markets, and now people were passing, rushing, really, hurriedly. Clearly the morning rush was in full swing.

"Am I in trouble for sleeping on the bench?" Shirri asked, gathering her robes about her. She hadn't even realized she was going to fall asleep here; she'd have preferred the couch back at Calene's, but somehow she'd wandered too far in the dark, and been overcome by weariness. Planning to sit for a moment, instead she'd sat right down and gone out.

Now it was morning, and guards were scowling down at her – except for the lead who'd shook her awake. There was no feeling on display there. "Come with us," he said.

This was not about sleeping on the bench, Shirri realized. "Fine. To the dockyards?"

The guard took the lead, but shook his head, leaving Shirri a worrisome feeling in the pit of her stomach. "Come with us," was all he said as they marched her away.

CHAPTER 95

Cyrus

The scourge wave reached the bottom of the Saekaj tower with the force of the tide breaking upon the shore, and yet, at least at first, Cyrus could scarcely tell they were there.

"Ripples in the pond," Terian muttered as the undulating mass stretching to the western horizon flattened out, and the wild growls of the scourge reached Cyrus's ears. They seemed to lose all character and definition, blurring into a sea of the dead, growing deeper, spreading out in a wide circle beneath the petals of the Saekaj tower.

To his side Cyrus heard the crank of the nearest catapult launch it dozenth shot. It sent a barrel with a flaming wick trailing a foot behind screaming into the mass of gray below. When it hit there was a thump, then a roar, and gray flesh scattered in every direction beneath a pall of black smoke.

The same scene was repeated in a rough circle around them, a dozen or a hundred undefined scourge bodies being torn to pieces some three hundred feet below at ground level. With every boom Cyrus felt the roar of it in his bones, the brightness scorching his eyes so he lost sight for a moment whenever he looked directly at one as it went off...

...Yet still, the scourge came.

"They're climbing," Baynvyn said, prone at the very edge of the platform, head hanging over. He stared down, down at the rippling wave, and Cyrus was reminded of a time when the tide had rushed past him on the shores of Luukessia. Water, in that case, though he'd experienced the same there from the scourge, now that he thought about it.

"Spikes aren't stopping them?" Terian asked.

"Oh, it's stopping quite a few of them – for now." Baynvyn lifted his head. "You're welcome to take a look, but suffice to say with the number that are coming behind them, the ones that have chosen to climb are being crushed into the spikes, and others are lifting themselves on their bodies, or rising on a pillar of newly-arrived scourge."

"Hm." Cyrus knelt, hanging his head over the edge of the platform, determined to see for himself.

It was as Baynvyn said; where before the base of the tower was black and covered in spikes, now the base was buried in scourge, the stem of the thing writhing and undulating as more gray beasts climbed like a seething, surging mass up, up, and closer to the lowest platform.

"You see my inevitability now," Malpravus's voice sounded over them, as if spoken from a thousand throats, vomited up by a hundred empty, long-dry skulls. "I am coming for you at last, Terian. Surely you knew this day would come?"

"I knew that a scorpion never misses the chance to sting," Terian said, his face twisted with hate. "But perhaps in my ambition to keep my people fed, to make them more prosperous, I put that lesson aside for a time."

"You always did embrace the truth of power a bit more

readily than meager Davidon," Malpravus said. "But you were always the poorer vessel for it, too. You never had quite the same potential, did you?"

That caused Terian to turn a resentful eye to Cyrus. "So I've gathered...almost my entire life."

"Worry not," Malpravus's voice echoed again, "for all of you will be equal in death. Equally forgotten, equally my slaves, your very essences turned to my noblest of purposes."

"What's noble about dying to serve you?" Baynvyn shouted. The voice, Cyrus realized at last, was coming not only from the Scourge below, beneath their clicking and scrabbling, but also...

...from behind him.

He turned slowly to find Niamh twitching, but her mouth moving along with every word that Malpravus spoke.

"Why...it is the only purpose that will be left," Malpravus said, and even through the pained grimace upon the Niamh-scourge's face, he could see the necromancer's smile, wherever the bastard was. "...for mine will be the only one remaining when this is done...and is there anything nobler than winning?"

CHAPTER 96

Vara

They discussed it for some time, back and forth, she and Isabelle, with no comment or word from the once seemingly-omnipresent Longwell, who had simply disappeared. But no matter how many ways they tried to hash it over, the ideas for leaving came down to one and one alone:

"Teleportation," Vara said. "It is the only way."

Isabelle sighed greatly. "I have told you, that spell is not safe."

"Staying here and slowly dying seems more dangerous still," Vara said, lowering her voice. "Look what time and waiting have made of him." She inclined her head in the direction where Longwell had disappeared. "Would you like to become half-mad and hopelessly craven, as he appears to be?" Without ceremony, she stood, clearing off the last bit of honeycomb she'd been indulging in while they'd talked it over. "Better we go – and soon."

"By 'soon' I think you mean 'now,'" Isabelle said, similarly getting to her feet. "Have you considered that perhaps there might be a middle course between yours and Longwell's?" She brushed dry grass off her robe, which had never really recovered from the crawl through Reikonos, and in addition to being gray with soot, had many, many holes, especially about the legs. "Something where we perhaps bide our time for another week, a month, setting a definite date where we will–"

"Every hour we delay, there is room for courage to falter and doubt to creep in," Vara said, stepping right up to her. "I don't mean to sound mad, but perhaps I do. Hesitation becomes habit. The longer we are here, this realm providing for us, the easier it will be, I think, to forget our chosen duty. Or at least – mine."

Isabelle turned her eyes down. "I never took duty as seriously as you people of Sanctuary, and my last thousand years have been...well..." She looked up. "...Dreadfully unfulfilling, if I'm being honest."

"You want to live many thousands more years in that way?" Vara asked. "Varren Perdamun, Cyrus's grandfather, was a human man, and he lived some ten thousand years before surrendering his blade and dying naturally. Imagine how long we might last, we three, in this place, with our weapons. No; I say let us charge boldly into our end, not mewl and loaf about for millennia."

"Very well," Isabelle said, and took a deep breath. She paced a few yards, blinking, and, Vara thought, remembering a spell probably long forgotten. "Where would you have us go? I'm thinking Phares–"

Something struck a heavy blow across the back of Isabelle's head, dropping her to the ground, eyes fluttering before she even landed. She was out, Vara knew, and Ferocis practically leapt to her hand as she turned, for she was already certain of what she'd find before she did–

Longwell. Holding Amnis, his grip reversed so he could grasp it just below the bladed tip. He'd swung the haft around wide, cracking Isabelle in the back of the head and sending her well and truly out.

Vara steadied herself, breathing a healing spell even as she gave Longwell a long, hard look. "So...are you Malpravus, then?"

Longwell wore his armor now, the true article, not some facsimile, but the dark blue armor of old, and his beard and hair had been hacked off so that he looked even barmier than ever – albeit at least like a dragoon again. "You were a friend, Vara, and dear to people I hold more loyalty to than any I have known in my life. More than my kingdom. And for that reason," and here he snapped Amnis around, grasping at the spear, preparing it for combat, "I cannot let you kill yourself like this."

CHAPTER 97

Cyrus

The first wave of scourge launched over the edge of the platform like fish leaping from the seas onto an open boat, and Cyrus was scarcely prepared for it.

They came in a great stinking mess, heaving themselves up on towers of their dead and near-dead fellows, all claws coated in black blood and reeking of corpses. Their teeth glistened with rancid saliva and their eyes were black emptiness as they clawed and leapt and fought their way onto the platform amidst the screams of guards and soldiers.

"Like an old-fashioned, magic-less castle defense!" Terian shouted, bringing his axe down like an executioner upon a leaping scourge. He caught it in the center of the forehead and it parted around the blade, each side of the creature curving off in its own direction.

Cyrus preferred the decapitation approach, taking the head off one that leapt up at him with jaws open. He caught it squarely, and the head went flying sideways like a struck ball, rolling down the hills and valleys of writhing scourge that were rising from below. "I never cared for those." He swung again, taking the head off another. "I got hired to do a few after graduating the Society of Arms. It's like guard duty, with some staring between crenellations thrown in for variety."

"Again, I am not sorry I missed the days of old," Baynvyn announced. He drove his blade into the chest of a leaping scourge, ripping it out of the air and hurling it back down onto the burgeoning tide.

Cyrus paused after slaying another, taking the time to glance momentarily at Niamh. She was up a level, having climbed the ladder while they were waiting for the tide to come, and now she stood beside Aisling, any noise she made lost in the choral growling of the scourge.

"She's holding on," Aisling called down to him.

"Great news," Terian said. "She'll hang on right up until we get too weak to slay another scourge, then she can come in and finish us off as we lay panting and exhausted on the deck."

"Maybe she won't be the one to do it," Aisling said. "All these years I've thought the title of Sovereign would look good on me."

"Hah!" Terian buried his axe in the stomach of a scourge, hurling it back down the growing tower of them. It struck and sent two more flying where it landed. "You should have said something about a thousand years ago, I probably would have stepped aside and spared myself a millennium of grief."

"Then what?" Aisling asked. "Join Bowe and Grinnd serving as the Sovereign's hands the world over?"

"I always did want to see Amatgarosa," Terian said, grunting as he swung once more. His breaths were coming heavily, and it was clear the battle was tiring him.

Cyrus could feel it, too, though his breathing was more controlled. "The tide rises." He slashed through another scourge.

"Yes, and you know what happens to the little sandcastle when it does," Malpravus's voice announced from a million scourge-mouths. "You are all of you grains of sand to me, and I am the ocean."

A scream down the line prompted Cyrus to look.

Just past Terian, a soldier had fallen, a scourge ripping at him. Another swiftly landed atop the first before leaping onto the next soldier in line. Within a moment, five more scourge had entered the platform at that beachhead. A scream behind Cyrus heralded the failing of another soldier, and he knew what that meant.

"They're coming over!" Baynvyn shouted, and another scream echoed down the line as yet another scourge made landfall upon their island in the sky.

Then another. And another.

Terian did not pause in swinging his axe, but he did look around to survey all around them. He was gray of face, and it was clear that the despair had gotten him, his axe hanging unused at his side. "We are finished," he whispered, heaving a great breath from his lungs.

Great gray masses writhed inward against the lines of soldiers folding upon the platform. The operator of a catapult screamed as three scourge got hold of him. The pop of launches ceased, vanishing into the cries of the dying.

A scourge leapt up and landed upon Terian's back, knocking the Sovereign off his feet. Its teeth glistened and struck for the neck, and Cyrus could see Terian's eyes looking accusation at him in that moment and he knew the thought upon his mind–

"If only you'd fallen that day," Terian murmured as the navy blue blood spurted from his wound, the scourge's teeth finding their way through his gorget and into the Sovereign's neck as the cries of the dark elven army being routed echoed all around them.

CHAPTER 98

Vaste

"Come on!" Vaste shouted, leading the three of them – Glaven, Aemma, and Qualleron – through the patchy fog draping the river road on the eastern edge of Termina. It seemed a madcap dash down the street, his boots slapping against the moist cobblestones, the heavy air condensing against them, turning them slick.

Qualleron's heavy breathing behind him suggested that they were keeping up; Vaste's heart was pounding and he was only still able to run with the help of Letum. It seemed to slow his pulse, to let him hurry along at a pace reasonably close to what the other three managed, but without taxing his bulky frame too hard.

Out of the mist ahead, a sudden glint–

Silver armor, laid in a formation. Termina Guard stretched to block their southern escape just beyond the grim outline of the Grand Span, where it met their road.

"Uh oh," Vaste muttered, and looked west, down the central road leading into the city. The chancel's scorched-out remains were like a ghost through the blanket of misty white. But before it were stretched another line of silver-armored guard, holding in place, blocking the path.

"Shit, shit," Vaste said, and wheeled 'round. Behind him, past the others, he could see motion in the mists from whence they'd come. Merrish and his boys were on their feet, and closing them into this box, with more troops behind them.

"Up the span," Vaste said, his decision made in a moment. He grabbed Aemma by the arm and hurried her up the gentle slope of the half-ruined bridge.

"But doesn't this one end?" she asked. "In the middle of the river?"

"It's either this way or through them," Vaste said. "And if we attack into the teeth of any of those lines of soldiers..." He was gasping for breath by this time, his legs burning and weary in a way he couldn't recall being since...well, perhaps the last time he'd been forced to hurry to this span to fight a battle.

"They snap the trap shut and attack our backs," Qualleron said, puffing a bit himself. "Of our limited tactical options, this was indeed the best."

"Sir Vaste the Wry is quite a skilled tactician," Glaven said.

"I learned from the best," Vaste said, feet hammering as he hurried up the span, thighs absolutely screaming at the run, at the incline. "By osmosis, perhaps."

"Is that meant to be a reference to Cyrus Davidon?" Aemma asked. She was not gasping for breath.

"Subtle, because his ego doesn't need the compliment," Vaste said, "but yes." He imagined Cyrus, and wondered if he had indeed met his fate in Reikonos. And Vara? Where was she? Somewhere in the bowels of this city? He should have sent Glaven to her manor with a message, should have been more focused and less exhausted, for he saw little chance of any other help within a thousand miles of this place.

Out of the mist, the end of the bridge came swiftly; the stones simply stopped, blackened and charred by the explosion that had brought it down, the way forward simply...ceased.

"Damn," Vaste said, letting his angry, churning thighs and furious calves stop their relentless labor. "Part of me hoped that somehow we'd run back in time a thousand years and find the span open, Santir waiting on the other side peacefully to receive my gorgeous green self like the hero I am."

"That is not the era we live in," Aemma said. "This is not a time of peace nor plenty." She turned to look back down the span, where silver shone in the misty morning light, heralding the approach of soldiers, more Termina Guard than Vaste could count. "It is a dark era you have entered, I am sad to tell you, filled with none of the hope you left behind." She favored him with a weak, watery smile, but her eyes were fixed on the trouble coming their way.

"I warned you to surrender, Vaste!" Merrish's voice came out of the mist, and as the guard drew closer, he could see the former lord at the fore. "Even with your skill, you can only do so much against an army."

"Lucky for me you're not an army," Vaste called back, though it was hardly necessary. "Armies battle, you see. They fight in defense of their city, their land. They don't plunder and despoil and slaughter unarmed civilians. We leave that to barbarians. So you see, I'm not facing an army." He hardened his gaze as the winged helms emerged into utter clarity, the mist at their backs, a wind coming now out of the east. "I'm facing godless savages, like the dark elves, the trolls of old – or the scourge."

"You will find no audience for your wordplay here," Merrish said, his face hard as stone. He drew to within ten feet of them and stopped, a look of pure, self-satisfaction upon his face. The blood from his wound dripped to his chin. "We know what we are doing, and what we are against. We fight for our people."

"You are taken by the madness of a riot," Vaste said, "no better than a pack of wolves – or them." He chucked a thumb behind him, where, presumably, beyond the mists, the scourge waited on the opposite river bank.

"The humans destroyed Reikonos," Merrish said, "but they blamed us in their rage, and destroyed our chancel. We responded in kind–"

"You responded by wiping them out," Vaste said, "then wiping out their families and everyone of their species in this city. There is no defense for what you have done. A reasonable reply would be to halt their mob, to try and imprison those guilty of the crime, not to annihilate them and all of their blood. That's not justice, it's genocide." He clutched Letum tightly. "I am not having this discussion with you. I would have better luck reasoning with an angry bear."

"You could make this simple," Merrish said.

"I could," Vaste said, but drew a deep breath, "but for you, you pile of woeful, wretched dragon shit – I will not."

And with a breath, he summoned forth all the strength he had, and cast a spell.

CHAPTER 99

.

Cyrus
One Thousand Years Ago
Vaeretru

The fangs of the serpent dug into Cyrus around the edges of his breastplate, and he muffled a scream to let it die before it reached his lips. Better to keep it within, to let his rage and pain build inside rather than let a foe know he felt it. Warm, wet, sticky blood ran down his chest and stomach, and he battered his sword pointlessly at the scales of the snake that had him squarely in its grasp.

"Cyrus!" someone shouted – Andren, he thought, but the rush of blood in his ears and the sound of the snake slithering across rock was like water rushing through a river.

This was it. He would die in the dark, whisked away into the den of this thing, where even the brave warriors of Sanctuary could not find him.

Just like Narstron.

No...no. Not at all like Narstron.

His blade clanged against the face of the serpent to little effect, Cyrus unwilling to give up in spite of the utter futility of his situation. Still, the hour grew late for him; funny, really, that his day would be ending before it had even begun–

A blast of flame reached around the jaws of the serpent and it seemed to scream, the fangs impaling him ripping free as the serpent's jaws opened wide in pain. Cyrus felt only the wash of the fire, the barest touch of it for a second before it died away, but it was like hot coals had been dumped over his arm, singeing his skin.

He didn't care. He fell from the mouth and struck out as he dropped – ten feet, then twenty, blade catching on something and then tearing its way down, warm blood spraying across him from the serpent's chest as he landed hard on rock.

The snake thrashed, trying to turn in the tight tunnel, and Cyrus was forced against a wall, the beast's weight pressing upon him. His armor made not so much as a squeal, but in the joints he felt the pressure as it writhed. More orange light burned bright against the walls, and Terian shouted a battle cry as the snake thumped with new weight upon it. It jerked to the side, and the unmistakable sound of blade against scale and bone came heavy like a thud.

A breath, the snake screamed, and another thud echoed through the cavern.

Cyrus tried to stab the creature, but could not. He was pinned, completely and utterly, until finally, the snake writhed to the side–

And Cyrus was free, stumbling, rolling, unable to get his feet beneath him but unable to stay where he was for fear it would spasm back. His armor clanged against the side of the cave, and he took his breath in great gasps, as though he'd just crawled from the Torrid Sea after a desperate swim. In truth, he felt much like he had, sweat drenching him.

With a final cry and thud, Terian landed next to him, his plated boots ringing loudly upon landing. Cyrus looked up to him, the dark knight in the spiked armor.

"You all right?" Terian asked, heaving his axe over his shoulder. The snake was not breathing; neither head was still attached, and one seemed to be burning. Niamh appeared overhead, running on air, Andren a step behind her. Vaste and J'anda were a second behind, the troll pausing to deliver a hearty thump of his stave to the dead, twitching body of the snake.

"Thought you'd bought it there for a second," Niamh said, hand to her chest, red hair flashing in the fire light.

"I was afraid we would be finding you in pieces," J'anda said.

"Or not at all," Andren said, face ashen. "Least til it was too late, the hour past."

"I...wasn't," Cyrus said. "Worried about that, I mean." He sat on his haunches on the cold rock. A twinkling of light across his abdomen from the hand of Andren soothed the snake bite.

"You were getting dragged away by a snake and you weren't worried about dying?" Vaste asked. "What, did our little adventure in the jungle reset your marker for what true peril is?"

"No," Cyrus said, catching a smile from Terian in the dark. The dark knight knew, of course, clever bastard that he was. "It wasn't that. Not at all."

"You knew we had you," Terian said as Cyrus took his hand, and the dark knight helped him to his feet. "That if all else failed..."

"...You wouldn't," Cyrus said. For that was, exactly, what he'd been feeling.

CHAPTER 100

Alaric

The slaughter was silent, Alaric's cool rage sustaining him as he worked up, deck by deck, through the *Yuutshee*. It was quick work, peeling them off, ramming his blade into the backs of their necks before they even knew what had happened, taking their heads like Edouard but with so much more speed and cause.

Above, he could hear the Chaarlandian captain speaking between the muffling floorboards. The pirates remained in firm control of the *Yuutshee*. He could not see them, not from here, and the moment he dared to stick his head up...

Well...he would find himself once more against the same problem: hostages.

Another path was needed. Through a cannon hole in the side of the *Yuutshee*, he could see the pirate ship still hovering, waiting, filled with some number of foes...

So he reached out to the ether...

...and he brought himself over.

There were fewer than he thought; so many must have fallen, only six had remained to crew the ironclad. He made swift work of them, from bottom of the ship to the top, and he finished at the wheel, burying his blade in the back of the head of the pirate who stood there, eyes on the sky.

As he sunk, Alaric was already gone, returning to the engine room of the *Yuutshee*. Dugras stared at him blankly as he coalesced from the fog of the ether. "How are you doing that, exactly?"

"Are the engines all right here?" Alaric asked.

"For now," Dugras said. "They'd make Xiaoshani for sure. Beyond that..." He made a face. "...well, it gets speculative."

"Good enough," Alaric said, and stepped up to the dwarf. "Hold on."

"To wha – AAAAA!"

They came out of the fog of the ether on the Chaarlandian vessel's quarterdeck, and Dugras stumbled immediately. He looked around, half-blinded by the harsh daylight, but Alaric quickly covered his mouth with a mailed fist. "Shh."

Dugras nodded, and once Alaric had removed the hand, he asked, "What do you want me to do here?"

"Take the wheel," Alaric said.

"Uh, won't the crew kill me?" Dugras asked, taking care not to step on the fallen helmsman. He was forced to straddle the corpse until Alaric dragged it away and tossed it easily over the side rail – away from the *Yuutshee*.

"The crew is quite dead," Alaric said, looking down upon the Chaarlandian vessel's deck. "Save for those over on the *Yuutshee*." He tensed. "And those...I'm afraid I'm going to have to come to grips with them quite soon."

Dugras held fast to the wheel, but peeked around its spoked edges. "Well, if you could lure a few of them over here, you know, split 'em off from the herd, it might help, right?"

"Yes," Alaric said, "what did you have in mi–"

Dugras jerked the wheel hard left, and a shudder ran through the Chaarlandian vessel, rattling the bridges stretched between it and the *Yuutshee*. When Alaric caught himself, the dwarf flashed him a grin. "That ought to get their attention."

Sharp words from the deck of the *Yuutshee* wafted up to them, and sure enough, Alaric could hear footsteps rattling the bridges, hurrying back to the Chaarlandian ship from below. He closed his eyes, drawing himself into the ether–

And there they were, three Chaarlandian pirates clambering up the onto the deck of their ship. Once there, they swiftly locked eyes on the wheel, and Dugras behind it.

All this, Alaric saw from within the embrace of the ether, sliding along the deck in a patch of fog like a stray cloud. Once behind them he sprang from it, slashing with all his force–

The three were felled with only a scream between them, and Alaric was gone again.

"What?" the Chaarlandian captain was below, the deck of the *Yuutshee* not vastly changed from how he'd left it. At the forecastle, one of the Chaarlandians had Guy and Edouard stripped the way Alaric had been, along with several other crew members. They huddled, naked, upon the deck before their captor.

Alaric emerged from the slinking fog and slashed the Chaarlandian down, cutting him to pieces with one swift stroke.

Guy looked up at him in swift surprise. "I thought you was dead, Alaric."

"Not yet," Alaric said, and he vanished back into the ether, almost tripping over Edouard before he did.

"Stop!" the Chaarlandian captain shouted, voice echoing over the deck. Four others of his crew were behind him, coming down from the quarterdeck at a run, but he had Mazirin in his grip, her hair held tight in his gloved hand. "You do that magic again...I kill her."

CHAPTER 101

Alaric

"You fight *me*," the Chaarlandian captain said, ripping open his leathers to display his bare, hairy chest, and then pounding it, knife still clutched in his fingers and almost grazing himself. "No magic." He pushed Mazirin back to one of his fellows, who caught her; she was immediately surrounded by the other three, and had knives and pistols thrust to her head and chest. "You fight me or she die. Yes?"

Alaric stood, the breeze over the bow rustling through his armor. There was no choice. "Yes."

"No armor." The captain stripped off his leathers to reveal his bare chest, keeping his knife clutched in his hand, then pointing it at Alaric. "No."

"No armor," Alaric agreed, pulling off his helm and tossing it aside. He shucked out of the mail and let it clatter, going through the motions rather than upsetting the–

"Show me magic," the captain said, pointing the knife at him again as he kicked off his own trousers. "Take off with magic."

Alaric stared at him, then smiled, and with the wave of a hand–

–his armor turned to smoke, and he was dressed in naught but a loincloth.

"Yes," the captain said with a grin. "Tonight I eat your meat." He undulated his tongue then clacked his teeth so hard Alaric could have sworn he faintly heard them crack from the pressure. From his pants the captain stooped and retrieved his axe. "I eat your magic."

"You're going to eat my sword," Alaric said, feeling the weight of Aterum in his hand.

"No magic," the captain warned again, axe in one hand, dagger in the other, "or she die. Yes?"

"Yes," Alaric said, and the captain came at him.

He was fast, even with Aterum at Alaric's disposal, an angry, hairy, tattooed bundle of energy. He whirled with great skill, taller than Alaric by a lot. He came in hard, feinting, then retreating, waiting to see what Alaric would do.

Alaric held his blade at low guard. His weapon gave him advantages, but they were hardly limitless.

"You not useless," the captain said with that same grin. "I take your magic from you dead." He pounded his hand against his chest again. "Make my magic." He lunged at Alaric.

There was time for a parry. "It doesn't work that way." The clash of sword against axe was loud.

"I make work," the captain said, coming at him again.

It was some strain to keep him back, but not impossible, not with Aterum in hand. Alaric fended him off handily, parrying his wild thrusts, striking here and there, in small measures. A slash to the ribs, a gouge in the captain's thigh. He hobbled, pain creasing his face.

"No," Alaric said, "I don't think you'll make it work at all."

"Yes!" Edouard called, as though cheering at some spectator event. Guy was beside him, Praelior back in his hand, keeping position with the rest of the crew, a dozen paces away, with Alaric and the captain between them and Mazirin and her hostage-takers. Alaric gave Guy a subtle shake of the head, and the smaller man nodded; he would not act on his own.

"Yes," the captain said, bleeding, and then he said something else, something in his own language.

"Yes what?" Alaric asked.

"Yes!" the captain shouted.

And it was drowned in a boom of thunder.

Pain lanced through Alaric's side; one of the hostage-takers had turned the pistol away from Mazirin and on to Alaric. Firing, he'd struck true, and now blood welled from Alaric's side, dribbling down his ribs.

"Hah!" the captain shouted, kicking out; he struck Aterum flat across the blade, catching Alaric by surprise and sending the sword skittering away.

"No!" Guy lunged in but a gunshot cracked as the pistol roared again; Praelior flew from his fingers and blood coursed down as Guy stumbled, clutching his crimson-soaked hand, and fell to his knees.

Alaric sank down, and the captain roared, kicking him onto his back with a hard boot-sole. Alaric slammed to the deck, and the captain stood over him, axe raised. "I eat your magic," he declared, and swung the axe high–

CHAPTER 102

Cyrus

"Terian!" Cyrus shouted amidst the cacophony of battle around the platform. He lunged forward at the bleeding, downed Sovereign, striking a half dozen scourge threatening to overrun the platform as he went.

The noise was like armageddon coming upon them, echoing off the tower and across the growling, writhing, living landscape. Seizing hold of the Sovereign's armor by the neck, he breathed a healing spell – the best he could make happen under the circumstances and then breathed another, tirelessly thrashing with his sword against the tide of scourge surmounting the platform even now.

"You know why I didn't fall that day, Terian?" Cyrus asked, gripping him tighter. The Sovereign looked up at him, half-dazed. "Because you were there."

Terian looked into his eyes. "When all else fails..."

"You didn't," Cyrus said.

"Cyrus," Terian said, desperation in his eyes, Noctus still in his hand. "You need to go–"

"Shut up," Cyrus said, grasping him by the armor and lifting him to his feet, breathing another healing spell. "Baynvyn! We need to retreat to the upper platform."

Baynvyn was hip deep in scourge, but slashing his way through them furiously with Epalette. "I have doubts that will do us much good." He hesitated, a line of black scourge blood splashed across his face. "But you're the general, I suppose. Retreat!"

"To the ladders," Cyrus shouted, giving Terian one last healing spell, then looking him squarely in the eyes. "Up with you."

"What?" Terian asked, blood dripping from between his lips. "Oh – no!"

Cyrus hurled him bodily up a level and heard the clank of the Sovereign's armor as he landed on the upper platform. "Retreat!" he shouted, wading into the fray and grasping hold of a terrified dark elven soldier and giving him the same heave-ho treatment as the Sovereign. "To the ladders! Re-establish the line up there!" A scourge lunged at him, slipping on the fallen bodies of two of its fellows and a soldier, and Cyrus kicked it. It flew back, bowling over four more that chose that moment to leap upon the platform, and between them they caused a wave of scourge to flow over the edge like a waterfall of dead souls.

"That's the spirit," Baynvyn said, and tried to mimic Cyrus's maneuver to much less effect. It sent one scourge over, and his face fell. "Oh. I guess it's harder than it looks."

"Key difference between a rogue and a warrior," Cyrus said, and charged, putting down his shoulder and giving all his strength to the move. "You strike tight and true, while I am a battering ram that hits all." He slammed into a scourge and ran it to the edge, pushing it and a half dozen others over with it.

"Cyrus, get up here!" Terian's voice cracked over him,

sounding twice as cross as he'd been before he'd gotten bitten in the neck. "It's just me, this time, and there's little chance I can save you from this thousand-headed non-serpent if you fall."

"Don't I know it," Cyrus muttered, and gave one more hearty shove against a flood of scourge coming over the edge. A few dozen soldiers were still climbing the ladders to the upper level, but that was it. Baynvyn was defending one of them, and Cyrus rammed his way through to the other, hacking and slashing, trying to cover the retreat of the few – damnably few – survivors.

"Cyrus!" Terian's voice came once more.

"I'm a little busy covering the retreat right now," Cyrus called back, not daring to look up. Covering this one, lone ladder was doable if he focused, like watching the entry to a bridge.

"Cyrus," Terian said again, and the seriousness in his voice made him look (after chopping through two attacking scourge). The Sovereign stood above him, looking down, with his hand reaching out to Cyrus. "Come on...it's time." The Sovereign reached out his offered hand, and breathed, all malice gone from his visage.

"You have to leave."

CHAPTER 103

Vara

"Longwell," Vara said, bringing her sword to a low guard in anticipation of him swinging his spear down or stabbing forward, "I don't believe you mean harm, but you have lost your bloody mind if you think I'm going to meekly submit to this mad dictum of yours."

His feet rustled in the grass as he started to circle to her left. "You must! You must, or you'll surely die." He twirled the spear in a loose circle, sweeping the haft around him when he was done, and it was clear he'd had much experience with it. There was anguish in his eyes as he said, "I cannot let you die."

"You cannot expect me to live like this," she said, watching him for movement. He would strike, that much was sure.

"I expect you won't live at all if you try and leave," Longwell said. "I heard Isabelle talking about magic's restrictions. She casts that spell – you die." He twirled the spear again, bringing the blade back in line with her.

"I stay here, I die a piece at a time," Vara said. She could feel magical energy within herself, ready to be used. And used it would be, if Longwell attacked, for it was her greatest advantage over him now that Isabelle was rendered unconscious. Vara could see the slow movement of her chest rising and falling with every breath beneath her soiled robes. "Or go mad, like you. I would rather have it over all at once, in good cause, than live forever for no reason."

"We could be here together, the three of us, and live fine," Longwell said, his eyes welling with concern, and possibly tears. "Is that not reason enough? I have been here a long time, Vara, it's true. But I see this thing clear-headed. What is the need for you to die pointlessly? Wait, if you think a stand needs to be made. Wait until someone comes, clears the wreckage outside, and leave that way. Don't try some spell that will kill you just so you can charge pointlessly into a dark world that no longer has any place for you."

"How would you even know what waits out there?" Vara shot back, keeping her sword steady. "Other than what we've told you, you've had no contact with anyone for a thousand years."

He stared at her blankly. "That's not true."

"You haven't left, you haven't talked to anyone," Vara said. "So tell me – what great news of the outside have you heard?"

He twitched, and that was all the warning she got. Longwell struck, bringing the spear forward in a stabbing attack. Vara knocked it aside only barely, for it came quickly at her. When she batted it away, Longwell spun, bringing the blade tip low at her legs.

Vara leapt, jumping neatly over it and landing, sacrificing her balance in favor of a chance to attack. She came at him and struck squarely, the edge of her blade slamming into his breastplate and knocking him back. The spear came like a raised flag as he staggered, trying to regain his footing and pinwheeling arms.

She kept in a defensive posture, sword up. "Do not make me stop you."

He had caught his balance by then, though, and brought the spear parallel to the ground at waist height, his other hand extended in front of him, palm out like he might cast a spell. "I must."

Again he struck without more warning than that, coming in high this time, stabbing at her face. "Not sure how you mean to save my life by ripping my throat out," she said, catching the tri-bladed spear between the tines and then shoving it back at him. This time he whirled out of it, spinning back around and coming at her once more.

It went like that for a short bit, parries and blocks, attacks and defenses. Vara let her sword be her guide, the clanging of blades singing out the song of battle once again.

When they were both perspiring and breathing heavy, they stood off, looking at one another. "What say you now?" Vara asked.

"I have nothing more to say," Longwell said. And he charged in again.

"I have something to say," Vara said, but he did not stop.

She lifted a hand, pointed it at his feet, and whispered the incantation for force blast under her breath.

Vara expected some small thing, a blast of the kind that might sweep his feet from beneath him, send Longwell plummeting to his face, trip him up perhaps.

What she got...was much more than that.

A bellowing force blast like that of the days of old churned up three inches of soil and filled the air with a haze of grass as it ripped toward the Luukessian dragoon. It took his feet from him but also sent him tumbling backward in a roll the like of which Vara might have expected from a man caught in a tornado. He rattled in his armor as he flew back twenty, thirty feet before settling, facedown, on the tilled earth.

Looking at her hand in surprise, she turned back to Isabelle, who lay quietly upon the earth. She had barely felt the draw of magic from within as she'd cast the spell, a very different sensation to how things had gone in Reikonos. Had this power been here all along, waiting for her to draw upon it in desperation? Her magic had certainly seemed normal enough, up to now. That fresh, welling spirit within her was like water from an endless spring, and she swiftly drew on it, casting a healing spell upon Isabelle.

Her sister stirred within seconds, raising a head with a bloody gash upon it. The crimson traced its way down her forehead, and her eyes had a slight cloudiness. "Did he...hit me?" she asked, turning to look all about.

"Longwell? Yes," Vara said. "But you needn't worry. I–"

Isabelle's eyes alighted on the path of destruction from Vara's spell. "Good gods, what did you do to him in return?"

"Hopefully nothing permanent," Vara said, and mouthed another healing spell, this one directed at Longwell. Again, she barely felt it.

His crumpled form was laid out upon the dirty ground, a light rain of dust and blades of grass slowly falling upon him like decoration upon his dark armor. When the white spell-light settled upon his fallen form, he stirred, raising his head. He blinked at her from beneath his helm, and murmured, "Unnghhh..."

"I'm afraid this is where we leave you," Vara said, offering Isabelle a hand. Her sister took it, getting carefully to her feet. "Magic does not appear quite as constrained here in this realm, which suggests that casting a teleport might not be quite the death sentence you anticipated." She brushed a few stray strands of blond hair out of her face and back under her helm. "Best of luck, Samwen." She nodded to Isabelle.

"No – Vara, no!" Longwell charged at her, kicking up dirt as he tried to rise, Amnis in hand.

Isabelle's teleportation spell rose in a glow of blue as Longwell leapt toward them. The world began to fade as he soared, a look of sheer panic upon his face that faded out as they vanished from the realm that had been his prison for nearly a thousand years.

CHAPTER 104

Cyrus

"Leave?" Cyrus would have laughed, but he was far too busy swinging his sword, delivering furious kicks that knocked back the scourge. But they were surging over every edge of the platform now, and the last two or three soldiers were almost to the top of the ladder. To his right, Baynvyn leapt, and the ladder fell behind him, landing atop the swarming scourge. "I'm not done giving Malpravus's puppets a piece of my mind yet."

"Your mind always was your strongest weapon." Malpravus's disembodied voice washed over Cyrus.

Cyrus didn't hesitate; if the necromancer was complimenting him, it was time to be worried. He leapt as three scourge snapped at him, flying through the place where he'd stood a moment before.

With a clunk, Cyrus landed heavily on the upper deck to find the soldiers already retreating toward the elevator. Only a dozen or so remained, a flood of dark elves moving swiftly, raggedly, the grand doorways already being pushed closed. On the side opposite them, visible through the open entry, the sound of a great bar that must have been the length of a ship slammed into place even as Cyrus rose back to his feet.

Terian was with him. "You have to leave. Now." He pointed to the ship on the opposite petal.

"Are you out of your mind, Terian?" Cyrus asked. Already the scourge were massing below, creating a small reproduction of the undulating tide that would soon carry them over the lip of this final obstacle. The end was not in sight, either; to the west all he could see was scourge. "We're not going to win this by–"

"We're not going to win this at all," Terian said, seizing him by the pauldron, the clank of his gauntlet upon Cyrus's armor like a gun shot. "This battle is lost."

"Terian," Cyrus said, "listen to me. I know I've screwed up in my life, and maybe releasing these things was the worst of all of them. But we don't win this by splitting ourselves apart–"

The Sovereign seized his other pauldron and clanked his helm to Cyrus's, putting them eyeball to eyeball. "I *am* with you. I'm sorry I doubted you. A thousand years holding the bag let me forget that before you were the god that everyone worshipped, you were the man who struggled just as much as I do." He let Cyrus go, but kept a hand on his shoulder. "I remember now that before we were legends–"

"We were brothers," Cyrus said.

Terian half-smirked. "To the end." His smile faded. "But this isn't it – if you get on that airship and get out of here."

"That's the end of you, though–" Cyrus started.

Terian shook his head. "There's a ton of Dragon's Breath waiting on the elevator below, and seeded throughout the tower. More in the entryway. We close those doors, retreat underground, and I'll blow it up, bringing this sucker down with a half million scourge alongside." He grinned. "Bury the bastards."

"What the hell good does that do, Terian?" Cyrus asked. "You'll be trapped in the earth."

"We've been trapped before," Terian said. "But no one was coming to save us last time. This time–"

"I don't know what to do," Cyrus said. The click of scourge claws sounded below, like the ticking of a mechanical gear rolling ever forward. "Our allies, Terian. They're–"

"Our *friends*, Cyrus," Terian said. "Brothers and sisters. Some of them are still out there." He grew serious. "Find Ryin. He'll be of great use."

"Where the hell am I supposed to find–?" Cyrus started, but a scourge leapt over the edge beside them and he swung for it–

Terian chopped its head off first, sending it plummeting back over, growls subsiding for a second. "Come." And he hustled Cyrus away from the edge.

Baynvyn met them before the last open gateway, which was closing, darkness falling upon the elevator hall within. He caught Cyrus's gaze as they approached. "I hear we're leaving."

"Yes," Terian said before Cyrus could answer, "you should go with your father." Cyrus felt his head snap around at the curious weight those words had. "Quickly – to the ship."

"What will you do?" Cyrus asked, feeling Baynvyn take up his arm, leading him away, though he felt a pull to stay by the great doors, even as they began to squeak shut, soldiers pulling them closed. Scourge were coming, almost to the lip of the last petal of the tower. "While we're gone?"

"Keep the earth between us and Malpravus," Terian said. "And do what all Arkarians have been doing for the last thousand years." He smiled, and there was no malice in it, only utter sincerity. "Wait for Cyrus Davidon to return in our hour of greatest need."

"Terian..." Cyrus said.

"I believe in you," Terian called after him, the doors down to a sliver, a line of light across Terian's helm allowing a glint in his eye. "Not as a god, not as the great savior – but as the man who stood beside me in a hundred battles and never lost his nerve. I had your back–"

"And I will have yours," Cyrus said as the great doors thumped closed. Even over the rotating blades of the distant airship, Cyrus heard the great bar fall, closing off Saekaj Sovar – and his old friend – from the rest of the world once more.

CHAPTER 105

Vaste

With all he had, Vaste conjured up a Force Blast and slammed the base of Letum into the bridge, angling it forward and letting the spell wash out from the tip. It struck the bridge's road bed and rushed out with a *WHUMPF!* rising off the cobbles like a hot wind on a summer night.

Merrish staggered back, a dozen of his minions doing the same, armor clanging as they bounced off each other. "Stop that!" he said irritably.

"You're the angry mob aiming to kill us, make me," Vaste said, and cast the same spell again.

The blast rushed forth once more, sending the front rank over into the next, armor clattering and clanging, joining the wind already blowing from over their shoulders.

"This display will not save you!" Merrish said, face purpling as he rose to a knee.

"I don't mean to be saved," Vaste said, casting another spell, letting it channel his rage as he slammed Letum again into the cobblestones and let the unleashed spell-force bounce off them. It sent the front rank of soldiers rolling backward, knocked over the second rank, and put the third on the back foot, unsteady and about to fall. "No one is coming to save me. I know I can't beat your whole city of enraged elves." He cast Force Blast once more, and now a few of them went flying a foot or three off the ground, smashing into each other like fruit in a canvas sack. "I fight now because I wish to. Because I'm angry." Again, and they flew once more. "I was dropped here after the worst night of my life and only wished to pass through, but no one would let me. But the problem is, Merrish – I am stuck. Stuck watching, stuck witnessing. I would have gone on, to what and where, I don't know. Brokenness, perhaps. That Duchy in Firoba where the women apparently just love troll men, maybe."

He cast again, and now they were truly rolling, madcap and out of control down the slope of the bridge, the elves' faces blurring as vomit spewed from some of them, screams penetrated the air, the ranks behind them broke into full flight and failed to escape, being rolled over by their armored brethren. "But no! I could not even escape this little war of yours, and a pettier war I have seldom seen. 'They took our land!' 'No, they burned our chancel!' 'Well, they destroyed Reikonos!'" Again, and his words somehow overcame the clanging and cracking and retching, the stones now slick with blood and sick as he pursued the rolling, screaming mob as they were all blown down the damned span. "You know who destroyed Reikonos?" Vaste shouted, sending another spell to drive them down in a rolling mass. "Malpravus! I saw it myself! Not human, not elf – ancient evil, here to destroy us all, and you – you fucking lackwits exterminate each other!"

The end of the bridge was coming, and they were piling up madly at the base of the slope. Arms and legs stuck out akimbo, and elves were vomiting unhindered, seasoning the pile of no-longer-glinting armor and men.

The rage was boiling within him, and Vaste thought to himself how pretty a picture this would be, this tableau of grasping arms and waving legs and screaming, puking faces, elven soldiers all trapped in a pile almost as tall as him – how much more beautiful would it be if he just conjured a fire–

And he did, glowing bright, burning huge above them, all his anger gone into it, the frustration of Birissa's secret, of Sanctuary tricking him, of the red spell-light ripping through the city of Reikonos, killing all in its path–

The fire glowed, large as a house, hanging above the pile of writhing elves. The orange glow came across their faces and drew their eyes up, like a massive sun overhead. He could but drop it, and it would fall upon them like Chirenya's spell against the dark elves on this very bridge, like something Quinneria herself might have cast under the circumstances–

"Vaste." Aemma was beside him, her hand gently upon his arm.

He was sweating furiously, and the rage had begun to drain out of him. The fire-light glowed, and the elves had gone silent. All the arrogance had bled from Merrish's face, and his horror-struck eyes were upon the burning death that waited suspended above his head like an axe waiting to fall...

"Where is your joy now, Merrish?" Vaste asked, his breath huffing out of him in great, anger puffs. "Your boundless arrogance, your unquenchable desire to wipe us out?" He gestured lightly with Letum, and the ball moved subtly toward them, drawing screams. "Hm? Where is that righteous superiority that pumps through your veins? Does it finally chill at the realization that no, if you get enough angry people together, you cannot overcome all?"

He dropped the fire but inches, and many of the elves cried out again. Vaste could feel the heat upon his face, scorching, like standing before an open oven. "Not so hardy when you're about to be roasted to death, are you? When you go from being hunter to hunted, and all your mighty long life has come to its end?"

Merrish stared at the fiery death awaiting him, and turned his eyes away, clenching them shut. "Do it, then!" he shouted, and he sounded hopeless. The wails that rose from the pile of elves at this, the mad scramble...

Vaste snuffed the fire and felt his legs weak, as though the effects of running had caught up with him at last. "No," he said, keeping his feet only with the help of Letum, "for I am not you, wretched and miserable and willing to kill all in my path."

A collective breath seemed drawn in on the other side, the pile of elves gasping to breathe. The topmost rolled down the heap, and those on the sides avoided being rolled on. It was a frightful clamor, and Vaste had little intention of standing there and watching the terrified, wretched assemblage pull themselves back together.

"Come," he said softly, pulling Aemma's hand. "Let us be off before they regain themselves."

Skirting the edge of the gradually unfolding pile of elves, he heard no anger. There were sobs, there were tears, and a hundred eyes watching him fearfully as he led his small group around their edge and down the span, hanging tight to the rail at the edge of the river, away and toward the airship docks, the stink of sick in the air.

Aemma walked alongside Vaste, snatching fevered looks at the elves. Her breathing was ragged, too, and she looked in wonder – at him.

"How do I look?" he asked, not daring to look back at the elves for fear they'd be gathering up again, charging at him from behind. "Old?"

She blinked at him. "You look the same as ever. Why?"

"Qualleron, do I look older?" Vaste asked, turning back to

the bigger troll. "I must have used an awful lot of magic just now, it should age me."

"You do not look any different," Qualleron said, his boots clanking on the cobblestones. The mist was coming off the river a little lighter now, a fierce breeze blowing through. "Save for perhaps a bit...sweatier."

The span hung there, the far edge where it ended visible now that the fog was clearing. And in the distance, across the water, Vaste could see...

He stopped, surprising his small party. Glaven let out a chirp, skittering sideways to avoid colliding with him. Apparently he'd been watching behind them.

But Vaste little cared about that. For across the river...

"Um," he said, "weren't there meant to be scourge...*everywhere* over there?"

Glaven clanged into the riverfront railing, accidentally gonging his rifle stock against the metal. "Yes, yes, always, for a thousand years."

But the far bank was bare, gray dirt and mud the only things visible for a hundred yards inland, then two hundred as the mist continued to clear...

"The dead are gone, and for the first time since they arrived on these shores." Vaste rubbed his head, a heavy truth ringing its way into his heart. "Of bloody course. Malpravus. Who else could command *the dead?*"

"What...what does that mean, then?" Aemma asked. She stood at his shoulder, looking as he did.

"It means that Malpravus has some other use for them," he said, and picked up his pace along the riverfront. "Which means..." His breath almost stuck in his chest. "...he's not done yet. Not nearly done." And whatever he was up to, it was surely not good.

CHAPTER 106

Alaric

The sun glinted off the Chaarlandian captain's axe held high; sweat glistened, mingling with the blood that coursed down his side as he swung the weapon down, down at Alaric.

On a straight line, the blade would make contact with Alaric's neck. The course was clear; there was no turning it aside.

The sting in Alaric's side was great; a bullet had crashed into his ribs, breaking bones, tearing flesh. A savage stood above him, weapon falling to kill him...

It thudded into the deck.

Alaric stared up at the captain, whose toothy grin dissolved into outrage...

...For Alaric's neck was ethereal fog.

"It would appear you are an inefficient headsman," Alaric said, disappearing into the fog and appearing a few feet away, behind Mazirin's captors. Aterum was back in his hand, and his armor was upon him, and he took the heads off of two of them and hit the others with a Force Blast spell that knocked them sideways. "But I know someone who isn't."

The Chaarlandian captain leered at him, trying to rip the axe from where it was stuck in the *Yuutshee's* deck. "What?" He was bent over, on one knee, he'd swung with such force in his bid to decapitate Alaric.

Edouard's scream was chilling, and Praelior swung true in his hands. The blade cut cleanly, taking the Chaarlandian captain's head off and sending it spiraling. It bounced once upon the deck, and then flew overboard.

Mazirin lunged down and grabbed a dagger, impaling the nearest – and only – surviving Chaarlandian who had taken her hostage. The look on her face as she buried the blade in his heart and gave it a twist...

...Well, Alaric considered himself lucky he was not on the receiving end of it.

He sank to one knee, already casting the healing spell. When it hit, he murmured to Mazirin, "The Chaarlandian ship is yours, captain."

She spun 'round on him, blood still dripping from the tip of the blade. "Say again?"

"I killed the remaining Chaarlandians," he said, healing himself again, then tossing in another for Guy, who was still clutching his wounded hand. "Before I came over. The ship – it's empty."

Mazirin took this in with a weary look, then nodded once. "What do you plan to do with it, then?" She brought the dagger down to her side, and still it dripped.

Alaric froze. "What do you mean? I left Dugras at the helm. I assumed you would take it over."

Mazirin shook her head slowly. "Amatgarosan law is clear on this. In the event of a pirate attack, whoever takes over the enemy ship gains possession of it." She looked at the giant ironclad hovering off the bow of the *Yuutshee*. "That vessel is yours now...captain."

Alaric took that in swiftly, and his answer was just as quick in coming. "I must go back to Arkaria. Malpravus is coming, and the other nations...they must be warned." He pulled himself upright; the pain had nearly receded. "My duty is clear."

She watched for a long moment, then nodded once. "As it should be," she said, but, as usual, it was hard to tell what she was thinking.

CHAPTER 107

Shirri

She was paraded into the council chambers with cold dread rolling through her veins. No one would speak, as though she were a leper and the disease could be spread by words. The guards moved along with her, the thumping of their boots and the rattle of their breastplates the only sounds as she was marched into the presence of the same scowling elves as had pronounced judgment on her only last night.

"Shirri!" her mother's voice broke with relief. Pamyra stood in the place before the council bench, dark circles beneath her eyes, a weary look upon her. Clearly, sleep had not come easily to her, either.

She acknowledged her mother with but a nod, for she had little to offer save that. Hiressam and Calene waited there, too, Calene's eyes puffy and near-closed, tiredness sketched across her rough, scarred face as heavily as if painted there by some great artist. She winced, brushing a hand against her head.

Hiressam said nothing, sitting gloomily in the quiet, either hung over as well or simply cowed by the thought of the judgment they seemed about to face.

Shirri joined them, detaching herself from the midst of the guards that escorted her. She looked up into the waiting faces of the council expecting judgment and realized...

...They weren't even looking at her. Not Arcaeny, not Gareth, not any of them.

"Goodness," Shirri said. "It's as though we face the death penalty rather than the exile we were promised."

That caused a slight stir on the bench; Arcaeny looked to Gareth. Other looks were exchanged as well, awkward, glancing, and it sent a chill through Shirri.

Something had happened. Something was...wrong.

"Where is Birstis?" Arcaeny asked, voice crackling high and clear across the chamber. "Send for him, will you please?" A page bolted from the room at a run that would not have been considered dignified, even in the midst of battle.

That was not good, at least not in Shirri's estimation. If they were dragging Birstis in for testimony against her...against them...

Shirri sighed. A night on the bench. Truly, she should have gone the day before, taken a ticket however she had to. The train through the Heia Mountain pass to Emerald, to the shore for a watership journey to Firoba without the airship, just...out of this place where they clearly hated her and everything about her.

She thought of the quiet market, of Tsawana. Had this additional conversation truly been worth the wait? Fighting the fight as she'd thought she would do, forever, if need be, against all odds, in the way that Hiressam, that Calene, and even her mother wouldn't...

That stirred something in Shirri, and her face flushed red with anger.

"While we're waiting," she said, patience slipping out like the page had run, "I might as well say a few things that I know this council doesn't wish to hear."

"Shirri," Pamyra said warningly.

"Oh, marvelous." Calene clutched her head.

"Please," Hiressam said. "You need not do this."

Shirri ignored them all. Hell, she took a step up on the nearest chair, then used it to step up on the table just so she could look the council in the eyes at their level. To the hells with them if they thought they could look down on her. Let them have the guards drag her down; what did she care?

If no one was going to listen to her, as far as she was concerned...they were all dead anyway.

"Malpravus is coming," she announced, matter-of-fact. A steely calm had come over her, oddly, a flush in her cheeks the only hint of real emotion driving her. "I know you don't want to hear it, don't want to believe, fear what others believing it might mean for you. But you know what?" Shirri smiled. "I don't care.

"I don't care," Shirri said, "because I've realized something – no one wants to hear the bad news, the news that contradicts what they believe. Everyone has an idea of what their day might look like, even if it's as simple as having no plan at all but to sit about at leisure while you wait for something to happen. No one wants to imagine the forces of their nation being marshaled to war–"

"Shirri, please, don't do this," her mother said. "We're in enough trouble as it is."

"–And I truly understand that," Shirri said. "I do. Walking down an alleyway in Reikonos, I didn't want to be ambushed by Machine thugs. I didn't want to have to call for help using the mystical prayer that was on my mind because I'd just read about it. I certainly didn't think I was conjuring up some manner of trouble that would upheave everything I cared about. Wouldn't have picked it that morning. Wouldn't have chosen to go that route. Wouldn't have borrowed the money."

The council had their heads down, barely acknowledging her. A few were talking amongst themselves.

"But I didn't get to ignore it when the problems started coming my way," Shirri said, and she got angrier the longer she spoke. "I didn't get to ignore it when the Machine took my mother. I couldn't just run away and leave her to it. And when that big red spell came crackling across the city, I couldn't just sit still and let it devour me whole."

"Devour your what now?" Gareth asked, blinking at her.

She gave him a funny look. "It eats souls. The spell."

"Oh."

"I know you don't want to hear this," Shirri said, and here she switched to a strange tone of almost-pleading, yet she could not find it in herself to debase herself before these people. "That things are going well for you while the rest of Arkaria falls apart, but you are a part of this land. And this trouble is going to come your way whether you want it to or not. Stick your head up your arse, hide it away for as long as you can, but you won't escape it.

"Malpravus is coming," she said, and somehow those words echoed with terrible finality. "And he's going to bloody well kill us all if he can."

Arcaeny raised her head at that moment, and there was a pained look in her eyes. "Yes. Thank you for that," she said, and looked down again.

"Sure," Shirri said, and stepped down. Her only surprise came in seeing the guards loitering a dozen steps behind her, without having made a single move to drag her from the top of the table. She would have thought a government bent on exiling her would have shown little reticence about throwing her against the ground.

A boom of doors flung open at the back of the chamber got

her attention. Birstis came in striding up with his silvery, miniature breastplate gleaming in the morning light, his red breeches and blue blouse catching her eye as he hustled up the aisle behind them.

Calene watched with a wary eye, and whispered. "Something's amiss."

"Ah, Birstis," Arcaeny said, looking almost relieved. "Have you confirmed it?"

"Confirmed what?" Shirri asked, but she was ignored.

Birstis nodded. "Aye, Councilwoman. We have."

"What is going on here?" Shirri asked aloud; the faces of Pamyra and Hiressam echoed her words, but perhaps more politely. Shirri, for her part, was done with politeness.

Arcaeny laid her eyes upon Shirri at last, and there was a squirming discomfiture in them. "Reports came in this morning that the scourge have moved, as one, from their customary place across the Perda from Termina."

"They're moving en masse in the direction of Saekaj Sovar," Birstis said. "There is no doubt, based on the testimony of no less than twenty-five unaffiliated airship captains. Either we are dealing with a large, mass conspiracy of a joke–"

"Or the scourge are moving in a truly coordinated mass," Shirri said.

"And who better to coordinate the old dead?" Pamyra asked, her voice cracking.

"Than a bloody necromancer," Calene finished. For them all, really.

"One with new magic and perhaps ideas of what to do with it," Hiressam said.

"Is it possible that they just sense life in that direction?" Gareth asked. He was rubbing his fingers together in front of his belly. "We know they're drawn to life, after all. The very breath of it, in fact."

Birstis shook his head. "That mass has been at the bank of

the Perda for a thousand years. They do peel off, some of them, at times. About thirty years ago there was an airship that crashed shortly after takeoff, just over the river. A hundred and twelve souls aboard, and the herd moved in that direction, but not all of them. Not like this. There is not a single scourge currently on the bank of the Perda. They're all gone. Watch stations all up and down the river are burning up the telegraph wires with the same report, confirmed by every airship captain coming in from that direction."

"And Termina itself?" Arcaeny asked.

Birstis hesitated. "We have lost contact with Termina. Reports from the city are...scattered, and perhaps best dealt with at another time." She gave the council a knowing look. "It is what we discussed before, and unrelated to this."

Shirri felt her eyebrows rise. All the scourge? And what was happening in Termina?

"It seems in this scourge matter we may have a problem we cannot ignore," Arcaeny said, and she lifted her eyes from the desk before her. "So...this leaves me with a question." And she looked right at Shirri. "Can you help us? Help us understand what is coming? Help us...prepare for it?" Her voice, before so strong when she'd pronounced judgment upon them, now sounded...weak, and so uncertain. "Can we even prepare for it?"

Shirri saw her mother look to her out of the corner of her eye. Calene and Hiressam, too, and none of them spoke. It was a curious feeling; the desperation within Shirri faded, like the fire in her eyes was turning to glowing coals. All the worries of the last day receded, and she felt an icy reserve come over her.

I speak for us all now, she realized. *Because I am the one who did not lose faith. Did not abandon the oath Alaric swore us to.*

She would speak for them now, for Calene stood silent, and so did Hiressam. This was not the moment for revenge, though, on them or the council; Arcaeny's desperation was echoed in every face along the council bench, staring down at her the way she'd looked at Alaric, at the others. They were legends, though, and dead–

But I am here, she thought, *and I am all these people – and maybe all the world – has.*

I remember, Alaric. And I always will.

I will carry this task to the best of my ability.

And I will see it done.

She caught the hint of a smile from Hiressam. Faith renewed.

"Well," Calene said, looking at her, smiling through a slightly pained grimace. "Go on, then."

Shirri took a deep breath, and faced the council. "Yes," she said, and believed it to her core. "We can prepare for what is coming. And..." this was the part was a little dicier, and yet somehow...

...the words of Alaric Garaunt came back to her, the vow she could not forget set her heart aglow with a newfound certainty. "...We can win."

CHAPTER 108

Cyrus

"Hurry!" Baynvyn shouted. The scourge were cresting the sides of the platforms now, and Cyrus was following him to the airship, which was already rising off the dock, a ladder hanging off the side for them as it reached thirty feet above the platform...then forty...

"You first," Cyrus said, and clapped Baynvyn on the back to move him along. The whip of the winds off the airship blades was furious, drowning out the howls of the scourge.

Baynvyn leapt, dagger in hand, and caught the ladder a mere ten feet below the keel of the airship. Twisting from his own momentum, he shouted, "Now you!"

The scourge were coming, and in numbers so great that Cyrus wondered if even in Luukessia he'd seen their like. It was Caenalys again, with the gray beasts climbing over every surface – over the airship docks, scratching at the doors, and moving – inexorably – toward him.

"Stay, Cyrus," Malpravus's voice reached him on the winds. "Your destiny is here."

"No," Cyrus said, "it's not."

And he leapt.

He caught the rope ladder some ten feet below Baynvyn, who was already scurrying up. The ladder, too, was rising, being hauled aboard by sweaty sailors, the smell of them already reaching Cyrus's nose.

"We will meet again soon, Cyrus," the scourge called in one voice. The airship was rising – two hundred feet, three hundred feet above the landing platform. "You cannot escape your destiny."

"You are not my destiny," Cyrus muttered. He caught a leg upon the bottom rung and started to climb, leaving the voice of the old necromancer behind, howling in the wind like the rasp of death that he represented.

When he reached the side of the ship, strong arms tugged Cyrus over the edge, and he landed on the deck with a clank. A thought occurred to him. "Oh, shit," Cyrus muttered. "The shipmaster–"

"Is not Hongren," came a familiar voice. "Not for this voyage, anyway."

He lifted his head; Aisling waited before him, her cloak pulled back, age lines wrinkling her mouth into a smile.

"Trusted advisor to the Sovereign, huh?" Cyrus pulled himself to his feet beside Baynvyn. Niamh waited behind Aisling, twitching, but less than she had been on the platform. The influence of Malpravus was fading, then.

"The most trusted," Aisling said, waving them to follow as she walked toward the quarterdeck. The wind swirled around her white hair, and up at the wheel a sailor gave it a long, spinning turn, the ship already plunging forward against the currents.

Cyrus felt something change in the air before he heard the

boom; the flash lit up the horizon behind them, and Aisling shouted, "Brace-brace-brace!" with such confidence that any apprehension he might have had with her in charge dissolved immediately and he knelt, taking hold of a rail as the ship rattled furiously.

The tower was covered in flame, an explosion thrice its size, fire giving way to cloud as a wall of gray dissolved, the scourge half-annihilated by the Dragon's Breath.

"The Gates of Saekaj and Sovar close once more to the world," Baynvyn said sadly.

"But not forever," Aisling said, putting a hand on her son's shoulder. "Perhaps not even for long."

Cyrus watched the fire of the explosion die like a candle being blown out. "No. Because we won't let them be alone in this. Not for long." He looked to Aisling, and for the first time saw her as the shipmaster, truly. "Where are we heading?"

She was looking forward at the sunset blazing behind the wall of gray clouds blanketing the western horizon. "To Emerald," she declared, and the ship's course moved not at all; she'd already known, already ordered it. "First, anyway."

Cyrus nodded slowly. "To Emerald," he said, trusting her to know where they needed to go.

And when they got there, whatever they found...he would find a way, at last to make this right. All of it.

CHAPTER 109

Vaste

They found the airship docks without further incident, a tall-walled yard just beyond the ruin that had been the Southbridge in days of yore. Vaste's legs had almost returned to normal by the time they reached it, striding through the empty streets in silence, the occasional crackling fire in a bin or shout in the distance the only audible clue that they were in a living city.

Or at least, half-living. Vaste ignored the stings of his conscience and wondered if he should have dropped the fire upon the Termina Guard. A hundred of them, more or less, against however many thousands or tens of thousands of humans they'd killed?

But he'd failed to do so, the flame hanging right there. Why?

He was still debating it even as he ushered his small party past a couple of suspicious-looking guards who said nothing to him, letting them pass into the yard where at least one airship's engine was already running, and was taking off in a slow rise to the south.

"Where do we go?" Aemma asked. She seemed quiet, though unbroken, with her eyes taking in all the movement in the yard. Airships being loaded and unloaded; in spite of the chaos in Termina, things here seemed be proceeding as though there were nothing but peace all about. The scent of oil was thick in the air.

"I don't know," Vaste said, at the ends of his own experience. "Emerald? Your Northern Confederation? Where might you be safe?"

"Possibly in a different place than you would be," Aemma said. "At least in this land. Emerald...I do not know how they would react to a troll, or an elf, in this time." She shot Glaven an apologetic smile. "I am sorry if I was unkind to you when I first arrived."

"I took little note of it, madam," Glaven said, inclining his head, "as I think we had bigger worries than minor slights in these last days."

Vaste looked to Qualleron. "I suppose you wish to remove yourself to Firoba and away from all this madness. Perhaps visit that duchy with all the friendly women?"

Qualleron stared him with a pinched look upon his large face. "Heavens, no. I'm not leaving. I have business with Malpravus, who used me for his own ends while pursuing genocidal efforts in his own city. This...I cannot let stand."

Vaste looked to Aemma. "He's right, and I need to find a way to help him reach his goal. Malpravus...he's trouble for us all. If you need to go help your people–"

"Vaste." And she caught his hand in hers. "My people died in Termina. Not all humans, I mean, but my band, the ones I considered my family...they died on the street that night. Going north...I'm not even from there. I was born on the border near Elintany, in what the elves consider their territory. My village was already scourged, the band was all I had left. With them dead..." She looked away for a moment, then back at him. "I have nowhere else to go. So...wherever you are going, let us go together."

"I don't know where I'm going," Vaste said. The airship blades were blowing a considerable wind down upon him, stirring his hair.

"Perhaps I could help you with that," a voice called, and Vaste turned—

"Merrish," he said, whipping Letum around.

The former lord held up his bare hands, empty of weapon. The blood that had run down his face from the bullet wound had mostly clotted, and he seemed to be alone. The arrogance that was prominent upon his cheekbones and haughty lips was gone like the mist that had hung over the river, and he kept a healthy distance. "You saw the other shore? When you left?"

"The scourge?" Vaste kept Letum well in hand. "How they're gone? Is that what you mean?"

Merrish nodded slowly. "The elders of the city sent word calling back the Termina Guard. Pulling them all back, reassembling – this long night for the humans is over. There are whispers all about – from Reikonos, from Amti, from Saekaj. They say something ill is coming."

"Something very ill is indeed coming," Vaste said. "Malpravus."

"I have sent that message along," Merrish said. "They will be hearing it about now, from one of my men, from some of the guards you..." he cleared his throat, "...dealt with so strongly. But without someone who knows of these things firsthand, someone who has seen—"

"You cannot be serious," Qualleron said, reaching for his own sword.

"Please," Merrish said. "I believe you, Vaste. That he has come back. That his threat is dire and imminent, else why would the scourge have left? But not all have seen the legends of your friends, of you, the way I did before." He self-consciously rubbed himself, a pained look coming over him. "Or have felt your power the way I have this day. They will need to hear from someone who *knows*. From someone they can believe."

"This could be but a ploy, Sir Vaste," Glaven said. "To trick you back into the city when you are close to leaving."

"Perhaps," Vaste said, and he lowered Letum. "But I'm afraid that given all I've seen, I'm going to have to do the stupid thing and walk into what could be an obvious bloody trap because..." he straightened his considerable carriage, "...if we don't have more help, Malpravus will win by default."

"And if he betrays you in order to kill the human?" Qualleron asked.

Vaste paused, then flicked his hand toward Merrish. "I must make arrangements to see my friends leave this place. It is too dangerous here for them."

"There is no danger to any of them anymore," Merrish said. "You have my word. But if you still feel you need to send them...I understand."

"I do," Vaste said, and beckoned Qualleron, facing away from him, in hopes that Merrish would not hear. "Can you make arrangements to leave? Several, I mean – find the transport leaving soonest, another leaving later, and be prepared to go if you do not hear from me."

"I can," Qualleron said. "Are you sure you would not rather I go with you?" He brandished his sword with its chipped edges. "I make a formidable ally."

"Without doubt," Vaste said, and took hold of Aemma's arm. "But I would not chance this being a trap." She started to speak, but he stopped her. "If this is truth, and Merrish is done with his pogrom and genuinely afraid...well, we need the help of the elves of Termina. I will try and convince them. But if they prove false there's no reason for all of us to die."

"But you will be going in alone?" Aemma asked, shaking her head.

"Not alone," Glaven said, muscling his way into the circle. "I cannot go to Emerald in any case. I will go with the master." He brandished his rifle. "If you would have me."

"I will, gladly," Vaste said, and gathered himself up.

"Are you sure about this?" Aemma asked, grabbing him by the arm. Her small hand felt warm upon his bare wrist. "They may kill you."

"Everyone tries that sooner or later," Vaste said. "But if they attempt it, it will go quite messily for them." And he favored her with a smile.

She watched him slowly walk away, standing beside Qualleron, so small next to him.

"Thank you for this," Merrish said, his bloodied jaw standing out on his well-tanned face.

"I can only hope you don't mean to try and have me killed," Vaste said. "As you have so many lately." Glaven was beside him, his weapon at ready – always, Vaste had a feeling, at least for the next while.

"I think I have killed enough for now," Merrish said as they walked through the yards, and toward the gates that opened up to reveal the misty, half-ruined city of Termina. "Enough that I may indeed regret my settling of accounts – and soon."

"Really? You just may give me cause to hope again, Merrish," Vaste said, the city of Termina laid before him, shining, the fog and smoke already on the wane. A wind blew through, rustling his robes, and the smell of burning was gone – for now. This fight was over. A larger one still loomed.

But that was not as much of a weight on his mind as Vaste would have thought; for truly, he had thought for certain his days of hope were now all past. But staring at the city, he found himself thinking that possibly – just possibly – there might be just the tiniest thread of hope remaining for him.

CHAPTER 110

Alaric

"I don't really know how to do this," Alaric said, standing upon the quarterdeck of the ironclad, his hands upon the wheel of his new ship. It moved smoothly, rattling the remaining bridge tethering the ironclad and the *Yuutshee*.

"Just like that," Dugras said. He'd yielded the wheel, and was now watching. "Take it slow or you might cost me my way back to the *Yuutshee*."

"I imagine she could not well survive without you," Alaric said with the trace of a smile. "Though I also question my ability to do so."

"This ship is in good shape," Dugras said. "I looked at her engines myself. She'll run without any trouble, at least long enough to get you to a port."

Alaric watched him shift his gaze away. "And then?"

Dugras adopted a pained look. "Well, you'll have to land her."

He shuffled his feet. "Hey – a good ship needs a name. What do you want to call this tub?"

It took Alaric only a moment to answer. "The *Raifa*."

"It's a good name," Dugras said with a nod. Below, on the main deck, Edouard and Guy stood, watching either side. "And, a, uh...adequate crew, I suppose."

"They don't know how to do anything," Alaric said. "And neither do I."

"Admittedly, that could be a bit of a problem," Dugras said, fiddling with his collar. "I wish there was something I could do to help, Alaric, I really do, but the captain's orders are clear–"

"The *Yuutshee* must proceed with all due speed to the Amatgarosan outpost at Xiaoshani." Mazirin's voice was like a trumpet. She stood at the bottom of the quarterdeck, and ascended slowly. "To inform the empire of what transpired in Reikonos, and, now, what is happening over Luukessia. And," she added softly, "what is about to happen in Arkaria."

Alaric felt a strange, hopeful feeling in his chest. "Do you now believe me that Malpravus is going to be a great threat?"

"I believed you before," Mazirin said, coming up to stand beside him. "Where we differ was in what to do about it. I believed reporting to my superiors superseded any response I could make personally."

Alaric cocked his head. "And now?"

"And now," Mazirin said, with a glint in her eye, "there are two ships." She turned to look at Dugras. "You will take command of the *Yuutshee* and proceed immediately to Xiaoshani, where you will inform them there that we have a–" And here she spoke some bit of her own language, then lifted her head, almost pointing her chin at him. "Do you understand?"

"Okay," Dugras said. "What about you?"

"I will be going with Alaric," Mazirin said. "A skeleton crew will remain on the *Yuutshee*." She barked out a sharp command,

and a dozen crew scattered across the deck of the Chaarlandian vessel. "I ask again: do you understand?"

"Not really," Dugras said with a sigh, "but I'll tell them."

"Good," Mazirin said. "Dismissed."

Dugras sketched a rough salute, then gave Alaric a nod. "Best of luck, Alaric."

"Thank you, Dugras," Alaric said. "I hope we meet again."

With a nod, the dwarf hobbled off, over the remaining bridge to the *Yuutshee*, and he was gone. A moment later, chains rattled, the bridge slipped free, and the *Yuutshee* started to turn, smooth, graceful lines arcing away as she angled south.

"Hey, Alaric," Guy called from below. His hand looked fine now, other than a crust of blood. "We bloody made it." Edouard was smiling beside him, a sword in one side of the man's belt, a holster in the other. He no longer looked at his feet, though he was hardly the strongest and most confident man Alaric had ever met. *Give him time*, Alaric thought. There was certainly plenty ahead of them he'd need to summon his courage for.

"So we did," Alaric said, smiling back. He turned to look at Mazirin, his hands still firmly upon the wheel. "Thank you, as well."

Mazirin stiffened. "I don't understand your land, your world – magic and swords." She hesitated. "But I understand you are a man of honor, and that you are trying to make things better in your own way." She lowered her voice. "And I don't find you...'Too old.'" She took up the wheel from him, guiding it expertly.

"I think quite the same of you," he said, and she looked mildly scandalized – then smiled.

He felt a tingle, and for now it was not the ether. Though that was a thing, too – for if it had returned–

Sanctuary – the ark – must surely still be alive.

"In fact," he said, enjoying the give and take of feeling the wheel spinning in his hand between his control and hers, "I feel quite young at the moment." To this she smiled, and for the moment, all seemed...possible.

For now...there truly was still hope. And with the aid of Mazirin, he turned the wheel toward the setting sun, and the ship began to move against the winds, back toward Arkaria.

Back toward home.

CHAPTER 111

Vara

The world felt like Vara was being pushed through a hard barrier, a strong and heavy layer of chain mail as deep and dark as the night's sky. She twisted, thrashed, and finally–

Landed on her knees in thick, deep grass, a layer of gray clouds hanging overhead.

"I think we...made it," Isabelle said, flat on her back next to Vara. The spell, and that last barrier to entry, had left them both on the ground and staring up.

There was a curious sick sensation in Vara's stomach, a deep-seated nausea not unlike a resurrection spell. Pushing a few blades of long grass away from where they lay over her face like tree boughs in a dark forest, she took a breath of chill, morning air. "Where are we?"

"Pharesia, I think?" Isabelle said, not bothering to get up. "I would have picked Termina, but..."

"I am in no mood for being chased by scourge and swimming the Perda to get to the city proper, thank you," Vara said, pushing herself up on her elbows. As soon as she did, and could see over the grass...

...She froze.

"You...you..." Longwell's voice pierced the quiet calm. He lay in a pile a few feet away, roughly where they'd left him when the spell had kicked in, ripping all three of them out of the Realm of Life. He looked as worse for the wear as they did, but that was not why she had paused.

No...it was the army around her that made her sit there silently. In uniforms of brilliant green, a mix of those long guns in hand as well as a few spears here and there, they were clearly men, and human ones at that.

The silence was thick, and Vara said nothing, the worry of half a hundred guns and spear tips pointed at her head leaving her quite stunned into silence.

Not so for Isabelle, though: "So much for 'making it' to safety."

"Yes," Vara said, finding the silence and the many guns more than a bit unnerving, "out of the frying pan and all that..."

The circle of soldiers parted to make way for one of them who stalked over to them from the surrounding legion, his gaze tight and piercing, and hefted a pistol in his grip. He pointed it directly at Vara, and with a steely eye spoke in the human language, not the elven. "In the name of the army of Emerald – I declare you elves under arrest."

The Sanctuary Series Will Conclude
(At least for now) in:

Rage of the Ancients
The Sanctuary Series, Volume 12
Coming in 2023!
(I hope.)

AUTHOR'S NOTE

Well...that was a hell of a thing. I appreciate your patience if, in fact, you were one of the patient. If you weren't...well...

Maybe you noticed on the previous page, maybe you didn't...the next book is the end for the Sanctuary Series, at least for now. Why? Because I clearly can't keep the series going in a timely manner. I have too many other books to write, ones which pay the bills or have the possibility of doing so. Also, a lot of the readers of Sanctuary bailed after book eight. Which is fair enough, it was a damned good end if I say so myself. Some don't care for the steampunk setting. Some have told me they just don't care for the new books (which begs the question why they're reading books they don't enjoy, but I've long given up trying to answer *that* one). For a guy who's still got a good few years of writing to pay the bills before I can retire (which probably just means writing less, and writing whatever the hell I want, whenever the hell I want), that makes it tough for me to justify starting the next quadrilogy while watching the sales continue to tail off. Writing four more books of epic fantasy in this series? It's a big commitment.

So does this mean the end forever? Not necessarily. I had a loose series plan that would carry us out to book 20, laid out in quadrilogies of four books each - 9 thru 12, 13 thru 16, and 17 thru 20 to wrap things up. It's not like I'm going to set fire to those ideas and spread the ashes to the winds. I'll put them in the back of the filing cabinet, and in a few years I might find myself unable to resist them. Or I could take a page out of Brandon Sanderson's book and do a Kickstarter to see if fans are interested enough in books 13-16 that they'd be willing to fund them amply enough in advance that I could plan to write them at the pace of one or two a year and know I'm getting paid well enough for them that I don't have to constantly panic and get back to writing a Girl in the Box book so I can get my next release out to goose sales/pay the bills.

Bottom line: there are possibilities. But the bigger possibility right now (failing a Kickstarter success, if I choose to even try one) is that in the next couple years, sometime close to completion of book 12 or shortly after, I'll write something else in the Sanctuary universe. It'll probably a trilogy, something that takes place elsewhere in the wide world, maybe in that Duchy in Firoba where the women like trolls. I've got ideas. It'll take place closer in time to the original series than books 9-12, and there will be magic, and swordplay, and a more high fantasy setting. I might write another one after that. It's a big world; some of your old favorites might show up at some point. Or maybe they won't. There's lots to explore in Firoba, in Bithrindel, in Amatgarosa, Coricuanthi, and so on. It's a world that lives in my head, and I'm likely to spend more time there, if not in Arkaria itself.

A lot of this hinges on you, though. What do you want to see? More high fantasy from me? Or are you done at book 12? Would you like a Kickstarter as a chance to show how much you want to see what happens in the potential books 13-16? Would you like hardcover copies of the originals (which would, unfortunately, also take a Kickstarter at this point)? I'm asking you because, if you've read this far, presumably you at least want something from this series, even if it's just a satisfying ending to this quadrilogy. Kindly seek me out on social media and let me know if you feel strongly about it one way or another, or just get on my mailing list and send me an email (you can just reply to the confirmation email, it'll get to me).

(Note: if you write me an angry, complaining email, I will not respond. I'm sure you have well-considered reasons for doing so, but it takes me an hour or better to respond to a negative email in the proper, considered manner, without biting back, and I just don't have that kind of time in my day. Soz, as the Brits say.)

If you want to know immediately when future books become available, take sixty seconds and sign up for my NEW RELEASE EMAIL ALERTS at my website, www.robertjcrane.com. I don't sell your information and I only send out emails when I have a new book out. The reason you should sign up for this is because I don't always set release dates, and even if you're following me on Facebook (robertJcrane (Author)) or Twitter (@robertJcrane), or part of my Facebook fan page (Team RJC), it's easy to miss my book announcements because … well, because social media is an imprecise thing.

Find listings for all my books plus some more behind-the-scenes info on my website: http://www.robertjcrane.com!

Cheers,
Robert J. Crane

Other Works by Robert J. Crane

The Girl in the Box
(and Out of the Box)
Contemporary Urban Fantasy

1. Alone
2. Untouched
3. Soulless
4. Family
5. Omega
6. Broken
7. Enemies
8. Legacy
9. Destiny
10. Power
11. Limitless
12. In the Wind
13. Ruthless
14. Grounded
15. Tormented
16. Vengeful
17. Sea Change
18. Painkiller
19. Masks
20. Prisoners
21. Unyielding
22. Hollow
23. Toxicity

24. Small Things
25. Hunters
26. Badder
27. Nemesis
28. Apex
29. Time
30. Driven
31. Remember
32. Hero
33. Flashback
34. Cold
35. Blood Ties
36. Music
37. Dragon
38. Control
39. Second Guess
40. Powerless
41. Meltdown
42. True North
43. Innocence
44. Southern Comfort
45. Underground
46. Silver Tongue
47. Backwoods
48. Home
49. Eye of the Hurricane
50. Ghosts* Coming June 2, 2022!

World of Sanctuary
Epic Fantasy
(in best reading order)

1. Defender (Volume 1)
2. Avenger (Volume 2)

3. Champion (Volume 3)
4. Crusader (Volume 4)
5. Sanctuary Tales (Volume 4.25)
6. Thy Father's Shadow (Volume 4.5)
7. Master (Volume 5)
8. Fated in Darkness (Volume 5.5)
9. Warlord (Volume 6)
10. Heretic (Volume 7)
11. Legend (Volume 8)
12. Ghosts of Sanctuary (Volume 9)
13. Call of the Hero (Volume 10)
14. The Scourge of Despair (Volume 11)
15. Rage of the Ancients* Coming in 2023!

Ashes of Luukessia
A Sanctuary Trilogy
(with Michael Winstone)
(Trilogy Complete)

1. A Haven in Ash (Ashes of Luukessia #1)
2. A Respite From Storms (Ashes of Luukessia #2)
3. A Home in the Hills (Ashes of Luukessia #3)

Liars and Vampires
YA Urban Fantasy
(with Lauren Harper)

1. No One Will Believe You
2. Someone Should Save Her
3. You Can't Go Home Again
4. Lies in the Dark
5. Her Lying Days Are Done

6. Heir of the Dog
7. Hit You Where You Live
8. Her Endless Night*
9. Burned Me*
10. Something In That Vein*

Southern Watch
Dark Contemporary Fantasy/Horror

1. Called
2. Depths
3. Corrupted
4. Unearthed
5. Legion
6. Starling
7. Forsaken
8. Hallowed* (Coming in 2023!)

The Mira Brand Adventures
YA Modern Fantasy
(Series Complete)

1. The World Beneath
2. The Tide of Ages
3. The City of Lies
4. The King of the Skies
5. The Best of Us
6. We Aimless Few
7. The Gang of Legend
8. The Antecessor Conundrum

*Forthcoming, title subject to change

ACKNOWLEDGMENTS

Thanks to Lewis Moore for the edits, Jeff Bryan, for the proofing, and Lillie of https://lilliesls.wordpress.com for her work proofing and compiling my series bible.

Thanks also to Karri Klawiter of artbykarri.com for the cover.

Thanks, too, to my family for making this all possible.

Printed in Great Britain
by Amazon